THE HERRON HERITAGE

The Herron Heritage

Janice Young Brooks

HEADLINE

First published in Great Britain in 1992
by HEADLINE BOOK PUBLISHING PLC

First published in paperback in 1992
by HEADLINE BOOK PUBLISHING PLC

10 9 8 7 6 5 4 3 2 1

ISBN 0 7472 3855 3

Printed and bound in Great Britain by
HarperCollins Manufacturing, Glasgow

HEADLINE BOOK PUBLISHING PLC
Headline House
79 Great Titchfield Street
London W1P 7FN

PROLOGUE

May 1946

Max Herron

'You are searching for Merlin, and you need look no further, for I am he. Now go to King Uther and tell him that I will make Igraine his if he will reward me as I ask; and even that will be more to his benefit than to mine.'

Malory's Morte d'Arthur, edited by Keith Baines, 1962

House parties weren't what they used to be before the war, Blanche Leland thought, looking out over the grounds. Guests used to be stunned by the sheer magnificence of Leland House before the parties even began. The lawns were so perfect – smooth, green, growing just to the knife-edge of the flower beds. The lobelia-bordered croquet rectangle used to be the best in the south of England. The gardens themselves had been mentioned in several guide books, and paintings of the Capability Brown lake at the end of the yew alley were familiar to anyone who knew England's best landscape painters. Now the grass was ragged, the entire estate faintly shabby. The lake had gone green and slimy, the yews desperately needed trimming. And the bank of delphiniums that were meant to provide an astonishing view from the main dining room had toppled over like dead soldiers.

The war had changed everything and Blanche didn't understand how or why. Of course, they'd lost the gardener and both his sons in the fighting and virtually all the maids had gone off to do war work, but being without help hadn't seemed all that bad during the fighting. Raymond had offered the house as a hospital for recuperating officers and, while everything had been topsy-turvy, it was understandable and sometimes even rather fun. Any number of the handsome young officers had fallen in love with her, which was amusing. And if the estate wasn't tended properly during those difficult times, who was to care? It was temporary, even patriotic.

3

Everyone made sacrifices and let their lives be turned inside out.

But now, damn it, the war was over. The handsome young officers had gone home and forgotten her. Her daughters had become big, knobby-kneed and rude-spoken and didn't require, or even want, her mothering. Raymond was preoccupied with his own concerns. Blanche had expected everything would return to 1938 – the best year of her life. But it hadn't. Not at all. For one thing, the workers hadn't come back. Some were dead, of course, but not all. Where had they all gone? It was impossible to get decent servants, and they wanted to be paid the earth and had become very much above themselves in their manners.

Life was so different. Not at all the bright, hectic round of parties and gossip and love affairs she'd thrived on before the war. So dreary and utterly boring. People were so serious. There were still shortages of nearly everything. And no one seemed young and gay anymore. Not even Blanche herself. She tried not to think about it often, but sometimes she was overwhelmed by the comparison. She'd been a slim, blonde twenty-five-year-old with a handsome, rich husband and two beautiful little daughters when Hitler did whatever he did to drag England into his nasty war. Now she was thirty-two, growing a bit plump. There were even a few loathsome white hairs in the sleek, fair bob. All her clothes were dreadfully out of date, and Raymond had become unreasonable about shopping.

As if conjured from her thoughts, her husband entered the room. A pair of greyhounds trailed him. 'Looking very pensive, my dear.'

'I thought you'd walked to the village, darling,' she said.

'Changed my mind. Or had it changed for me, rather. Bit of a problem down on the beach. On call, don't you know.'

'Raymond, why? The war is over. The army has no right to keep interfering in your life.'

4

'No bother, really. They found what they believe may be some mines washed in. Got the bomb fellows down, but might want me to pop down for a look later.'

'You can't go. We're having guests.'

He didn't answer. Instead he knocked the dead ashes out of his pipe into an ashtray and went to fix himself a drink. Blanche watched him. She'd learned not to try to help. He got awfully uppity when anyone treated him as if he were an invalid. Good thing it was his left arm he lost, not his right. He'd have had an even worse time managing for himself if he were dependent on his left arm. But she never looked at that empty sleeve without resenting it. It was as if God had plucked her out of the dreary vicarage existence and made her a fine lady with a perfect husband only to make everything go wrong after one glorious year just to spite her.

'I'll run down after dinner then. Who are the guests this time?' Raymond asked with a hint of weary resignation.

Blanche bristled. He used to like house parties every bit as much as she did. 'The usual crowd. Bunny and Leo Smithe. Sissy and John Wilson. Evelyn and Harold. Harold's sister Helen – you remember her? She's lost her husband and has become terribly serious. Harold thought a weekend here might cheer her up. Then there's that peculiar American professor, Dr Taylor Lisle, who's been staying with the Wilsons.'

'Good man. Heard him give a talk once. Near the end, it was. About returning prisoners of war. Psychology and all that rot, but quite good, actually. Made sense.'

'And there's another American, Max somebody. Max Herring – no, Herron, I believe.'

'Why's he coming if you don't even know his name?'

'He's a distant cousin of a school friend of mine. Apparently she visited America during the war, met him and invited him to get in touch with us if he was ever nearby. He's here in England, and I got a note last week asking if he might drop in before he goes back. I thought,

5

if we had to have him, it would be best to invite him with a crowd. He can spread his boring Americanisms among more people that way if he's a dreadful sort.'

'Oh, not all Americans are dreadful. I met a chap ...'

He went on with his reminiscence, but Blanche wasn't paying attention. She was thinking about the ham. It was so difficult to get decent meat and while it was quite a large cut, she wasn't sure she could stretch it far enough for all the people she'd invited. She'd have to remind Raymond not to slip bits of it to the dogs under the table.

Max Herron had driven down from London and stopped to gaze at Leland House before officially arriving. He always made a point of getting a fix on a situation before throwing himself into it. Vast formal gardens, a little ratty from neglect. A huge manor house done in herringbone brickwork. Acres and acres of rolling land. Must cost a fortune to keep up a pile like that, he thought. All that wasted land. Not even used for grazing that he could see. Granted, it was impressive looking, but when were these old families going to realize that they had to make use of what they had?

If it were his, he'd make a different use of it. Put in homes. Decent, affordable housing for all those families cropping up everywhere. Practically every woman of childbearing age in England seemed to be pregnant or carrying an infant – or both. And in a year or two, they'd all want to get out of their crowded flats and into nice little houses of their own. A smart man could make a bundle with a place like this. Of course, you'd have to put in hedgerows and windbreaks to keep from having to look at it, but still ...

He'd keep these opinions to himself, even if he choked on them. It was the sort of forward-looking American opinion that he'd learned didn't go down at all well here. When you talked common sense to these people, they tended to get a look like the drains had backed up and they were trying to ignore the smell.

Another car was approaching. He let out the clutch and pulled off the road to let it pass. As it did so, the solitary passenger in the back turned and waved. For a second Max couldn't place the familiar face, then he remembered.

Dr Lisle. Taylor Lisle. What in the world was he doing here? A perplexing, fascinating man. A person Max half liked, half feared – without any idea what inspired either emotion. Though only in his early forties, little more than a decade older than Max himself, Lisle had been a friend of Max's father. No, not a friend. A business advisor of some sort. That in itself was odd. Samuel Herron had never asked anyone's advice that Max knew of, and yet he seemed in awe of the mysterious, eccentric Lisle. Max had heard his father half-jokingly refer to him as a sooth-sayer. Lisle was said to have an understanding of human nature that amounted to a gift of prophesy.

When Max was fourteen, he'd been sent to spend the summer with Lisle at a great sprawling house in New Mexico. He hadn't wanted to go, had never understood, even in retrospect, why he'd been sent. There had been three other boys there for the vacation, only children of wealthy fathers like himself; they'd all been packed up without regard to their wishes and assigned to Dr Lisle.

Not that any of the boys regretted the visit. In fact, it was one of Max's fondest memories. It was the only time he'd really known the outdoor life – camping, hunting, riding, mountain climbing. There was something rugged and exciting going on all the time. He learned to shoot a rifle and hand-gun, attended the only rodeo he was to ever see, and lost his virginity to a doe-eyed Mexican girl. It had almost seemed that Lisle was conducting a con-test of some sort. Or perhaps an experiment. He ques-tioned the boys a lot. What had they learned? What had they liked best? What lessons about life had they got from fishing, or camping, or sleeping out in a rainstorm?

But whatever it was about, it was over too soon. In September the boys had all gone back to their families –

7

sun-browned, calloused and swaggering, but no wiser. If someone had won the contest, it wasn't announced. If the experiment had been successful or not, they never knew. He wasn't asked back and had had little further contact with Lisle, but his father kept in touch and through the years often mentioned having heard from him.

And so now, after all this time, here he was at a house party weekend in England. What a strange coincidence.

It might have been a pleasant enough dinner party if Helen Eversleigh hadn't considered herself an intellectual. Instead of light conversation, she had engaged Dr Lisle in discussion of the 'meaning' of the war. 'My late husband was in Intelligence, Dr Lisle, and said you were invaluable to England in winning the war. He heard you speak once and was most impressed. Something about officials using patriotism as a tool of conflict. I'm afraid it lost a bit in the translation. Would you mind elaborating?'

Lisle laid down his fork. 'I'm afraid I'd bore the table to death, Mrs Eversleigh. Perhaps later?'

'Yes, of course. But one thing – he said you spoke of the need to make constant psychological assessments of why the war was being fought. Now that it's done, what's your own assessment?'

'The war was fought to preserve a political system, of course.'

'And a way of life,' Helen's brother Harold put in. 'Would you mind passing the salt?'

'No, not a way of life. That's the myth the war-makers must use. And used magnificently, I must say.'

'But a political system and a way of life are the same, aren't they?' Helen asked, shoving a salt shaker in the general direction of her brother.

'Not for most of us,' Lisle said. 'For the Jews, of course, Hitler's system was catastrophic, and we Allies pretended that we were fighting partly for the Jews, which is nonsense. But for the average German, life

8

would not have been much different under Hitler, had he prevailed, than life was for the English before the war. The average person isn't concerned on a daily basis with ideals. His needs are for food, shelter, someone to help him teach his children to earn a living. Nearly any system of government can and must meet those needs.'

'Surely you're not saying the Allies would have been as well off had Germany won the war,' Helen said, growing very pale.

'No, nothing of the kind. I'm just pointing out that a political system is like a living organism. It has an inherent need to save itself. Any other system is perceived as a threat. Even a superior one. The Allied powers didn't invest tens of thousands of lives in fighting Hitler's and Hirohito's political philosophy. The only part of their philosophy we cared a fig about was the part that said they would take over things we felt belonged to us. If two neighboring cave men meet over a dead bison, they don't sit down and evaluate each other's cultural evolution to determine who's best qualified to the kill. They simply bash away at each other with any weapon handy to get the whole bison to themselves. We aren't so very different. There are just more of us with better weapons.'

Harold signaled the serving girl to bring another serving of ham. Blanche watched in despair as he took the largest slice. Even though she'd banned the dogs from the dining room, there wasn't going to be enough left for sandwiches for tea tomorrow. She'd have to talk to the cook about cucumbers.

Max was seated so that he could appear to be looking at Dr Lisle while actually gazing past him at Blanche. Even with that slight frown, she was the most ravishing woman he'd ever seen. She had precisely the sort of icy, serene beauty that most attracted him. Her skin was as smooth and lustrous as ivory silk and his palms itched with the desire to rub his hands over her. Such exquisite beauty wasted on that poor stick of a husband. Raymond Leland looked like a skittish, overbred racehorse. No, he looked more like those sissy, silly dogs of his; a stereotypical British milquetoast.

As Max stared at Blanche, her gaze shifted and their eyes met. His stomach lurched with the intensity of the look that passed between them. Yes, she knew what he was thinking – and her cold, bold eyes told him she didn't mind a bit. He glanced briefly, ever so briefly, at her full, pillowy bosom and the corners of her mouth moved upward ever so slightly. Max had a sudden vision of himself rising from his place, pulling her from her chair and taking her right there in the middle of the table in front of everyone.

'Don't you agree, Mr Herron?' Helen Eversleigh asked.

'I'm sorry,' Max said. 'My attention had wandered for a moment. Please excuse me. I'm so taken with the beauty of the ... surroundings.'

'I was saying that war brings out the nobility in mankind. Dr Lisle disagrees. Were you in the service?'

'Yes, but I saw precious little nobility and a great deal of suffering.'

'Then you don't think, as I do, that Hitler caused us to search our hearts and find the good in them?'

'I'm afraid I thought little of Hitler. My war was with Hirohito.'

Helen Eversleigh lost interest in him. She had hoped to find an ally. 'Dr Lisle, I'm frankly surprised at your attitude. It seems quite cynical.'

'Cynical or realistic. They are often the same.'

'I take it you think there is no good to be found in human nature – if war can't bring it out, nothing can.'

'My dear lady, you are wrong on both counts. There's enormous potential for good in mankind. But war suppresses it; peace can nourish it.'

'Can? But doesn't?'

'Not often enough.'

'I understand you're from Kansas City, Mr Herron,' Blanche said, using the brief pause in Helen's inquisition to divert the conversation.

'Yes, I am. Third generation.'

'Such a fascinating place, America. So – so manly,' Blanche said with a slow smile.

'Nothing like the soft, voluptuous charm of England.'

Bunny Smithe, who had been doing a workmanlike job of quietly getting drunk at the far end of the table, laughed shrilly. 'Voluptuous! Oh, I say, Mr Herron! Nothing voluptuous about Merry Olde.'

'I disagree,' Max said slowly. 'England is serene, lush, well-manicured. Rolling hills, dark, secret valleys. And under it all, a raging passion for life.' He stared directly at Blanche as he spoke. The air between them fairly shimmered.

Dr Lisle slowly folded his damask napkin, glancing slowly and thoughtfully between Max and Blanche. Then he rubbed his forefinger along the near edge of his plate and smiled, as if reading something there that pleased him.

'Tell me about her,' Max said later to Lisle.

There was a foursome of bridge players, and the rest of the guests were watching the game and making languid conversation. The two American men had taken up a distant stance by a fireplace in which a fitful fire burned.

'Blanche Leland?' Lisle asked, though he knew perfectly well who Max meant. 'She's the daughter of a second son who took orders and, most uncharacteristic for the British, took them very seriously. Burned his bridges with the family by taking up a position in a rather shabby section of London. His wife died shortly after Blanche was born. She was brought up by cousins on her father's side. I imagine they made pretty clear that she was being educated for a life she'd never live as a poor parson's daughter. Then she met Raymond Leland and married into even better circumstances than they enjoyed. Must have been a fine poke in the eye.'

'Are there any children?' Max asked.

'Two girls. But they don't count. Can't inherit. I imagine they're off at school somewhere. There hasn't been a sign of another child for years, people say. Possibly the war took more than Raymond's arm. Estate's entailed. Since there are no sons, someday it will belong to Raymond's younger brother, who loathes Blanche.' Lisle paused for a moment, then said pointedly, 'You're not married yet, are you?'

'No,' Max said, looking at him sharply. 'How do you know so much about Mrs Leland?'

'Oh, I pay attention.'

Max knew he'd get no better answer than this.

'Do you want her?' Lisle asked.

'You sound as if she were yours to give,' Max said, startled and offended.

'Perhaps. Perhaps,' Lisle said, squinting a little as he studied Blanche, who had just taken the final trick in the bridge game. Seeming to forget Max Herron, he strolled over to join the card players.

PART ONE

Spring 1965

Anthony Wentworth

'The best thing for being sad,' replied Merlyn, beginning to puff and blow, 'is to learn something. That is the only thing that never fails. You may grow old and trembling in your anatomies, you may lie awake at night listening to the disorder of your veins, you may miss your only love, you may see the world about you devastated by evil lunatics, or know your honour trampled in the sewers of baser minds. There is only one thing for it then – to learn. Learn why the world wags and what wags it. That is the only thing which the mind can never exhaust, never alienate, never be tortured by, never fear or distrust, and never dream of regretting.'

The Once and Future King, T.H. White

Chapter One

Anthony Wentworth was brought to the admissions office at Harvard at the age of fifteen by the renowned psychologist Dr Taylor Lisle, who introduced himself with ponderous modesty as the young man's tutor. Slavedriver, mentor, surrogate grandfather, almost anything would have been a more accurate description of the man Anthony always called 'the Prof' than 'tutor'.

Office underlings who were obsessed with mundane trivialities such as compulsory education laws and transcripts were brutally flung aside and the Director of Admissions himself was finally routed out to deal with the intruders. The Director recognized Taylor Lisle and was aware that the university had been courting him for years. Accordingly, the Director agreed to test the boy for admission.

Anthony not only passed the tests, he passed with such high marks that the Director, after double-checking the test results and catching his breath, said he saw no reason for Dr Lisle's protégé to take any of the introductory freshman courses.

'No, he needs exposure to the youngest students,' Dr Lisle said.

'To catch up socially, you mean. That may be a wise idea,' the Director said.

'No. To discover for himself how immature the others are.'

The remark was typical of Lisle. Arrogant and abrasive. Of course, his bragging about Anthony was really bragging about himself. Anthony was his product, his life's work, his grand experiment come to glory.

Anthony lived up to Taylor Lisle's academic expectations, easily completing a four-year double major in business and psychology in three years. It wasn't a popular thing to admit in those days, but Anthony really loved studying, collecting facts like other people collected money or stamps or butterflies. Compared to the amount of study he'd been subjected to most of his life, Harvard was a breeze. He was confident in class, but outside class, that was a different matter entirely, a matter Lisle hadn't prepared him for.

Anthony wasn't one of the bespectacled nerds the media likes to do heavily ironic fillers on when they go to college at a preternatural age. His biological parents must have been giants, for Anthony was edging past six feet when he started college at fifteen. He'd dwarfed his adopted dad, older brother and the Prof for three years before that. Besides being big and unusually mature in appearance, he was strong, lean and tan from growing up on a working ranch. He didn't look like the social misfit he was.

The Prof had spoken slightingly of the maturity of college freshmen and, in an intellectual sense, Anthony agreed. After all, he told himself, what kind of fool chugalugs enough beer to nearly vomit his heart up and considers it fun – or manly, for God's sake? How can anyone with a brain find genuine amusement in stealing a girl's panties? And yet, however loudly his intellect told him this was stupid, he ached to be part of it and enjoy it as mindlessly as the others. But he couldn't get into it without a part of himself standing aside, observing and sneering. *Well, will you look at that – Anthony Wentworth, with all his gifts, risking life and limb to crowd seventeen people into a Volkswagen. Whoopee, what fun,* the voice of reason drawled contemptuously.

That first summer after Anthony started college, he went home eagerly. The ranch: real life. The land actually belonged to the Prof, but it had always seemed like the Wentworths' to Anthony because his father was the ranch manager. Dr Lisle only lived there between speaking and teaching engagements and let Jeb Wentworth run it with a free hand. Rory's mother – Anthony's adoptive mother – had died when the boys were both too young to remember her, leaving the family a society of men. Anthony and his brother Rory had always been expected to work as hard as any of the hands, even though the boys had a heavy load of studies which Lisle supervised. Sometimes he taught them himself, other times he hired tutors to come in. In spite of the correspondence courses Anthony was expected to complete over that first summer break, he had three glorious months of riding and roping and breathing the clear air as if he were trying to soak it up to take back to Massachusetts.

Rory hadn't gone on with his schooling. Nevertheless, Anthony was surprised to learn how thoroughly his brother abandoned learning. He never saw Rory touch a book that summer and was surprised that the Prof didn't seem to mind. That was when he started to realize what he should have always known: that their education was for his sake. Rory had just been along for the ride. And hadn't much liked it.

He put Rory out of his mind in the fall. When he went back to school he decided that since he couldn't revel in the frivolous, he'd reject it. During his second year he grew his hair long, which made him look like a tanned, blond Beatle, and took up with the socially conscious crowd. He carried around *Silent Spring* like a Bible, protested, picketed and made love a couple times with a militant Asian girl named Ming who shaved her pubic hair as an expression of some feminist principle – he never could figure out just what.

Then he took up the banner of segregation, this bright, protected boy who'd never attended a public school or eaten at a lunch counter, nor for that matter known a Negro except for a few dignified, aloof African students at Harvard. Sometimes even he suspected that

17

he had a colossal nerve thinking he knew anything about race relations. But mostly he enjoyed feeling worthwhile.

One long weekend in October he was part of a couple carloads of boys who drove down to Georgia to work for voter registration. He learned something important, though he didn't understand its significance to his own life until years later. He'd been going door-to-door in a dismal black slum all day, handing out flyers, giving the rah-rah pitch to anybody willing to open the door to them. One 'housewife', a girl who couldn't have been any older than he was, opened her tattered screen door and impatiently ordered him inside. There was a naked child clinging to her leg and another one wearing a disgusting rag of a diaper at her breast.

'Wha' you want, white boy?' she asked over her shoulder as she stirred something she was cooking.

He launched into his spiel, but she wasn't listening. He got only a few sentences out before she put the spoon down and dislodged the infant, who started screaming as she deposited him in a cardboard carton on the floor. She shooed the naked toddler out the door and gestured at an unspeakable mattress lying on the floor saying, 'One dollar before you starts and make it quick. My man, he comin' home for lunch.'

It took Anthony a moment to realize what she was talking about, and then he was appalled. He stared at her speechless. She stood there, one high, round breast exposed, a glistening drop of milk oozing from the nipple.

'That's ... that's not what I'm here for!' he croaked.

She looked genuinely perplexed, then shrugged and went back to the stove. The child kept screaming. Anthony started talking again, quickly, almost hysterically: '... your constitutional rights as a citizen ... control of your own community affairs ... blah, blah, blah ...' And even as he was rattling along, he was thinking of two other things. One was that she wasn't old enough to vote – for

18

that matter, neither was he, so what the hell was he doing this for?

The second thought didn't register consciously at first. He was talking like a madman and she was stirring something on the stove. She bent down and picked up a crumpled, torn bag and poured something from it into the pot. Anthony was about four more sentences along before he realized that it was dried dog food.

Dog food!

His mouth started watering with nausea. He gulped convulsively and lurched toward the door, pausing long enough to find his billfold, shove a twenty-dollar bill at her and gasp, 'Buy some real food!'

That evening, back at the hotel, the idealistic young men sat around and talked about their experiences that day. All but Anthony. He listened, but didn't talk. He hadn't the words for the feelings that girl had aroused in him. He hadn't the maturity even to understand the hammer-blow emotions that still gripped him. He sat sipping a Coke while the others repeated complacently to each other the fine and noble things they'd said during the day. There was a lull while room service was delivered. A young man rolled a trolley cart in and started removing dish covers. Steaks, hamburgers, pork chops, sandwiches.

But no dog food.

That's when it hit him.

The key to it all was money. Money. Not flyers, not high ideals, not prissy white boys reeking of expensive aftershave intruding on neighborhoods where they were unwelcome freaks and boring the socks off people with six syllable words. The difference was money. If that girl had money she wouldn't be stretching out her family's dinner with dog food. If she had enough money, she wouldn't be turning tricks on a filthy mattress on the floor for a dollar. A dollar, for Christ's sake. If she had money she'd have shoes and education. She was just a kid. She ought to be giggling with other girls in the high school corridors, not living as she was. God! She must have got pregnant when she was twelve or thirteen. A baby herself. And all because there wasn't enough money.

But he had no money of his own to give, other than the occasional twenty, and that wasn't enough to change anything except for a few days for one person. Nor did he have any idea how to put forward the concept except to a bunch of friends who had no more assets, financial or political, than he did. So he did what any immature, conscience-stricken sixteen-year-old boy wonder would do: he gave up. Fled from the knowledge of poverty as if it were a disintegrating corpse reaching out for him. He assigned himself the safe, organizational jobs for the movement. Stuffing envelopes, running errands. Anything to save him from coming face to face with another girl like that. And then, by the end of that second year in college, claiming a heavy class load, he gracefully managed to back out entirely.

The second summer home was truly saddening. Though a working ranch looks pretty much the same to an outsider from one year to the next – probably from one generation to the next – there are actually constant, if subtle, changes: new fencing round a corral; old horses put to pasture and new ones broken in; the dimensions of the kitchen garden altered; the ancient battle-scarred raccoon no longer coming to beg dinner scraps, but two young ones in his place. They were such little things, but the ranch was changing without him. He was becoming the outsider, come to visit.

The saddest change was in Rory, his brother. Anthony had always known that the classical education Dr Lisle had inflicted on both of them hadn't taken with Rory as it had with him, but now Rory had shed it like an unwanted skin. He was turning into a 'good ol' boy' with a ferocious, deliberate intensity. He'd bought the requisite beat-up pickup with the gun rack in the back window, had started using chewing tobacco and had the beginning of a beer belly. He'd taken up with one of the Mexican ranch hands' fifteen-year-old daughter.

'She's under age, Rory,' Anthony told him. 'You better stay away from her before you both get in trouble.'

Rory gave him a look that was just half a step from physical violence. 'Mind your own beeswax, college punk. Just 'cause you've got your dick in a book—'

'Hey, you're talking to me, not some effete tourist at Marvel's Grill.'

Rory gazed at him through half-closed eyes. 'Jeez, hard to tell the difference, these days.'

Anthony let it go. Not through restraint or wisdom, but out of sheer shock. He'd become one of 'them' to Rory. An outsider. And in a way, he was right. But he cared about Rory. They'd learned to ride together. They'd skinned their first rattler together and been caught in a fierce, terrifying snow storm and seen meteors in the vast bowl of Southwest sky together. They'd taught each other all the dirty words they knew. Rory was part of Anthony and they'd grown apart. It made him want to kick things.

Anthony went back to school that fall a different person and yet still an unformed one. Until then, he'd never really thought ahead very far, never wondered what niche he was to fill, or create for himself to fill. He'd imagined his schooling as a pleasant interlude before taking up his final role at the ranch. But now he knew there was no role there. Rory was his father's eldest son. His real son, come to that, not that Jeb Wentworth ever made anything of Anthony's being adopted besides sitting him down at the age of six and telling him. But if Jeb were ever to retire, Rory would take over his job. Not Anthony.

So what in hell am I to do when I finish school? Anthony found himself wondering. Apply all the principles he was learning to some business, obviously. But what? What are you going to be when you grow up? kids ask each other. Now Anthony was asking himself. He was about to be 'grown up' before he was ready. The only business he knew about was ranching and if he were to go into that, he should have been at some Midwest ag college, not Harvard, for Christ's sake!

He'd come to feel that he had to do some good, improve the world in some way, that having a good brain and first-class education incurred an obligation. But his experience in the voter registration drive had taken the idealistic sparkle off him. Still, if he kept his mind and options open, surely he would find out what he was meant to do.

During that last year of college he was in a state of constant anticipation. Like someone waiting for a caller, imagining the doorbell ringing, running to look out the front window at intervals. Surely, he thought, something would grab his imagination, signal to him: this is it, this is the beginning of a compelling lifelong interest, here's what you want to do with your life. This is how you can make the world a little bit better place.

Then one day they were playing 'Pomp and Circumstance' and someone was handing him a diploma and he still had no answer.

Jeb Wentworth and Rory were there for the graduation, as was the Prof. Jeb was uncomfortable in the Ivy League setting and Rory was, as Anthony told him later, a flaming asshole. He wore a plaid shirt, string tie and a sneer to the ceremony. At least he didn't spit tobacco juice on anyone, for which Anthony wryly supposed he ought to be grateful.

The next day the four of them started the long train ride home. The Prof always insisted on train travel. He said it was because you saw the country and met real people on trains. Jeb and his sons knew it was because he couldn't admit to being afraid of anything.

'So, Anthony, what do you have in mind next?' the Prof asked as the train pulled out of town. Rory and Jeb had gone to the club car and Anthony and Lisle had the double bedroom compartment to themselves.

'Not a damned thing, Prof,' Anthony admitted.

'Good. It leaves you free.'

'Free to go to Vietnam and get blown to bits, most likely.' Anthony had followed the step-up in the United States' involvement in Vietnam with obsessive fear. And then just the month before, Johnson had sent troops to the Dominican Republic. Anthony knew enough of history to sense what this could signal. One way or another, Johnson was going to wipe out a generation, Anthony feared. His generation. Possibly starting with him. The Prof in one of his 'prophetic' moods had once mentioned Vietnam and made a remark about how the very name was someday going to be a blot on a generation's conscience.

'No, that's taken care of. I've talked to your draft board.'

Anthony didn't even ask how it had been 'taken care of'. He was too overwhelmed with relief to question it for fear that his safety might be snatched from his grasp. Once the danger of military service was removed, he suddenly realized how large it had loomed in his subconscious. He sensed that it was part of the reason he hadn't made a more concerted effort to establish a course for his life. A soft, oily voice in the back of his mind had been telling him that he probably didn't have much life left anyway, why worry about it?

'We'll have a week at the ranch for you to come back down to earth, then there are some people I want you to meet,' the Prof continued.

'What people?' Anthony asked, still only half with him. He wasn't going to die in a rice paddy or a sugar cane field. Thank God!

'All in good time.'

A week later Anthony and Lisle were headed back east again. Anthony had no idea where they were going or why,

23

but that wasn't unusual. It was so rare to get a straight answer from the Prof that the Wentworths had all got out of the habit of asking many questions. It was like trying to grill Socrates – or Freud.

'Where are we going?' Anthony would ask and Dr Lisle would say, 'Where do you think we're going? Study the train schedule and tell me where you think we might disembark and how you'd feel about it.' A proven teaching tool, but damned tiresome when all you want is a simple answer. With the Prof there weren't ever simple answers.

Sometimes, however, there were what Anthony could only term 'prophesies' – usually the garden variety: 'You'll get caught in the rain if you go out now,' or 'Rory will just get drunk if you let him off early today, Jeb.' Those were just common-sense warnings, Anthony told himself, but they were always right. *Always.* And sometimes the Prof's predictions went beyond mere logic. Only the year before, he'd warned Jeb against buying a herd of supremely healthy looking cattle – which mysteriously died the week after someone else purchased them. He'd also warned Jeb against housing his prize bull in a specially-built barn. Jeb didn't listen that time and the bull died when lightning hit the structure. Anthony resented the Prof's 'fortune telling', though he wasn't sure why. That was the reason he didn't want to discuss his own lack of direction; he didn't want the Prof to tell him which way to go. He wanted to find out for himself.

After Grand Central and a car rental office, they fetched up just outside Bridgeport, Connecticut. Anthony had made something of a point of not asking the Prof anything. Just waited for him to turn the information loose. That made Lisle uneasy and, oddly enough, Anthony found himself enjoying the Prof's discomfort.

'Aren't you curious?' Lisle finally asked.

It cost him, that question.

'You'll tell me when you're ready,' Anthony said calmly. He didn't know why he suddenly wanted to exert this peculiar power over the older man, but it was heady stuff.

Lisle scowled at the road for a mile or two. Then, as if he'd worked something out in his own mind and was pleased with it, he turned and smiled. 'I wondered when you'd start rebelling.' He laughed, then said, 'I want you to meet an old friend of mine. Max Herron.' He waited. Anthony said nothing. It damned near killed him. This was all obviously important to him in some way he couldn't guess, but he was set on a course of not asking questions.

'Max is from Kansas City. Money in paper mills. I knew his father.' He gave Anthony a sly glance and Anthony smiled – enigmatically, he hoped. Fatuously, he feared.

They drove through winding lanes and the Prof managed it as though it were familiar territory. Finally they crested a slight rise, the trees parted and Anthony found himself looking at what he first took to be a school of some sort. An enormous, mostly three-story Tudor building with wings and additions and outbuildings, all in the same style. Did the Prof think he was sticking him into a teaching position at some posh private school? If so, he was going to be disappointed. Anthony didn't know what he wanted to do, but he knew it wasn't teaching.

'Nice place,' he said coolly as trees closed back in on the lane.

They stopped in front of the big wooden double door and a white-jacketed attendant descended the steps, made the slightest bow and took the Prof's car keys. 'Welcome to Birches, Dr Lisle,' he said with genuine warmth. 'I've put you in the Martha Washington suite, if that would suit? And the young man in the Grover Cleveland room?'

'Excellent, Sinclair. I was sorry to miss the forsythia this year.'

'Mr Max regretted that, sir. It was a truly fine display.

A bit of trouble with the tourists taking pictures, but Mr Max hates to deny them the pleasure in spite of the nuisance.'

So, the Prof was a frequent fixture here. And he himself was expected, Anthony thought. Apparently it wasn't a school. Those facts didn't satisfy his curiosity, only honed it to a sharper point, but he'd declared a minor war of sorts on the Prof and had to maintain his battle line. Instead of asking any of the questions battering at the back of his teeth, he satisfied himself with gawking like one of the poor tourists. Birches looked like what you'd get if you did the Hearst Castle at San Simeon in tasteful Tudor and set it in the lushly proper Connecticut countryside.

They were ushered into a great central hall. 'They're in the study, Dr Lisle,' Sinclair said.

'We'll find our own way, thank you,' he said. A pair of large carved doors to the left were open and Anthony followed the Prof through. The older man stopped, giving Anthony the opportunity to study the room before anyone noticed their presence. There must have been a dozen people there. Some were chatting in groups. Three men were watching a golf game on a television. Two women on a sofa leaned toward each other, sharing what must have been a funny secret, for they were stifling laughter. But it was obvious which one was Max Herron. Everyone, no matter what they were doing, seemed to be keeping half an eye on him.

He stood talking with two other men by the french windows. He was a big man, well over six feet with broad shoulders. He had the look of a former athlete just beginning to lose his battle with age. The striped golfing shirt strained a bit at the waist, there was a hint of jowls, a fan of gray in the dark blond at his temples. As he gestured toward the television watchers, his gaze caught the visitors.

'Dr Lisle! You've arrived,' he said, striding forward. 'Blanche is around someplace. She's been worried that you wouldn't make it in time for dinner. I told her you never missed one of Pierre's meals if you could help it.'

'How are you, Max?' Dr Lisle asked. It sounded more like a real question than a polite one.

Herron gave the query its due. 'Pretty good. Pretty damned good. This must be Anthony.'

'Anthony Wentworth, Max Herron,' the Prof said.

'How do you do, Mr Herron.'

'No, Max to you, my boy,' he said heartily, pumping Anthony's hand.

A silence fell while they studied each other. Max Herron kept hold of Anthony's hand in both of his. Little old ladies sometimes do that, hang onto you once they've got you, but seldom men, Anthony thought. It was oddly disconcerting. *He's ill*, Anthony realized. Under that healthy, rich man's tan there was a pale shadow of sickness. His hands were dry and cool. Just a degree too cool. The insight surprised him. He didn't usually have insights.

He was introduced to the others. 'Anthony Wentworth, everybody. Anthony's just graduated from Harvard. Just turned eighteen years old in February and already graduated,' Max Herron said. *He's well-informed*, Anthony thought. The Prof hadn't said anything about his age or graduation; he must have spoken to Herron before visiting. *What the hell am I doing here?* he wondered wildly. This was stranger than most of the Prof's machinations.

'Ah, Blanche!' Herron said halfway through the introductions.

A fiftyish woman with platinum blonde hair had come into the room. Unlike the other women who were in tennis dresses or expensively casual slacks, this one was in what was once called a 'tea dress'. Floral, drapey, very old-world lady of the manor. In another setting, with different clothes, she would have been fat, but she was so sleek and well-groomed that she merely seemed plump. 'Look, Blanche, Dr Lisle is here with Anthony.'

'How do you do, Anthony,' she said dismissively.

'Dr Lisle, I've had Pierre fix that eggplant dish you're so fond of.'

Anthony had never seen the Prof eat eggplant.

'Blanche, will you just look at the boy. Only eighteen and already graduated from Harvard. Isn't that impressive?' Herron said.

'Quite. How nice for you,' she murmured. She couldn't have made it more clear that she didn't give a damn.

'Where's Faye? I want her to meet Anthony,' Herron asked.

'Out riding, I believe,' Blanche said.

The Prof hadn't said a word during all this. Now he spoke. 'It's been a long trip, Max. Do you mind if Anthony and I change clothes and rest a while? Of course, Anthony doesn't need rest after a trip, but I do.'

'Yes, please. Of course. Anthony, help yourself to whatever you like. There are stables, a swimming pool, tennis courts. Even a small putting green. Watch television. Roam around. Make yourself at home. Cocktails here at seven. Oh, Anthony, is that shepherd's hut still up in the hills to the north of the house?'

That took the young man by surprise. For a second he thought he meant here, then he realized Max Herron was talking about the ranch. 'Yes, sir. It is, but it's about to fall down from age.'

Max chuckled. 'I thought that, too, when I was a boy. I went up there and pretended I was a Spanish explorer discovering the land and facing the elements alone. That was a long time ago, wasn't it, Dr Lisle?'

'Not so long, Max,' the Prof said gently. They smiled together over some old memory.

A servant hovered, waiting the opportunity to show them their rooms. Anthony's was a cool, airy combination bedroom and sitting room on the third floor with a balcony that overlooked the stables and woods. The Prof was down the hall from him. Anthony's suitcases had been unpacked and, still puzzling over Max Herron, he stripped out of his clothes and headed for the adjoining bathroom. A brisk shower was what he needed, he told himself. It would clear his mind.

He stepped into the bathroom and discovered a very attractive young woman looking in the medicine cabinet. She whirled, looked him up and down slowly, appreciatively, and smiled. 'Oh, my, my, my, what have we here?'

Chapter Two

Anthony forced himself slowly to grab a towel, trying to keep it from looking like an hysterical lunge for protection. Wrapping it round his waist as casually as he could manage, he said shakily, 'Do you mind telling me who you are?'

God, what a prig he sounded to himself! Pure Don Knotts.

The young woman was smiling as she leaned back against the sink, still frankly studying him. She had long blonde hair with a sort of preppy/hippy headband. Her tailored denim skirt was short and although she didn't seem to be much over five feet, her legs went on for ever. She wasn't the least disconcerted by Anthony's state of undress. In fact, she seemed to be enjoying his discomfort. 'Darling, I'm so sorry, I thought this was someone else's room. I was looking for some clear nail polish to fix a run.' She extended one of her great legs to prove it; twisted her foot a bit and gazed down in self-appreciation. 'You don't have any, do you? Nail polish?'

Oh, for something witty to say. Instead, he muttered, 'No, I don't,' and turned to leave the bathroom.

She followed. 'I do believe you must be Anthony Wentworth, since I know everyone else here this weekend. What a surprise. I thought he was a dreadful, pimpled little *wunderkind* with knee socks and slide rule.'

'Sorry, I left the slide rule at home,' he said, sounding surly. She was laughing at him. There's nothing more defenseless than a naked man being laughed at, Anthony

31

realized. He hasn't any concealed weapons.

'Nice to meet you, Anthony Wentworth,' she said, taking his hand and shaking it briskly. His towel was beginning to slip and he needed that hand, but she didn't let go. 'I'm Betsy Graves.'

'Glad to meet you, Betsy.' He almost said 'Miss Graves'. She intimidated the hell out of him.

'I'm making you uncomfortable, aren't I, darling?' she said with a voluptuous chuckle.

Let go of my hand, he thought wildly, but tried to look worldly wise.

'Take your bath, Anthony Wentworth. We'll meet again.'

She finally liberated him and ambled toward the door, short skirt swinging, delicious legs looking as good from the back as the front. And no sign of a run, as far as he could see. She paused, looked Anthony over once more and slipped into the hallway.

Anthony had learned about sensory overload in his psychology classes, and now experienced a brand of it firsthand. Who were these people? What was he doing here? How come everybody knew about him and he knew nothing about them? He figured it was probably some grand psychological laboratory the Prof had tossed him into to test him in some way. Well, dammit, he was sick of being a guinea pig. He fumed and muttered and by the time he'd scrubbed himself nearly raw, anger had been replaced with curiosity.

Max Herron – obviously a man of wealth and power, a man accustomed to the limelight socially. A sick man, too. Jeb Wentworth had had the same gray-under-tan look for a while after he had his gall bladder out. Herron was also oddly familiar. Strange, that. Anthony knew he'd never met him. He had the vague sense that he'd seen him many times. He must slightly resemble someone he'd seen a lot. Some movie or television person probably. Who?

Never mind who he looked like, who was he? Anthony went over his impressions of the house. Was there a clue there? Photos, plaques, trophies, diplomas? The Prof had taught him some memorization techniques and he used them to tour the house again in his mind. Lots of very pricey art and furnishings, but nothing that gave him a clue to the man himself. The house could have been put together by a decorator. Or Herron's wife. Decorating was usually left to the woman of the house.

Anthony temporarily abandoned the puzzle of Max Herron and mentally examined his wife, Blanche. She was easy to dispose of. Cold, rich, bitchy. English accent. She seemed to be the only one of the principals of the place who didn't give a shit about him. Herron found him interesting and even Betsy Graves had heard enough about him to remember his name and be surprised at meeting him in the flesh.

Unfortunate phrase.

Anthony went out to sit on the balcony, grinning like a Cheshire cat, remembering Betsy Graves. Now that he was over his first shock, Betsy seemed quite a nice little armload of woman. Hot to trot, no mistaking that. No kid; she was probably twenty-five and clearly knew her way around a bedroom. He started to get an erection thinking about her. But then, he could get an erection thinking about almost anything. Yes, Betsy might make this perplexing visit a lot more entertaining. His room or hers? He'd have to find out where hers was.

After dressing, he went exploring, keeping his distance from the rest of the guests. He wasn't up to any more surprises. There was a swimming pool of stupendous size, but it was thickly peopled with rich, bronzed strangers, so he veered off to a cluster of buildings that included a stable, thinking he'd be more at home with the horses. But as he approached, so did a rider, a girl in her early twenties. She was petite, almost fragile, but very wholesome, dressed in a soft white shirt, khaki jodhpurs and riding boots. She floated down off the horse then spoke with some intensity to the groom, pointing to her mount's right foreleg. The two of them then knelt down to examine it.

It was clear they'd be a while, and curious as Anthony was about the condition of the horse, he didn't want another human encounter until he'd adjusted to the last few, so he went back to the house. The Prof was there. 'Been looking around?' he asked. 'What do you think of the place?'

'Not quite like the ranch, is it?'

'Do you like it here?'

What difference does it make? Anthony thought. 'Yes, it's all right.'

'What do you think of Max Herron?'

'Hardly anything,' Anthony said, resolved to stop being the 'test subject'. Let the Prof answer a few questions for a change. 'Who is he?'

'An old friend of mine.'

'No, I mean what does he do? What supports this place? Why does he seem familiar?'

'He comes from paper money in Kansas City. Paper manufacture, that is. Still has a place there, too. And Palm Springs. And in the Bahamas. Nowadays Max just keeps the money earning money. Mainly investments in shopping centres, I think.'

'How do you know him?'

If Taylor Lisle minded being on the receiving end of the questions, he didn't indicate it. 'I knew him when he was a boy, then met up with him again just after the war. We've kept in touch through the years.'

Anthony thought that was an understatement. The servants knew Lisle as well as if he lived here. 'What am I supposed to think of him?' Anthony asked testily.

Lisle looked uncomfortable at that one. 'Whatever you like, my boy,' he said, recovering quickly. 'I'm going to look over some new gardens they've put in. Do you want to come along?'

'Thanks, no.'

The Prof took himself off and Anthony was left wondering, as he so often did after their conversations, 'What the hell was that all about?'

Taylor Lisle found Max Herron sitting on a concrete bench in a small arbor where new growth had only just begun to cast shade. 'What do you think of him?' he asked.

Max moved over to make room for the older man. 'He's a fine boy. Fine.' He was smiling.

'Aren't you ready to tell him?'

Max didn't answer right away. 'I have to explain to Blanche first. I've thought of a hundred ways of starting, but —'

'He has the right to know.'

'Of course he does. But I owe it to Blanche ...'

There was so much Lisle wanted to say, but it was all obvious. Max had undergone surgery for cancer only a few months earlier, so mentioning that he might run out of time was not only unnecessary, but cruel. Max was convinced, and the doctors seemed to agree, that they'd got it all. And, in truth, Max was looking better. Still, anything could happen.

'Max,' Lisle said as mildly as he could, 'you've had many years in which to tell Blanche about him already.'

'I know. I know. But the time's never been right.'

'What makes you think it ever will be?'

'It will. I promise. Soon.'

Anthony stuck around his room for another hour before wandering down to join everyone for cocktails. He kept an eager eye out for Betsy Graves, but there was no sign of her. Blanche Herron offered him a drink and asked his preference, but wandered off to talk with someone else without fixing him anything. Her attitude toward him seemed to be evenly balanced between suspicion and utter boredom.

'You must be Anthony Wentworth,' an unfamiliar voice said as he was pouring himself a soda. Anthony

35

turned and was startled speechless. The speaker was a man in his late twenties with straight black hair, lapis blue eyes and the most powerful physical presence Anthony had ever come across. Even though all Anthony's hormones were in the right places, he had an almost uncontrollable urge to touch this stranger, he was so beautiful. Or perhaps beauty was the wrong word, implying femininity. There was nothing girlish about him. He was just handsome to the point that it almost hurt to look at him. More surprising, he didn't have the self-assured arrogance most good-looking people have – that aura of 'look at me and weep, mortals'.

'I'm Steven Packwood,' he said, putting out a hand that looked like it belonged on a concert piano keyboard; big and strong, but somehow sensitive. 'Max says you're remarkable.' He said it with a grin.

'I'm remarkably confused, if that counts,' Anthony said.

'It's an odd, inbred group,' Packwood said, glancing around indifferently at the others. 'They don't mean to make you feel like an outsider. But they do exude an air of smug superiority, don't they? I assure you, though, if they didn't consider you one of them, you'd be in slivers on the carpet by now.'

'I think Mrs Herron would reduce me to slivers except I'm not worth the bother.' Anthony had no idea why he was spilling his guts to this man except that he seemed to understand.

'Blanche? Don't worry about her.'

'Who are the rest of these people? Who are you, come to that?'

Steven Packwood laughed. 'My grandfather and Max's father started the paper manufacturing company that's the kernel of Max's empire. Herron Paper Products. You've heard of it?'

'Sure, but I'd never made the connection.'

'So that's me. The scion of half of Herron paper. Let's see who else is around. Have you met Faye?' He gestured

36

toward a slim young woman talking to Blanche. She was the one Anthony had seen riding earlier. Now she was in a pale blue cotton dress with her fine blonde hair pulled back in a ponytail. She wore no make-up or jewellery and was the essential wholesome upper-class girl. Fragile and yet tomboyish

'I saw her earlier. Who is she?'

'Faye Leland. Blanche's younger daughter. I'd introduce you, but you're about to meet the dragon lady.'

A tall, angular woman was indeed bearing down on them. 'Good evening, Steven,' she said in a clipped mid-Atlantic accent. 'This must be Dr Lisle's protégé Anthony. I'm Lillian Smith, Mr Herron's private secretary.'

'How do you do, Miss Smith. I'm Anthony Wentworth,' he said. She shook his hand in a fierce grip.

'Of course you are. Are you enjoying yourself?' The funny thing was, she seemed actually to care about his answer. Or maybe it was just her manner. She leaned forward as if afraid she might not hear him properly otherwise.

'I am, yes. It's a beautiful house,' Anthony said.

'Oh, the house.' She waved away thirty bedrooms as a mere roof over one's head. 'What do you think of Mr Herron?'

Well, that's direct, Anthony thought. What a disconcerting woman. Before he could frame a reply, a soft voice from somewhere behind her said, 'Mother, you're putting Mr Wentworth on the spot. That's not fair.'

Miss Smith – or, rather, Mrs Smith – stepped aside a bit and a little mousy person slid round her. She couldn't have been quite five feet tall and had a round face, round granny glasses and no special colour hair pulled into a frumpy bun at the back of her head. She looked about fourteen, but sounded older. 'I'm Nina Smith. I'm awfully glad to meet you,' she said putting out a tiny hand that had a grip almost as powerful as her mother's.

'Hi, Nina. I'm Anthony Wentworth.'

Fortunately, before Anthony could be forced to make any more awkward conversation with this odd, owlish little person and her formidable mother, a servant announced dinner and Steven Packwood said, 'We best get along, Mrs Smith.'

She nodded curtly as if she acknowledged the dismissal but only of her own volition.

'She ran the Hitler Youth,' Steven said in an undertone as he led Anthony toward the dining room. Anthony glanced at him sharply. 'Just kidding,' he said. 'But it would have been a job custom-made for her talents. It's a wonder Nina turned out halfway human.'

'Nina?'

'Her daughter. You just met her.'

'Oh, yes.' He'd met Nina and forgotten her a few seconds later. She was about as memorable as a sparrow. But then, he had no idea what she would come to mean to him.

Seating for dinner was a scramble. Eating with the Herrons was normally quite formal with place cards, individual menus and the whole Emily Post routine, but there had been a domestic upheaval behind the scenes. Blanche Herron, white with rage, had to let the guests choose their own places. Unfortunately, Anthony lost sight of both Steven Packwood and the Prof, the only two he wanted to sit near. He sensed that there was probably a pecking order to who sat where, and he was hoping someone would guide him to an appropriate place when he felt a small hand on his arm.

'Why, it's Anthony – with clothes on, for a change,' Betsy Graves said with a rippling laugh. She had on a white eyelet summer dress with skinny straps and a deep – extremely deep – dip in the center of the front. Her bikini tan line was visible cutting across between her breasts. There was something fantastically sexy about that thin white line against her perfectly tanned skin. It was all Anthony could do to keep from tearing her clothes off.

'Let's sit down,' he said.

She glanced down at the front of his trousers and smiled wickedly. 'Yes, maybe we better – before someone gets the wrong impression. Or the right one.'

She was a slut, there was no question in Anthony's mind about it. He never fooled himself. But then neither did she. Intellectual compatibility or even the mildest sort of affection didn't come into it; there was absolute dynamite between them. A salad was served and Betsy and Anthony made meaningless conversation about the weather. Somehow she even managed to make the barometric conditions sound sexy. 'I do love hot weather, don't you? Such a pleasure to lie naked in front of a window fan, but air conditioning isn't any fun at all.'

By the time the main course was being cleared, her hand was on his thigh and edging toward his crotch. With her other hand – God, she was a cool number, he thought – she snapped open the catch on a little evening bag and said, 'Darn it, I'm out of cigarettes.' The man on her other side offered her one of his, but she said, 'Thanks, but I'm terribly partial to my own. I'll just run upstairs and grab a fresh pack. Anthony, would you mind keeping me company?'

Before he could even agree, which was never in doubt, she'd more or less dragged him to his feet and out the door. They all but ran through the ground floor rooms and up the main stairway.

'We've only got a minute,' she said, breathlessly opening the door to Anthony's room.

Anthony Wentworth was no prude, but he was frankly shocked. She closed the door, pushed him back against it and started undoing his pants. As she leaned forward, he put his hands on her shoulder straps and eased them down her arms. Her breasts practically popped out and they were magnificent. Even fuller and silkier-skinned than he'd imagined and his imagination had been working overtime. The nipples were small and erect and there was untanned skin about the size of a lemon round them. He nearly came right in her hands and probably would have except that she shoved him into a brocaded straight-back chair by the door. There he sat with his pants down round his ankles, like the traveling salesman in a porno flick. Straddling his legs, she lifted her skirts and lowered herself onto him.

She gasped as she was penetrated and Anthony could see her climaxing with him. She threw her head back, eyes closed, and shuddered with pleasure. He put his hands round those fantastic globes of flesh and sucked one nipple fiercely while kneading the other. He just kept coming and she was making a panting, whimpering noise. It was over in a few seconds.

Finally she sighed, leaned forward and wrapped her arms round his head. 'Not bad,' she said, laughing.

She started to move and Anthony said, 'Wait. I don't want it to be over.'

'It's not over. Just an intermission. We have to get back to the table. This was just the appetizer.'

Anthony groaned and she slowly got up and went to the bathroom. He started putting himself together, amazed that it had all been so fast and efficient that he was hardly wrinkled. He heard the toilet flush, then she came out of the bathroom looking as if nothing unusual had happened.

'I hope Blanche is serving cheesecake. Her cook does it divinely,' she commented languidly as she left the room, Anthony trailing behind her like a stud horse being led back to the stables.

Nobody seemed to have noticed their absence – why should they? They were only gone five minutes at the most – except a sour-looking man about four seats down from Betsy.

'Where have you been?' he asked querulously as they passed.

'Don't fuss. I just ran upstairs for some cigarettes.'

'Who was that?' Anthony whispered as he held her chair out.

She seated herself primly and smiled politely at the

woman across the table. 'Just my husband.'

The weekend was a sexual circus. They did it in bed, in the pool, in the woods behind the stables and once, at four in the morning, on the dining table where they'd eaten that dinner. She was voracious and seemed all the more passionate at the prospect of getting caught. Oddly, Anthony liked her less and less with each session. He knew she thought of him as hands, lips and dick. Nothing else about him made any difference or interested her in the least.

Anthony thought he was sexually precocious before that weekend, given that he was only eighteen years old. But he guessed that few men of fifty had had sex in as many positions, variations and with as many auxiliary artifacts as he could claim after two days with Betsy Graves. She was amazing, the nymphomaniac he and his friends had fantasized about in the dorm but didn't believe really existed.

Naturally enough, he didn't remember much about that stay after the first dinner. The Prof left, which he noticed only because his unexpected departure meant one less person paying attention to him, which was fine.

'It's a crisis for a corporate board I serve on. Three members have resigned in a huff and replacements have to be found immediately. But I'll be back Sunday to fetch you,' he said after dinner. 'Will you be all right on your own here?' he asked like someone leaving a four-year-old at a birthday party.

Would he be all right? Anthony nearly laughed.

The only other thing that stuck in his mind was an odd little incident at dinner the second evening. He was, naturally, sitting next to Betsy and noticed that her attention had wandered to the head of the table. Max Herron was in conversation with Faye, the wholesome blonde girl Anthony had first seen riding. She was leaning toward him, all smiles and cute animation. He was patting her hand and laughing.

'How adorable. Daddy's little darling,' Betsy said. There was chilling viciousness in her tone. 'She's got Max wrapped round her little finger. It's disgusting.'

It wasn't the words so much as the look of venom on her face that made Anthony feel sort of sick. For God knew what reason, Betsy hated Faye with the same intensity that she liked sex. That was when he first realized that Betsy was frightening; this was a person who felt everything with dangerous intensity. He'd have left the table right then except that she quite literally had him by the balls – just a little entertainment under the concealment of the tablecloth. A moment later the expression of loathing on her face was replaced by her usual smooth, sneering sexy look and Anthony put aside the brief conversation. But it kept haunting him.

Dr Lisle turned up bright and early Sunday morning. 'Have you enjoyed yourself?' he asked.

'Enormously,' Anthony said, trying not to look as smug and sore and exhausted as he felt.

'Have you talked to Max?'

'No. Was I supposed to?'

'Not especially. I was just hoping you'd get to know each other.'

For once Anthony wasn't even curious about his meaning. He had other things on his mind.

They went down to breakfast, served buffet-style round the pool. Max Herron detached himself from a conversation as soon as he saw them. 'Help yourself to all you can eat,' he said heartily and clapped Anthony on the shoulder. 'Growing boys need lots of food. Dr Lisle, are you sure you won't change your mind and stay longer? I have to go back to Kansas City tonight, but Blanche and some of the others are staying. She'd love to have you both.'

'No, we'll be getting along,' the Prof said.

'Oh, Betsy said to tell you goodbye,' Herron said offhandedly.

'Betsy— ?' Anthony had been about to yelp, 'Betsy's

gone?' but Herron misunderstood.

'Betsy Graves. My stepdaughter. You did meet her, didn't you? She remembered you and said to give you her best wishes. I think she's coming round, Dr Lisle. Not so wild. This weekend she was as quiet and well-behaved as you could want. I hardly saw her. I think it's the kids.'

His stepdaughter? Oh, shit! He'd been screwing the host's stepdaughter? 'I thought Faye Leland was Mrs Herron's daughter,' he said.

'Yes, both of them are. Amazing how two girls could be so different and neither of them is anything like Blanche. Betsy's been a trial, but Faye is the sweetest little thing. You'll come back, won't you, Anthony?' Herron was saying.

'I'd like that, sir.'

'We're going to bolt our breakfast and run, Max,' the Prof said. 'We've got a train to catch.'

'Still not flying,' Herron said, laughing.

'Not when I can help it,' the Prof answered, bristling up like he did whenever anyone made fun of his fear.

'You don't mind flying, do you, Tony?' Herron asked.

The 'Tony' took him by surprise. No one called him that. 'No, sir. I enjoy it.'

'Good, I've got a plane I keep in Kansas City. Maybe you'll come up someday and let me buzz you around in it.'

Anthony felt guilty as hell. This nice old guy was going out of his way to be hospitable and he'd not only ignored him all weekend, but spent the time screwing his brains out with his stepdaughter. 'That'd be great!' Anthony said, trying to cover his dismay.

Herron clapped Anthony on the shoulder and beamed at Dr Lisle. 'He's a fine boy, isn't he? Just what I expected. A real credit to you.'

'And his father,' the Prof said.

Herron just looked at him as if at a loss for words.

They left an hour later. Steven Packwood came up while

Anthony was packing. 'Not leaving already, are you? Where have you been keeping yourself?' Steven asked.

'Here and there,' Anthony said, trying to make it sound jokey. Now that Betsy wasn't around he was feeling worse and worse about himself, wishing he'd got to know Herron and Packwood better while he'd had the chance. But he'd blown it.

'I saw Betsy panting after you,' Steven said, shattering Anthony's illusion that they hadn't been obvious. 'You like her?' he asked bluntly.

Anthony looked up from his packing and met those startling blue eyes. 'Not much,' he said.

'Good. She's dangerous goods. Runs poor Ned ragged. Someday he'll reach the breaking point and strangle her. He might strangle whoever's in bed with her at the moment as well.' It was clearly a warning.

'Ned's her husband?'

'Poor sap, yes. And jealous as hell. She keeps him in a frenzy of rage all the time. You know they've got a bunch of kids.'

'She has children?' Anthony found that appalling news, though he didn't know quite why.

'Boys. Three or four, I forget exactly.'

'How old *is* she?'

'Twenty-eight. Doesn't look it, does she? The story is that she and Neddy had it off behind a potted palm at her boarding school tea dance. True or not, old Ned took the blame for knocking up this fifteen-year-old who was probably sleeping with half the men in a fifty-mile radius. People say Ned's family was frantic, he was only nine-teen and on an academic scholarship at Princeton, and hers was thrilled to get her off their hands. Who wouldn't be?'

Yeah, Anthony thought. *Who wouldn't be glad to be rid of her?* He'd had a narrow escape. It was the first time he realized that sex could be a double-bladed weapon.

44

Chapter Three

Anthony didn't see or hear anything of the Herron crowd for three years, with two exceptions. The first came almost a year after he and Lisle made their mysterious visit. Anthony had been working at the ranch and growing daily more unhappy and unfocused. Rory's status as elder son meant that Anthony was his underling. And Rory never let him forget it. Anthony knew as well as Rory how the ranch was run and what had to be done, but Rory was for ever telling him to do things he'd already begun.

One afternoon when he went to town for the mail, he got a letter on expensive pale blue stationery. He slit it open without even bothering to look at the return address. It was a printed birth announcement for some baby born a couple of weeks earlier. Name: Martin Westgate Graves. For a second Anthony couldn't place it, then he noticed the parents' names: Elizabeth and Edward Graves. Betsy and Ned.

So, Betsy'd had another baby, Anthony thought. Why the hell was she bothering to tell him? He'd managed thoroughly to forget her. After that memorable weekend, he'd felt nasty and 'defiled', Puritan though that sounded, for weeks. The very thought of her made him feel like an over-sexed idiot.

He dropped the card into the wastebasket next to the stamp machine and it fell face down. That's when he noticed the handwriting on the back. Just a few lines in a spidery, sprawling hand. 'Darling, he's yours. But Ned's taking credit. B.G.'

His hands were shaking so badly that he could hardly

fish it back out of the wastebasket. He read it over and over, frantic to find some alternative meaning in it, but there wasn't one. The bitch was saying he'd fathered this kid. He staggered out to the truck. Jesus! He felt cold, but was sweating like a pig and his stomach was roiling. He was two miles past the ranch before he realized he'd missed the turn.

He had two days to agonize over it before the Prof came back from another of his trips. Anthony didn't want to tell him but didn't know what else to do. He *had* to talk to someone. All his fancy education and Mensa mentality didn't give him a clue to what a nineteen-year-old kid is supposed to do when a married woman tells him he's the real father of her child. He knew he should have been going to his father, but he couldn't bear the thought of admitting to him that he'd let him down so badly.

And, too, in a vague way Anthony held the Prof to blame. Why in hell had he thrown him in with those people? Like tossing a kitten into a stock tank to see if it sinks or swims. Well, Anthony had sunk all right. It was a normal human need to shift the blame, but by the time the Prof got back, Anthony had figured out that it was entirely the old man's fault and that he, Anthony, was the aggrieved party. He went to pick up the Prof at the train station in a fine, martyred rage. Cool, noble, and put-upon, he slammed the luggage into the truck and drove a couple miles before pulling over to the side of the road.

'You're very mysterious today, Anthony,' the Prof said. Smugly, Anthony thought.

'I have to talk to you before we go home.' Now that the moment had come, he had no idea what to say. He'd kept the birth announcement in his pocket, afraid to let it out of his sight. He took it out now, unfolded it and handed it to Lisle. Like Anthony, Lisle read the front and shrugged. 'Look at the back.'

He stared at it for a long time, then looked with absolute horror at Anthony. 'Is this ... can this be true?'

'Yes, it *can* be. I don't know if it *is*.'

'Oh, my God. This is awful.'

'You're telling me!'

'No, it's worse than you think.'

'Oh, great! Just what I needed to hear.'

'Anthony, how could you?'

'How could I? Jesus! It was damned easy, Prof. She threw herself at me.'

He considered Anthony for a moment and sighed deeply. 'Yes, of course she would. I'm sorry.'

'What do I do?'

'Stay away from her.'

'Jeez, as if I hadn't thought of that! Betsy doesn't matter—'

'She matters!'

'No, it's the kid that matters.'

'Cut the sarcasm, Anthony. I mean it. Don't ever have anything to do with her again.'

'But what about the kid? What if it really is mine?'

'*He'll destroy you.*'

He said this in an eerie voice that made Anthony's skin crawl, like an Old Testament prophet pronouncing a curse. They sat in silence for a long time. The Prof looked ten years older. Anthony felt miserable, closer to tears than he'd been since he was a child.

Finally the older man spoke again, in a defeated voice. 'You haven't heard anything else from her, have you? No phone calls or other letters?'

'No. Do you think she'll ... do anything. Make trouble?'

'God only knows. Let's go home. I'll make some calls.'

They didn't talk the rest of the way, but it was, in an odd sense, a comfortable silence. They had a problem, but had got past blaming each other. Now it was a joint concern. Anthony had someone on his side, whatever his side was.

The Prof holed up in his office for a couple hours, making phone calls, then invited Anthony to check some fences so they could talk privately. Anthony had no idea who he'd been talking to on the phone.

'As far as I can tell she sent you that announcement to validate her torture of Ned,' Lisle said.

'What do you mean?'

'She hasn't told anyone else that the child isn't Ned's. She's apparently using this story of the child being yours to get back at him about some indiscretion of his.'

'So it's not true.'

'Nobody knows. Probably not even Betsy.'

'But the Herrons and their friends don't know she's saying I got her pregnant.'

'They don't know and they wouldn't care whose child it is. Don't forget, Anthony, they all know her. Nobody would think badly of you over this if they knew.'

'I don't care what they think of me, but if it's true, I should take responsibility.'

'No! You can't. You mustn't.'

'Why not?'

The Prof took a deep breath. 'Look, Anthony, consider this rationally. What can you do? First, the child could be yours or Ned's or the mailman's. Betsy's blatantly promiscuous. Even if we had some way of knowing the baby were yours, she and Ned have a sick, tortuous relationship that they're satisfied with. She's not going to leave him for you.'

Anthony shivered. He'd been thinking about doing something for the child. It hadn't crossed his mind that Betsy might come with the deal.

The Prof went on, 'Ned's a masochist who gets something out of having a wife like Betsy. If he were going to get rid of her, he'd have done it years ago. This is nothing new. She started rumors about her last child being someone else's, too. She thrives on causing scandals about herself, then rubbing everybody's nose in them, especially poor Ned's.'

'She's disgusting.'

'It's more than that. She's truly evil. Or perhaps she's truly innocent.'

'Betsy! Innocent!'

'I mean in the sense that she sees something she wants and she takes it. She thinks something, so she says it. That is a sort of Neanderthal outlook, a primitive innocence. Like an infant, but with cunning. That's why you must never have anything to do with her again. Or the child.'

'Don't worry. I've learned my lesson, Prof. Besides, I'm not likely to ever run into her again.'

The Prof shook his head. 'I wish that were true.'

Anthony was so emotionally drained by the conversation that he didn't press him to explain that remark. But he should have. It was a moment when Lisle might have been sufficiently shocked to put aside an old and solemn promise and tell Anthony a great deal.

Anthony wasn't sure how much Betsy Graves' bombshell had to do with it, but he soon realized it was long past time for a change. Working at the ranch was pointless. He had no future there. For the past year he'd just been killing time waiting – waiting for what, he had no idea. The future wasn't going to come looking for him; he'd have to look for it.

'I want to go away,' he said one night at dinner. He'd chosen a time when Rory was out whoring and drinking so it was just him and his father and the Prof.

Jeb helped himself to a piece of apple pie and nodded like it was something he'd been waiting to hear, not eagerly, but with resignation. 'You've been like a horse with a burr under his saddle for weeks,' he said.

'Where are you going?' the Prof asked. He sounded pleased at the decision.

'Europe. I'm strong and smart enough to get odd jobs. I know a lot of French and a smattering of German. If I stay in youth hostels, I ought to be able to afford it.'

The Prof was all but rubbing his hands together. 'You want some company?' Anthony stared at him. Somehow the idea of the Prof waiting tables and staying in hostels

49

was too absurd to absorb. Lisle saw the amazed look on his face and laughed. 'I don't mean me, Anthony. You remember Steven Packwood?'

'Of course.'

'I got a letter from him the other day. He's combining an extended business trip with a strange kind of intermittent sabbatical from work. England and France mainly. I don't imagine either of you want a full-time companion, but you might want to arrange to touch base from time to time.'

'Have you got his number? I'll see how he feels about it.'

It was easily arranged. They met in New York and flew to London where Steven had appointments with several office suppliers. Anthony acted as right-hand man and secretary to him, toting cases full of paper samples, typing letters and such. And he enjoyed it, in spite of the occasional wry thought that the local business college would have probably prepared him better than Harvard did for his current occupation. But at least he had an occupation instead of just filling empty boots at the ranch. It wasn't a lifetime thing, thank God, but it was better than being pushed around by Rory.

Between appointments, they 'did' London. The Tower, the Houses of Parliament, Big Ben, the whole touristy business. They even took a boat trip up the Thames to Hampton Court where Anthony got utterly lost in the maze despite his intellectual contempt for something so childish. He'd read that if you kept your left hand on the hedge, you couldn't get lost. After he was rescued, he vowed that if anyone ever told him that again, he'd laugh in their face.

Anthony didn't get to know Steven very well at first, though he liked him better with every day. It wasn't that Steven was standoffish. Quite the contrary. He was very talkative and observant, but there was a subtle reserve to him. As if he was talking about what he saw, but not what

50

he thought of it down deep. Not that Anthony tried to dig deeply into his soul. It wasn't the sort of thing he knew how to do.

When the business part of the visit was over, they took to the countryside. They enjoyed a fantastic train north to Edinburgh, then slowly worked their way south in a rented car. Anthony later claimed they'd visited every castle and church in the whole of England, Scotland and Wales. It was the churches that made Anthony start thinking about the layers of Steven Packwood. It wasn't that Steven talked about religion, nothing middle-class and embarrassing like that, but while Anthony was rummaging in the guide book for the history of the churches, he seemed to just let them soak into him. Inside a church, he seemed to shed the present and himself. He became serene and slightly vague. Even at places like Tintern Abbey, which was just a half-shell of a building with vines growing through open windows and ferns in the cracks, he dropped his voice and stood a little straighter, as if a service was going on. Anthony found Steven's behavior more interesting than most of the places they were visiting.

Anthony wanted to ask him about it, what he was feeling, because it was obviously something Anthony didn't grasp. But he didn't quite know how to open the subject and it seemed like prying. He'd grown to like Steven so well that he didn't want to impose on the friendship for fear of damaging it.

It was odd; Anthony had always thought that a 'sensitive' man, if there could be such a thing, would be a nerdy loser. A hairdresser, or momma's boy, or something. But he was beginning to sense that it might be possible to be sensitive and still be strong and manly. At least Steven struck him that way. He did nice things. Very *little* nice things, like casually sticking a clump of moss back where he'd accidently kicked it loose without even seeming to notice he was doing it.

Once, when they were at a village market, a little girl ran into him. She had long hair and was slobbering all over a lollipop. Some of her hair was stuck to the sweet and Steven, who was talking about a local battle he'd once studied, bent over and untangled her hair. Then he told her to spit on a handkerchief and gently cleaned up her face. All of this without missing a word about Bonnie Prince Charlie and Culloden. Anthony honestly didn't think Steven knew he was doing it. A sort of auto-pilot thoughtfulness.

Weird. And fascinating.

He seemed so sure of himself that Anthony let him determine their course most of the time. Steven had been to England several times before, so it made sense to let him decide where to go and what to see. One morning about two months into their leisurely tour, Steven said, 'Let's go see Leland House today.'

As they set out, Anthony consulted the guide books and wondered about the trip. Leland House was hardly mentioned except some nostalgic bits about what wonderful gardens it used to have. Nothing important happened there that he could discover. It wasn't a very old house, probably early 1800s, and nothing compared to the 'stately homes' they'd visited. A big place, but cheesy-looking, in Anthony's opinion. As if it had gone to seed and somebody had tried to fix it up on the cheap. As if the paint had come from Woolworth's. 'What are we doing here?' he asked when they drove through the gates and paid their fee to take the tour.

'I told Max I'd take a look while I was here.'

'Max? Max Herron? Why?'

'This is where he met Blanche. She was married to the owner at that time.'

'Blanche was married before? Oh, yeah, she has daughters from an earlier marriage,' Anthony said, forcing Betsy back out of his thoughts. 'The place looks like her. I mean, if it were fixed up.'

'Apparently she was pretty obsessed with it for a while.

52

She and her first husband only had Betsy and Faye, who couldn't inherit. They say the husband's brother didn't get along with her. There would have been a battle royal if the baby had lived.'

Anthony was in the dark. 'What baby?'

'Blanche and Max's. I thought Dr Lisle had told you all this.'

'No, what's the story?'

'Well, I don't know how much of it's true. I got most of this from my mother, but her gossip is usually pretty reliable. It seems that Max and Dr Lisle came to visit here a year or so after the war. The night they arrived, Blanche's husband went out to check on an unexploded bomb somebody had found. The thing went ka-blooey and killed the husband. Max and Dr Lisle stayed on to help her make funeral arrangements and such. But in the midst of it, the dead man's brother came dashing in, rubbing his hands over what he'd inherited. It must have still been pretty nice then. Blanche put up a big stink, crying, hysterics, all sorts of carrying on. Poor fatherless girls and their widowed mother being thrown to the wolves, etc. Max stood by her, patting her hand and keeping the brother-in-law from tossing her out. Then, to everyone's surprise, she ups and marries Max. Not quite two weeks after her first husband died.'

'Really?' Blanche Herron didn't seem the impulsive type from what Anthony had observed.

'The story gets better. Max took her to London to recuperate and see lawyers and a month later she's sending the brother-in-law's solicitors a medical report saying she's pregnant. The brother-in-law must have gone nearly berserk at the idea of Leland House being snatched from his grasp.'

'What? I don't get it.'

'Blanche was claiming the child was her *first* husband's and therefore would be the heir to the estate if it was a boy. A posthumous Leland baby.'

'Ohhh – was it true?' This conversation gave Anthony

an eerie sense of *déjà vu*. Once again he shoved Betsy Graves out of his mind.

'Nobody ever knew. Max whisked her back to Kansas City to have special medical care. She had a hard time with the whole pregnancy and the birth. Of course, the gory gynecological details of that part of the story are what my mother likes best, but I tuned them out.'

'So did the baby inherit this place?' Anthony asked.

'No, it was a boy all right, but there was something wrong with it. It died a week or so after it was born. Or maybe right away, I'm not sure. Blanche went haywire, my mother said. Complete breakdown. Months in a mental hospital. Everybody else must have been pretty relieved, especially poor old Max.'

'Why was Max relieved?'

'Anthony, if the kid had lived, Blanche would have made everyone's life a living hell trying to prove it *wasn't* Max's. Max told Mom once that he knew it was his, but he was pretty well potted at the time or he'd never have said a word. Even people who didn't like him much felt sorry for him over the whole thing. He wanted a son so badly and here's this dead son that Blanche would never have admitted was his anyway – and there was never another child. Not for them, anyway, though there was some gossip later about Max having a child by a mistress. I don't think that was true. Anyway, Blanche finally came round and started talking about adoption, but he wouldn't hear of it. Instead, he became the best father he could to her little girls. They really are like his own daughters.'

'Betsy and Faye.'

'Yes,' Steven said drily. 'At least Faye appreciated his efforts. Although I think she's as strange as Betsy in her own way.'

'How do you mean?'

'I can't sum it up. I've known her nearly all my life and I don't like her. She's married now, you know.' Steven put the Herrons aside and said, 'Let's park here and see if anybody's revived the gardens.'

They followed a tour guide through the gardens and house. As they left, Anthony said, 'I don't see what all the fuss was about. Would *you* get into a lifelong battle for this place?'

'Not the way it is now. But it must have once been elegant. My dad visited once before the war and said it was beautiful. Blanche's brother-in-law got clear title to it, or whatever the British equivalent is, after Blanche's baby died, then he lost his money in a uranium scheme, or was it gold? Let the place go to ruin, then had to move into the servants' quarters and open it to tourists. Max has been trying to buy it back for Blanche for years, but the old guy won't part with it if it means Blanche getting to lord it over him.'

'Which she would.'

'Would she ever!'

They traveled throughout England for another two months before Steven had to get back to work. As the day they were to head for Dover and then France approached, Anthony began to sense that Steven wasn't thrilled. He had an odd kind of extra intensity, an overstated appreciation of the places they were seeing. Anthony's imagination, such as it was, leaped to the conclusion that in some sense Steven was as 'lost' as he was. For all his apparent assurance, was it possible he was seeking an elusive *something* too? Or was Anthony just trying to find a similarity between them where none existed?

'You don't want to go to France, do you?' he asked Steven one morning.

'Of course I do. France is fascinating.' They were driving toward Dover and he spoke without taking his eyes from the road. Just ahead of them something vast and gray loomed up out of the mist. 'There it is. Dover Castle.'

As many ancient monuments as Anthony had seen, none of them had impressed him more. There they were, speeding down a busy four-lane highway, cars and trucks and fumes surrounding them, and that great, magic castle that figures in so much of Britain's history gradually took shape high on the horizon. Anthony forgot the conversation he'd tried to initiate. They bought the guide books, took the tour of the castle. Centuries of human feet had made hollows in the wide stone steps. They climbed to the top and looked out over the Channel. As they were coming back down the circular staircase, Steven said, 'How odd. It winds the wrong way.'

Anthony had just slipped and nearly fallen. 'It sure does something wrong.'

'No, don't you see? A castle staircase needs to be built for defense. If you're invading, coming up the steps, I'm coming down. I've got my sword in my right hand, and I have to be able to put my left against the wall for support. But here, I'd have to be at the narrow end of each tread to reach the wall with my left hand. I'd slip off the treads, just like you did. It's an invader's staircase, not a defender's. Unless the defenders are all left-handed,' he added. 'It's important to be able to put your hand out and have support close by.' He paused and repeated, 'Very important.'

'What are you really talking about?'

Steven looked at him with surprise. 'Myself, I guess. Or you. Or life. How about getting sandwiches and eating them on the cliffs?'

They found a pub that packed them ham salad sandwiches, pickled eggs, crackers, cheese and apples in biscuit tins. Steven also bought some beer. Quite a lot of beer. They drove to the edge of the cliff and sat overlooking the lighthouse. They wolfed down the sandwiches and eggs, then started on the cheese and crackers. 'Why don't you want to go to France?' Anthony asked.

Steven started the automatic denial, then paused and said, 'You're more perceptive than I gave you credit for. It's not France. It's the work.'

'You don't like it?'

'Oh, it's all right, but it doesn't mean anything.'

'What is selling tons of paper products supposed to mean?' Anthony asked.

'Exactly.'

'Steven, what are you talking about?'

Steven brushed cracker crumbs off his hands and leaned back on his elbows, frowning slightly. Anthony wondered if he was thinking that his perception wasn't so great after all. He hoped not. He'd been inordinately pleased at what he took to be a compliment. 'Anthony, as far as we know we're only given one life, unless the reincarnation people are onto something. Right?'

'As far as we know. Yes.'

'Well, that one single life in the course of all history ought to be worth something, shouldn't it? But what difference does it make to the world if I sell four reams of sixteen-pound bond paper or four hundred thousand?'

'To your company, a lot of difference.'

'But not to me.'

Steven needed to explain himself as much as Anthony needed to hear someone else's view that was so much like his own. Steven sat up, fished out a pocket knife and looked out to sea while peeling an apple and talking. 'I like my job. It's interesting and I'm good at it. I have a younger brother who could do it every bit as well, but I can't quit the race. I don't know who I'm racing exactly, but I've got to win. But sometimes I think – no, I hope, there will be a turning along the way and I can dash off that way.'

'Is it the money?' Anthony asked.

He laughed. 'God, no! I'm what they call filthy rich. My brother and I were the only grandchildren on both sides. We inherited bundles. No, I don't need the money, but I have to do something and as long as I am doing it, I have to do it well. You see that, don't you?' He put away the pocket knife and offered Anthony the apple.

'That's what I'm doing here,' Anthony said. 'Trying to figure out what it is I need to do.' Between bites of apple, he sketched in the background of the ranch, Rory's present and probable future role and his own sense of uselessness. Steven listened with interest. 'It sounds egotistical, but I'm certain I have the brains and drive to do very well at anything I take on, but I want to take on something I really care about and then throw my entire soul into it.'

'Then you *do* see.' Steven sounded genuinely surprised. 'You want something of your own to do. A place of your own to carve out and make something of. Have you any idea what it is?'

'None whatsoever. I have a degree in psychology—'

'You do?' Steven stopped himself just short of laughing.

'Since I didn't have anything else in mind,' Anthony said defensively, 'I let the Prof influence me into it. But I don't much care about the subject. I know all the textbook stuff, but you need more than knowledge, you need some instinct for people and I haven't got that.'

'It's very admirable, and fortunate, that you know and admit your shortcomings.'

He meant it as sincere praise, even though Anthony had hoped he would deny the self-assessment. 'It doesn't help me figure out what to do.'

Steven sat forward suddenly. 'But you're looking. That matters. A year or two on your own, trying things out, will help. At the very least, it might help you know what you don't want to do.'

'Are you speaking from experience?'

'As a matter of fact, I am. I thought I knew twice. Once it was religion; once it was a woman. I was wrong both times.'

Anthony was dying to know more about this, especially about the woman, but it was clear that confession time was over. He opened two bottles of beer, which they both drank too fast, and opened another two. 'Don't you have a sense of what general kind of thing you're looking for?' he asked.

'No. Do you?'

58

'Sort of. I want to do some good. For someone else. But I believe it all hinges on money and I haven't any. If I had gobs, like you, I'd be trying to do something with it.' He knew that sounded superior, but he was getting drunk and was starting to feel belligerent.

'Like what?'

'I've no idea,' Anthony admitted. 'I guess I'm looking for two things, really, an enjoyable way to earn a lot of money, and then a good cause to put it into.'

'Oh, God! I've got to go back to work tomorrow.' Steven flung himself back on the grass dramatically, self-mockingly. 'Sometimes I hate paper. Give me another beer, would you?'

They applied themselves to getting moderately drunk, telling a few dirty jokes along the way. Then, not trusting their balance, they crept carefully to the cliff edge, laid on their stomachs and tossed pebbles over. Somehow, in that hour, their relationship underwent a subtle change; Anthony lost his awe of Steven, and Steven abandoned the faintly fatherly air he'd always adopted with Anthony.

'Do you know what I want?' Steven finally said seriously. 'I want to *be* good.'

'Aren't you?' Anthony asked, inching back from the edge.

'God, no!'

'What have you ever done that's so bad?'

'Nothing. But not doing wrong isn't the same as being good. It's an internal thing.'

Anthony looked at him for a long minute, then said, 'That sounds to me like spiritual jerking off.'

Steven looked at him furiously for a second, then started laughing. 'Jesus! You're right, dammit!' Still laughing at himself, he got up and started tossing the last of the crackers to a crowd of seagulls who'd been sitting and watching them from a safe distance. They fell on the scraps with hysterical squawks.

Anthony stayed in Europe for over two years. He worked

at half a dozen jobs, never finding anything compelling. He did office work, acted as a tour guide, labored in the vineyards of France and drove beer trucks in Germany. All he learned was what he *didn't* want to do. Then one morning he woke up knowing it was time to go home. He had no idea what he was going to do when he got there, but he'd turned twenty-one many months before and his age was hanging over him like a noose. He had, in a sense, excused his own aimlessness on the grounds that his chronological contemporaries were still in college and didn't have to make lifetime decisions yet. But even if he'd had a normal school history, he'd be on his own shortly.

He didn't have enough money to get a ticket right away so he couldn't get home for Christmas as he'd hoped. Booking at the last minute was too expensive. He had to book a flight two weeks later. He telegrammed his plans to the Prof and had his Christmas dinner with the little monkeyish man who owned the tour business he'd been working for. They ate crêpes and drank a great deal of wine. As he later recalled, they both wept pretty copiously at the end of the evening.

He was to change planes in New York, but as he stepped from the jetway, the Prof was in front of him. For a second he thought the jet lag, or more likely the over-whelming perfume his seatmate had doused herself in, had got to him and he was hallucinating. 'Prof, is that really you?'

'Thank God!' the Prof said, 'I was afraid I'd miss you. Get your luggage. I have tickets for us on a flight to Kansas City in half an hour.'

'Us? You're flying? What's happening?' He felt like his stomach had turned to ice.

'How many bags are we looking for?' Lisle asked, grabbing Anthony's elbow and hurrying him toward the baggage claim.

'It's not bad, is it?'

He paused. 'No. It's Max Herron. He wants to see you.'

'Me? Why me?'

—The Prof sighed and seemed to sag into his clothes. 'This isn't the time or place.'

Anthony hadn't realized how independent of him he'd become until that moment. Nor how desperately alarmed. 'It damned well is! I'm sick of you jerking me around without telling me the reasons. We're not going anywhere until you tell me why in hell Max Herron wants to see me, of all people.'

'*Because you're his only child and he's dying.*'

Chapter Four

Anthony never remembered exactly what happened next. He had a faint recollection of the Prof grabbing his arm and propelling him through the airport. They must have claimed his luggage and reboarded another plane, although he never could recall those actions. By the time he collected himself enough to speak, they were in the air, on a flight to Kansas City. He turned to the Prof, who was sitting rigidly, his hands locked like vises to the armrests and his jaw clenched so tightly that his facial muscles were twitching. He'd forgotten Lisle's horror of flying. 'Prof?'

Lisle just shook his head in a slight, but jerky, side to side motion. 'Later,' he whispered through gritted teeth.

Anthony's mind was whirling. Now that he'd been told, it seemed so obvious that he wondered why he hadn't realized it long ago. It explained so much. This was why the Prof had taken him to Connecticut that time. Max Herron wanted to see how his child had turned out. He knew so much about him, and now Anthony understood it was because Max must have kept up with his progress through the years. And Max Herron had looked so familiar, like someone Anthony had seen many times. He had; in the mirror. He looked like a younger version of Max Herron.

Anthony recalled the story Steven had told him at Leland House. Steven had mentioned gossip about another child, an illegitimate child of Max's. Steven had dismissed the possibility, but it had been true. Max *had* fathered another child, Anthony, and had had him raised secretly under the wing of his friend Dr Lisle.

But who was his mother?

Could she have been one of those tanned, well-bred, professionally lifted faces at the Herrons' house party? Had someone besides Max looked at Anthony and thought, 'That's my son?' Had she been willing to part with her child because she belonged to that social set and couldn't stand the scandal? Or was she an unsuitable woman? A dancer? Secretary? Or worse?

Had Blanche known? Anthony thought back over that Connecticut weekend several years before. She hadn't suspected who Anthony was anymore than he had. He was sure of that. Her attitude toward him had been neutral, bored.

Anthony went through a range of emotions: indignation, astonishment, anger, maudlin tenderness, confusion. He supposed that all adopted children must occasionally be furiously insulted that their biological parents didn't care enough for them to own up to their existence. He'd gone through that stage when he was eight or nine and thought he was cured of it. But now that part of him was martyred and injured all over again. How could Max Herron, who so wanted a child to replace Blanche's dead infant, have abandoned him? On the other hand, he'd seen to it that he was placed with a trusted friend who would see that he had the best. A friend who would keep him informed about his boy, send progress reports and pictures. Anthony thought back to that weekend. Herron bragging on about his early graduation, showing him off to his friends. Poor old guy. He must have wanted to shove him forward and say, 'Look what I've done! This is my son!' but he couldn't.

Only now, dying, could he ask for his son. Acknowledge him. At least between the two of them. Jesus! How unfair. If the Prof was right that Herron was dying, Anthony would never really get to know his true father. He'd had one chance and he'd wasted it fooling around with Betsy Graves. Damn her! Damn her to hell!

Had his adopted father known whose child he was rais-

64

ing as his own? Probably not. He was a quiet man, not given to asking questions. Besides, questioning the Prof was usually a pretty fruitless exercise.

Shit! What a thing to lay on someone without any warning, Anthony thought angrily.

He nudged the Prof. He shook his head in a clear 'don't-talk-to-me' gesture. 'Who knows this?' Anthony asked him, nudging him again.

Dr Lisle took a deep breath. 'You. Me. Max.'

'That's all?'

He nodded stiffly.

Anthony thought they'd get to talk after the plane landed, but it didn't work out that way. He had to practically carry Dr Lisle off, he was so unstrung by the experience. A uniformed chauffeur was waiting for them and whisked them straight to a limo. As they sped toward Kansas City through the bleak, watery winter afternoon, the Prof lay back, so pale that Anthony was beginning to get seriously worried about him. Still, he had to know some things. 'Prof?'

Lisle half opened his eyes, pointed at the limo driver and made a shushing gesture, finger to lips. Grudgingly, Anthony recognized that he was right. This wasn't business that was appropriate to discuss in front of one of Max's employees. But when? They pulled up in front of a large hospital complex. The chauffeur hopped out and opened the door for the Prof. 'I left a boy to claim your bags, sir. I'll go back for them and take them to your hotel.'

'Thanks. Just give me a second on firm ground,' he added, stepping out and taking a few long, deep breaths. His color was a little better. The bitter cold wind buffeted life back into his face.

'Oh, there you are! I was waiting at the wrong door, Dr Lisle,' a voice said. A young woman in a baggy brown poncho-coat, granny glasses and a knot of sparrow-colored hair at the back of her neck rushed up. 'Mr Wentworth, how nice to see you again.' She saw Anthony's blank expression and added, 'Oh, you probably

65

don't remember me. I'm Nina Smith. We met once. My mother is Mr Herron's private secretary.'

'Oh, yes. Of course. It's nice to see you again.' She was only the slightest bit familiar. He remembered her mother, but not her.

'Dr Lisle, you look tired,' she said. 'Would you like a wheelchair?'

'Certainly not!' the Prof barked.

'I'm so sorry. I didn't mean to give offense.'

'None taken, I'm sure,' he replied in a voice that clearly meant the opposite. 'How is he?'

'A little worse. He'll be glad you're here. Beware – the ladies are distraught. Mother, Mrs Herron, her daughters.' They'd stepped into the warmth of the building and her glasses fogged up. She wiped them with the end of her distinctly hand-knitted gray scarf as she spoke. She had fairly pretty eyes, Anthony noticed in a distracted way.

'They would be. Does the press know yet?'

'I'm afraid so. The hospital just started getting calls. Come along before they catch you.'

The were taken to an elevator hidden round the corner from the main bank of them. It had only one button and went to the top floor. As they glided upward, something dreadful fell into place in Anthony's mind. He couldn't imagine why it wasn't the first thing that occurred to him, but he'd been so swamped with the emotions of learning who his father was that he hadn't thought beyond it.

Betsy Graves was his sister.

He'd slept with his sister. Half-sister. Stepsister. Something. What did it matter? He felt acid bubble into his throat and thought he was going to throw up. He leaned back against the wall of the elevator, unable to breathe for a moment. He was still trying to sort it out when the doors opened and they stepped out into what looked like a luxurious private penthouse, but with a uniformed nurse behind a desk in the foyer. 'Dr Lisle and Mr Wentworth,' the Prof said.

66

The nurse looked questioningly at Nina Smith, who nodded her agreement. 'Please go in,' the nurse said.

Anthony forced the thought of Betsy out of his mind, just like he'd learned to force terror out of his mind when breaking a stallion. Veering mentally from the profound to the trivial, he suddenly realized what he looked like and how inappropriate it was. He was wearing his beat-up pea jacket, jeans and sneakers. And they'd entered a waiting room that wouldn't have disgraced Versailles. Tall ceilings, flocked walls, brocade-covered sofas and chairs. Even a fireplace with a paneled drink cabinet beside it. He couldn't believe this was part of a hospital, of all things. This, he supposed, was where multi-millionaires came to die.

Blanche Herron was on the sofa in front of the fireplace, sitting bolt upright, silk-clad legs crossed, expensively manicured fingernails drumming on a cherrywood side table. Her daughter Faye was sitting next to her, crumpled and red-eyed. Anthony never quite forgot how she looked then, broken and crushed by the imminent loss of the stepfather who had adored and spoiled her.

Betsy Graves in a figure-clinging sweater and Pendelton plaid skirt was across the room, casually flipping through the page of a magazine, as if merely waiting for a hairdresser appointment. She glanced up languidly and gave Anthony a seductive half-smile. He shivered involuntarily. She revolted him. He revolted himself. Her husband Ned, who looked more primeval and brutish than Anthony remembered him, was pacing back and forth in front of her and stopped to glare at Anthony and Lisle.

Mrs Smith, the intimidating secretary, was standing by a window, holding back the sheers and looking down. She turned as they entered the room. 'Dr Lisle, I was afraid you'd be too late.'

Blanche stood and walked over on spiky heels. Her bosom bounced with indignation. 'What is this all about?' she demanded of the Prof.

'Max wanted to see Anthony,' he said in a voice he

undoubtedly hoped was calming.

It didn't work. 'Why? Who the bloody hell is this boy to intrude on us at such a time?' She sounded very British, almost Cockney.

'Mother,' Faye said plaintively.

'Max asked to see him,' the Prof said. 'Would you deny him anything now?'

'Of course not,' Blanche said, slightly abashed. 'But you can't go in now. They're doing – something.'

At that, a door behind her opened and a bevy of nurses came out. One carried a bundle of linens, another a tray of instruments, a third a white plastic bag through which they could see wads of stuff with nasty biological-looking stains. A doctor followed them. 'He won't let me give him any more morphine until he's seen a visitor he's expecting,' he said to Blanche.

Blanche gestured angrily at Anthony. 'That's the boy.'

'Good. I'll wait. He's in great pain and there's nothing more we can do but spare him that.'

Lisle took Anthony's elbow and steered him toward Max Herron's room. It was furnished and decorated as elegantly as the sitting room, but it was impossible to disguise its function. There were lots of switches, machines, and a heavy antiseptic smell overlaying a sweet-sticky odor of illness. The bed, though dressed with a luxurious silk spread, was a high hospital bed that looked like a torture instrument. Max Herron was stranded in the middle of it. A big man, now shrunken, he lay half-curled against the pain. His face was the color of cooked pasta, his lips were bluish. Tubes ran into both his arms and one large one ran in under the bedclothes to go God knew where.

Anthony followed the Prof as he walked round to the far side of the bed, which was the direction Herron was facing. 'Max. I'm here,' he said.

The man's eyes fluttered open, then closed against a stab of pain, before opening again. He tried to nod his head in acknowledgement.

'I flew to New York and back. Can you believe it?' the Prof said.

68

Herron made a dreadful obligatory smile.

'I've brought Anthony. I've told him.'

This time it was a slight but very real smile.

The Prof pulled over a chair and gestured to Anthony to sit down. It put him close to Herron, with their faces on a level. He almost gagged at the terrible odor of dying that surrounded him. Max reached out an impossibly thin, blue-veined hand, into which a needle was taped. Anthony met his hand with his own.

They stayed that way a long time, the dying man's cold fingers lying intertwined with his son's. Anthony didn't know if Max was sleeping or dead except that a machine he assumed read his heartbeat kept blipping. Finally Max's lips started moving, but no sound came. He shifted, cringed, cleared his throat – the worst sound Anthony had ever heard in his whole life – and tried again. 'I – had – to – call – you – son – Tony –' he said in a croaking whisper.

'I know. I'm glad,' Anthony said. 'I'm glad you're my father.'

The fingers clenched round his with an instant of incredible strength, which immediately ebbed.

Anthony started crying. Not a single tear trickling unnoticed down his cheek, but really crying. It was all he could do to hold back noisy sobs. And he didn't know what he was crying about, except that this man whose genes he shared was about to escape from him. He was Anthony's history and he was taking it with him. Anthony was losing something he'd never known he had. Partly it was because Max called him Tony and nobody else in the world did, as though it were an old intimacy between them. One Anthony had never known about.

Or maybe he was crying because he'd slept with his stepsister.

The Prof handed Anthony a handful of tissues. With one hand, he mopped his face and blew his nose. He eased his other hand away from Herron's. He was clearly sleeping or unconscious now, his mouth slack and drooling, his breathing labored but regular. Anthony stood, mortified, his knees almost buckling under him, and went to the bathroom where he washed his face and stared bleakly at the mirror for a moment. Just then he looked more like Max Herron than ever before.

Max Herron died three hours later. Lisle and Anthony waited there at the hospital penthouse suite with the rest of them. Most of the time Blanche and her daughters were in the room with Max and the doctor. Mostly, it was just Anthony and the Prof and Betsy's husband Ned in the big fake living room. Mrs Smith, the secretary, went several times into the room where Anthony's father was dying. Anthony had the impression that her daughter was there part of the time, but she was such an inconspicuous person he couldn't be sure where she was.

Anthony wanted to have a private talk with the Prof, but there was no question of a personal discussion with scowling Ned Graves hovering, so Anthony removed himself as much as he could without actually leaving the room. He pulled a heavy chair round half facing the window and sat staring out at the sky. Dr Lisle, pretty shaken himself, tried to make sporadic conversation with Ned about the whereabouts and welfare of a number of their mutual acquaintances, especially someone named Charlie, whom Anthony took to be Faye's missing husband. According to Ned he was on his way from someplace. But their talk kept lapsing into silences.

Around seven there was a muffled shriek and the sound of sobbing from the next room. After a moment, the door opened and the doctor came out. 'I'm afraid it's over. He went very peacefully,' he said to the room in general; then, after a respectful pause, he left.

Ned got up and went in. Anthony and Lisle stayed put, not looking or speaking at each other. Suddenly the secretary's daughter, the brown sparrow, was at Anthony's side. She must have been there for some time and he hadn't noticed. 'I'm very sorry ... Anthony,' she said softly, then faded back into the scenery.

They stayed that way, frozen into mental and physical immobility, for long moments. Finally the door to the other room opened again and Betsy came out. Her face was an icy mask. Ned was behind her with his arm round Faye, who was sobbing her heart out. Blanche was behind them, her eyes red and make-up streaked, but utterly composed. Mrs Smith brought up the rear of the procession. Her daughter went to meet her. 'I'll sit with him until the funeral people come, if you'd like,' the brown sparrow said.

Mrs Smith nodded and put a hand on her daughter's cheek for a second. A message no one else could hear passed between them, and they glanced at Anthony. Blanche turned to Mrs Smith. 'You have a copy of his written instructions for the funeral, don't you? Good. If you'll come by the apartment at nine thirty this evening, we'll go over the details.'

Then they were gone. Anthony went into the hospital room to say his final goodbye. There was a nurse there, taking away the last of the medical paraphernalia. Nina Smith was sitting by the window, hands folded in her lap, serene gaze on Max. With the pain gone, the lines in his face had relaxed. Someone had rolled him onto his back, straightened his limbs and tucked the silk bedclothes neatly across his broad chest. Nina turned a little, a subtle movement that said she was standing guard, but trying not to intrude. Anthony didn't know what to do now that he was by Max's side.

'Did you like him?' he asked Nina. He felt it was a stupid thing to say, but it came out before he thought.

She considered the question carefully before answering. 'I didn't always like him. But he was a good, good man. My mother adored him.'

This side issue was just the sort of distraction he needed. 'What will your mother do now?'

'Retire. Mr Herron provided for her very well. Of course she'll stay on to help his successor in any way she can for as long as necessary. So will I.'

'You? Did you work for him, too?'

'In a way. I was my mother's assistant.'

'The secretary's secretary?'

She smiled and Anthony was surprised at what a cute, elfin sort of girl she was when she smiled. 'More of an apprentice,' she answered. Then she got up and, as if he'd proved himself in some way, she said, 'I'll leave you alone with him for a while, if you'd like.'

Anthony didn't want to stay, but he did because she seemed to be granting him a privilege it would be tacky to reject. He stood there for a long time, looking at the dead body and wishing for something miraculous to happen. The Prof was always having mysterious insights and Anthony laughed at such nonsense, but now he wanted to believe; he desperately needed some sign or psychic message or great thought. But nothing came and finally he turned away.

To Anthony's astonishment, the Prof insisted on going from the hospital to the Herron apartment. It was the top three stories of an awning-canopied, marble-walled building overlooking the Country Club Plaza, an elegant, old-world shopping area. 'Those people don't want us around,' Anthony protested.

'No, but it's important that you be there. Just to make the point.'

'What point, for Christ's sake?'

'That you were his son.'

'Do they know?'

'Not officially.'

'What the hell does that mean? Listen, Prof, I'm getting sick of all this mysterious stuff. I want some real answers from you. What the hell are we imposing on these people for? So I'm Herron's son. Who cares but me? If his wife cares, it's only to hate me. And I'd just as soon never lay eyes on Betsy Graves again, if you don't mind.'

'That's a problem.'

'A problem! God, Prof! I had sex with my stepsister.

That's like some disgusting Greek play!'

Lisle rubbed his face as if it hurt.

Did it really matter that she was his stepsister? Anthony suddenly wondered. He was the child of Max Herron and some unknown woman. Betsy was the daughter of Blanche Herron and her first husband. He and Betsy were no real relation whatsoever. No genes in common. It was still a nasty situation, but not as nasty as he'd been thinking.

He had so many other questions to ask, but he gave up out of sheer emotional stress. Emotion wasn't something he liked or knew how to deal with. He liked the sort of emotions one deals with in the study of psychology; they were all someone else's feelings and motives, not his own.

They made their courtesy call on the Herrons and were received just as coldly as he'd expected they would be. Dr Lisle offered to be of any help he could; did they want anyone called? Were there any services, floral or anything, that he could arrange for them? Every offer was turned down frostily. The Prof seemed impervious though Anthony was in agony. They finally made their escape.

They had a suite at an expensive downtown hotel. Their bags were already there, and Anthony had started lethargically unpacking his when the Prof popped in his door and said, 'Anthony, I'm going to leave for a bit. You'll be all right on your own, won't you?'

That infuriated him. He'd just come back from years of hitching round Europe and now Lisle started treating him like a child. 'Yeah, I'll be fine,' he said. He meant to be arch and sarcastic. It just sounded surly. What the hell.

As soon as he left, Anthony flopped onto the bed to think. But his thoughts were so confused he couldn't focus on anything. Closing his eyes, he gave in to a little nap. He could have sworn he was in the same position when he woke up in the morning. The Prof was shaking his arm. 'Anthony, wake up. You've got to shave and dress for the funeral.'

'Huh? Funeral?' For a long moment he couldn't place where he was or what funeral he was talking about, then it fell into place with a sickening thud. 'Today? What time is it?'

'Nearly eleven. You were exhausted. Jet lag, I imagine.'

Anthony was stupefied with sleep. Staggering to his feet, he said, 'The funeral can't be today. He only died yesterday.'

'It was his request. He didn't want to be embalmed. The only way to avoid it is to be buried within twenty-four hours of death.'

Anthony flung himself together and arrived at the funeral home still half asleep. He felt drugged, which was probably better than going through it with his senses sharp. He was kept from any sort of grief by his extreme discomfort. First, he wasn't dressed right. He had one beat-up suit that he'd hauled around for a couple years just for emergencies. It looked like he'd slept in it. For a week. Everyone else in this rich crowd was dressed in the height of funereal fashion.

In spite of that, the Prof kept shoving him forward. He wouldn't let him lurk in the background inconspicuously. Lisle pushed him right into the first row with the Herrons. And they hated it just as much as Anthony did. If it hadn't been for her British upper-crust training, Anthony thought Blanche Herron would have spat at him. He could have killed the Prof, and the Herrons probably would have cheered him on.

There was an endless service, a walnut casket, mercifully closed, and quite a mob of mourners considering the short notice. Afterward, a few reporters slunk in close and got off a few pictures of everybody being herded out of the service into limos. That was where Anthony drew the line. Lisle tried to push him in with the family again, and he dug in his heels like a mule. Shaking off the grip on his elbow, he said, 'No. Stop it.'

Lisle looked surprised and oddly pleased. 'Very well, Anthony.'

They hung back at the end of the procession to the cemetery. Anthony refused to crowd in under the canvas canopy where the family and their friends stood shivering in the cold, snow-flecked wind. As soon as the last words of the service were spoken, Anthony hustled Dr Lisle back to their own car. The chauffeur was missing, and they sat in silence for a long time.

Finally Anthony said, 'Why?'

'Destiny,' the Prof answered.

It wasn't the answer to his question, but then he wasn't sure exactly what his question had been. As for destiny, it was one of Lisle's typical, pseudo-mystical responses. Anthony wasn't having it. 'What the fuck *is* this all about? Why force me on those people? This is awful – for me and them.'

The Prof put both hands up to his face massaging away the weariness. 'Oh, Anthony, it's such a long, long story. I thought I'd have more time to tell you about it. I promised Max I wouldn't until he was ready. I've regretted that promise for years. Now there's no time and I'm not sure you need to know it all anyway.'

'What do you mean, no time? It's over. He's buried. Tell me now.'

'Not yet. We have one more thing to do.'

'Does Dad know who I am?' It had been preying on his mind.

'No, Jeb doesn't know. Only you and me and Max. Though surely Blanche has caught on by now. To part of it.'

'Yeah, that I'm her husband's bastard.'

As he said this, the chauffeur opened the door and peered in. 'I'm so sorry, Dr Lisle. I didn't see you come down the hill. Are you ready to go now?'

They drove off. 'Where are we going?' Anthony asked.

'To Max's office.'

Anthony's only feeling, beside confusion, was relief. The dreaded family would undoubtedly be going back to their penthouse. As long as the Prof wasn't trying to crash that grim little post-funeral party, he didn't care where they went. He figured another two or three hours of this mysterious crap, then it would be over and life could get back to normal. Whatever normal was going to be for him now.

Their car pulled up at an office building downtown. Entering the foyer, they were once again met by Nina Smith. The sparrow girl seemed to be everywhere. She took their coats and almost disappeared under them. 'You'll find it rather quiet today. Most of the employees were given the day off out of respect for Mr Herron.'

They went up an elevator to the fifteenth floor and came out into a small, richly appointed waiting room. It appeared that Herron's offices had the whole floor. A receptionist who was sniffling into a tissue greeted them with a watery smile.

After Nina disposed of their coats, they were shown into a hallway with several offices off each side. Most were empty or had but a single worker in place to hold the fort. Those few were polite but subdued, apparently in genuine mourning. On the walls between the doorways were framed examples of paper products, some rather yellow from age. Each had explanations of the year and content and other historical notes. Anthony stopped and read a few and wished he had more time to study them. They were really interesting.

'Those were the general offices. The warehouse is down in the bottoms by the railroad tracks,' Nina Smith said as they turned a corner down another long hallway. 'And in here are the sales reps cubicles. Most of them have their real offices at home or in the field.' She gestured to a large room with low dividers marking out several dozen mini-offices. 'Here is my mother's office and the charity office.'

'The charity office?' Anthony asked. What a weird thing.

'Yes, Mr Herron "inherited" the presidency of a local charity from his father. He does – did – what he could to keep it going. Here is Mr Herron's office.'

They entered through impressive double doors that

looked like they belonged in a castle. Another receptionist was in place. This time there was no introduction. 'They are all here,' the receptionist said to Nina.

'Good. Come along, gentlemen,' Nina said, ushering them into the inner sanctum.

It was all Anthony could do to keep from saying 'shit' aloud when he saw who was causing the low buzz of conversation within. It was the whole goddamned Herron clan again. Blanche, her dreadful daughter Betsy, Faye, scowling Ned, a freckled ex-Ivy League man who must have been Faye's wandering husband, Mrs Smith and, sitting at Herron's desk, an older man Anthony had noticed at the funeral.

'Is *this* who we've been waiting for?' Ned growled.

The man at the desk stood up and, ignoring Ned, came round to shake hands with Dr Lisle. 'I'm glad to see you, Taylor. And this is Anthony. I'd have recognized him anywhere. I'm John Athalon, your – uh, Mr Herron's personal attorney. Please, sit down.'

Everybody was seated in an informal half-circle round the desk. Anthony took an empty chair, the Prof on one side of him and Nina Smith on the other. Anthony was rigid with fury. How dare the Prof do this to him yet again? And what the hell was everybody doing here? These people should have been at their pricey penthouse having a catered buffet with the other mourners. The whole thing stank of something nasty.

The lawyer went back to the desk and started handing out a stack of bound folders. Ned tore into his like a starving man into a rump roast. Anthony opened his more slowly and saw that it was titled 'Last Will and Testament'.

Athalon had taken his seat behind the big desk. 'As you know, this unconventional meeting was part of Max's final instructions to me. I know there are people waiting for you and that you're all perfectly able to read the document at your leisure, but I'm bound to go through it with you. I'll be as brief as I can.

'The last section of the copies you have is the most comprehensive list of assets I could manage at short notice. This is, of course, approximate. The values are as of last Friday. When we file the official evaluation with the court as of the date of death, I will make sure you all have copies. It's a matter of public record, anyway.'

Anthony had closed the folder and let the attorney's words wash over him. Herron had probably made him a token bequest. That accounted for why he was here, but he felt like an intruder even listening to the rest. The attorney could have just sent him a letter. This simply wasn't any of Anthony's business. He'd just tune it out like he used to do in college when he was studying and his roommates were talking.

Athalon went on, 'Beginning on page 7, paragraph 4, you'll find the relatively minor bequests.' There was a shuffling of paper as the rest of them sought the place. 'Dr Taylor Lisle is to receive one million. Mrs Smith is to receive $750,000 in addition to her pension plan, and the rest of the list is household employees and the amounts in cash or equivalent stocks or bonds, the choice of which is assigned to me.'

These were the 'minor' bequests! Anthony thought. And he wasn't included. In a way, he was glad. He didn't want even the most tenuous financial tie to these people.

'Now, as to the family, it's rather complex, but I'll try to simplify it slightly. Of course I will be available to any of you to explain in more detail in a few days if you'd like. First, Blanche. You are to have the proceeds of a trust of close to ten million for your lifetime. That is, the interest on the investments is yours to do with as you like.'

'Ten million?' Ned yelped. 'That's chicken feed! Blanche's expenses—'

Athalon put up a hand for silence. 'There is a separate trust that maintains the properties and pays wages. This is entirely Blanche's discretionary money. If you'll let me finish.'

Ned subsided, but was still angry. Anthony was stunned. Imagine people having the gall to say that the interest on ten million dollars was 'chicken feed'?

'Upon Blanche's death, the trust reverts to the estate. Both Faye and Betsy have a similar five million dollar trust. In their cases, however, the assets go to their children upon their deaths. But in both cases, the expenditure of the monies must have the approval of the trustee.'

Interesting, Anthony thought, in spite of his resolve not to listen. Max Herron had provided generously for his wife, and it was damned nice of him to give so much to her daughters. After all, they were no relation to him at all. But as this crossed Anthony's mind, he realized the tension in the room was thick enough to cut with a knife. What was the matter with them all? They'd just inherited stupendous amounts of money. Blanche's eyes were wide and horrified. Faye was practically gasping for air and Ned was literally turning purple.

'The balance of the estate, and the decision-making power in regard to the trusts goes to –' He picked up the document to quote directly from it and read – 'goes to my beloved son, Anthony Wentworth.'

There was a terrible silence. Anthony assumed the balance truly was 'chicken feed' but decision-making power over the trusts? Why the hell would Max put him in charge of his wife and daughters' money? It was crazy. He didn't care what they did with it.

'The balance?' the Prof said with cool inquiry.

'Yes, you'll find the figure at the bottom of page 16 of the addendum,' Athalon said. 'It's approximate, of course, as I said earlier, but it's in the neighborhood of two hundred million.'

They were all staring at Anthony with loathing. He could hardly breathe. Nina Smith, the little brown sparrow, put her hand over his forearm and smiled.

PART TWO

1968

Nina Smith

'And near him stood the Lady of the Lake
Who knows a subtler magic than his own –
Clothed in white samite, mystic, wonderful.
She gave the King his huge cross-hilted sword,
Whereby to drive the heathen out. A mist
Of incense curl'd about her, and her face
Wellnigh was hidden in the minster gloom ...'

Idylls of the King, Tennyson

Chapter Five

Nina's heart, though not half so tender as most girls', broke for Anthony. He looked like he'd been poleaxed. She could have sliced up that bastard Taylor Lisle like bacon for not telling him in advance. It was criminal to let anybody be hit with something like this without warning. Anthony Wentworth, unknowing heir to millions, must have felt dreadfully betrayed. Lisle's doing this to him was like shooting a guinea pig full of dexedrine in front of a crowd of hostile scientists. It was terrible.

For Anthony's good, as well as her own pleasure, she'd have to peel Lisle off him, no question of that, but he wasn't the first priority. That could wait. What couldn't wait was getting Anthony safely out of that room full of Herrons before he could speak. She'd have to get him where he could think it through and compose himself. She wasn't about to let him say anything he might later regret. He looked like he was about to speak. Nina put her hand over his arm quite firmly and smiled as warmly as she could. 'Didn't you say you had a call you had to make, Mr Wentworth? If you'll come along, I'll show you to a phone.'

She didn't think he registered what she was saying, but he was well brought up enough automatically to stand when she did. Then it was just a matter of steering him out like a tugboat shoving an ocean liner around. In the hallway, he hesitated and was about to say something, but she said, 'You want to get out of here, don't you?'

'More than anything.'

'Then hurry.' She had him into his coat, out of the

building and into a cab before he knew what was happening. It was a simple matter to fly by the hotel where he was staying to pick up his clothes. He didn't remember what hotel he was in, but she'd made a point of knowing. Then she found a good, but not Herron-style extravagant hotel, flashed a few company credit cards and got him into a suite under the name Anthony Smith. She didn't want Taylor Lisle to be able to call round and find him. Anthony followed along like a machine, too stunned by the revelation in Max Herron's office to know or care where he was.

Once she got him to his rooms, she hastily ordered up drinks and sandwiches and sat down across from him to wait for him to want to talk. Now that it was time, he had nothing to say, or perhaps too much to say to know where to start. He stared at Nina, or more accurately through her, for a long while. He'd never really noticed her yet, but there was all the time in the world. Finally, he shook his head and said, 'Is all this true? Can it be true?'

Nina nodded.

'Then ... Oh, God. I don't even know what to ask.'

'You'll think of the questions and I'll be here, or wherever you want me, to answer them.' Nina the Ubiquitous. He might as well start learning that now.

'Where are we? What am I doing here?'

She told him the name of the hotel. 'I thought you'd want to get away and think things out on your own time, at your own pace.'

He nodded. 'That was exactly what I wanted, but I didn't know it. How did you?'

'I guessed. It's my job – or at least I hope it will be.'

'What?'

'I'm your private secretary. I mean I am if you want me to be. That's what my mother and Mr Herron have been training me for for the last several years.'

'Then you knew? About me? About the will?'

'Only Mother and I knew. No one else. Except Mr

Athalon and Dr Lisle, of course. At least I assume he knew.'

'The list grows!' His face had hardened at the mention of Lisle. 'That was the worst thing the Prof ever did to me!'

'I'm sure he had what seemed like a good reason,' she said. 'I know you have a lot on your mind, Mr Wentworth, but do I have the job? As your secretary?'

'What? Oh – do you type?' He looked surprised at himself for a minute, then burst out laughing. 'What the hell do I care? I don't have any idea what to ask you to type.'

She joined his laughter and went to sit beside him on the sofa. 'Look, Mr Wentworth, you've sustained a dreadfully shocking surprise. But now you're on your own. Your time is yours alone. Nobody else knows where you are or will until you instruct me to tell them. Just relax,' she said soothingly. 'Let your thoughts sort themselves out at leisure. I've taken the room next to yours. I'm going to go away for a while, but I'll be available whenever you want. If I could suggest it, perhaps you should just lie down for a while. Rest. Let your mind wander where it will.' She took a scrap of paper from her purse. 'Here's my room number. Call me whenever you're ready.'

He didn't take the paper. She leaned over and put it in his shirt pocket. It was a rather intimate gesture, but he didn't seem to notice. As she started out the door, however, he called to her. 'One thing.'

'Yes?'

'Please stop calling me Mr Wentworth. I'm Anthony.'

'I'd be happy to call you Anthony when we're alone. But in front of others, it's important that you be Mr Wentworth.'

He nodded as if he understood the subtle complexities of this; she wasn't sure he did. But he would in time. He was very smart, even if he was stunned into stupidity at the moment.

She went to her room, called her mother and reported in. 'You did exactly the right thing getting him out,' her mother said softly. She was at her office desk and didn't want to be overheard. 'And just in time. All hell broke loose. Blanche had hysterics, Faye went berserk, and Ned actually punched a hole in the wall. It was dreadful. Athalon left here looking like death.'

'What do you think they'll do?'

'There's nothing they can do. John Athalon knows how to write an unbreakable will. What do you think of him? Your Anthony?'

'I think he's what we hoped,' Nina said. 'Did you see his face when he realized? Surprised, but not greedy. Composed, considering. Angry, if anything.'

There was a concerned silence for a moment from the other end of the telephone line. 'Not a rebel, do you think?'

'No, I don't think so. You know his college record as well as I do. If he were going to go off the rails, he'd have done it then.'

'You're right, of course.' Lillian Smith signed, sounding tired. 'In a way, dear, I envy you. Just starting. And having such good material with which to work. On the other hand, I'm glad to be done.'

They signed off affectionately. Nina always felt sorry and a little contemptuous of other people who complained of how their parents didn't understand them. Nina Smith and her mother understood each other like two halves of a peach pit. Nina supposed it was because it had always been the two of them against the world. Their lives, thoughts, ambitions and habits were so interwoven it was impossible to tell where one left off and the other began. What a shame Anthony hadn't been graced with a mother like that to raise him, Nina thought. Instead, he had that cold fish bastard Dr Lisle. Nina found herself feeling uncharacteristically frazzled just thinking about Taylor Lisle. She'd thought he was a creep since she was a kid, long before she had any real reason to dislike him. His pretentiously 'knowing' attitude had always galled her.

Time to regroup. Taking off her glasses, she sat down

crosslegged in the middle of the room, closed her eyes and concentrated on relaxing. Toes, ankles, calves, knees – up her body. As usual, by the time she got to her head, her mind was nearly blank. A quarter of an hour of deep relaxation did as much for her as eight hours' sound sleep.

But she was interrupted this time by a knock on the door. 'Do I have any money?' Anthony said without preamble as Nina opened it.

Nina goggled. What a question!

'I mean cash.' He was wearing a beat-up pea jacket, a sweatshirt so faded that the original message was merely a ghost, and ratty jeans. He looked exhausted.

'Oh, yes. I've opened a personal checking account for you at First National. All I need is for you to sign the signature card.' Nina riffled through her briefcase and handed him a card and a ballpoint pen.

'You were ready for this,' he said, sounding impressed and just a shade angry.

'It's my job. Or at least, I hoped it was going to be,' she replied.

He glanced at the check register, where she'd written in the opening deposit of ten thousand dollars. 'What in hell would I need this for?' He was really angry now.

'Anything you want. Or nothing. It doesn't have to be spent. It's just there if you need it.'

That placated him a little. He was mad now about the money. Furious that it belonged to him and that so much had gone on behind his back. That was natural. It would pass. Then they would get down to business. 'Where are you going?' she asked, trying to sound casual instead of demanding. It would also take him a while to realize just what their relationship was to be and that she must know all the time where he was and what he was doing.

'Out,' he said curtly. 'I don't know where.'

'I'll be here, waiting for you.'

He had a momentary look of panic, as if a blind date suddenly started talking about the wedding plans.

87

Then it passed. He'd mentally dismissed her.

He was gone the rest of the day, and all the next day. By the third morning, Nina was getting panicky. She was considering calling the bank to see if any of the new checks had cleared, thinking she might get some idea of where he'd gone. Perhaps he'd written a check for an airline ticket or something that would help her find him. But she didn't want to alert anyone, not even a clerk at the bank, to the fact that she'd lost him. Lost him, like whatsername leaving Ernest in the lost luggage at Victoria Station! What was that Oscar Wilde line? Nina thought wildly. 'To lose one parent is a tragedy; to lose both smacks of carelessness.' Losing Anthony certainly smacked of carelessness.

Lillian was keeping in touch. Everyone was harassing her. John Athalon was trying to find Anthony, Ned Graves (not a good sign) was after him. Taylor Lisle was so frantic he was actually reduced to shouting. Well, of course he was. His life's work had vanished. He'd built Anthony brick by brick, and Anthony had escaped him 'What are you telling them, Mother?' Nina asked.

'That Anthony has gone on a private retreat, taken you along as his private secretary, and will let them know when he's ready to see them. They're taking it badly. Especially Lisle. And Nina, Steven Packwood called Anthony.'

The name hung in the air for a minute. Lillian Smith knew how her daughter felt about Steven even though they'd never talked about it outright. 'What did he want?' Nina asked with admirable calm.

'Just to express his condolences. He dashed here from Montreal as soon as he heard of Max's death. He's in town. He left a number.'

Nina took it down, her fingers trembling a little. 'Steven knows the situation? The will and all?'

'Nina, dear, the world knows about the will. Haven't you read this morning's papers? The press is having a heyday. *Time* and *Newsweek* have both called this morning. The *Wall Street Journal* is camped in the reception room, interviewing secretaries. I put them off, but you'll have to deal with them sooner or later.'

'How can I do that when I've *lost* Anthony?'

'You'll find him,' Lillian said with assurance. Nina wished she had the confidence in herself that her mother did.

As it was, he found Nina before she found him. The phone rang about ten. Nina leaped for it.

'Hello, Nina. Anthony here.'

'Thank God. Where's here?'

'I'm not sure. We need to talk.'

'Yes. I'll come to you if you'll just tell me—'

'No, I'm on my way back. I'll be there within the hour. Here's what I want – a hot bath, clean clothes and a steak lunch. Well done. No mushrooms. Then I want you to give me a concise overview of the assets. Can you do that?'

'Of course. I have it all h—'

'Good. By three we'll have a statement for the press. The papers are full of this, and they might as well have the truth. At least as much of it as they need to know right now. And do you know where Steven Packwood is?'

'Yes, he's in town.'

'Good. Would you ask him if he could meet us at six at the hotel? But he's not to mention it to anyone else.'

'I'm sure that will be fine. He called you. Anthony, where are you?'

'Nina, rule one: no matter who else you're fending off, I'm always available to Steven Packwood. *Always*. Do you understand?' Nina started to make the justifiable remark that she could hardly have told Steven where he was when she didn't know, but he swept over her. 'I'll see the Prof at nine, but don't tell him where. Just tell him you'll send a car for him.'

'Yes, I will.' Lisle wasn't going to like that a bit. Good.

'Nina, are you up to this?'

'I certainly am,' she said, a grin in her voice. She was practically rubbing her hands together in glee. *Here we go!* she thought. He was a new person, just the person she'd hoped for. Brisk, decisive, bright.

Then he really took her by surprise. 'Nina, do you know who my mother is?'

He didn't know? Oh God, was it up to her? If Taylor Lisle had been within reaching distance, she'd have strangled him with her bare hands.

'Nina? Do you know?'

'Yes.'

'Good. You'll tell me over lunch. Have my clothes and steak ready. I'll be there as soon as I can get a cab. There aren't many in this neighborhood.'

This neighborhood? What in hell did that mean?

But she didn't get the chance to ask. He'd hung up.

Nina's mother had been widowed a month before Nina was born. Lillian's husband was an ambitious young man from the wrong side of the tracks, but with great ideas. Lillian Smith had seen herself as the wife who would make it all possible, then it was gone. In his first venture, he'd made an error in moral judgment and had been caught out. He couldn't face it and killed himself. Lillian had no idea he had the strain of pride and predilection to depression that could cause him to take his own life.

Though she had sincerely loved him, she'd also seen him as a lump of fine-grained clay, capable of being molded into something grand and important. But when he died, broken by a fatal flaw, barely two years into the marriage, she'd been left with an artist's hands and vision and no material. She briefly considered her infant daughter Nina as a replacement, but in those days women were thought of differently, and thought of themselves differently. A woman wasn't something on her own, she was the driving force behind a man. Nina had absorbed a lot of her mother's thinking, and it made her out of step with most other women of her generation. But Nina didn't mind following a path of her own, especially when she'd seen through her mother what a satisfying path it could be.

After Nina was weaned and the savings started to run

out, Lillian Smith went back to being a secretary. As luck and her own superb instincts would have it, she got a job with Herron Paper Products. She was part of a secretarial pool, but within a month of starting, Max Herron's secretary quit to get married and Lillian was given the job of temporary secretary to young Mr Herron until someone more qualified could be found. She did so well that he kept her.

Here, at last, was Lillian's new supply of rich, supple clay waiting to be worked into something magnificent. Max Herron was smart, wealthy, attractive. He was not an introspective brooder like her husband had been. Max Herron could become a Great Man. She always said it that way, in caps. And, thanks to her, he almost did become great. At least he became very much richer and socially prominent. But Lillian had always hoped he'd use his gifts to enter politics. She had it mapped out: a state position, to get his feet wet and learn the ropes; senator, then governor, then on to the national level. She alluded to cabinet posts, but Nina believed her mother was secretly aiming for him to be President.

But it simply didn't interest him. He was a very intelligent and hardworking man and graced with enormous charm, or charisma as they'd say these days. However, he lacked that spark of extra drive, super ambition and reined-in fanaticism that a politician must have. And she couldn't instil it in him. He became important in industry, wealthier than ever and there was a great deal of satisfaction in that for her. When he turned fifty, she gave up part of the dream. It was hard for her to admit that her ambitions for him had limits and that he'd reached the fringe of them. Then, when she learned about the cancer, she gracefully and willingly abandoned her goals and set out to make the rest of his life as pleasant as possible.

That's when she started taking a sincere interest in Anthony Wentworth. She'd known about him all along, of course. She'd done all the paperwork for the adoption, but now she looked at the file of pictures Lisle had sent over the years, studied the transcripts, examined the lines of age in her own face – and gazed thoughtfully and speculatively at Nina. They were to have another chance, she and her daughter. With Anthony. Anthony Wentworth, with the right woman behind him, could be a Great Man.

And Nina had been raised to be that woman.

Not as a wife. Never as a wife. A wife has her own agenda and priorities. No, Nina was to be Anthony's private secretary, the woman who (if she's any good at her job) should be more important than a mere wife. A great man's wife is only an ornament, a procreator, a sometime bed partner. But a good secretary is a business partner, source of vital information, confidante, decorator, sounding board, advisor, protector, fashion consultant, spy, priest, battering ram, travel agent, physician, historian, dietitian, librarian, scribe, and translator. She must know his thoughts and moods and preferences better than he himself.

And Nina was ready. Lillian had seen to it that her daughter knew Herron Paper inside and out. From the time Nina was little, Lillian had involved her in her work. She had to; there was no time for her to be the ordinary mother, making cookies and taking her little girl to the park. She had to work and so Nina helped. She'd stuffed envelopes, learned to type by copying the letters Lillian had typed for Max Herron. From the time Nina was thirteen, she worked summers and vacations for him. In the mail room, running errands, filing invoices. Lillian sent her to the Barstow School for Girls for several years, on Max's advice (and with his financial aid), to get necessary social polish, then Nina was sent to take secretarial courses to polish her technical skills.

With the cancer verdict, Nina started a new level of training. 'I want you to make Mr Herron's travel arrangements for this trip,' Lillian would say. 'He likes a window seat, left side of the plane, first class. He doesn't like to arrive any later than three in the afternoon, but he doesn't mind taking extremely early flights. No evening flights. The limo driver is to hold up a sign that says, "MH". Just that. No name. No company name. Oh, and no Asian drivers. Their driving scares him. Be sure he has two fresh shirts and four handkerchiefs in his travel case. Also a deck of cards so he can play solitaire while he's on the phone. It relaxes him.'

That was when Nina started learning the difference between a secretary and a private secretary. It had little to do with typing or shorthand and everything to do with human nature, with knowing a man more intimately than a wife ever could.

Nina used the extra key to Anthony's room and got to work. Going through his clothes, she noticed those with red in them were more worn. Presumably he liked red. A red tie, then, to replace the shabby one he'd worn to the funeral. She checked sizes, made notes and telephoned Jack Henry's, where her mother got Max's clothes. They had a selection ready when she got there and she was able to make her choices like a whirlwind. She was back in forty-five minutes with a basic wardrobe for a day or two. A new suit, casual wear and a thick maroon velour robe with matching silk pajamas. She'd get them mono-grammed when she had more time.

She had everything laid out, down to underwear and socks, fifty-five minutes after his call. His luncheon had been ordered and would take only a quick phone call to bring up. She ran back to her room to wash her face and throw on a clean dress. She met him in the hallway when she returned to his room.

He looked a mess. He was still wearing the same jeans and sweatshirt, but they were filthy. He hadn't shaved or combed his hair since he'd left. There was a splatter of something unspeakable down the sleeve of his jacket. He looked like a bum. All but his face. There was a light in his face. The haggard, angry, confused boy was gone and in his place there was a dirty, happy, energetic man.

'I'm a little late. Sorry,' he said. He fumbled for his key, but she had hers in the lock before he could find it.

'Where have you been?' she asked, as he strode in and through the parlor of the suite.

'Around. I didn't know where I was most of the time.' It was clear he wasn't going to tell her. He kicked off his sneakers, peeled off his socks and was struggling to get out of his sweatshirt by the time Nina caught up with him in the bedroom.

'When were Max and Blanche married?' he said through muffled folds of fabric.

'June 1946,' she said, quickly turning away as he unzipped his jeans.

'Uh-huh,' he said. 'So Betsy is what I was afraid she was,' he said.

What did he mean by that? She heard his pants fall to the floor, the change in his pockets rattling, and then the bathroom door closed. She extracted his checkbook from the pocket of his jeans, picked up all the dirty clothes and flung them into a drawer, then went to call room service. She'd already called her mother to ask her to set up the meetings with Steven and Dr Lisle. Now Nina called her back to confirm that she'd got them. It was all set up.

Just as she hung up, Anthony emerged from the bedroom. He was so clean he almost sparkled. He'd nicked himself shaving and kept dabbing at the blood on his chin with the corner of the towel he was drying his hair with. She'd bought him three casual sweaters and, as she suspected, he'd picked the red one. The gray cord pants fitted perfectly, she was glad to see. He noticed her eager attention and said, 'This is great. How did you know the sizes?'

'I'm psychic,' she said with a laugh. It was gratifying to have the first personal job she'd done for him recognized as well done.

He yanked open the drapes (remember that, she told herself, he likes lots of natural daylight – corner rooms in hotels with many windows) and chatted about the miserable winter weather while they waited for the food to arrive. This was good. He was in control. He'd mapped out a schedule and they were going to keep to it. First lunch, then serious talk.

He ate all the ghastly well-done steak like a country person does, even the fat. He quit eating the baked potato when he ran out of sour cream. But he left the green beans untouched. She'd see to it that there was always plenty of sour cream and that nobody ever served him green beans.

He was done when he realized Nina had just been watching him. 'Aren't you eating?'

'I had a sandwich earlier,' she lied. There wasn't time for her to eat. She was watching him. Learning about him. She was working.

He shoved the room service trolley into the hall and put the 'Do Not Disturb' sign on the outside doorknob. Then he sat down across from Nina and ran his fingers through his still damp hair. He looked tousled and very young.

'Can I assume from the date of their marriage and the date of my birth that I am Blanche's child?'

So cool, so businesslike. She nodded.

'God, I was a dolt not to figure that out sooner. I just bought the illegitimate child gossip and never questioned the dates until today. Does she know?'

'I'm certain she doesn't.'

'Steven Packwood told me the story, which I'm sure he believed, of Blanche's child dying. That was me, wasn't it? What happened?'

Nina took a deep breath. 'I only learned this a few years ago myself, when Mr Herron found out he had cancer. And I learned it from my mother, so some of the "facts" may be merely her opinion.'

'It's a starting point. Tell me.'

'When the baby was – I mean, when you were born it was a very difficult birth. You were a "blue baby" or something. The doctors told Mr Herron you were certainly

95

brain damaged and would probably not live more than a few days, if that. Mrs Herron was near death herself. Mr Herron didn't think she could stand the added strain of knowing she'd given birth to a – well, a vegetable. He decided it was better if she never knew and just thought you died right away. He really believed you would be dead in a couple days anyway.'

'Don't justify him, Nina,' he said grimly. 'Just explain.'

'Well, he put Dr Lisle in charge. Put money for medical expenses into an account for him to draw on and so forth. My mother helped set it all up. The few days passed, and then a week. It looked like you'd live after all. But Mother says the doctors were still telling him you'd never walk or talk or have any mental capacity. It was a terrible time for him.' She paused. She was justifying again. 'So he had Dr Lisle arrange for your adoption. You were about a month old when it was all completed—'

'Wait a minute. How could that be done without Blanche knowing? Did they have a funeral with no body?'

'Anthony, almost anything can be done with enough money. Blanche was very ill, nearly comatose, and when she was well again he must have just told her he'd taken care of everything.'

'I'm hardly a vegetable.'

'No. You thrived. Mother says that by the time you were a year old, you were obviously not only well, but very healthy and smart.'

'But it was too late to tell Blanche the truth?' He said it like a challenge.

'I guess so. Mr Herron's one lie had turned into a year's worth of daily lies. And there was something else.'

'Good God, what?'

'Well, it's rather complicated and I'm not sure I've got it right, but Blanche had married your father within a very short time of her first husband's—'

'Oh, yes.' He held up his hand for silence while he pondered something. 'Steven told me and I didn't pay enough attention. Of course, neither of us had any idea he was talking about me. Steven said she was claiming that I was her first husband's child. Was that the story? To keep some inheritance away from somebody.'

'Leland House, I think.'

'So Max had a secret child, but if he owned up to my being alive, Blanche would have claimed I wasn't Max's son, but her first husband's.'

'Yes, I think – it sounds crazy – but I think he let her go on thinking you were dead because that way you really remained his son, no question from anybody.'

'Even though I'd been adopted and I didn't know him?'

'But he knew you. He kept up with every detail of your life. Mother has a whole file on you. Pictures, letters from Dr Lisle. Max Herron did love you, Anthony. In his own way.'

'His own bizarre way.'

'Love is always bizarre, isn't it? You do know you're really his, don't you?'

'Yes, having seen him. I don't doubt that part of it.' He stood up abruptly and started walking around the room, head down, hands clasped behind his back. Nina didn't say anything, though she didn't think he'd have noticed if she had. He probably wouldn't have been aware of her if she'd been pacing right on his heels.

'So Betsy Graves is my half-sister,' he said. 'We have the same mother.'

'Yes, but what difference does that make? She's dreadful, but you don't have to get along with her. After all, they've never known you before, they'll hardly be hurt if you don't come into the family fold.'

Suddenly he picked up a legal pad and sat down. 'Let's go over the business,' he said.

That surprised her considerably. She'd thought – dreaded – going on and on about his parents. But apparently he'd put that matter into a compartment to study later. That's what she would have done, anyway. Her mind was a perfect rabbit warren of neatly identified compartments, a few of which she was very careful not to open very often.

Nina got her briefcase and began. She was pleased at how well he understood. He knew business; not Herron Paper, of course, but business in general. It wasn't just a matter of being familiar with the terminology, he was on top of the concepts. She'd been prepared to talk on the most basic plane, but he kept impatiently waving aside her simplifications as if to say, 'Get on with it!'

With lightning speed they skimmed the high points. Suppliers, transportation, labor relations, sales staff, cash flow, advertising, real estate, production facilities, bank loans, investments, debts, billing and collection procedures, corporate structure. And as she spoke, he took copious notes in a bold, sprawling hand on the legal pad. He asked relatively few questions, but she saw big question marks appear frequently in his notes. This, clearly, was just a preliminary overview. The questions would come later.

There were, she discovered to her considerable distress, quite a large number of gaps in her knowledge. 'I'm sorry, I don't know,' she had to say too many times. It damned near killed her to say it.

But he was cool and brisk about it. 'Then we'll both find out. Make a note.'

From the beginning, he was interested in which items, debts and assets were the responsibility of the paper company partnership which Steven Packwood's family owned half of, and which had been Max Herron's alone. Paper or private, they started designating them. They moved along quickly, both taking notes. By two forty-five, they'd briefly flown through nearly every aspect of his inheritance. It was surface, like a two-page outline of a fat complicated novel, but he had the gist of it.

'All right,' he said, sitting back and laying the legal pad aside. 'Let me see if I've got this. The paper company, substantial as it may be, is primarily the source of the funds with which Max built his own considerably more substantial investment empire.'

As concise a summary as you could make. 'Yes, that's true.'

'And I assume the other half of the partnership has done the same over the years.'

'That's my understanding, although I think Mr Herron had somewhat better luck with his investments than the Packwoods have. And I think that back in 1930 both your grandfather and Steven's put their own private resources into the company to keep it afloat during the Depression, but since then—'

'Yes, yes. I see,' he cut her off.

'It's quarter to three and you've promised a press release at three. Hadn't we better work on it?'

He flipped to the back of the legal pad and tore out a page. 'I've already done it. You can polish it up.'

There was very little to polish. It was a brief statement of the obvious: that Anthony Wentworth had inherited the considerable holdings of Max Herron, including his half-interest in Herron Paper Products. Mr Wentworth, aged 21, a native of New Mexico and Harvard graduate, would have no further statements to make until he had become familiar with the estate and the paper company. As far as could be determined at this point, no changes were planned for the company and Mr Wentworth would have a statement at a later date as to the status of his private holdings.

Why would anyone expect a statement about the private holdings? Nina wondered. Only *Time* magazine, with its gossipy attitude, would be interested in those. The rest, the *Wall Street Journal*, the *New York Times*, *Business Week*, with their investor readership wanted to report on any possible upheaval within the paper company. But she didn't question it, merely printed it up neatly, corrected a misplaced modifier and sent it by messenger to her mother, who would release it from the office.

When she'd completed this task, she sat down across from him again. 'What do you want to go back to and review in more detail?'

'Nothing at the moment. You left something out.'

'Have I? What?'

'The charity.'

'Charity?' Her mind was skittering. What was he talking about?

'When you showed me the office, there was a room you said housed the charity business.'

'Oh yes, of course. Samaritan. I'd forgotten.'

'It's called Samaritan? Nice. Tell me about it.'

She had to rummage through her mind. 'I don't know very much about it. I think your grandfather and Steven's started it very early in their partnership. Something to do with scholarships for former paper boys. Newspaper delivery boys, that is. Early on, their biggest paper buyer was the *Kansas City Star*, you see.'

'Does it still give scholarships?'

Scramble. Scramble. Come on brain cells, don't fail me now. 'I think so. And it helps other people, too. I believe. Sometimes, at least. I remember Mother making a draw last year for some people who'd lost their house in a tornado or flood or something.'

'How's it funded?'

'Wait a minute.' She riffled through her paperwork. There was bound to be something about it somewhere. Of all the weird things to be interested in. The most minor, trivial aspect of the whole estate. 'Here it is. Stocks. A.T.& T., Bethlehem Steel, Loew's. Good stuff. It's a trust, administered solely by Mr Herron or his designee. You now, of course. Annual income, about thirty thousand dollars. Nonprofit incorporation, naturally. Hmmm, this is odd. I see no mention of the Packwoods in what I have here. I must have been wrong about the partners founding it. It must have been started by your grandfather alone. I can get you the paperwork.'

'Would you do that, please?'

'What? Now, you mean?'

'Please. And Nina, before you go, have room service send up a hamburger. I'm starving.' He grinned wolfishly.

He wasn't the stunned, horrified, confused automaton she'd brought here a few days ago. This was a young man who'd grabbed life by the shoulders and was ready to shake its teeth loose. She just hoped he didn't rattle them all to bits in the process.

Chapter Six

It took Nina several hours to find all the material Anthony had asked for. She tried not to think about the implications of his interest in Samaritan, because the whole thing scared her to death. What in hell was all this interest in the most insignificant aspect of the enormous financial empire he'd inherited? No, don't worry about it, your job is just find the documents, she told herself. Put those questions in a compartment and latch the door.

When she got back from the office, it was six thirty and Steven Packwood was already there. 'Hi, Steven,' she said, trying to sound casual. It wasn't easy. She'd been crazy about Steven since she was a kid. The lock on the door labeled 'Steven' wouldn't hold for long. Her mother knew how she felt, and disapproved, because Lillian Smith saw in him the same troubled introspection her husband had succumbed to. 'He thinks too much,' as she expressed it. Nina knew she might be right, but her feelings for him were in her heart, not her head.

They'd been friends for many years when one disastrous moonlight and honeysuckle night at the Herron Connecticut house, she'd impulsively let him know she was in love with him. He'd drawn back as if bitten by something poisonous. He'd thought of her as a little sister. She should have realized that he wasn't ready to regard her as a woman. She'd made her move too soon, and for the last three years she'd been trying to recoup her loss. Back to casual friendship until he was ready for her, was her philosophy – if he ever would be, a sinister voice in the back of her mind said. She ignored it. Though he grew more wary with her as time passed, she was still waiting patiently.

'Hi, Nina. We've been wondering what became of you,' he said without looking up.

'Have you got the information?' Anthony asked. He didn't even glance at her either.

There was no large table to work at, so the two of them were sitting on the floor with paperwork spread on the carpet between them. They looked like a couple of college boys trying to put together a term paper. Anthony was adding some figures. Steven, his coat, tie and shoes discarded, his shirt open at the neck, was searching through sheets of legal pad paper. He looked so casual and boyish it made Nina's heart hurt. She set the folder of documents on the floor between them. They both reached for it, but Steven laughed a little and drew back, letting Anthony go through it first. As Anthony glanced at each paper, he handed it to Steven. 'Yes, yes. That's good,' he said.

'Look at this,' Steven said, handing one back and jabbing a finger at a densely printed paragraph.

'What about the articles of incorporation?' Anthony asked. 'Are there any limitations that will require me to refile?'

'What are you doing? Can I help?' Nina said, sounding pathetic. *Come on, guys. Let me play.*

That's when he said it. Anthony just glanced up as though it were a trivial matter and said, 'I've decided to give my money away to charity.'

'*What?*' Nina shrieked. Beyond the ringing in her ears, she heard Steven laugh, although what the hell he thought was funny she couldn't imagine. Had they both gone mad? Had they been messing with LSD or something?

Anthony got up, grinning. 'Not all of it, Nina. Don't pass out. I'm not nuts. But look, nobody in the world *needs* two hundred million dollars. Max couldn't even make a dent in spending it. The more they spent, the more he was worth at the end of each year.'

Nina's teeth were chattering. Her whole body was

chattering. She was afraid she was having a stroke. 'Anthony, please tell me ...'

He launched into a story about working on a voter registration drive back in college and something about a young black woman and a mattress on the floor and dog food. Nina hardly took it in, but thought it was a dreadful, dirty story. The gist of it seemed to be that if the woman had been given money, she wouldn't have to eat dog food.

'But it takes more than money, Anthony, to change people's lives,' she said. 'It takes education and—'

'But education costs money too. Believe me, Nina, money's at the heart of it all. I've thought about this a lot. I went down to the slums the day of Max's funeral ...'

Little men were standing in the open doors of the various compartments of her mind. All were vying for her attention. One little man was observing that while Nina referred to Max Herron as 'your father' or 'Mr Herron', Anthony always referred to him as 'Max'. Another was screaming, 'Stupid honky boy. It's a wonder he's still alive!' and another was drawling, 'There he goes, Nina, your Great Man has escaped you.'

The babble in her head was deafening.

'Anthony, what are you talking about?' she said.

'Listen, Nina, I didn't really trust my memory of that girl. I was awfully young when it happened. So I spent a couple days just talking to people in the slums. When I asked them what they needed to make their lives better, it all came down to money. Money to get warmer clothes, to send their kids to school, buy food and medicine. There are all these people who need money, and here I am with literally hundreds of millions more than I need. I've explained it all to Steven and he understands. He's going to work with me on this. And we're going to need your help.'

'What do you intend? To just convert it to cash and hand it out!' Nina said, trying to keep her voice down, but failing miserably.

Anthony wasn't about to be rattled by her reaction. He said calmly, 'I'm going to keep my half of the paper company. The income from that alone is more than I ever dreamed of having. And I'll keep the properties for now and enough assets to keep them staffed for the time being. But everything else, the stocks, bonds, real estate, everything's going to be put into Samaritan.'

'But Samaritan only gives a scholarship or two a year.'

He grabbed her shoulders and grinned. 'Yes, up until now. But with my seed money, plus what can be raised from other people, it can be a fully fledged charity and do an enormous amount of good for a great many people.'

If Nina had been a Victorian lady she'd have swooned. She couldn't make a great man out of someone with $250,000 a year from the paper company. That was just mildly rich. She got up and went to the window, actually tasting something bitter in her mouth. She thought for a second that she might disgrace herself by being sick. But as she stood looking out at the snow-silted sliver of sky in sight between buildings, something in the most remote recesses of her brain whispered, 'Rockefeller ... Pulitzer ... Carnegie ... Ford ...'

Of course! Except for Ford, all of those great men were remembered more for the charities they endowed than for the source of the money that funded them.

She turned and found them staring at her as if they were anxious for her approval. Well, they ought to be. She was the one who could make it work. Idealistic people are contemptuous of practical people, but they're the ones who make the idealists' dreams come true.

'All right,' she said, smiling encouragingly. 'What do you have in mind?'

They both looked relieved. 'I'm going to turn the assets over to Samaritan,' Anthony said. 'It will have a board to administer the distribution—'

'Hold it,' Nina said, putting up a hand like a traffic cop. 'Who's on this board?'

'Well, we hadn't really got to that.'

'What do you mean? That's the starting point. This is yours. You have to make certain from the onset that you're in charge. Imagine how you'd feel in a few years if you turn it over to other people and they start giving away money in ways you think are foolish or immoral?'

'But honorable people—'

'You can't speak for anyone's honor but your own.'

They looked at each other. 'She's right,' Anthony said with a degree of surprise that wasn't altogether flattering.

'She always is,' Steven said.

'Anthony, you must remember that this is your money,' Nina said to drive home her point. 'You can give it away if you like, but it's yours, like it or not. That makes you responsible for giving it away in the best possible manner. You have to be permanent president and chairman of the board. I believe that's the way it's set up now. Don't make any change in that.'

'But—'

'You can create as many sub-units as you like to administer various aspects. But they must all ultimately have your approval. You get your trusted, honorable men to run them. Give them almost full autonomy, but reserve the final word for yourself.'

'For himself or for you?' Steven asked.

That hurts. I only want what Anthony wants. 'I'm just making suggestions,' she said softly.

'That's right. You're not being fair to Nina, Steven,' Anthony said. 'Where do we find the good people we need?' This was to Nina.

'You have the best right here in this room. Steven. There's nobody more honorable.'

'Of course Steven's involved,' Anthony said, apparently missing the undercurrents flowing between Steven and Nina like a rip tide. 'I couldn't even consider doing this without him. But we'll need to hire other qualified people.'

'Well, yes, to do the day-to-day work,' Nina said. 'But

the top men have to be volunteers. Raid the boards of the national corporations headquartered here: Hallmark Cards, TWA, Stover's Candy, Hudson Oil. Moneyed men and women like yourselves who do such things out of civic duty. You'll get more work out of volunteers than employees. You'll understand that the first time you watch your own people at Herron Paper working themselves to a nub for a Christmas party.'

'Do you really think so?'

'Anthony, your own money, substantial as it is, won't be able to make as much difference in the world as you obviously hope. I'd bet the welfare organizations of this city alone use up the equivalent of your whole fortune every few months. You can see how little good it's doing. You have to use the money creatively, and it's going to have to be augmented. Fund-raising is going to have to be a large part of the operation for it to grow. Rich men are the best fund-raisers because they know where the money is and how to extract it. But you have to give them some power over how it's spent once it's raised. Or at least they have to think they have that power.'

There was a knock on the door. 'Bring it in here. Thanks,' Anthony was saying to room service.

Steven strolled over to her while Anthony dealt with a mistake in the order. 'Nina, leave him alone to figure it out himself.'

'Leave him alone? I'm his private secretary. It's my job to be as helpful as I can. I'm doing my job the best way I know. He's very young, Steven.'

'Yes, and you're as old as time.'

Nina didn't know what he meant by that, but she didn't like it. Why was he always criticizing her, generally in ways she didn't even understand? She wanted him to love her or at least admire her as a start on that road, but all he could do was find fault.

'Steven, it's too much money to experiment with blindly.'

'It's not the money.'

'It is. It's all about money.'

'But it shouldn't be. You even saw that yourself for a second before you lost the vision.'

'There, I think we've got it sorted out,' Anthony said. 'I'll share Nina's sandwich while they're bringing up another.'

'Ah, she's the Earl of Sandwich, not Warwick,' Steven said.

'What's that supposed to mean?' Nina asked.

'You know. Wars of the Roses. Warwick the Kingmaker.'

Nina saw red. How dare he judge her? Judge against her for trying to help Anthony reach his greatest potential. 'Are you going to give your money to Samaritan, too, Steven? No, I guess you can't. You have Gary to think of,' she said and could have bitten off her tongue the minute the words were out of her mouth.

Steven looked like he'd been struck by lightning.

'Steven, I didn't mean—'

'Who's Gary?' Anthony asked casually as he divided up the club sandwich.

'Since Nina's obviously going to gossip about him as soon as I'm gone, I might as well tell you.'

'No, Steven, I wouldn't ha—'

'Gary is my illegitimate son.'

Anthony nearly dropped the plate. 'Your what?'

'I have a son. Maybe Nina'd like to give you all the details. She knows everything. I was stupid enough to tell her.'

'Oh, Steve.' Nina felt like shit, which is just what he wanted. But this time she knew she deserved it. She shouldn't have flung Gary's name around like a threat. She'd only wanted to remind him that they were old friends, not enemies, she told herself, but she'd done it the worst possible way. She could see that Anthony was truly stunned. Oh, for a time machine and the ability to go back to five minutes ago.

'There's no need for anyone to tell me anything about

109

it,' Anthony said tactfully. 'Let's eat while we talk out management structure ideas.'

They did so and by the time dinner was finished, everyone had forgotten, or was pretending to have forgotten, the earlier flap. They got back to work. Anthony's vision of Samaritan's role was sweeping. He saw it as ultimately funding medical projects, disaster relief, education, housing for the needy, youth activities, but he had the intelligence to realize he had to start small, make careful initial selections of beneficiaries who were not only worthy, but would gain the public attention to raise significant funds. Nina was getting genuinely excited about the ramifications. Anthony was euphoric. Steven was optimistic, but restrained and thoughtful. As usual.

By quarter to nine, mindful that Taylor Lisle was due shortly, Steven said, 'I'm brain dead. I'm going home. If Nina can type up notes of the major points we've settled on, we can review them tomorrow and start the wheels rolling.'

Nina started gathering up notes as the two men congratulated each other on their plans. As soon as Steven was gone, Nina said, 'Would you excuse me a moment?' to Anthony and ran down the hall. She caught Steven at the elevators. 'Steven, wait. I'm sorry. That was despicable of me. Please forgive me.'

He looked tired. 'There's nothing to forgive. You are what you are, Nina.'

To her disgrace, she felt tears come to her eyes. 'And what is that? A bitch? Is that what you mean?'

'No, not at all. You're just incredibly single-minded. And you've got your mind set on – God knows what.'

'On helping you and Anthony with Samaritan. It's my job to help Anthony do whatever he wants to do. And I'm not stupid, Steven. I'll be really helpful—'

'If you could just help a little less intensely – but you can't do anything halfway. You know, in some ways I envy you. You glance around, see what you're after and go for it no matter what's in the way. You're so sure of everything. It's a shame you can't bottle some of that up and sell it. I'd be your first customer.'

'Steven, can't you like me a little?'

'I do like you, Nina. We're just so very different.'

'But differences are what makes the world interesting.'

The elevator doors opened and Dr Lisle, his face a mask of fury, strode out. 'Where's Anthony?' he demanded of Nina. He didn't even seem to notice Steven.

Nina pointed. 'Turn left. Last room on the right.'

She was still watching him when she realized the elevator doors had closed and Steven was gone.

Nina knew something about Ellen MacLaughton and Gary before Steven told her the whole thing from his viewpoint. Ellen was a 'boho', a Bohemian, as they called those 1950s precursors of hippies. She was Nina's art teacher's assistant at Barstow. It was a private school or Ellen wouldn't have been allowed on the premises because she was a 'fallen woman', and made no secret of it. She had a child, but no husband. Shocking! Scandalous! Fascinating. The girls adored her. Not only did she have a titillating private life, but she was talented, wonderfully beautiful and eccentric and only a few years older than they were. They all aspired to be like her. They took to wearing pale or no lipstick, black clothes and tights and their wardrobes broke out in a rash of woven headbands and long beads. Every time the art teacher stepped out of the room, they'd drop their pens and brushes and surround Ellen to pry details of her life from her. And she was all too willing to oblige. She found herself every bit as intriguing as they found her.

Her elderly father was a successful writer of science fiction novels under several pseudonyms. Blessed with a private family income as well, the two of them were able to live a luxurious life. There was never mention of a mother in her stories and Nina had no idea what had happened to her. Ellen's doting but clearly peculiar father raised her to make her own decisions about society and

111

the way to live her life. When she was seventeen, she met a boy her age and got pregnant. The girls had the impression that he was from a family they knew (the very wealthy and their supernumeraries like Nina formed a great sticky web of acquaintances), but Ellen would never hint at who he was.

'Why didn't you get an abortion?' they'd ask. Their own parents would have whisked them off to some expensive clinic where such things took place secretly but routinely.

'Because I knew my son was destined to be a great man,' she said, tossing back her long dark hair. They got shivers, the spooky way she said this.

'Did the boy offer to marry you?'

'Offer? Oh, he begged. He was a very responsible person and would have been a wonderful father to Gary.'

'But why didn't you get married?'

'Because he didn't love me passionately, and marriage without passion is immoral,' she said didactically.

The schoolgirls were thrilled.

'What happened to him? Do you ever see him?' they asked.

'He's studying to be a priest,' she said.

They gasped. How romantic.

What a fool Nina felt not to have realized that Ellen was talking about Steven. Even then she was in a state of despair at his having converted to Catholicism and entered the seminary. But Nina didn't make the connection. She just didn't realize that her Steven, whom she'd worshipped since she was eight years old, was biologically male. He was purely a romantic figure to her. Actual genitals didn't figure in her dreams at that age.

The girls' obsession with Ellen's private life, about which she was so frank, eventually reached some parents' ears. The school didn't condone this sort of education. It was very modern to let her be around the girls, but a different matter when she appeared to be influencing them. One day Ellen MacLaughton just wasn't there anymore. The art teacher claimed she'd taken a job elsewhere, but the girls knew she'd been canned. That made her a martyr in addition to her other attractive qualities. They talked about her reverently for a year or so, then someone else more interesting came along and they forgot about her.

It was some years later that Nina heard the other side of it. Steven had left the religious life and, after completing college, went to work for Herron Paper Products. Nina was just out of secretarial school and they were at one of Max Herron's Christmas house parties in Connecticut. Steven, normally a teetotaller, had a few drinks to blunt some private sorrow; quite a few drinks, in fact. While the others were passing out sheet music for a grand session of carols, Nina saw him slip away to the library. She followed and found him slumped on the sofa nursing a brandy and staring at the fire. She sat down next to him.

'I should be spending Christmas with my son,' he mumbled.

She nearly slipped right off the cushion. His son? But she was afraid that if she showed her shock, he'd think her a child and not talk to her anymore. 'Where is he?' she asked. She actually sounded calm.

'With his mother someplace. I try to keep track of them, but Ellen lives like a gypsy.'

That's when Nina put it together.

He told her the whole story, but it sounded different from his viewpoint. Of course she was older and wiser and had escaped Ellen's magic by then. As he spoke, she realized that Ellen wasn't romantic and fascinating at all. She was selfish, self-obsessed and reveled in being deliberately weird, even at Steven's expense. That was unforgivable, hurting Steven. He'd wanted to take his responsibility as the father of the child, partly because it was the done thing, but partly for reasons Nina didn't quite understand, although he tried to explain.

'A child is a reason for living, a future that isn't your own,' he said. It seemed to her that he had plenty of reasons for living and a very nice future indeed before him. But she nodded as if she were with him in this.

113

Steven said that Ellen wouldn't marry him because he didn't love her enough. He was baffled by this, he told Nina. He tried to convince himself he was madly in love with her so that he could convince Ellen of it, but the harder he tried, the more difficult and demanding she became. Eventually even her father took Steven's part, but it did no good. She had the baby by herself and even put 'unknown' on the birth certificate where it asked for the father's name.

What an unmitigated bitch! Nina thought, but even as he was telling the story, Steven was oddly tolerant of Ellen. 'She knew her mind. She played by her rules. I didn't understand them or agree with them, but she was true to her morals and you have to admire that,' he said.

The hell you do, Nina thought.

Over the years, they'd kept in touch, Steven said. But even then Ellen refused officially to acknowledge Steven's role. She'd send pictures of Gary, he told Nina, and say 'I thought you'd like to see how my son is coming along.' Not *our* son. *My* son.

It was shortly after the baby's birth that Steven underwent some kind of religious conversion or awakening. That's when he went to the seminary. He never talked about it. Nor did he explain himself when he left that life and returned to work for Herron Paper Products.

And this heartfelt, heartbreaking confession was what Nina had so stupidly and callously flung in his face in front of Anthony. God only knew how long it would take her to regain his trust.

Nina headed back to Anthony's suite. It was just as well that she'd dawdled, mired in her own thoughts, and missed the initial meeting between Anthony and his one-time mentor. They had a lot to sort out without her taking any part. She opened the door of the suite and donned her protective coloration – that of a drab, mousy, no-personality secretary. 'Good evening, Dr Lisle,' she said pleasantly, but very softly. The docile little nobody.

'Ah, Nina. Sorry I rushed past you like that in the hall. I was so anxious to see Anthony.'

'Of course. Don't give it a thought. It's good to see you, sir. If you gentlemen don't mind, I'll just take this typewriter to my room and get on with those notes.' She grimaced as she tried to lift it.

'It weighs a ton. You can work here, if we won't disturb you,' Anthony said.

'No, I don't even hear voices when I'm typing,' she said. *And if you believe that, I have a bridge in Brooklyn I could sell you.* She got busy typing, her ears pricked. Apparently Lisle had seen Anthony's enthusiasm for the charity plan and recognized it was wise to go along with it – or perhaps he genuinely liked the idea. There was no way to tell. Anyway, he was listening to Anthony expound the concepts he'd worked out with every appearance of approval. Occasionally he'd point out a seeming drawback, but thanks to their preparation, Anthony had responses to all of them.

The dynamics of the conversation were interesting to Nina. Anthony was clearly in charge, not asking Lisle's advice particularly, but anxious to impress him. There was one especially interesting exchange. Anthony had been talking about the medical research aspect of his plans and Lisle raised some objections she didn't quite catch. Anthony said, 'What do you mean by that?'

Lisle said, 'I'm sure you'll see, if you think about it.'

There was an electric pause, then Anthony said, quite firmly, 'I'm sorry, Prof, but as much as I'd welcome your thoughts, I'm not going to get into a guessing game to figure out what they are.'

Again, a pause. Lisle cleared his throat – Nina guessed a lump of pride was stuck in it – and said, 'I only meant that you'll probably want to stay away from "established" diseases like cancer and heart disease or you'll run the risk of double-funding and run-ins with the charitable societies specializing in those. You don't want to be an interloper.'

'Yes, that's a good point,' Anthony said. 'Nina, will you make a note of that?' She kept on typing as if she hadn't heard. 'Nina?'

She made him repeat her name twice before she let it sink in that she was being spoken to. But she could not have been entirely convincing, because after they'd covered the main points of the charity plan, Anthony said, 'Now there's some personal stuff we need to talk about.'

Nina's ears practically stood out from her head.

'Nina, I'm afraid we *are* bothering you,' he said. 'I'll carry the typewriter to your room for you. You'll work better without us yakking.'

It was obvious that no protestation was going to help. She might as well give in gracefully. She gathered up her paperwork and trailed along after bidding Dr Lisle goodnight.

She thought about trying the drinking glass to the wall trick, but decided it was an unworthy act.

Besides, it probably wouldn't work.

Chapter Seven

The Herron women had always regarded Nina Smith as something between a household pet and a mechanical device: something one let out of its pen or flipped a switch to turn on when the occasion demanded, otherwise a being of no senses. At combination social-business gatherings, which is where she most frequently crossed paths with them, she would be dutifully engaged in a few moments of excruciatingly polite conversation, then she'd be unplugged as far as they were concerned.

Nina understood this and didn't feel especially martyred. She knew it wasn't personal, and it was done with such sophisticated courtesy that it was impossible justifiably to take offense. It was simply the way they operated. She'd heard women of their class exchange the most shocking, intimate confidences in the back seat of a limousine with the chauffeur – presumably deafened and unsexed by the social gap – only a few feet away. Of course, she wasn't at the same level of non-being as the more lowly employees. She was on a fuzzy-edged plane of her own. Like governesses used to be; not quite family, not quite servant (after all, she'd gone to the same schools they had), but bobbing uncertainly somewhere between.

Her mother had taught her that this could be an advantage. The private secretary is, above all, her employer's extra ears and eyes. All the better if others believed her incapable of sight and hearing. She had all this in mind when she called on Blanche Herron.

It was ostensibly an after-funeral courtesy call. Actually it was a spy mission into the very heart of the enemy camp.

She knew they would give Anthony trouble; she was trying to ferret out just how much trouble they had in mind. To her good fortune, she caught all the women, Blanche and both her daughters, at home in the penthouse. 'How very sweet of you to call, Nina. You must join us for luncheon.'

'You're looking very well, Mrs Herron, considering the terrible loss you've sustained,' she said very softly.

'You mean Mr Herron, of course,' she said, looking at Nina suspiciously.

'Naturally,' she gushed, acting just the tiniest bit shocked that she could think otherwise although both knew the loss of the money was an equal or greater grief to her.

Blanche had good reason to be suspicious of Nina. The way gossip traveled within the family, Nina felt certain she knew that Lillian Smith's daughter had taken the role of secretary to Anthony. Nina was counting on Blanche's ego to make her think Nina couldn't possibly be loyal to anyone but her and her own concerns. This proved to be quite true.

'I suppose you've been awfully busy showing that dreadful young man all the secrets of my husband's business, but of course what else can you do?' Blanche said sympathetically as they entered the sunlit informal dining area that overlooked the Plaza. 'Jerome, please lay a setting for Miss Smith.'

'Not so very busy, Mrs Herron,' Nina lied. 'Mr Wentworth understands business fairly well, I believe, and Steven Packwood has spent the last several days with him explaining about the paper business.'

'Nina, you're such a good girl. So tactful. Your mother must be very proud of you. No, I'm certain he's down at the office rubbing his hands and positively drooling.'

Nina dropped her gaze modestly, not committing, letting Blanche draw her own conclusions.

'Hi, Nina, escaped from the salt mines?' Betsy said, coming into the room and taking a place at the luncheon table with her back to the million-dollar view. She wore faded jeans and a clingy red turtleneck that did wonders for a figure that hardly needed help. It was almost impossible to believe that she was the mother of five boys, the oldest a teenager. She barely looked twenty herself – unless you got close enough to see the hard lines around her mouth. That was new, Nina reflected, that sign of age and dissipation. 'I suppose you've come to throw us all out to beg for our suppers on the street.'

'Betsy,' Blanche warned.

'Mother, don't let's be silly around Nina. You know Anthony's in charge of paying your rent, and he's unlikely to keep on paying for this place. Why should he? We're nothing to him.'

'Oh, I'm sure he has no intention of stinting you on anything,' Nina said sincerely. She had briefly mentioned to him that it seemed a little extravagant to keep paying to staff and maintain four luxurious homes in various parts of the world, and he had briskly set her right on that. They were what his father wanted for Blanche and they were hers for as long as she had the slightest interest in them. He didn't come right out and say, 'Like it or not, she's my mother', but that was the implication. Nina also knew he'd put out feelers about buying Leland House for her, perhaps in the hope that she'd move back to England and keep her distance from him.

'That was the most unforgivable thing Max did,' Betsy put in, 'leaving all the property in that boy's hands.'

'No, it wasn't,' Faye said from the doorway. Nina hadn't heard her come in and was astonished when she saw her. Faye had faint blue circles under the eyes and even her hair looked tired and lifeless. She was in a flannel robe and nightgown. She rushed over and gave Nina a hug, such an uncharacteristic action that Nina stepped back in surprise. 'How could Max have done this to me?' Faye asked plaintively.

Nina didn't know exactly what she meant, so she just patted her shoulder and looked sympathetic. 'I'm sure he didn't mean to hurt you, Faye.'

'But he knew how fascinated I was with business. It was always understood that I'd be put in charge. All those times I went with him to the paper mills and the brokers' and—' She paused to blow her nose on a tissue she pulled from the pocket of her robe.

Good God, she'd considered herself his business heir, Nina thought with amazement. Who would have guessed? Of course Max Herron had taken Faye on business trips. But it was, Nina had always assumed, because neither Blanche nor Betsy was willing to jaunt around, and he liked to have his family with him. But Faye had apparently taken this as the act of a mentor. Nina had never much liked cool, superior Faye, but for a fleeting moment she felt genuinely sorry for her. What a blow it must have been to her to hear Athalon turn it all over to Anthony, a stranger.

Nina noticed, too, that Betsy was looking at Faye with what appeared to be genuine sympathy, the first time Nina had ever seen any of the gentler emotions on Betsy's hard face. Even in Nina's brief brushes with the family, it had been obvious that Betsy was wildly jealous of Faye. Max's betrayal – in their view, at least – had brought Faye down to Betsy's level. Nina was sorry to see it. They could make a formidably bitchy combination if they joined forces.

'You've got to make him understand he has to turn down the inheritance, Nina. It simply isn't moral to accept it just because Max lost his head and slept with some floozy ages ago and felt bad about it the day he happened to be making a will.'

It took Nina a minute to figure out what Faye was talking about, then realize that she had answered one of Nina's most pres-sing questions. They had no idea who Anthony's mother was. At least Faye didn't. What about Blanche? Had she figured it out, or been told?

'A person can't turn down an inheritance,' Blanche said grimly.

'Yes, they can, Mother. It's perfectly legal. I've checked with my lawyers,' Faye said.

So she'd already engaged attorneys, Nina thought. That

was revealing, and a little frightening. Not quite as frightening as the fact that she appeared sincerely to believe that Anthony could be made to give up everything.

'Faye, I don't think—' Nina began.

'He must be made to understand that it's wrong to accept. We all know he's probably not really Max's son anyway. Whoever the awful woman was, she convinced him her brat was his, and Max wanted to believe it. I don't know why he was so damned desperate to claim a son when he had me. I'm as good as any son.'

Nina glanced at Blanche, who was nodding. Jesus! This was deeper water than Nina had anticipated. The truth about Anthony's birthright hadn't even occurred to them. If they pursued it, they were bound to find out. What had been wrong with Max Herron? To keep the secret of Anthony's birth from them, even Blanche, the child's mother, all these years, then set up his will so that they'd have to be told when he was safely out of the way? Was he, at heart, a coward? Nina had always felt he was very courageous, but had she been wrong? Had they all been wrong about him?

'I'm sure you are as good as a son,' Nina reassured her. Faye had taken hold of her sleeve. Nina could hardly just go on goggling at her in amazement. She said, 'Don't you think, however, that Max wanted you to be free to have a life of your own? Marriage and children?'

'No, that wasn't it at all. I think this Wentworth person had been applying pressure to him. Moral blackmail. Max was so ill toward the end. He didn't know his own mind. And this man must have nosed around him, playing on his desire for a son. I have detectives checking on his movements.'

'But Faye, he's been in Europe for the last couple years,' Nina said. Faye was on a headlong downhill run, and Nina felt she owed it to everyone to stop her before she got to the bottom.

'I know that's what we're told. But transatlantic flights are nothing these days. I'm sure he was slipping back and meeting Max. Probably even blackmailing him. My people will find the proof.'

Nina glanced, appalled, at Blanche and Betsy. They were just listening complacently. They'd heard all this before and were backing her, or at least making no attempt to dissuade her of her rash accusations. They were actually willing to go to court and claim that Mr Herron had been incompetent and had been unduly influenced by a gold-digging bastard son. Max Herron was lucid until the end. Nina knew it; they all knew it, and yet they were ready to degrade his memory by claiming he was nuts.

The thought of the publicity that would generate was staggering. It was no comfort knowing that later, perhaps years later, they'd be proved wrong in court; the press never made any attempt to correct the wrong impressions they'd given. The stigma of the gossip they'd start would cling to Anthony, and Samaritan, for decades to come.

'Well, I'm sure something can be worked out,' Nina said feebly.

'Something had better be worked out and it better be to my complete satisfaction,' Faye said. She wasn't sniffling anymore. She had the look of the fanatic in her eyes.

'Jerome, you may serve now,' Blanche was saying as Nina stared in horror at Faye. She wanted to run back to Anthony and report this conversation, but she was stuck there to endure a girly-girly luncheon with Anthony's worst enemies.

Anthony took the news of Faye's attitude more calmly than Nina had. 'I didn't want to have to get into the past,' he said thoughtfully.

'You have to. They're going to invent a truly sleazy past if you don't tell them the truth. Think of the adverse publicity!'

'I'll have to talk to the Prof about it,' he said, and Nina's heart sank. This would have to stop, this dependence on Lisle. 'I've got to get out of this damned hotel, Nina.'

'I can find you someplace to live.'

'I don't want to buy, just rent.'

'In Kansas City, I assume?'

'Yes, for now. But not in the city. I can't stand the smell and the sense of being shoulder to shoulder with so many people. It'll have to have grounds and plenty of room and privacy. I'll be conducting business there. Lots of guest rooms. I'm going to maintain the face of family unity as long as possible. See to it, would you, Nina?'

Nina had never been sent looking for a house before, but she didn't want to show any chink in her armor. 'Of course.'

She managed it in one day by using her high school alumni roster. A few well-placed phone calls and by nightfall she'd leased a fourteen bedroom mansion between Ward Parkway and State Line. It was the property of the scion of a meat-packing fortune who had moved to Switzerland and had been trying to sell it for two years. He was desperate enough to lease for a while. It was even furnished – extraordinary good luck.

'You're great, Nina! How did you do it?' Anthony marveled.

'It's my job,' she said modestly. 'The owners have put their more valuable art works in storage, along with the good silver and china and, of course, their clothing. Some of the furniture is a bit shabby, one bathroom is catastrophic and the linens are pitiful, but other than that, you can move right in.'

'When?'

'Right away. Tomorrow, if you'd like.'

'I'd like. Can we be ready for a family party in a week?'

'A family party?' she asked warily.

'With attendant attorneys,' he said with a wry smile.

They moved Anthony to the mansion the next morning. 'Jesus Christ! It looks like Dracula just moved out!' he said, surveying the gloomy, dark-paneled entry hall. 'Can we take these drapes down and open up the windows? And get some hundred-watt bulbs.'

Anticipating that he'd want some changes, Nina had already hired a skeleton staff. She put them to work while Anthony and Lisle explored the place. She summoned a dry-cleaning establishment to arrange for cleaning and storage of the miles of velvet curtains. A senior sales officer of Macy's sent a woman to make an inventory of the bedding and towels. When she was done, Nina placed a gigantic order for replacements and also hired a cleaning firm to take on the mammoth dusting, polishing and window-cleaning job.

'Mr Wentworth likes lots of light and it's especially important in this dark house that every window is spotless, inside and out,' she told them and ignored their alarmed looks at the blustery weather outdoors.

By noon she was feeling quite smug about her accomplishments. *I love my job*, she murmured, hugging herself.

'Let's have some lunch,' Anthony said, coming down the front stairway. 'Where's a McDonald's?'

Nina cringed.

A week later the place was hardly recognizable. Nina hadn't made any major changes that violated the lease, but a brutally thorough cleaning and the temporary storage of many of the heavier, shabbier pieces of furniture had made a world of difference. The place really looked quite elegant. The only arrangement she didn't care for was the adjoining rooms that Anthony and Taylor Lisle had staked out. Lisle showed no sign of moving on.

On Anthony's orders, she'd sent out invitations to the family for a house party. All the Herrons and their attorneys as well as her mother, Steven Packwood and Dr Lisle were to be there for a late dinner and brunch the next day. It was rather formal and ambitious and was a test of Nina's organizational skills.

'Are you ready?' Anthony asked when she checked in with him in the top-floor room he'd fitted out as office.

'I think so. The caterers are already in the kitchen.'

'And all the guests are coming?'

'I believe so. Blanche sent her acceptance first. She must

124

have given orders to the others. Betsy's bringing her whole brood, including a nursemaid or nanny or something. They weren't invited, but I think she's doing it to make everyone as uncomfortable as possible. Do you know, she and Ned have given – or sold – one of their boys to Ned's missionary uncle – in Africa, I think.'

'You're kidding,' Anthony said, shaking his head in disgust. 'You've got all the documents in the safe?'

'Originals and copies. I think the originals ought to stay there.'

'Yes, I can see them tearing up things as dramatic gestures. Good thinking, Nina.'

That was the best thing about working for Anthony. He was really appreciative of her skills and unstinting in his praise.

'I've rented you a tux, but I think you really ought to own two of your own, so one is always ready while the other is at the cleaners.'

'A tux. God! Do they really dress like that for family dinners?'

'They will for this one. It's hardly a happy barbecue in the back yard.'

He turned the swivel office chair round and stared out the window. 'Why the hell are they coming? Aren't you surprised that they all accepted?'

'No, they've probably convinced themselves that you've come to your senses and have invited them over to give Mr Herron's money back to them, or that they'll be able to make you do so.'

'Are they all really so greedy that all the millions they've got the use of aren't enough?'

'It's not just the money itself. It's the power it gives them. Or would, if it were theirs.'

He turned back round, angry. 'What power? They don't want to do something worthwhile with it, as I do.'

Nina wanted to be omniscient, to give him all the answers, but she didn't have them. She understood these people only as a careful observer; she wasn't one of them. 'Anthony, they expected to receive it, and it's been taken from them. That's all they can see.'

'Well, if they're coming here to get it back, they're certainly in for a number of nasty surprises.'

Chapter Eight

Betsy was the first to arrive. 'Well, Nina dear, the clan assembles,' she drawled. Her boys, all of them except the one who'd been sent off to do missionary work overseas, were scrambling out of a second rented limo that had followed hers. 'Well, well, well,' she said, looking over the front of the house, 'dear Anthony certainly has caught on to how to spend Max's money, hasn't he? Did you know, the first time I met him he was naked.'

Naturally, Nina was fascinated with this tidbit, which was probably an outright lie, but she wouldn't give Betsy the satisfaction of knowing. 'The house is only rented,' she said.

'How very frugal. Ned's coming out later. He had an appointment this afternoon in the city. I do hope you've put us in separate rooms with the heathens at the opposite end of the house. Boys! Will you pipe down!'

Faye arrived a quarter of an hour later. She had her husband Charlie with her. They pulled up in a little red sports car which he drove himself. Instead of waiting for help, he hoisted a single small overnight bag out. Nina liked him for that. None of the rest of them seemed to have grasped the concept that they were physically capable of lifting anything heavier than a gold cigarette case or a stock certificate.

Steven followed Faye and Charlie. 'What a mausoleum!' he said.

Naturally, Nina took this as a slight on her abilities. 'It's a lot better than when we moved in. You should have seen it with seventy acres of dusty moss-green velvet drapes.'

He shuddered. 'Where's Anthony?'

'In the office upstairs. Nobody is to know.'

'Your secret's safe with me,' he said and disappeared up the stairs to visit Anthony. Nina remained on guard at the door. John Athalon along with Blanche's lawyer and Faye's lawyer arrived together deep in an animated conversation about a golf course on some island in the Caribbean. The three of them showed no signs of being on conflicting sides of a battle. That always amazed her about lawyers, that they could compartmentalize things even better than she herself could. They were capable of trying to annihilate each other all day in court, then go off arm in arm to play golf or attend the opera.

She was brooding over this when Blanche arrived. The chauffeur handed her out of the car as though she were delicate crystal. She looked up at Nina, who was shocked. She couldn't have looked worse if she'd been beaten up. For the first time Nina realized Blanche was an old woman. 'Are you unwell, Mrs Herron?' she said, concerned.

'Just one of my beastly headaches. My maid's at the chemist's. She'll be along shortly. If I could just lie down and rest?'

Nina saw her to her room and helped get her settled in the absence of her maid. Blanche was the Edwardian-type lady who actually had to undress to her slip to put on a cream silk wrapper and matching satin mules to take a nap. As Nina got her into bed, wondering if she ought to provide her with a cologne-soaked handkerchief to complete her headache toilette, the maid arrived from the drugstore with a bottle of pills. Nina abandoned Blanche to her ministrations.

Lillian Smith was next and Nina suddenly felt a great deal better, just knowing her mother was nearby. 'You mustn't worry, darling. If Anthony's the man you think, it will all go very well. If he's not, it doesn't matter.'

Ned didn't arrive until nearly seven. 'I hope this charade won't last very long. I have an early appointment tomorrow morning that I'd like to be rested for,' he barked, flinging his coat at the butler.

Nina rushed upstairs to report to Anthony one last time. 'They're all here,' she said breathlessly.

He and Steven were playing what looked like a hand of gin rummy. As if there were nothing more important to do.

'Have you fireproofed the house?' Steven asked. 'You should before you invite in fire-breathing dragons.'

'No, but I'm sure Nina has a bucket of water under each dining room chair to fling at anybody who turns incendiary,' Anthony said.

The image of sloshing Betsy or Faye with a bucket of water struck Nina as so funny she became nearly hysterical. She laughed so hard she had to sit down and mop her eyes. Her laughter was contagious and pretty soon the two men were hooting and shouting with mirth.

They were the only people in the house who found anything to amuse them. The evening didn't promise much in the way of giggling.

There's a lot to be said for the veneer of good breeding. It may be a very thin layer of civilized behavior, but it's often remarkably durable. The cocktail hour was proof of that. An outsider might have sensed an undercurrent of unease, but only if he were very sensitive. Anthony was utterly calm, utterly charming, utterly in charge. He wore his rented tux as if he'd been born in one and set a tone of urbane ease. He inquired solicitously of Blanche whether her headache was better and offered some folk remedy that involved pinching the web of skin between one's first finger and thumb. Whether it was the headache or the bizarre situation, Blanche accepted his concern with astonishing meekness. He avoided speaking to Betsy at all, but did it so suavely that Emily Post herself couldn't have found fault. Women usually found Betsy revolting, but most men were fascinated with her vulgarity. Odd that Anthony disliked her so intensely, Nina thought.

Steven, looking so handsome Nina could hardly keep her eyes away from him, deflected Ned with a discussion of the space program, a subject upon which Ned was fanatically supportive. Nobody was inclined to join in or rescue Steven. Betsy and Faye were by the fireplace, soaking up the warmth and gossiping with malicious animation about the previous owners of the house. Faye's nice husband was talking about airplanes with Betsy's dreadful boys. They were spiffed up for the cocktail and hor d'oeuvres hour, but it had been arranged that they would be hauled off before dinner to eat with their nanny in the playroom.

Finally, after a nerve-wracking three-quarters of an hour, dinner was announced, and the heathens were dragged off. The adults entered the dining room. Nina felt she had done a good job there, and glanced at her mother for her approval. Lillian smiled and nodded. Nina had made the seating arrangement originally, but when she showed it to Anthony for his approval, he'd juggled it completely.

'No, not you at the foot of the table,' he said. She was hurt at first, until he added, 'I need you next to me.' He pencilled in 'Blanche H.' at the hostess end of the table. 'Thirteen of us,' he mused. 'Not only unlucky, but quite gauche, I imagine, having so many more men. Still, nothing to do about it. It's not an occasion we'd invite strangers to just to even up the numbers. Since we can't alternate, move Steven up to my other side. And as long as we're doing it all wrong anyway, make sure Betsy has to sit next to Ned. That'll be good for her.'

They found their places and settled into the salad course. Nina could hardly make herself eat, she was so nervous. She noticed that most of the rest of them toyed with their food as well. All except the attorneys. They packed it away like lumberjacks. After what seemed like eons, the raspberry mousse was taken away, the dishes were cleared, the gentlemen were served their port and the ladies their sherry. The room fell silent.

Anthony stood. With a self-deprecating laugh, he uttered the cliché, 'I guess you're all wondering why I've asked you here. Nina, could we have some real lights?'

Nina flipped the switches, then before taking her seat, slipped a packet of papers from where they'd been concealed in the walnut sideboard.

'Look here, Wentworth, I assume you've had time to see reason,' Ned said gruffly.

'I have indeed, Ned.'

Ned nudged Betsy. 'What did I tell you?' She arched one eyebrow contemptuously.

Anthony looked down one side of the table and up the other, as if wanting to memorize their faces as they were before he went on. 'I have a number of extremely important things to tell you, and I'm very glad to tell you now. But if there are dramatics, and people storm off, I won't tell you again.'

'Well!' Faye snorted.

'Only once,' he reiterated, looking straight at her.

She glanced at her attorney and smiled. 'Do go on, and when you're finished, I have a few things to tell you.'

Did she really have a ploy, Nina wondered, or was it all bluff? Faye was capable of the most extraordinary bluffs, with her fragile, freshly scrubbed look.

'You'll be welcome,' Anthony said. 'Now, there's a bit of history to dispose of first. Immediately upon or shortly before her marriage to Max Herron, Blanche Herron conceived a child—'

'Dear God, a gynecology lecture,' Betsy sneered.

'I wouldn't dream of trying to instruct *you* in biology,' Anthony said to her coldly.

'What the hell's that supposed to mean?' Ned said, starting to rise.

Betsy dragged him back down. 'It means I'm a slut, my dear. Shut up. I can't wait to hear this story. Mr Wentworth has a flair for the theatrical.'

'It was a difficult birth.' Anthony was apparently unperturbed by the interruptions. But he had his right hand on the edge of the table and Nina could see the tendons standing out with stress. 'The baby, a boy, died.'

There was a murmur of bored assent around the table.

'Except, he didn't,' Anthony went on. 'The doctors told Max Herron his son would be a mental incompetent if he lived at all, which seemed unlikely.'

Faye glanced questioningly at her mother, as if to say, 'I never knew this part of the story.'

'So Max, wanting to spare his desperately ill wife the pain of possibly coming to love the baby before ultimately losing it or, worse, given the people involved, having to actually raise such a child, Max told her the baby had died, and had it put into a children's hospital to quietly pass out of their lives.'

Now he really had their attention. He looked at Blanche and the rest of them followed his eyes. She was gazing down at her hand, pleating a napkin between her fingers.

Anthony continued, 'But contrary to medical opinion, the child didn't die. It survived and the hospital soon told Max they couldn't keep it any longer. It would have to go home. Max was in a bad spot then. Here was this extraordinary defective child to account for when his wife already believed it dead. So he arranged for its adoption.'

'Are you trying to say this son of Max's, this imbecile, is *still* alive?' Faye asked, outraged.

'Very much alive. And not an imbecile.'

'I don't believe a word of it,' Faye said, leaning forward and glancing round at the others to get their agreement. 'This is just a complicated trick. But it's not going to work.'

Dr Lisle spoke for the very first time. Very quietly, but with tremendous effect. 'I arranged for the adoption. It is quite true.'

'You?' Faye looked back and forth between him and Anthony several times and the realization – hateful, dreadful, unthinkable – visibly dawned on her. It was a repulsive sight, the way her polished, innocent face turned ugly and terrified.

'No!' she said, standing up suddenly. 'Mother! Say something! This awful man is claiming to be your *son*!'

Blanche finally looked up, one tear rolling down her ravaged, rouged face. 'Faye, dear, he *is*.'

'No!' Faye ran round to her, threw herself to her knees next to her mother. 'No, you mustn't believe this! You can't. It isn't true.'

'I didn't know until today,' Blanche said very slowly and very softly. The rest of them only heard because they were so tense and over-attuned. 'There are documents. My attorney had people search for papers to discredit him as Max's son and they found ...'

Betsy spoke to Anthony in a dead-sounding voice. 'Then you're—'

Anthony looked straight at her. 'Your brother.'

'Oh God!' Betsy put her hand up to her mouth and suddenly leaned forward as if gagging. She took a long, rasping breath and waved off Ned's attempts to find out what was wrong with her.

'I have several copies of the documents for your attorneys,' Anthony went on, very deliberately ignoring Betsy. 'I have more to tell you, but I imagine you'd like to talk to each other first. For now, I think it might be best if we left you Herrons alone for – let's say half an hour? Prof, Steven, Nina, Athalon, shall we excuse ourselves? Mrs Smith, you might wish to stay.' He gestured curtly for Nina to give copies of the birth certificate and adoption papers to the attorneys.

By the time she had done so, Anthony had already disappeared. Lisle followed Nina out, going straight for the cigar humidor in the library. Steven and Athalon were just ahead of him. Nina headed for the nearest bathroom, but the door was closed, and she could hear someone in there being violently sick. Anthony.

The rest of the evening, though startling by normal standards, was somewhat anticlimactic by comparison – but only by comparison. Anthony's party trudged back into the dining room precisely thirty minutes after having left.

133

The Herrons fell silent. Whatever had transpired, whatever their plans were, they had apparently decided that for the present at least they'd behave with frosty decorum. This was probably because their lawyers had verbally beaten them into it. Faye's eyes were bloodshot and her face blotchy, but she had herself under control. Poor old Blanche looked like she'd been left out in the rain for a year or two. Ned was nearly twitching with fury, but even he – what a wonder! – was still and silent.

In a sense, Nina was in as much nervous anticipation as they were. She knew of only one more thing Anthony had to say to them. But he obviously had several items to cover from his private agenda. What could they be?

He resumed his place at the head of the table, but he sat down this time. He looked down at Blanche for a long while. Without using any form of direct address to her, he said, 'I'm sorry to have caused our "reunion" in such a public way. I hope that later, when there's time, we can get to know each other.'

She inclined her head regally. Nina had seen more animated expressions on mannequins.

'This afternoon I made an offer to buy Leland House. The offer was accepted. It'll be yours. I hope you'll make it your home.'

It was at once the gift she most desired and a banishment. She knew it. 'Thank you,' she said in a quavering voice.

He looked round at the rest of them. 'I'm removing from you, and myself, the bulk of the fortune that Max Herron left me. I'm keeping my share of the paper company, and of course your trusts are to remain untouched, but the majority of the assets are going to be put into a foundation. A charitable foundation.'

He gave them a few moments to take this in. Betsy was looking at him with loathing. Faye was clutching her husband's hand and looking frantic. Anthony went on, 'Nina has some paperwork here outlining the basic structure and aims of Samaritan. She'll hand it out so you can study it at your convenience. Max, my father, left me in charge of the disbursement of the money set aside for your allowances and the upkeep of the many properties and employees you are accustomed to use. I think there was a reason for this, perhaps a reason he didn't truly know at the time. I believe it is my responsibility to use this – this "power", if you like, to benefit you.'

They were looking at each other and him in confusion and alarm.

'I've decided my father would have wanted me to help you in more than the strictly financial sense. Even if it's not what he intended, it's my obligation. Samaritan has the potential to help not only the recipients of its bounty, but the providers of it as well. To be involved in helping others is, well, an ennobling process.'

They were still staring at him blankly. There was a haze of sweat on his forehead in spite of the chill of the big, drafty room. He sighed and plunged in. 'Let me put it simply: the extent to which I co-operate with you in disbursing the trust funds will depend on the extent to which you support Samaritan.'

Faye gasped. 'That's outright blackmail.'

'If you want to call it that, you may. But benevolent blackmail. It is, I genuinely believe, for your own good. I don't expect you to contribute any funds to Samaritan. Only your support, your help, in finding and encouraging others of your circle to give. You know how; you've all been involved in fund-raising for symphonies and hospitals and the like. You'll see, being intimately involved in helping others will truly help you. Doing good is good for the doer.'

'Bullshit!' Betsy said. 'What a goddamned goody two-shoes you are. This is the most outrageous thing I've ever heard.'

'Betsy's right,' Ned said. 'You're a fool! And you're trying to make fools of us! And I, for one, won't have it.'

Anthony calmly opened a folder and glanced at the contents. 'Ned, your law firm keeps you on as a courtesy to your late father, who founded it. You have no clients and an honorary income of twenty thousand dollars a year from the firm. Just about enough for Betsy's clothes, I imagine. You have debts of over a hundred and fifty thousand dollars that I was able to discover in a few days. There are, no doubt, many more, including an unspecified amount promised to your missionary uncle. You have no home, no cars, no employees, no school tuitions that were not paid for by Max. Now that responsibility is mine. If you think I'm foolish, that Samaritan's foolish, I can't force you to support it. You are free to walk out of here this minute and fend for yourself. But if you stay, if you show the world, and *me*, the appearance of genuine support, you may continue to live, let us say, as "gracefully" as ever.'

Nina had been slipping round, handing out the Samaritan fact sheet. Faye's husband, Charlie, had been studying it while Ned was being eviscerated. He looked up now. 'Say, this looks exciting. No, really!' he said as Faye nudged him brutally. 'I'm with you, Anthony. I'd like to be a part of this.'

Ned was so white they thought he was having some sort of seizure. He was breathing hard through his mouth and looking like a fish. Finally, he found words. 'I'll ruin you, you fucking bastard.'

Anthony stood and leaned forward. Suddenly the fresh-faced Harvard brainchild disappeared and there was a strong, rugged ranch hand in his place.

'Try it, Neddy-boy,' he said menacingly. 'Walk out of here now and earn your own living, then come ruin me if you can.'

Ned roared to his feet, flung his chair against the wall and stormed out. There was a collective exhalation of breath.

'Betsy?' Anthony said. 'Are you going with him?'

She said nothing for an excruciatingly long moment, then, 'I believe I'll stay where the money is,' she said with languid venom. 'After all, I do like nice things.' She held out a diamond-clad hand and studied it. 'But I am free to loathe you, aren't I?'

He acted as if he hadn't heard her. 'I'm not condemning you to this for ever,' he said to all of them. 'If, after two or three years, you don't feel that you've benefited from your forced association with Samaritan, you can walk away and there will be no argument, no reprisals.'

'So you say,' Faye sneered.

'So I say. When I give my word, I mean it. Take it from goody two-shoes!'

'Are you done with us?' Faye asked coldly.

'Not quite. One more thing. Twice a year, at a place of my choosing, there will be a week-long meeting, a "retreat" if you wish, of the Samaritan people. You will all be there, being the charitable, loving family. Now, Samaritan's first meeting will be a week from Friday in Max's old office. I hope, for all our sakes, to see you there.'

He rose to leave, Nina started to gather up her remaining papers. As she did so, she noticed Steven. He was staring at Anthony's retreating back with an expression of positively astonished admiration. Taylor Lisle came up behind him and put his hand on Steven's shoulder. His look was smug. He'd known all this. It might have been his plan, or at least his suggestion. He was still very important to Anthony. More important than she was, Nina realized. But it didn't matter. She had lots of patience. He was old and she was young. She would win.

As Nina started out of the room, Faye rushed up to her. 'Nina, how could you let him do this to us?' she said, her voice almost out of control.

'I didn't know,' Nina said softly. It was not only what Faye wanted to hear, it happened to be true.

PART THREE

1968–1974

Steven

'What sort of picture do people have of Sir Lancelot from this end of time? ... He was a knight with a medieval respect for honor ... But the curious thing was that under the king-post of keeping faith with himself and with others, he had a contradtictory nature which was far from holy. People have odd reasons for ending up as saints. An ordinary fellow, who did not spend half his life torturing himself by trying to discover what was right so as to conquer his inclination towards what was wrong, might have cut the knot which brought their ruin.'

The Once and Future King, T. H. White

Chapter Nine

Steven Packwood had underestimated Anthony Wentworth.

He'd thought Anthony's goodness was niceness, mere trivial naiveté. But that night in the drafty borrowed dining room with the Herrons hovering like vultures, he found out Anthony had a true virtue that was simple, strong, brave, perhaps a bit wrong-headed, but deeply sincere. He sat watching the younger man trembling at his own audacity as he made his ultimatums and Steven fell in love with him. Not in a sexual sense, for Steven was tragically heterosexual, but in that he had found someone to anchor himself to. Someone who had found Right. Someone who stood closer to his own ideal than he had ever managed to define, much less attain.

The irony nearly overwhelmed him. He'd always patronized Anthony, felt fond of him, but superior. While they'd both been 'searchers', looking for a purpose in life, Steven had assumed that with his sensitivity and tortured determination, he'd find it, whereas Anthony, so smart but without cleverness or complexity, would soon abandon the search and settle into being a lawyer or a stockbroker and live in a nice house in the suburbs with 2.5 children, and be content.

When Steven learned that Anthony had inherited Max Herron's money, he'd been glad for him, but anticipated that he'd soon turn into another version of Max himself: complacent, successful, somewhat more ethical than the average multi-millionaire. Then that day in the hotel suite when Anthony started talking about Samaritan, the young heir had surprised him, pleased him, kindled an excitement in his soul. Here, thanks to Anthony's concept and funding, was something Steven could believe in. It was good and generous, there was no doubt of that, but even then Steven had underestimated the sincerity, the fervor, with which it had been done.

To attempt to force the Herrons into the fold, to make worthwhile people of them by association with generosity, that was downright heroic, and probably quite doomed. They'd fight him tooth and nail. Anthony wasn't stupid, he knew that. And yet he had the self-assurance, the confidence in the Rightness of Samaritan, to force them into the bosom of his precious project to do their worst. He was that convinced they would benefit spiritually, and that devoted to his obligation to benefit them.

Steven tried, later, to explain to Nina what he'd come to understand that night. 'I thought Anthony wanted to do good so he'd be *seen* to be doing good. Most of us do. But that night I realized that he wanted to do good for its own sake.'

But Nina misunderstood. 'There's nothing wrong with being seen to be an admirable person.'

'No, but real virtue is for its own sake. It needs no acknowledgement, Nina.'

She stared at him as if he were a trifle mad, which he sometimes suspected himself. She was so practical, so straightforward in her fanaticism to make Anthony a great man. She and Steven were like the differences between Eastern and Western philosophy. He felt inner greatness was the whole point of life and screw the world's opinion; she recognized that it was nice enough, but the show of greatness was the vital thing.

And yet, she fancied herself in love with him. Steven was amazed by that. How could she think she loved him when she hadn't the tiniest sliver of understanding of him? Now that she had Anthony to devote herself to, maybe she would stop looking at him with those great, sad, lovelorn eyes.

Putting Nina out of his mind, he rose from the table that night and followed Anthony. He caught up with him on the stairway to the third floor. Another man would have wanted to sit around with his partisans, gloating over his victory, being petted and made over. But Anthony was trying to escape.

'Anthony,' Steven called.

The younger man turned. He was pale, shaken.

Steven stood on the step just below him. 'Anthony, I will do anything I can for you. Anything,' he said simply.

Anthony put his hand on Steven's shoulder. 'Thank you.'

They stood that way a moment, awkward, moved. Then they embraced quickly, uneasily, pounding each other on the back the way men do to disguise love.

After the meeting in Kansas City, Steven went home to see his father. The older man agreed that Steven's younger brother was perfectly well suited to uphold the Packwood interests in Herron Paper Products, leaving Steven free to devote himself to Samaritan. 'Dear God, I hope this will make him happy,' he said to his wife later. 'Why can't he be happy?'

Steven's mother had no answer. In fact, the first years of Samaritan were a time of uncomplicated joy for her son, the longest period of inner peace he'd ever known.

Unlike Anthony, Steven wasn't free to put his fortune into Samaritan. Although he hadn't heard from Ellen for a long time, he still had a moral, and someday perhaps a financial, obligation to their son. More pressing, the senior Packwoods had another son nobody talked about. He was the youngest, now a grown man, so severely handicapped emotionally that he'd nearly murdered another child in his kindergarten and had been institutionalized since he was six years old. The most expensive experts that money could buy had all told the Packwoods there was no hope of the patient ever being able to function within society. The costs of private care for him were staggering. Someday, when Steven's parents were gone, they would be his debt. But now he could give Anthony and Samaritan his heart and brain and time, which is all that Anthony wanted from him.

They devoted themselves to building and planning the scope of the great charitable organization they felt it could be. Sometimes their dreams leaped into unreality and they'd laugh at each other and go out for hamburgers and greasy fries to come back down to earth. Nina Smith and Taylor Lisle were always standing by, ready to help them find the practical way of implementing their dreams.

The first step, Lisle said, was to make well-placed donations that would garner attention and make Samaritan a familiar name in the circles of society that had money to give. The first project was one hundred thousand dollars given to a Carnegie library in southern California to restore smoke-damaged books from a fire. The suggestion for this donation came from Lisle, and Anthony originally objected. 'This isn't what I have in mind. Not that restoring books isn't worthwhile, but that's in a community of wealthy people who can well afford the restoration themselves.'

'That's the whole point,' Lisle said. 'We make them aware of us and, more important, make them feel a twinge of guilt that we stepped in when they didn't.'

'If you and Steven go out there to make the presentation and spend a week allowing yourself to be wined and dined, my guess is that you can get them to commit half again as much to Samaritan,' Nina said.

Grudgingly, Anthony and Steven went. They were young, handsome, well-bred and utterly irresistible in their bright-eyed enthusiasm for Samaritan. In a country crawling with uncouth, dirty hippies, if the evening news were to be believed, the old California millionaires were charmed by these two shining examples of American youth.

They returned to Kansas City with checks and commitments for checks totalling nearly $300,000.

Nina was ecstatic. Steven said, only half jokingly, 'The biggest donation was from a rich grandmother of two of the homeliest young women I've ever seen.'

'Did either of you promise to marry them?' Nina asked matter-of-factly.

'No!' they chorused.

'Then it's all right.'

Anthony was more serious. 'But she really did give for the wrong reason.'

This remark touched a nerve in Taylor Lisle. 'Anthony, you've got to clear your mind of the idea that you have either the right or the duty to judge people's motives in giving. It's up to you to see that the money is spent well. That's all. That's plenty.'

Steven was surprised at the outburst. He, like all of them who'd known Lisle over the years, had come to expect vague psycho-babble questions from him rather than this kind of blunt, authoritative talk. Moreover, he wasn't sure he agreed with the pronouncement. Wasn't it unwise to accept money that came tainted by a hint of blackmail, however subtle or minor?

But in those first years there were so many clearly good, exciting things happening that Steven didn't often allow himself to drift into doubt. Highly visible gifts were given to a small town in Mississippi that had suffered devastating flood damage; a Jewish children's hospital in New Jersey in danger of closing because of expensive structural instability in their ancient building; an historical restoration of a pre-Revolutionary village in Virginia; and most profitably, a soil conservation program in windy, oil-rich Texas that allowed farmers and the oil men to make use of the same coveted land. The funds came in in astonishing amounts. Steven and Anthony were able to put aside any concerns about the sources in the excitement of determining worthy causes and seeing good done.

Surprisingly, the Herrons were, if not overtly helpful, not as obstructive as they might have been. Blanche went quietly to her exile in England. Betsy showed up like a

145

malignant spirit at the meetings she was required to attend. She sat at the table, filing her nails and giving heavily ironic looks to anyone misguided enough to speak to her. When the meetings were over, she strolled out, not to be seen again until the next meeting. But she was living up to the minimum standard Anthony had set.

Charlie Brent, Faye's husband, was extremely supportive. He not only gave a substantial amount of his own money, he solicited large sums from friends of his. He even took time from his own highly lucrative brokerage firm actually to participate in Samaritan in practical ways. It was he who discovered a small cancer research lab in Maine that was about to disappear because the funds had been siphoned off by an errant financial manager.

'They're on the point of a breakthrough,' he told Anthony. 'Not the Cure, but an important step in that direction. I've already hired experts to check on this claim and they say it's true. They need seventy-five thousand to get them over the hump. I can contribute about a quarter of it if Samaritan can carry the rest.'

'If you believe in it, that's good enough for me,' Anthony said.

'There's one thing.' Charlie hesitated. 'Would you mind very much if Faye made the formal presentation at the press conference when it's all set up? She'd love it. She's very enthusiastic about Samaritan.'

Steven sank back in his chair and tented his fingers. He was an idealist, but that didn't make him a fool. When Charlie had gone, he said to Anthony, 'Be careful of Faye. I don't trust her. She's being too co-operative.'

'Oh, I don't know,' Anthony said. 'Maybe my attempt to make her a better, more generous person is working.' He stared at Steven for a long moment, then added, 'Or maybe I'm an asshole.'

Steven laughed. 'Entirely possible. I saw her at a restaurant last week with Ned Graves.'

'He's her brother-in-law.'

146

'He's your enemy.'

Ned Graves had made a pest of himself, as he'd threatened. Every month or so someone from his firm filed one nuisance suit or another against Anthony and Samaritan. They were groundless actions, attempts to question the tax exempt status of Samaritan with the IRS, and appeals to the probate court to disqualify Anthony as executor of his father's estate. Nothing was too trivial for him to fasten on as a means of annoying and harassing Anthony. He even attempted to get a consumer group to protest against the quality of Herron Paper. These suits, handed over to John Athalon to deal with, were easily dismissed. Partly, as Athalon explained, because Ned was imposing on his partners for legal freebies which made them both resentful and professionally embarrassed at being made part of his personal vendetta.

Strangely, while Steven, Nina and Lisle raged against Ned for his behavior, Anthony was detached, almost understanding. 'He hates me. He's lashing out the only way he can. He could be carrying around a gun and taking pot shots at me in the street. I'm lucky this is all he's doing.'

'He hasn't any reason to hate you!' Nina objected, maddened by Anthony's refusal to be as upset about Ned as she was.

'He thinks he has.'

'But he's not a Herron. He couldn't have inherited. Even his wife is no blood relation to Max. It's ridiculous for him to resent you for inheriting from your own father.'

'That's not why he hates me,' Anthony said, but refused to explain further. 'To tell the truth, I kind of admire him. He's the only one who stood up to me. My mother went off meekly to Leland House, Faye's demeaning herself to the point of working one day a week doing boring office stuff for Samaritan, and even Betsy's pretending to be supportive. But Ned had the balls to say no to me in no uncertain terms. You have to like that.'

147

'I don't have to!' Nina said. 'Besides, your threat to cut him off financially isn't even working. He's living as well as ever on what you supply Betsy.'

'Not quite as well. Betsy's not as generous with him as Max was. He's been forced to give up a very expensive mistress and three racing cars.'

'That hardly makes him a pauper.'

Nina appealed to Steven later. 'We've got to make him see that Betsy and Faye are dangerous. They're wicked and he should cut himself away from them. That last lawsuit, the one questioning the reincorporation procedure of Samaritan, came about because Faye was in the office and heard us talking about it. She ran right to Ned and tattled.'

'Anthony knows that,' Steven said. 'But they're his family.'

'I see how he feels an obligation to help support them, but he could just have checks sent, without having them around snooping and causing trouble.'

'Nina, you don't have brothers and sisters and a gang of cousins. It's amazing the lengths a person will go to in order to maintain a pretense of family affection. It's even worse for Anthony because he didn't know them for so long. He's trying to make up for lost time.'

'If that's true, how do you explain that odious Rory?'

Steven just shook his head. Rory Wentworth was a mystery to all of them. The week after the fateful family meeting when Anthony made his ultimatums to the Herrons, he'd gone to New Mexico to visit his adoptive father and brother. No one knew what had transpired, but the speculation was that he'd made some sort of promise to the senior Wentworth to provide for Rory, who'd apparently decided that ranch life didn't give enough scope to his talents, whatever they were. All Anthony would say was, 'I always thought Rory really loved the ranch and was looking forward to being the manager, but he wanted to come back here with me. God knows what we're going to do with him, but we have to find something!'

So Rory Wentworth drifted through the growing Samaritan offices, making lewd suggestions to the secretaries, sneering at Anthony, squabbling with Nina and offending everyone. He was worse than useless. He had no social graces, so he couldn't be sent to luncheons and dinners to impress people into giving money. There was no sense of charity in his soul, so he contributed nothing worthwhile at the meetings during which they considered the relative merits of potential recipients of Samaritan's benefits.

'There has to be a niche for him,' Anthony lamented at a meeting with Steven, Nina and Lisle.

'Just give him a paycheck and send him away to spend it,' Nina suggested.

'I can't do that. I can't pay him from Samaritan's funds unless he's doing something worthwhile.'

'Anthony's right,' Lisle put in. 'That's exactly the kind of freeloading that can bring down an organization like this.'

'Then what do you suggest he do?' Nina asked sharply.

'Well, I've found that he's as stingy with other people's money as he is with his own,' Lisle said.

'Yes,' Anthony said, his eyes widening with a memory. 'Remember the fence posts?' Anthony explained to Nina and Steven: 'Years ago we had a flash flood on the ranch while Dad was in the hospital with his gall bladder. The Prof was gone and Rory had to replace the fence posts. Instead of buying new ones, he found some army surplus junk that looked like shit but cost almost nothing and was indestructible. Those posts are still there.'

'So if we ever need fence posts for Samaritan, we know who to go to?' Steven asked with a laugh.

'Well, we don't want someone stingy in charge of handing out charity, but it wouldn't hurt to have a tightwad in charge of the office expenses,' Anthony said. 'To keep an eye on the stationery bills and luncheon expenses, getting bargain typewriters.'

'Some charities spend as much as ninety per cent of

their funds on raising more money and only ten per cent on the objects of the charity,' Lisle said.

'Ninety per cent!' Steven exclaimed.

'It's legal,' Lisle said. 'We're running twenty-seven per cent so far.'

'That's too much,' Anthony said. 'It should never exceed twenty per cent. That's what professional fund-raisers charge if you hire them from outside.'

'Your brother has no accounting credentials – except the fence posts.'

'He'd have to have some formal training in accounting,' Lisle agreed.

Anthony turned to him with a grin. 'Well, you've been in charge of his education so far. I'll depend on you to force him to take classes.'

The battle between Lisle and Rory raged for days. At one point Rory stormed into Anthony's office and tore his paycheck up into shreds then demanded the plane fare back to New Mexico. But eventually Lisle prevailed. In spite of his vulgar manners, Rory was intelligent and knew how to work hard. Once convinced he had to have a degree, he threw himself into getting it with depressing ferocity.

The first year passed. The *Wall Street Journal* had two short but highly complimentary articles about Samaritan's work. *Time* magazine ran a sidebar on the origin of the organization when Samaritan paid the medical bills of a severely burned child. *Forbes* ran a piece on charities and mentioned Samaritan as one of the smaller, newer ones that showed promise of handling its finances well, though they asterisked it as being somewhat unfocused in its aims.

The first annual meeting came and went without any emotional fireworks. Anthony prevailed upon Blanche to host the meeting at Leland House in England. Betsy and her children attended, all except the one who lived in Africa. Faye and Charlie were there. Rory was persuaded to leave both his books and his string ties behind to attend.

Part of the reason it went so well was the presence of non-family members. Anthony had already recruited a handful of like-minded men to help and advise on Samaritan's activities. Primary among them was Rhys Jones.

Rhys Jones was an amiable eccentric. Short, plump, sandy-colored, he was in his early thirties when Anthony first met him. It was he who had brought to Taylor Lisle's attention the smoke-damaged library books. Most who knew him only slightly regarded him as a likable oddball; but those who troubled to know him better soon learned that the pleasantly fatuous exterior concealed a wide-ranging knowledge, especially in the arts.

Blessed with a substantial inherited income, he lived half of each year in Europe, going from one ancient capital to another attending operas. It was his belief that there was a perfect opera somewhere, an opera in which the structure of the music, the story, the characterization and the staging all reached the optimum of quality. He'd never found it, but lived in perpetual hope. While he searched, he refreshed himself with the imperfect, familiar works, which he thoroughly enjoyed in spite of their minor failings. But let some village company high in the Swiss Alps put on an original or little known work, and Rhys would be in the front row on opening night. Should an angry, experimental composer in the Eastern bloc defect with a portfolio of scores, Rhys would see that he was housed and fed in freedom.

A pleasantly rounded wife and two roly-poly sons accompanied him everywhere. Sitting in line in the front row of some obscure theater, they looked like a line of freshly painted Russian nesting dolls, rocking slightly in time to the music.

But his interests extended beyond opera. He was an expert on medieval bookbinding techniques; he'd written the definitive work on Fabergé's fabulous eggs and owned two of them; he had a degree from the Chicago

Art Institute where he had shown great talent and little motivation to produce works of his own.

At Taylor Lisle's invitation, he'd joined Samaritan as a volunteer director. He was to be the art expert. 'Let the public support things like saving the pyramids,' he said. 'We should save the things nobody cares about now but might prevent World War Three.'

'What do you mean?' Steven asked when they met at Leland House.

'Some old illuminated manuscript that's crumbling and fading might contain the advice we need to conserve our society. A church where Charlemagne or Cotton Mather once prayed could inspire some world leader to redeem us from conflict. Even now, some impressionable child who is going to be a world leader in half a century might be gaining an insight into human nature from a fragile Russian icon.'

In spite of his obscure philosophy, his actual suggestions to Samaritan were practical. An old doctor's entire medical library, which ran to thousands of volumes, many of them valuable rarities, had been willed to a small Midwestern medical school. They had neither the experts nor the funds properly to catalog it. Rhys suggested that Samaritan help. It did. Likewise, at Rhys's suggestion, a depressed West Virginia mining community received the funding to save a statue of a Revolutionary War hero which was about to topple over in the town square. The good will and publicity generated far exceeded the modest cost of jacking up the plinth upon which the old hero stood.

Rhys was also an enthusiastic fund-raiser. Appealing to other like-minded, well-heeled connoisseurs and benefactors of the arts, he started bringing in substantial sums from the beginning. There was no question that Rhys Jones was a valuable addition to Samaritan.

The problem arose because Rhys was, in addition to his other interests, an avid golfer.

* * *

Lisle objected to hiring Rhys. 'But, Prof, you brought him to us,' Anthony said. 'What's wrong with him?'

'Nothing's wrong with him. It's the destiny …'

'Come on, Prof,' Anthony said, angry at this vague, spooky talk.

The Prof bowed his head and said, 'Any great tragedy, when it occurs, resembles the mouth of a great river in flood spate – a turbulent, incomprehensible, overwhelming force that a solitary person cannot grasp or overcome. And yet a river, like a tragedy, is made up of hundreds, perhaps thousands, of tributaries. The geographer, if he traces back far enough, eventually winds up standing by the source – often little more than an insignificant, intermittent trickle dripping from between two layers of stone.'

'What in hell is that supposed to mean?' Anthony was nearly shouting. This kind of talk made him furious. 'Are you trying to tell me you have one of your premonitions that he's going to do something wrong?'

'Not deliberately.'

'Then I'll chance it,' Anthony said firmly.

Chapter Ten

Everyone associated with Samaritan always credited Rhys Jones as the creator of the celebrity golf tournament concept. While trying out a golf course south of Houston (a community theater was doing an original musical called *Gusher*) Rhys met a pair of astronauts. They quite liked Rhys ('The tubby little weirdo,' as they described him to their friends over Sunday barbecue). Rhys dashed back to the Kansas City headquarters with the idea bubbling over.

'They're a new aristocracy,' Rhys told Anthony and Steven. 'Outwardly ordinary men, but they've been somewhere none of us will ever be. Explorers of the Universe! They are Columbus and DeSoto and Cabot. Wouldn't you have given ten or twenty thousand dollars to meet *them*?'

Rhys was able to bag three of the astronauts and plans for the Samaritan Tournament were undertaken. A course in Virginia was chosen. By a process both alarming and mysterious, Ned coerced his law firm into putting up the twenty-thousand-dollar donation for him to play in the tournament. This upset Nina dreadfully. 'He's up to something terrible.'

'I don't think so,' Anthony said. 'He'd sell Betsy and their kids, in the unlikely event he could find a buyer, just to get the chance to actually speak to an astronaut. He won't start something ugly in front of his idols.'

Anthony was right. Ned was on his very best behavior. Euphoric in the presence of the astronauts, he was even offhandedly pleasant to Anthony. He'd brought along his own cheering section: three of his sons. 'You remember the boys, don't you?' he said casually to Anthony as they sat side by side putting on their spiked shoes.

Anthony glanced up and was surprised at how much they'd grown. The oldest, Wayne, was nineteen now. Dark, handsome, smiling but vaguely sly-looking, he shook Anthony's hand. 'How do you do, sir.'

'Fine, Wayne, but that "sir" makes me feel old. Just Anthony,' he said.

Wayne grinned, obviously pleased to be treated like an equal.

A blond boy only a year younger stepped forward. 'I'm Harry,' he said.

'Nice to meet you again, Harry. I though you were in Africa.'

'No, that's our brother Donald.'

'Sorry I mixed you up. Are you a golfer, Harry?'

'Not much of one. We're just here to watch Dad.' He jumped and whirled in surprise. 'What are you poking me for?' he said to a very fair sixteen-year-old.

The boy, so blond he looked almost albino, sneered. 'Have you forgotten me, Mr Swell Manners?'

'I wish I could,' Harry said before he remembered where he was. 'Anthony Wentworth, this is my brother Van.'

Anthony held out his hand. 'Glad to have you here, Van.'

The boy looked at Anthony's hand. 'Yeah, I'll bet you are.'

I won't allow this, Anthony thought. Before Van could withdraw, he took his hand and pumped it vigorously. 'Maybe you'll all be playing in a few years.' He released Van and sat back down. He asked the boys about their schooling and other sports they played. Wayne and Harry were glad for the interest and, used to Van's sulks, answered for him as if he were mute rather than merely rude. As Anthony checked over his clubs, he noticed that Ned was gone. As casually as possible, Anthony said,

'Wayne, there's one more of you, isn't there? A younger brother?'

'Yeah – I mean, yes. Martin the Toad. He's a little creep.' He grinned as he spoke.

'The baby,' Van said with genuine nastiness.

Harry seemed embarrassed by his brother's behavior. 'Well, he *is* a baby. He's only six, sir.'

'Yeah, and Mom thinks he walks on water,' Van said.

'Your mother isn't here today?' Anthony asked uneasily.

'No, sir,' Harry said before Van or Wayne could say anything. 'She's staying with some friends of hers in Palm Springs.' The glance he gave his brothers was fraught with warning. They either didn't know where she was or didn't want anyone else to know.

Anthony found them occupying the back of his mind while he met and greeted the other players. The Graves children had ceased to be an anonymous mob of kids in the last two years. They were becoming individuals. Harry seemed a really good kid. Wayne might be. That slightly shifty look might be superficial. Van was a hateful little jerk, but it could be a stage. Raging hormones and all that. Anthony found himself thinking of them warmly as family and wondering what he might do to help them out and get to know them better.

It went well until the fifth hole. No matter what accusations were tossed around and how the legend grew over the years, it was a pure accident. A freak accident, but truly an accident. The spot where they were to tee off was at the edge of the course, backed by a fence, a narrow field, a train track and then a weathered cliff. In front of them was a long drive, narrow and heavily treed on both sides. It called for a powerful, straight shot. Ned went first. His style and carriage were brutish, but effective. Muscles bunched and face contorted, he swung. The ball curved left slightly.

The crowd applauded politely.

Rhys was next. While he liked golf enormously, he

wasn't much good, nor did he take it as seriously as most players. In his view, it was, after all, a game. He stepped forward, shaded his eyes and pretended he couldn't see the end of the long, narrow vista. The spectators laughed. He clowned a bit more, taking a few mock swings, each more violent than the one before. Though silence among spectators is a rule of golf, Rhys discouraged it. People were still muttering to each other about what a funny guy he was when he stepped up to the tee. It was probably the undertone of muttering and everyone's concentration on Rhys that kept them all from noticing the rumbling approach of the thirty-car freight train on the track behind them.

Three things happened simultaneously: Rhys began a madly powerful swing, the freight rounded the cliff edge and blew its shrill whistle, and a startled woman spectator screamed.

Rhys's nervous system, if not his conscious mind, meant to check his swing, but it was impossible. Some neuron misfired or his muscles misunderstood the command. He hit the ball, followed through and released the club. It flew away from him at a terrific rate, and like an awkward but deadly spear struck Ned in the throat.

There was another scream from someone as Ned collapsed, a spurt of blood spraying those standing nearest him. Another blast from the train whistle drowned out words for a moment. There was a second of tableau-like stillness, then chaos. People surged toward Ned where he lay in a heap on the grass. His boys fought their way through the crowd. NASA's security people clung to the astronauts like magnets and whisked them away as if by magic. One moment they were there, the next they'd disappeared into thin air.

Rhys stood looking at his hands, wondering where in the world his golf club had gone.

A number of players were physicians. Two of them immediately knelt by the fallen man. Another two looked on while Anthony and Steven tried to keep everyone back.

'Let him have air,' Anthony said, but he knew from the one look he'd had at Ned that air wasn't going to help him much. He was clearly unconscious if not dead and there was blood all over everyone and everything near him.

It was Steven who saw Ned's blond son Van hurl himself at poor Rhys. 'You've killed him. You son of a bitch. You've killed my dad!' the boy screamed as he flung Rhys to the ground like a stuffed toy.

Steven leaped forward and yanked the distraught boy off his victim. Rhys scooted backwards, terrified, holding one hand to his head. Steven could hardly keep hold of Van. The boy had gone berserk and was shrieking and flailing wildly. He managed to land a blow to Steven's ear before Steven got him under physical control. Suddenly Van sagged and began crying – horrible gasping, wrenching sobs. Steven turned him round, holding him up and letting him cry against his chest. 'Now, now. You're not helping your dad this way,' he said.

Van blubbered something incomprehensible.

Steven didn't know what to say. He couldn't mutter platitudes about how Ned was going to be all right because it was clear he wasn't going to be. The blade of the club must have severed the carotid artery and Ned was either bleeding to death or already dead. Steven, like Anthony, had had only the most fleeting look, but it was a dreadful sight. Van was still sobbing out words. Steven now caught a few of them. 'That fat bastard killed my father!'

Steven grabbed Van's shoulders and looked into his anger-misshapen face. 'No, he didn't. It was an accident. You know that and don't you forget it.'

'He hated him, just like you all do. You just don't see that he was smarter and stronger and better than any of you!'

'Rhys hardly knew your father and he certainly didn't hate him. You're upset, Van. You don't know what you're saying so shut up.'

'You're as bad as the rest,' the boy spat out. 'I think you all planned it. Maybe you planned it yourself. You're a bastard, too. A murdering bastard!'

'Shut up, you little fool. People can hear you. You're making an ass of yourself.'

Van's arms suddenly shot up, breaking Steven's grip. His face was inhuman with grief and rage. 'I'll get you for this!' he hissed. 'I'll get you if it's the last thing I do!' He whirled away and disappeared into the crowd. Steven shoved people aside, trying to get to him, to stop him before he hurt himself or someone else, but Van, small and slight and driven by mad rage, evaded him. Finally Steven spotted him heading back to the club house. A man and woman were with him. The woman had her arm round him and he was leaning against her as they walked.

I was a great comfort, Steven thought. *I should have just let him say any nasty thing he wanted to get it out of his system instead of arguing with him.* Still, it wouldn't have been right to let him go on about Rhys that way.

Anthony, meanwhile, was dealing with Wayne and Harry. They were just as upset as Van, but handling it much better. 'Boys, we've got to find your mother. Do you know where she is?'

They looked at each other uneasily.

'Never mind. Don't tell me if you don't want to. Tell Miss Smith and she'll find her. Nina, come here.'

She took them aside. They whispered something to her and she wrote in the small notebook she always had at hand. Then they came back to Anthony. 'I hear the ambulance,' he said as the faint sound of a siren wafted across the course. 'You can't all ride with him. I'll take you along behind. Where's Van?'

'Is Dad going to be all right?' Wayne asked.

'I don't know. I hope so,' Anthony said. 'But we all have to stay out of the way so the experts can take care of him. You two find Van and come back to me.'

As the boys went off, dazed, Nina said softly, 'She's spending the weekend in Las Vegas with a singer.'

'And they didn't want anyone to know?'

'Right.'

'Then make sure no one else does. I don't know it either.'

It was a mild rebuke and Nina knew it, but pretended she didn't.

'I'll meet you at the hospital as soon as I've reached her.'

Wayne found Van pouring out his accusations to an older couple who had been friends of Max Herron. They were letting him rage, as Steven had been unable to do. 'He doesn't know what he's saying, darlin',' the woman told Wayne. 'Y'all just go on along with Mr Wentworth and we'll bring Van when he's calmed down. Ah wonder if just the tiniest little drink ...?' she inquired of her husband.

Steven and Anthony went with Wayne and Harry. Harry was crying quietly and the rest of them were silent. As they pulled up to the emergency room entrance, a physician came out to greet them. 'Mr Wentworth?'

'I'm Anthony Wentworth,' he said, getting out of the limo.

'Are these Mr Graves' sons? Let's find somewhere to talk.'

Anthony knew what that meant. The doctor broke it to the boys very nicely. Everyone had done everything they could, but it was too late. Their father had passed away on the way to the hospital. The boys looked helplessly at Anthony. He spoke for them. 'Doctor, we're all away from home. Could we just have a room with a telephone for an hour or so?'

When Van arrived he was in icy self-control, like a hostage who's decided he can't fight it but is keeping notes on the evidence to convict his kidnappers later. Steven found his frigid glare unnerving, but Anthony seemed hardly to notice. A nurse brought in Cokes and candy bars, which the boys consumed automatically in spite of their shock and grief. Anthony called their schools and explained that they wouldn't be in class the next week. There was some discussion of whose job it would be to tell their Aunt Faye. Harry assumed it would fall to Anthony, but he sensed that Wayne was starting to chaff at all the help. 'Wayne, you're the oldest. Would you mind speaking to her?' Anthony asked, and was rewarded with a look of gratitude.

Nina hung up the phone and sat very quietly in the small private room the country club had given her to use. Her conversation with Betsy had been grisly. First Betsy had laughed, apparently thinking it was a joke. When she realized it really was Nina on the phone and that she was serious, Betsy said, 'Dead? Ned dead? What have you people done to him?' Speaking to whatever man she was in bed with, she screamed, 'My God! My brother has killed my husband! Get out! Get out!' The only hope Nina could hold out was that Betsy was thoroughly drunk, and when she sobered up she'd realize the truth.

There was an uproar outside the door and she was going to have to deal with it. Putting Betsy into a mental compartment, Nina came back to the immediate problem of the golf tournament. She sighed, slipped her notes into her purse and tucked her blouse in before opening the door. The mob hovering in the lobby enveloped her. It was mainly players and their friends and families, but the questions being shouted at her were from the sprinkling of reporters. They were as chipper as squirrels. They'd been assigned a boring story to cover and it had turned into something gory and peculiar.

'One moment, one moment,' Nina said, holding up her hands and looking around for something to stand on. There was a folding chair against the wall and she climbed onto it. The room grew slightly quieter. 'I'm deeply sorry to say that Mr Graves has died.' She waited for the rumble of talk to go quiet. 'The tournament, of course, is canceled out of respect for him. I have no information yet on whether it can be rescheduled.'

'In the meantime, Samaritan keeps the money?' an especially greasy-looking reporter shouted.

She could have kissed him. 'Of course not,' she said,

feigning shock at the very idea. 'Samaritan never takes contributions under false pretenses. The many good works the organization performs are all funded with entirely voluntary contributions. The money will be returned to all participants. Some of them may wish to leave it with Samaritan in honor of Mr Graves' memory, but that is up to them.'

'Where's the wife?' another reporter asked.

'Mrs Graves has been informed and is on her way back to the family home in Kansas City. We'll make an announcement as to when and where the funeral service will be held when that decision is made. The people of Samaritan had the greatest respect for Mr Graves and join with all his friends in expressing our grief at this tragedy,' she said, not quite choking on the words.

But one of the reporters wasn't having any. 'Respect? Wasn't the guy always suing your outfit?'

Nina glared at him and said smoothly, 'This is all the information we have at this time. Any further announcements will come from Mr Graves' family.'

Everyone started drifting away. The reporter who had asked the last, awkward question started to approach her, but she gave him a look of such unyielding malice that he shrugged and backed off. The lobby gradually cleared of all but employees and one lone figure sitting by the fireplace.

'Dr Lisle,' Nina said. In the rush and confusion he'd been forgotten and left behind. He looked genuinely glad to see her. He took her hand as she joined him. She let him keep it. 'I'm on my way to the hospital. May I give you a ride?'

He nodded. 'I knew he'd die young.'

Nina had never held with this spooky psychic shit Lisle sometimes came up with. 'It's a tragedy,' she murmured.

'Not in itself,' Lisle said, looking past her. 'But so many dangerous seeds are planted now and there's nobody to stop their growth. Not you. Not even me.'

She could have slapped him. She loathed this sort of

163

talk. It frightened and confused her and neither emotion fitted into her life. 'It was just a terrible accident. Nothing more.'

'Nina, Nina, it was much more. Don't you sense it? Don't even you feel the foreboding?'

'Even me? All I feel is tired and hungry. And you look exhausted. Come along. Let's go see how Anthony and Steven are holding up.'

Nina told Anthony she intended to call on Betsy when she returned to Kansas City.

'The woman is capable of any sort of scene,' Anthony said. 'If she's planning one for me at the funeral, I won't go. Better to have her get it out of her system in private. I'll go by her apartment this evening, too.'

Nina went to see Betsy some hours earlier than Anthony. The family was assembled: Betsy, Wayne, Harry, Van, Faye and Charlie. Little Martin was sitting on the floor in front of a television playing cartoons with the sound turned down. Betsy looked dreadful, wrung out and beaten down. An outsider might have thought she genuinely grieved for her husband. Perhaps she did in some peculiar way, Nina thought, but it was more likely she'd just been hauled away from a weekend of marathon sex and hadn't pulled herself together yet.

'Betsy, I'm so terribly sorry,' Nina said, embracing her in a formal, token way. 'At least it was very sudden. He didn't suffer.'

'Tell us,' Betsy said. There was a nasty, hungry tone to her voice.

'I told you already,' Van put in. 'Rhys Jones flung a golf club at him and killed him in cold blood.'

'Oh no!' Nina exclaimed. 'Rhys had just begun his swing when a train whistle blew. It startled everyone, especially him because he'd been concentrating so hard. He dropped the golf club – at least he would have dropped it, except that he was already swinging so hard that instead of falling to the ground it flew through the air. It struck your husband in the throat, Betsy, but it was purely

164

accidental.'

'Bullshit!' Van said.

They ignored him, but Nina responded, 'It was an accident. Van, even if Rhys had wanted to do your father harm, which he didn't, how could he have timed such a thing? How could he have taken such careful aim? It's ridiculous to even consider.'

There was a subtle change in the atmosphere of the room and Nina quickly realized her mistake. She'd come to be a sponge, to absorb impressions of them in her usual manner, but had lost her head and expressed her own views. She didn't like them, or anyone, to know where she stood. To cover her gaffe, she quickly said, 'What about Donald, Betsy? Is he going to be able to come from Africa for the funeral?'

'Dear Donald,' Betsy said vaguely.

Faye rose and stretched. 'I've been on the phone since I heard, but I haven't been able to get through to him. Apparently he and Uncle John have left the mission to go to some village. There isn't time to get him here now, even if we did reach him.'

Wayne, who'd been pacing at the end of the room through all this, walked by and snapped the television off. 'It's awful. We should all be at our father's funeral.'

Martin, deprived of his entertainment, went to the sofa and snuggled into his mother, rubbing his face against her breast in a way Nina found downright creepy. It was like an infant nuzzling for a nipple, but Martin was six years old. He was an eerily beautiful child with his pale blue eyes and Beatle-like mop of straight blond hair. 'I'll be at Daddy's funeral, won't I, Mommy?' he said.

'Right by me, darling.'

Out of the corner of her vision, Nina saw Wayne roll his eyes in disgust. 'Might I use your bathroom?' she asked, wanting to get herself well out of the limelight but without actually leaving.

It worked. By the time she came back, they'd forgotten her and were arguing among themselves about funeral flowers. Unresolved, the discussion moved on to music, upon which Betsy and Faye disagreed. Betsy's boys took her side as though it were a matter of life and death. Nina let the conversation swirl around her, wondering how Betsy engendered this fierce loyalty in her sons. They obviously adored her and would swear black was white to agree with her. With the exception of Martin, she'd ignored and neglected them all their lives. She made no effort to make them happy or set a good example or earn their respect. She made no sacrifices for them, gave them no hugs, kisses or approving smiles. Nina had never seen her show any of them but Martin the slightest affection, yet they loved her unreservedly.

Martin had gone back to the television. As the picture came into focus, Charlie said with alarm, 'Martin, turn up the sound. Something's happened.'

The cartoons were gone and a newscaster was talking over a film clip of a mob scene in a shopping center in Maryland. George Wallace had been shot, he was saying.

Nina sighed with relief. If she'd ever spared George Wallace a thought, it was to dismiss him as an inconsequential, red-necked bigot. But shot, he was big news, big enough to keep the press away from Ned Graves' funeral and Samaritan's connection with his death. She slipped away quietly while the rest of them watched the news. She was smiling as the elevator descended.

Chapter Eleven

Anthony decided to attend Ned's funeral no matter what Betsy might be planning, but not the visitation the night before. Steven took that duty. 'Hideous,' Steven reported later that evening. 'Betsy decked out in acres of black. The boys scowling and trying not to cry. Faye being gruesomely gracious.' He'd stopped by the Kansas City mansion which Anthony had finally purchased instead of leasing. Nina was there, doing paperwork, but she slipped into the background, her favorite locale.

Anthony smiled. 'I don't get it. You've got such a thing about Faye. She's a fine worker. She's raised a lot of funds for Samaritan and is always there when there's a crisis. Remember how she straightened out that civil war between Rory and the secretarial pool?'

'I know, I know,' Steven said, shrugging. 'She got it sorted out and kept them from all quitting, but they hate Rory more than ever.'

'You can't blame her. Rory makes himself easy to hate,' Anthony said, smiling. Rory's devotion to keeping Samaritan's internal costs down was obsession. No one, including Anthony, spent a penny without having to explain it to Rory's satisfaction. It had become policy for Samaritan staff always to be sated before dessert at business luncheons because it was impossible to justify to Rory why a person who'd just eaten a full meal needed a slice of chocolate cake at the end.

'You can pick up a candy bar on the way home if you really need sugar,' he'd grouse. 'Bad for your health anyway.'

'Faye's deep down nasty,' Steven went on. 'I can remember from the time my cousins and I were kids and spending summers at Birches, she pretended to be friends with everybody, but by the end of the first week she had everyone at each other's throats. I never could pin down how, but I know she was responsible.'

Anthony fastened on a side issue. 'Summers at Birches. That seems odd to me. I was utterly unaware of any of you, but you all knew each other from childhood.'

Steven knew what he was thinking and cut him off with a cynicism rare for him. 'Don't get all warm and fuzzy about it. Max and my dad got along fine, thought the world of each other, but Blanche and my mother could barely endure each other and we kids were savage. It wasn't long summer evenings of friendly kick-the-can games. It was constant competition and snarling. And lessons! Swimming and rowing and golf for us and the girls had dancing and baton and God knows what. Summers were more hectic than the school year. And Betsy was trying out sex for as long as I can remember. Used to bore us boys senseless when we were little and wanted to be fishing or exploring the woods, then we grew up a bit and went around doubled over in frustrated agony all summer.' He shuddered at the memory.

'So maybe it wasn't perfect,' Anthony said, and they both laughed.

'Anyway, I've done my duty and I'll be off in the morning,' Steven said. They'd planned a meeting with some West Coast fund-raisers and the business of Samaritan had to go on. Anthony had canceled his participation, secure that Steven could handle it himself.

'Rhys isn't still thinking of going, is he?' he asked as Steven started patting his pockets for car keys.

'I hope not. He still doesn't get it that the Graves are blaming him. He feels awful, but knows to the depths of his soul that it was an accident. Stick close to him.'

'I will. He might need protection. Goodnight.'

Nina, whom both of them had forgotten, waited until

he was gone. 'Is Dr Lisle going to the funeral?' she asked.

'The Prof! Oh my God, I forgot ... Call him, would you, Nina. Tell him I'll send my car for him.'

'It's a bit late.'

'Well, first thing in the morning then.'

Nina smiled to herself. She knew she would have been blamed if Anthony had completely forgotten Lisle. But thinking of him at the last moment was just as dismissive. Anthony wouldn't understand the subtlety, but Lisle would. His days were numbered, it just remained to ease him completely out of the picture.

Ned's funeral was conducted with Episcopal decorum. Ned, as befitted his social station, was a patron though not a practicing member of the church. Anthony slipped in just as the service was starting, to avoid any unnecessary contact with Betsy. Standing at the back with the Prof and Nina, he spotted Rhys. Nodding to acquaintances, he made his way briskly down a side aisle and slid in beside him. Everyone moved a bit to the left to make room for the three of them.

Rhys shook his hand and looked at him with gratitude for a moment. A man from Ned's law firm was reading a eulogy. His heart obviously wasn't in the rolling phrases of praise, but he was doing the best he could. Anthony eased his gaze sideways, vaguely wondering who else was in attendance. Rhys leaned back a fraction and that was when Anthony first saw the young woman sitting beside him.

She was gorgeous in a timeless, other-worldy way. Tiny and very slim, but with an extremely well-endowed figure, she had a shining, heavy coil of red-gold hair at the nape of her neck. She was wearing a silky gray dress that looked so old-fashioned and Edwardian it could have almost been a costume – or an heirloom. Anthony wondered who she was. He knew he'd never seen her before. He'd have remembered.

Taylor Lisle noticed Anthony gazing at the young woman. He shivered with apprehension. He'd never seen her either and didn't know her name, but he knew instinctively what she was. She was the woman at the center: Helen, Lucretia, Guinevere, Juliet, Cleopatra. The woman whose very existence would change things. The key that would open the door to destruction. His head was pounding, impressions swirling like tornadoes. He knew there was nothing he could do to change things. But he knew he would try anyway.

A soprano was singing 'Amazing Grace': I was lost but now am found; was blind but now can see. *But I'm appalled at what I've found*, Lisle thought, *and horrified at what I see. And there is nothing I can do to stop it unfolding. It is as inevitable and ruthless as the change of seasons.*

The immediate family was led out a side door to get into waiting limos to lead the procession to the gravesite. The others were left reverently to file out of the sanctuary and either flee or mill about until the hearse was ready to lead. As they stood in clumps in front of the church, the young woman spoke quietly to Rhys. So she's with him, Anthony thought. Who can she be?

Anthony wasn't going to the gravesite, but he hung about anyway. 'Anthony, the car's waiting,' Lisle said.

'I think I'll wait. You go ahead with Nina. I can get a cab.'

Nina knew a dismissal when she heard one. She clutched Lisle's elbow and said, 'Fine. I'll look for you in half an hour or so?'

'Or so,' Anthony agreed.

Lisle looked back at Anthony working his way through the crowd toward Rhys and the young woman.

'Rhys, you're not going to the cemetery, are you?' Anthony said.

'I feel I should. After all, I was responsible.'

'You were not. A train was responsible.'

'That's what I told him,' the young woman beside him said.

170

'Oh, I'm so sorry,' Rhys said. 'Gilly, this is Anthony Wentworth. Anthony, my niece, Gillian Powell. Gilly, Anthony is head of Sama—'

'I know who Mr Wentworth is, Uncle Rhys,' she said, putting her hand out.

Anthony took it. It was like shaking hands with a child, she was so petite, but there was strength and firmness, too. Her skin was cool and soft and he had to force himself to let go. 'How do you do, Miss Powell – or is it Mrs Powell?'

She smiled as if he'd made a joke. Anthony loved her teeth. They were a little bit irregular. Just enough to give her a pixie-ish look. 'It's miss and please call me Gilly.' She pronounced it as if it started with a J. She had a surprisingly low, warm voice for one so tiny. Very small women tended to be either whispery or shrill, in Anthony's experience. And she spoke with the slightest hint of an accent, but Anthony couldn't quite place it.

'Are you Welsh, Gilly?'

'What else could a niece of Rhys Jones be?' she said with a laugh. 'Actually, I'm American, but I was born and lived in Wales until I was seven. I'm on my way there now, once I get Uncle Rhys away from this dreadful funeral. But I won't leave until I know he's out of harm's way. Oh, I am sorry. I'd forgotten. They're your relatives, aren't they? How tactless of me.'

'Not at all,' Anthony said, charmed by her. 'A person doesn't choose their relatives and can't be held accountable for them.'

She laughed as though he'd said something very clever and for a moment he felt as though he had. 'I suppose you'll be going to the cemetery,' she said.

'Not if you held a gun to my head.'

'My feelings exactly. Well, Uncle, you've been outvoted. You must come away. Perhaps Anthony would join us for luncheon. I don't have to be at the airport until five.'

'You two go along,' Rhys said. 'I really think I ought to—'

'We wouldn't consider leaving you behind.' There was nothing Anthony would have liked better than to get this luscious young woman to himself, but he had a duty to Rhys. 'Let me just call home and alert my housekeeper. We can have lunch at my house.'

He called home before anyone could object. Rhys snagged a cab. As they pulled into traffic, Anthony asked, 'Why are you going to Wales, Gilly?'

'It's a long story that involves my whole family history. Too dull for words,' she said.

'But I'd like to hear it. Please.'

Gillian shrugged. 'You'll be sorry. My mother was Uncle Rhys's sister and on one of his trips back to Wales he took her along. She met my father, married him and had me. They were divorced when I was seven and I came back to the United States with Mother. It was an amiable divorce. I visited Da every summer until I was twenty or so, but I haven't seen him for several years. My mother died two years ago.'

'Oh, I'm sorry. I didn't know. Rhys has been keeping a lot of secrets from me.'

She smiled. 'Uncle Rhys,' she patted his knee affectionately, 'has been good to my mother and me. Anyway, I haven't seen Da for years and he's researching a book and needed my help and asked me to come over.'

'Researching a book? Your father isn't Owen Powell?'

'He is! Don't tell me you've heard of him?'

'Of course. His biography of Edward II is a masterpiece. The first Prince of Wales. I loved the story. Edward I had conquered Wales and had promised them a prince who was native-born and didn't even speak English. They thought he meant one of their own, but he meant his infant son who had just been born on the campaign. Naturally he didn't speak English. He didn't speak anything.'

'You're a student of history?'

'Only in passing, and usually by force. But I took a course in college on medieval Britain, and your father's

172

book was part of the supplementary reading. I liked it so much I bought it instead of sharing the library copy. He has a real gift for making the past come alive. It was one of the few history books I read that made me feel like I was getting to know a real person. Owen Powell's daughter, imagine.'

'I'll tell him how you feel. He hates it that most historians write to impress each other, not to enlighten the public.'

'And he's working on something you're going to help with?'

'Yes, a book on Henry VII this time. He was Welsh, you know.'

Rhys had been silent throughout this conversation, looking out the window and thinking his own thoughts. But now he joined in. 'Gilly is quite a scholar in her own right, Anthony.'

'Uncle! You should be ashamed. I'm no such thing. I'm a librarian, that's all. When I say I'm going to help Da, I mean only as a dogsbody. Running parcels of books back and forth to the post office, copying out passages of notes, that sort of thing. Oh, is this your home? It's enormous, isn't it?'

They'd turned in at the gates, and Anthony suddenly saw the vast house through new eyes. It was impressive, for size alone. And Nina saw to it that it was kept in excellent condition. 'It's as much a place of business as your office and must reflect the attention to detail that Samaritan means,' she said as she ordered workmen to make repairs to the bricks and stucco. But Anthony suddenly saw it as it really was – a huge, Tudor house with no heart, no soul. It was just a structure, not a home.

'What's the matter?' Gillian said, looking at him. 'Did I say something awful?'

'What? Oh, no. I just suddenly realized the place hasn't any – any life.'

'That's because there are no flowers,' Gillian said

matter-of-factly.

'That simple?' Anthony said, smiling at her.

'It's not simple at all. A house is just a box to put people in, but flowers give it life.'

'I'll hire a garden service.'

'Oh no! That would be like hiring a robot to raise a child. You need a gardener.'

'That's what I said.'

'It most certainly is not,' she said, getting out of the taxi and looking around critically. 'A garden service is a group of ghouls who come in and poison as much of nature as they can and you end up with nothing but grass and a lot less of your money. A gardener, a real one, will give the house a soul. He or she will make it look serene where it needs to be and turbulent where it needs a jolt to the eye. He'll make it smell different in the morning and the evening. You see this glare? This is where you need coolness – lobelia, if it will grow in this climate. Does it?'

The cab pulled away. 'I haven't any idea. What's a lobelia?'

She looked at him as if he'd asked who God was. Then she leaned down and examined a leaf on the shrub by the door. She shook her head in disgust.

'Where do you live?' Anthony asked after a luncheon of spiced chicken salad on greens. It seemed a sissy meal to him, but Gilly was complimentary. He was glad that she ate like a real human without any silly feminine fluttering over her food and insisted on going into the kitchen to thank Mrs Roush in person. He liked her for that. In fact, he liked everything about her.

'I've been living in Seattle with Mother since we came to the States. But I sold our house there. I won't go back. Mother was such a part of it to me. It wouldn't be the same without her.'

Rhys was fixing them glasses of cognac. 'She says she sold her house as though she did it the way normal people do.'

'What do you mean?' Anthony asked as Rhys handed

174

him a glass.

'Uncle Rhys is making fun of me,' Gilly said, smiling up at him.

'Well, it was crazy. I'm surprised the authorities didn't put you in a mental home.'

'It was my house to sell as I liked. I had an obligation to Mother.'

'What are you talking about?' Anthony asked.

Gilly slipped off her shoes and curled her legs gracefully beneath her. 'I put a reasonable price on the house so that I would have a lot of potential buyers to choose from. Then I interviewed them to see if they met my standards. Or rather, the garden's standards.'

'She practically gave them proctored tests. I was there once when she put some poor fool through his paces. It was embarrassing,' Rhys said, but his tone belied his words. He was proud of her.

'I just had to make sure the buyer would do right by the gardens. Mother and I spent years on them. I couldn't sell to someone who was just going to go out and mow them down and plant grass seed. Or worse, that terrible woman who wanted nothing but roses.'

Anthony fell on this. He *knew* what a rose was. 'You don't like roses?'

'Of course I do, just as I like pickles once in a while. But who could live on a steady diet of pickles?'

I could live on anything with you, Anthony thought and almost blurted it out. 'So you're moving to Wales permanently?' he asked.

'Probably not. I've become too thoroughly American. But I'm not terribly good at long-range plans, except with plants. Da and I might be at each other's throats in a week. He's a very firm-minded, outspoken person. Used to his own ways.'

'And Gilly isn't,' Rhys said wryly.

'Oh, Uncle, I'm a marshmallow. You know that.' She glanced at her watch. 'I really must get on my way. Anthony, it's been wonderful meeting you. Uncle has

175

talked about you so much I felt I knew you. You're as marvelous as he says.'

Anthony didn't feel marvelous. He felt dull and childish. He'd hardly been able to speak in her presence. And now she was getting away from him, possibly for a long time. 'I hope we meet again,' he said.

'I'm certain we will,' she said as she rose and slipped on her shoes. 'I understand your mother lives in England. Do you ever visit her?'

'Yes, occasionally. In fact, I'll probably be going over later in the year,' he said, although he'd forgotten about Blanche until Gilly mentioned her and hadn't planned to visit her anytime soon.

'Let me know when you're coming. I'll be ready to go screaming away from Da for a while. We could go to a show.'

'Or Kew Gardens,' Anthony said, inspired. All he knew about Kew Gardens was that they were in England someplace.

'I'd love that. I'll give you my address,' she said, fishing in her handbag for a pencil and paper.

'I'll take you to the airport,' Anthony said, taking the scrap of paper as though it were gold.

'Please, don't bother. Uncle Rhys is seeing me off and I know you're busy. It's going to be a race, what with picking up my bags at the hotel.'

'At least let me send you in my car.'

'I'll be glad to take you up on that, Anthony.' She was making her way briskly toward the door with the two men doing their best to keep up with her.

Anthony had the car brought round. Rhys held the door open for Gilly and she turned to Anthony, taking his hand. 'I'm very happy that we've met. I hope ...' She shook her head. 'Never mind. Thank you for lunch.'

As they emerged from Anthony's car at the airport, Gilly sighed. 'He's not engaged or anything difficult like that, is he?'

'Anthony? No, not that I know of,' Rhys said.

'Good. That will make it less complicated.'

'Make what less complicated?'

Gilly took his arm and said, 'I'm going to marry your Mr Anthony Wentworth, Uncle.'

'You hardly know him!' Rhys protested, but not very strongly.

'I know all I need to know.'

When Anthony got back to the office, he stopped to talk to Nina. 'You know that florist in London where you get flowers for Blanche?'

'Yes?'

He scribbled a copy of the address Gilly had given him. 'Have him send a lobelia plant to this address, will you?'

'A single lobelia plant? Is it a joke?'

'I didn't mean it to be. Why?'

'Well, a single lobelia plant is a straggly, pitiful thing. You need masses of them.'

Anthony threw up his hands. 'Then send masses!' This morning he'd never heard of the damned things. Now it sounded like the entire female population of the world was intimately acquainted with lobelias from birth.

'Anthony, I've been waiting for you to get back,' Taylor Lisle said, coming into the office.

'Hi, Prof. What's up?'

'I'd like to talk to you, if you have a few minutes.' *How am I going to explain this without sounding like a madman? It doesn't matter. I have to try.*

'It's a gorgeous afternoon. Let's go for a walk, Prof. I need some french fries from the McDonald's down the block.'

Lisle shuddered. Anthony had been served food prepared by some of the greatest chefs in the world but couldn't be cured of his yen for McDonald's food.

When they were seated in a corner booth, surrounded by the usual late-afternoon mob of tough-talking teenagers, Lisle took a few careful sips of his coffee and watched in amazement as Anthony wolfed down a Big Mac and two orders of fries. 'I'm starving. I only got a fancy little lunch,' Anthony explained between bites. He finally shoved aside the assortment of plastic and greasy papers in which the meal had come wrapped. 'So, what's up?'

Lisle took a deep breath. 'That girl at the funeral—'

'Gillian Powell,' Anthony said enthusiastically. 'She's Rhys's sister's daughter. She's also the daughter of Owen Powell. You know, the writer?'

'Is she indeed?'

Anthony didn't notice his mentor's obvious air of gloom. 'She's beautiful, isn't she? Old-fashioned and romantic looking. She's a librarian and a gardener. Interesting combination. Sort of little old lady-ish stuff, actually. Girls these days don't seem to care about flowers. I never thought about it until today, but it's a shame.' He glanced up at a girl passing them with a tray. She had straight hair to her waist, tight jeans, a snug teeshirt under which she obviously wore no underwear and a grubby headband. 'Gilly's certainly different,' Anthony mused happily. 'She seems immune to trendy stuff. I'd like you to meet her, but she's on her way to Wales right now.'

'Good.'

That brought Anthony up short. 'What did you say?'

'Anthony, you've got to forget about her.'

'What in the world are you talking about, Prof?'

'She's dangerous to you.'

'Bullshit.'

'No, I mean it.'

'What do you mean dangerous?'

'I'm not sure, but I know it's true.'

Anthony leaned back, getting control of his temper. He hated this kind of crazy talk. Maybe the Prof was slipping mentally. For as long as Anthony could remember the Prof would occasionally come out with these weird pronouncements. Usually they were real downers – like all that flood stuff about Rhys and ominous, vague warnings. Of course, he'd been right, in a way, about Rhys. But that was just coincidence. Nobody could have known what was going to happen at the golf tournament. Sometimes the weird prophesies were positive. Predicting that Anthony was destined for great things. Nice stuff like that. Stuff you could take more as a compliment than a 'prediction'. Good God, was he about to take a turn to seances and voices from another world? Start hanging around with fortune tellers? Could he be getting senile? How old was he now? Seventy-one or two?

'Prof, are you all right? I mean, you're not feeling bad or having headaches, or anything, are you?'

Lisle bridled. 'I'm not senile or unbalanced, if that's what you mean!'

'Sorry, but this kind of talk—'

'Listen, Anthony. I know you don't understand this. But you have to believe me. I *know* things. I can't comprehend just how I know them, but I do. And I know she's dangerous to you. If you become involved with her something terrible will happen.'

'To me or her?' Anthony said, sincerely trying to play along with this instead of telling the Prof he was nuts.

'To everybody. Everything. You, Steven, Samaritan.'

'What's Steven got to do with it?'

'I can't see the details, but you must believe me. This is as true as if it already happened.'

Anthony sighed in frustration. 'You want some more coffee?' he asked.

'Yes, thank you,' Lisle said, giving them both time to think.

When Anthony returned, he had two cups. Stirring in three packets of sugar, he said, 'Prof, I don't believe in this knowing the future stuff, but I know that you do. So, just for now, I'm trying to imagine I buy it. Now, the way I see it, if there really is something awful in my future, it's already there. There's nothing to do about it. If it's supposed to happen, it's going to happen no matter what, isn't it?'

That was just what Lisle feared. He despised the concept of predestination. It reeked of dour Calvinists. It denied free choice, ambition, virtuous acts.

'See, I hate that idea,' Anthony was going on. 'I guess that's why I can't accept it. It would mean that nothing we do, good or bad, makes any difference. It would mean we've been put into a slot to shoot through some vast maze without any choice at all, even if we stupidly think we have alternatives. Life can't be that dreary. So I have to believe, instead, that the future is just some amorphous cloud of nothingness, waiting for us to shape it and make it the present, and eventually let it turn into the past.'

'I hope that's true.'

'So if my future's mine to shape, I have to make the best choices I can as I go along. I can't be terrified that something that looks like a good choice is a potential catastrophe. Nobody could. We'd all go mad if we thought that way all the time.'

'I'm not trying to make you unhappy, Anthony. Only to warn you. If you saw me walking along blindfolded and knew there was a precipice in front of me, you'd warn me, wouldn't you?'

'Sure I would, but I'm not blindfolded, Prof.'

'But you are.'

'Why? Because I don't get spooky feelings that something awful's going to happen? Something awful will probably happen to all of us. It does from time to time. Rhys letting go of that golf club was awful, but it was just something that happened. That's all. Did you see that coming?' Anthony asked, forgetting Lisle's ominous warning about Rhys.

'No, that wasn't what I saw. But I should have seen that coming.'

'No, you shouldn't,' Anthony said angrily. 'Look, Prof. I met Gilly Powell and I liked her. That's all there is to it now. Maybe I'll get to know her better and find out that she picks her nose in public and sleeps around with winos and hates me. If so, that'll be the end of it. But

180

maybe that won't happen. Either way, I absolutely refuse to forget her just because something might go wrong someday to someone.'

'You've outgrown me.'

That took Anthony by surprise and he answered. 'I'm supposed to, aren't I?'

Lisle stared at him for a second, then started briskly gathering up their trash. 'Yes, you are. And I'm glad to see it,' he said heartily. 'I'm sorry, Anthony, I think you're right. This is all just the mental meanderings of an old man. I probably just need a vacation. Forget I said anything.'

'You're pissed at me.'

'Not at all. It was just something I had to say to get it off my chest. Now I have. You're right. It was silly of me. Now, don't you have work waiting at the office?'

'Sure, but there's no hurry.'

'Get along. I'm going to finish this abominable coffee. I'll follow along.'

'I'm not leaving you.'

'Why on earth not? I'm not helpless. You're going to get out of here, Anthony. Take that as a prediction or a threat, whichever you choose.' He said it with a smile.

'You're sure?'

'Sure.'

Lisle watched him leave, his smile fading and his heart aching. He'd botched it. Anthony was going to marry this Gilly Powell, and it would be the beginning of the end. And there was nothing he could do about it. For that matter, there was nothing Anthony could do about it. It *was* predestined. And it was just as well Anthony didn't believe it. He'd been right about that, life wasn't worth living if you were just biding time, waiting for fate to catch up with you.

'But I can't stand to stay around and watch it happen,' he said aloud.

A girl with a sequined peace symbol appliquéd on the back of her denim shirt looked at him warily, obviously wondering if the crazy old man talking to himself was dangerous.

Chapter Twelve

Two weeks after he met Gilly, Anthony got a large package with her Welsh return address. He ripped into it and discovered a box of a dozen books, all by Owen Powell. They were all Welsh-related subjects: the life of Owen Tudor, the building and history of Harlech Castle, The Mabinogion and Arthurian legend, the Edward II book he'd liked so much, and history/travel books on several specific areas of Wales. At the bottom of the parcel was a book on flowers with the corner of a pale apricot-colored envelope showing. He opened the envelope and a photo and a note fell out.

The photograph was of an enormous mass of airy dark green foliage covered with tiny, deep bluish-purple blooms. Millions of them and so rich a color that the eye could hardly focus on them. And in the center of the flowers, Gilly's face. She was posed so that she looked like she was struggling though the dense foliage. She was smiling, but with a bit of mock panic to the grin.

Anthony stared at the picture and laughed out loud. He picked up the note.

Dear Anthony,

Thanks enormously for the lovely flowers. I was touched that you remembered the name of them. They brightened up my arrival amazingly. I was feeling homesick after the long trip and your flowers made me happy.

Da was impressed that I'd met someone who

spoke highly of his work. So impressed that he insisted on unloading these back copies on you. He has a huge stash of them. I believe he thinks there may be a nuclear war and when the dust settles and the libraries are all gone, he can get a corner on the book market with them. Anyway, you're stuck with them now and I'm afraid if you do get to visit us in our remote corner he'll expect a review on each.

I don't mean to scare you away with that remark. Do visit. I'd like to see you again and I don't know when I'll have the excuse or the freedom to come back to the States. Da is desperate for help and has let his files get into a terrible snarl. I may have a life sentence here.

Well, doesn't THAT sound pitiful!

Anthony, I enjoyed that afternoon at your house. Uncle had spoken of you so fondly and you lived up to everything he said. I sincerely hope we meet again.

Yours truly,
Gilly Powell

P.S. Look at page 37.

Page 37 was about lobelias and Anthony read it over twice. Then he reread her letter and gazed for a while at the picture. He couldn't remember ever feeling happier.

Anthony tried repeatedly that year to get away, but was thwarted at every turn. As he was opening Gilly's package, hurricane Agnes was working its way toward the eastern US. Within a week the winds were battering the coast and for ten days the terrible storm moved inexorably north, causing billions of dollars of damage and untold human suffering.

Everyone at Samaritan went on overtime. There was so much need they hardly knew where to start. But as always, when the need arose, funds came in to more than meet the need. They set up a temporary headquarters in

Georgia where Anthony and Steven directed the work. They were there for over two months.

Meanwhile, the usual work of the organization went on. Anthony put Rhys in charge on the home front. He did an admirable, if somewhat conservative, plodding job, which is just what Anthony hoped for. He checked in with Rhys by phone every day and flew back to consult with him in more detail every two weeks. On the whole, he was pleased with the older man's efforts. Faye threw herself into the work and made herself invaluable to him.

Anthony was uncomfortably aware that the Prof was probably taking Rhys's appointment as a slight. Anthony wished it could have been Lisle holding the fort for him, but he didn't feel complete confidence in his old mentor anymore. It wasn't only the peculiar conversation they'd had about Gilly. The Prof had missed a couple of important meetings that Nina assured Anthony she'd told him about. Worse, he didn't even admit to missing them, but claimed never to have known about them.

'Don't let it upset you so,' Nina had advised Anthony. 'At his age—'

'He's not that ancient.'

'Age is relative,' Nina said.

Anthony let it go. He had more pressing matters to deal with. But he did Lisle the courtesy of telling him about his decision to appoint Rhys before going ahead with it. 'You're looking tired, Prof, and it's going to be a big job. God only knows when Steven and I will be back for good. Rhys has more energy than he knows what to do with.'

'Nina *didn't* tell me about those appointments I missed,' Lisle said snappishly.

'Come on, Prof. It's not like her to mess up.'

'Nor is it like me, in case *you've* forgotten.'

'Still ...'

'Yes, of course. It's up to you.'

Anthony felt he'd handled it badly, but didn't know what else he could have done. Samaritan's smooth

185

operation meant more than the Prof's hurt feelings or Anthony's guilty ones.

By the time the hurricane operation was finally winding down, there had been a shocking massacre at the Munich Olympics. Fear was in the air. A rumor was circulating that the Arabs had threatened to start blowing up transatlantic plane flights.

'That doesn't make sense!' Anthony said.

'Munich didn't make sense,' Nina responded. 'Several of the directors have mentioned their fear of anyone in the organization making transatlantic flights for a while. Your talk of going to England worries them.'

'Nina, I can't be locked up because of other people's fears.'

'But Samaritan's structured around you. That's what locks you up,' she persisted. 'If you were going for some important purpose—'

'I'm entitled to a vacation,' he argued as a child might with a parent who had already refused permission.

'It's up to you,' she said, disapproval quivering in her voice.

He railed at Steven about it. 'Imagine her trying to tell me I couldn't go! She's gotten out of hand.'

They were in Steven's car, heading for the Plaza for a round of tennis. Steven slammed on the brakes when a car stopped suddenly in front of them. He swore briefly and said, 'Where do these people get licenses? I think Nina's right.'

'About planes getting blown up?'

'No. About everyone worrying about it. You're vital to the whole operation. They'd be quaking in their boots the whole time you were gone. It wouldn't be good for morale. We've put in a hard year, but so has everyone else. Their nerves are frayed. They'd be in a panic about who your successor would be if you ended up in little pieces all over the Atlantic.'

'But you're obviously my successor if something should happen.'

Steven hit the brakes again, but this time it wasn't because of traffic. 'Oh no! Not me. I don't want it. And I'd be lousy at running the whole show.'

'You'd be terrific.'

Steven shook his head emphatically. 'No, you think that because you like me. I'm not a leader. I'm hard pressed to know where I'm headed most of the time. I don't want to be responsible for taking somebody else with me.'

Anthony shook his head. 'If you thought half as much of yourself as other people do, we couldn't get your head through doors.'

'Nice, but no cigar. Have you got your racquet?' he said, pulling into the parking lot.

They'd played for twenty minutes when Anthony shouted across the court, 'All right. I won't go this year.'

Taylor Lisle wasn't ready to make a formal exit from Anthony's life. He spent the rest of 1972 with a round of busy activities that had nothing to do with Samaritan. He accepted lecture invitations at various universities, something he hadn't done for years. Between times, he went back to the ranch.

Jeb Wentworth had hired a new man to replace Rory as successor to his job. Jeb was pleased with his work. 'I'd rather have Rory here, but this boy's workin' out good. He knows his way around horses,' he told Lisle.

'Jeb, we need to talk about the ranch.'

'You puttin' me out to pasture?'

'No, quite the opposite. I've never told you, but you're my heir to this place.'

Jeb sat down heavily in the chair across from Lisle. 'No, sir. That ain't right.'

'It's entirely right. I have no family but you and Anthony and Rory. But I've been thinking about it. I want you to have the ranch now. I'm having an attorney draw up the papers. I'm selling it to you for a dollar.'

'No. This is your place.'

Not any more. It's served its purpose, Lisle thought. But

how could he explain to a simple, unimaginative man like Jeb Wentworth that he'd never loved the land like Jeb did? That the ranch was simply an isolated setting, a vast laboratory in which to raise a brilliant man – Anthony. Lisle had never loved the isolation and the howling loneliness, except for the fact that it allowed him to shape and mold Anthony with a minimum of outside influence.

Nor would Jeb understand the awful knowledge that was seeping into Lisle's consciousness – the knowledge that he was about to be walled up in a claustrophobic way that he couldn't picture, but which caused him often to wake in the night, sweating with terror. Like Anthony, Jeb found the concept of foreknowledge offensive. Jeb's only interest in the future was to wonder what tomorrow's weather would be like and if it meant he ought to move the cattle down from the hills to a protected valley. No, there were things he couldn't discuss with Jeb, even though he'd been a loyal friend and employee for many years.

'Well, it's going to be your place,' Lisle said. 'I'm going away soon. I want you to have it now.'

Jeb knew determination when he heard it. 'It's up to you. But I don't think it's right, selling a person a spread like this for a dollar.'

'You deserve it.'

'Charlie, do you know where I put that notebook with the orange cover?' Faye asked, rummaging through a stack of paperwork on the desk in their bedroom.

Charlie, half his face covered with shaving cream, stuck his head out of the bathroom door and gestured with a razor. 'On the dining room sideboard. Where are you off to in such a hurry?'

She followed him into the bathroom and sat on the hamper to put on a pair of warm, ribbed pantyhose. 'The office, of course. We've got that meeting on the amputee clinic that wants funding.'

'The meeting isn't until eleven. It's only seven thirty and there's a blizzard outside.'

'Is there? I hadn't looked. I've got some research to go over. I'm not quite prepared.'

Charlie finished shaving and washed his face. Toweling it, he trailed along as Faye flung a few things into her purse and searched for the missing notebook. 'Faye, honey, I'm worried about you.'

'About me? Why?' she asked, still on the run.

'You don't need to work so hard at this. You're wearing yourself down. You've been putting in twelve hours a day at this for a year.'

She stopped and smiled. 'Are you saying I'm turning into a hag?'

He put his arms round her and she snuggled against his chest.

'You couldn't if you tried.'

She looked up at him. 'It's worthwhile work, isn't it? You wouldn't be putting in the time and effort either if you didn't believe in Samaritan.'

'Of course it's worthwhile. But—'

Faye kissed him and slipped away. She knew he was leading up to the same old discussion about how she ought to stay home and have babies – the last thing in the world she wanted to waste time on. 'Must rush, darling. We're having Betsy and Martin for dinner, remember. Don't be late.'

'Can't Betsy ever eat at home?' he groused, but she was already gone.

Faye didn't, however, go straight to the Samaritan offices. Instead, she had the taxi let her off in the circle drive of a large stone house a few blocks from Anthony's home. The door opened before she reached it. She rushed in. 'Dear God, it's cold out there!'

'You wouldn't have been out in the cold if you'd stayed here last night like I asked you to,' her host said. He was a solid-looking man in his forties. Wearing only a heavy maroon silk dressing gown, his perfectly cut dark hair and subtly manicured nails announced his wealth. But his features were heavy, primitive, and there was a permanent scowl line between his brows. He could have been a cartoon representation of the fat cat banker, which was what he was. Joseph Fiore was the second largest stockholder and head of the trust department at Jackson County Bank and Trust, one of the largest banks in the city. He was said to have mob connections, but without any real proof.

'You know why I couldn't stay,' Faye said, slipping off her coat and letting it fall to the floor. 'Charlie knew Betsy was at that dreadful fund-raiser and I'd already said I wasn't going. I couldn't have pretended to be with her.'

Joseph was helping her unbutton her blouse and not being very careful about it. A button came off and pinged on the marble entryway floor. 'Why don't you quit bothering with that nothing husband of yours?'

'Why should I? Would you divorce your wife – if you could find her?'

'You know I can't. I'm—'

'Catholic,' she sneered, pulling loose the tie of his dressing gown. She looked down with a hungry smile. 'I know. But only Catholic enough to stay married to the bank president's daughter, Hail Mary. You don't want to give up your nice, safe marriage and neither do I. Charlie is handy.'

'I hate it when you wear these things,' Joseph said, fumbling with the catches on her bra.

'Not here, Joseph. It's cold.'

'I'll make you forget the cold,' he said, scooping her up and striding into the adjoining dining room. He set her down, pulling down her elastic-waistbanded skirt and pantyhose. She lifted herself onto the edge of the heavy oak dining table, and he stripped the clothing the rest of the way off her legs. Then he hastily spread her legs and shoved her shoulders back. Faye lay down, holding onto the edges of the table and grinning fiercely as he entered her. She and Joseph liked their sex fast, often and rough and they liked to see each other when they did it. That was why they always started off at the dining room table.

The lighting was good and the table steady. She could watch him sweat and heave as he hammered his pelvis at her, and he could watch her breasts flop and jiggle with her ragged breathing. He especially liked the very nearly ugly look of agonizing pleasure that contorted her face when she climaxed.

They almost never kissed.

Later, they had coffee and sweet rolls in his kitchen. Still naked, because they both liked her that way, Faye poured him a cup of coffee and set it down with the one hand while reaching to pull aside his dressing gown and fondle his genitals with the other. 'I don't know why you buy this foul-tasting foreign stuff,' she said of the coffee.

He picked up a sweet roll and smeared the sugary top against her breast. 'It's classy, you silly slut,' he said before sucking the sugar off her nipple.

'I bet you can't drink the whole cup,' she said. 'Wait.' She knelt and crawled under the table and positioned her head between his legs. 'Now try,' she said. Then she took him in her mouth.

He nearly choked to death on the last swallow.

When she was dressing to leave, hardly three-quarters of an hour after arriving, she said, 'You know, someday you can dump that fat bitch of a wife of yours.'

'Oh, yeah?' he said, lethargically fondling her as she struggled back into the pantyhose.

'Joseph, you and I are going to own Samaritan. Then we won't need her money or Charlie's. You'll be able to buy the whole damned bank.'

'So you keep saying. But when's it going to happen?'

'When the time is right. Not before.'

'Sure. And how's it going to happen?' He lit a cigarette.

'I'll tell you when the time comes. I'll recognize the opportunity when it comes along. I've got all the patience in the world.'

'You must have, to stick with that stupid prick of a husband.'

'Oh, Charlie is a nice guy.'

She looked at him and they both burst out laughing.

The meeting didn't take long. Faye had reduced reams of documents to a pithy twelve-page report on the amputee clinic. 'So there's no question that they're doing fine and necessary work,' she summed up. 'We sent in one of our own, undercover. He's a Vietnam vet who lost a hand, and we instructed him to be as difficult as possible. They treated him with enormous patience and skill. Their staff, particularly the psychiatric division, is excellent. As you can see from the report, my only hesitation is in regard to their financial management. They're paying more rent than they ought, and there's definite sloppiness in the inventory control. My recommendation is to provide the funding they're asking, but with the provision that we choose new personnel to oversee their finances.'

'Wasn't the vet you sent in one of Rory's protégés?' Anthony asked.

Faye was surprised, as she often was, at the depth of Anthony's knowledge. That hadn't been in the distilled report. He must have read all the relative documents beforehand. 'Yes, one of his treasures. If he's willing to part with the young man, he'd be a good choice. Not only is he good at his job, but he's a convert to the work they're doing.'

'Did you visit the place yourself?' Anthony asked Faye.

'Of course,' she said.

'I thought I'd never get her home,' Charlie put in. 'She was so touched by what they were doing she cried herself to sleep the first night.'

Only Steven involuntarily raised an eyebrow disbelievingly at this and Anthony didn't notice. 'Then that's good enough for me,' Anthony said. 'With the provisions Faye's suggested, are we agreed?'

He glanced round the table. Everyone was nodding.

Anthony watched the snow falling outside the window

and glanced down at the letter he was writing to Gilly. When he first learned that her father refused to have a telephone and the only way to hear her voice was to ring up the village postmistress and have someone fetch Gilly from her house a mile away, he went nearly mad with frustration. But in the following eight months, he'd acquired a great reverence for the stately, old-fashioned habit of writing, and receiving, letters. He felt silly and dull when he reread his own before mailing them, but loved getting hers.

Gilly had inherited her father's gift for language. Her letters were chatty, lively, breezy for the most part. Sometimes, too, she talked about the bleakness and grandeur of the Welsh landscape when she and her father had been traveling. Her description of Carnarvon Castle had made him feel he'd not only been there, but that he'd been there centuries before.

She talked, too, about her gardening and whenever she mentioned a specific plant, she'd refer him to the proper page in the book she'd sent him or enclose a picture from a seed catalog. Anthony had come to believe he could actually become interested in flowers if she kept it up for another decade or so.

There was always something enclosed in her letters as well, which made them fun. Sometimes a pressed flower to show him what she was talking about. Once it was a fabric scrap from a dress she said she was making. Often there were snapshots: the view from her window, her father's scruffy dog in a stand-off with an enormous neighborhood cat, a dramatic shot of a roiling black storm rolling in toward the sunlit meadows.

Anthony loved all her little bits and pieces and wished his own life generated such things that he could share. Instead, he wrote to her about what Samaritan was doing and sometimes he told her how he felt about things. It was odd that he should turn introspective with her. He'd never been inclined to examine his own feelings. He told her about growing up on the ranch, about his respect and

193

affection for his adopted father. He even told her, albeit briefly, about the shock and anger he felt at discovering he was Max Herron's only son.

The only thing he didn't tell her about was Betsy – and Martin. That was something he couldn't tell anyone. He still didn't know if he believed that Martin was his child. He'd only seen the boy a handful of times. There was a resemblance between them, he supposed. Though Anthony found nothing distinctive in his own appearance to look for in the child, their coloring was the same and the boy showed signs of being tall. But that certainly wasn't enough to prove a relationship. And it was not something he was prepared to talk about, not even to Gilly.

He turned from the window and went back to the letter.

... Faye presented a good case for a clinic that treats amputees. Psychological counseling as well as fitting artificial limbs, help with job placements. She seemed genuinely moved by the work they're doing and her husband confirmed it. She caught up with me later, embarrassed about it. Told me she didn't want her own feelings to have influenced me. Of course, we're in a business in which people's feelings should count for a lot. I told her that and she actually got tearful.

That made Steven go haywire. I can't understand why he dislikes her so much. It's not like him to dislike anyone. He is really the most forgiving, generous person I've ever known. I can't wait for you to meet him. I hope you'll like each other as much as I like both of you—'

'Excuse me,' Nina said from the doorway of his office, interrupting his thoughts. 'Wayne Graves is on the phone asking for an appointment.'

Normally Nina didn't consult him about his appointments, but she'd been instructed to let him know when

194

it was any family member. 'Business or personal?' Anthony queried.

'He said a little of both, mostly business.'

'Do I have anything for dinner tonight?'

'Not on my schedule.'

'Then ask him to come to the house for dinner at seven and tell Mrs Roush. Something hearty to eat. It seems the fancier the food the smaller the portions.'

'A beef stew and dumplings?'

Anthony smiled wryly. Given her head, Nina would run every aspect of his life. And Mrs Roush didn't like interference. 'No, just tell her hearty food. Let her decide.'

Wayne arrived a few minutes before seven. Anthony had never considered him as an individual before, only as one of Betsy's brood, and had to remind himself Wayne was the oldest. He'd turned into a remarkably handsome young man. He was medium height, but still rangy, like a big puppy that hasn't filled out yet. Still, he was going to become what used to be called a lady-killer. He had his mother's slightly sleepy looking eyes, but was dark-haired like Ned. Was he Ned's child? Anthony found himself remembering a conversation from years ago, the weekend when he met the Herrons at Birches. Betsy had forced Ned into marriage by becoming pregnant, but whoever told him the gossip claimed the child wasn't even Ned's. This was that child.

'We ought to chat politely for a while,' Anthony said, helping Wayne take off his heavy winter coat, 'but I've been smelling dinner for an hour and I'm starving. Do you mind talking over food?'

'It smells great. Let's eat,' Wayne said. He brushed a few snowflakes out of his thick, dark hair.

'What are you doing here in Kansas City?' Anthony asked over salad. 'Do you have a break from college?'

'No, I'm done. As of yesterday. I took a lot of summer classes because I wanted to graduate early like you did. Get on with real life.' He was talking round his food which he was wolfing down as if he hadn't eaten in days.

'And what does real life hold for you?' Anthony asked.

'A job with Samaritan, I hope,' Wayne said bluntly.

'I see.' It was a shock to him to realize that the next generation, which was how he thought of Wayne and his brothers, was coming of age. 'How old are you, Wayne. Twenty?'

'Yes, sir. I'm not asking for a great job. Any scut work you have until I can prove my worth.' He reached into an inside pocket of his sports coat and pulled out a few folded papers. 'Not exactly a formal submission, but I thought you might like to see these.'

They were copies of his transcript. At a quick glance Anthony could see that he was an excellent student. Heavy class loads each semester, almost straight As. There was a B after 'Art Appreciation'. Anthony glanced at him. 'What happened in art?'

'Damned stupid requirement,' Wayne said with a wry grin.

The rest of the classes were as business and science oriented as possible. No other arts, no English but the requirements. Three semesters each of French, German and Spanish. 'Interesting combination,' Anthony said.

'I was preparing myself for Samaritan,' Wayne said.

Mrs Roush came in with the stew. Anthony set aside the flimsy sheets, but continued to glance at them as he and the younger man attacked the fragrant food. 'Explain that, would you?' he asked.

'The business is obvious. Samaritan, for all it's good works, is a business. The science, well, that was mainly for my dad. And because I like it, but it can be helpful in things like the clinic my Aunt Faye was investigating.' He glanced at Anthony as if for approval. Anthony nodded for him to go on.

'The language – well, sir, I think you're going to see the day when Samaritan is a more international organization. There is also a great deal of foreign money available that hasn't been tapped.'

'We can't cure the ills of the world, Wayne. We limit ourselves to American concerns.'

'I know that, sir, but that's what I'm talking about. For example, that town in Nebraska last fall that had the tornado damage to the hospital – the population is largely German. They have a sister city in Germany. Funds could have been solicited, but weren't, because Samaritan thinks in purely American terms. The same was true in that town in western Texas that has the pollution problem with the water supply. The population there is fifty-six per cent Mexican immigrants. Mexican aid could have been sought. I'm not so sure it would have been forthcoming, but it might have been worthwhile to try.'

'I see,' Anthony said calmly, trying not to let the boy see that he was both excited at the ideas and embarrassed that he and his own advisors hadn't thought of them. He leaned back and said, 'While you're making suggestions, what else would you do?'

Wayne sensed that he'd been arrogant, but couldn't stop. 'Well, sir, I'd take a long look at Samaritan's investment portfolio.'

'Why?'

'Because what you've got is great stuff. Solid, conservative, safe. But without a significant added risk, you could be getting an overall two to three per cent higher return with some changes. And I don't mean putting millions in weird, trendy things. Even if you only made a few changes and got an additional one per cent, that would be enough added income to fund a number of projects.'

'I see. If it were up to you, what would you put money into?' Anthony asked.

'Computers to start with,' Wayne said without hesitation. 'The day isn't far off that every house will have one.'

'You mean every office.'

'No. Every house.'

'Wayne, I'd bet less than one household in twenty even has a typewriter.'

'I'm sure you're right, but a typewriter is just a fancy

197

pencil. A computer thinks. It can be your secretary, your filing system—'

'All right, I'll consider that. Why do you want to work for Samaritan?'

'Because I think I can be valuable to—'

'No, that wasn't the question. I didn't ask how Samaritan can benefit from you, but how you can benefit from Samaritan. Why this company? Why not IBM or a brokerage house?'

Mrs Roush came in just then to remove their plates and serve a rich chocolate cake with fudge icing – Anthony's favorite. It gave Wayne time to think about the question and Anthony was sorry about that. He'd have rather had a spontaneous answer. 'Let's take this in the living room,' Anthony said, thinking of the fireplace there.

They took their plates and their coffee along. Mrs Roush had set out brandy and snifters. 'Well?' Anthony said when they'd settled into place.

Wayne put his cake plate aside. 'Several reasons. One, I think I can make a difference. That's important to me, to make a difference. I'd rather shoot myself than turn into a drone that just fills a spot in some company.'

'Couldn't you make a difference anywhere else?'

'Not where it would matter as much to me.'

'Go on. Why else?'

Wayne shifted uneasily. 'Because of you,' he said softly. 'I know it sounds like I'm trying to be an oily little creep, flattering the boss, but I admire you. I like you. I'm glad we're family.'

Anthony leaned back in his chair. That was the first time any Herron had ever suggested pleasure of kinship. He hadn't realized until that moment how desperately he'd desired the recognition. He was so touched he couldn't speak for a moment. Then he said softly, 'I'm glad to hear that, Wayne.'

'I mean it.'

'I think you do. Thanks. Does your mother know you've come to see me about a job?'

That took Wayne by surprise. 'Yes,' he mumbled.

'And she doesn't approve?'

'She doesn't approve of you, but you know that. But I'm not defying some maternal edict, if that's what you mean. After all, Aunt Faye and Uncle Charlie work for Samaritan, too.'

'But they aren't her children.'

Wayne suddenly leaned forward. 'Look, I'm sorry about you and Mom. People don't understand her. She's really a wonderful person, but she's got, well, eccentric ways. And that puts people off. I know she's been pretty unpleasant to you.'

'Wayne, do you know what's between us? Why your mother hates me?'

The boy fumbled with his brandy snifter for a minute. 'She, uh, she says Martin is your kid. That you raped her. I don't mean to criticize Mom, but I don't believe it. About Martin.'

Anthony's heart was pumping with outrage. Damn her. Damn the bitch. Raped *her*! He forced himself to be calm. 'Why not?'

'Because he's a nasty little creep and I don't think a son of yours would be like that. We were all kinda wild, but Martin's really mean. Van's got some of that, too.'

'I'm not trying to set you against her and we won't ever talk about this again, but I'm telling you the God's truth: I didn't rape your mother, Wayne.'

'I believe you.' He looked Anthony straight in the eye as he said it and Anthony could tell it was hard for him to admit to a belief contrary to what his mother said. To allow them both to come to terms with their emotions, he got up and put another log on the fire and pushed it around. 'Is there anything else, Wayne? Any other reason you want to work for Samaritan?'

'I don't know – not that I know how to say. But I can promise you I'd bring my best to it.'

'I think you would.'

'Does that mean you'll hire me?'

199

'It means I'll think about it and let you know within the week.'

Anthony couldn't get to sleep that night, a rare thing for him. He'd waited for Wayne to say he wanted to work for Samaritan because the organization was worthwhile. And he hadn't. He'd given him every opportunity. That was a disappointment. Still, that was an emotional reaction, not a legitimate business consideration. You didn't have to be a fanatic to the cause to be a valuable contributor. Rory was a prime example. Rory didn't give a damn about doing good for the recipients of Samaritan's largess. He regarded them more as a necessary evil when he acknowledged their existence at all. And yet Rory's value was unquestionable. Morever, he wouldn't be any better at his job if he were a convert. It brought to mind something the Prof had said near the beginning, that Anthony wasn't qualified or entitled to judge people's motives for giving, that it was the giving that counted. The giving and the use to which the gifts were put.

Wayne was, in a sense, a gift of brains, enthusiasm, education, a very pleasant presence. He had drive and was eager to please, to make his mark. Anthony tossed and turned until quite late and finally decided to give Wayne a try.

Chapter Thirteen

'Prof! Where have you been?' Anthony asked, shaking hands warmly with the older man.

'You're busy,' Lisle said, glancing around Anthony's office. Stacks of paper were everywhere. Folding tables had been brought in to make extra room for the tottering piles.

'It's an annual report. I've let Wayne have his head on this one. I hired Wayne a couple of months ago, you know. Wayne Graves.'

'I know who Wayne is,' Lisle said sourly.

'He lobbied for a slick booklet to hand out to donors. They're going to be stapled up five thousand at a time so the center section, which is current financial status, can be updated frequently. The expensive color part of the booklet won't go out of date for years. Good thinking, huh?'

'If you convinced Rory, you've got my vote. You've redone your office, too.' The old-fashioned office had been gutted, a wall had been removed, making it much larger. Instead of the worn gray carpet, there was now a vast expanse of rich maroon pile that picked out a line from the beige, tan and maroon striped wallpaper. There was new furniture, too. Very modern. Clean lines.

'I'm surprised you can see enough of it to tell. What with the mess. Let's sit down.'

Anthony led Lisle to the new part of the room, an informal seating area with a big slab coffee table surrounded by deep, comfortably upholstered chairs. 'Nice,' Lisle mumbled. 'Rory must have had a stroke.'

'Samaritan didn't pay for this. I did,' Anthony said. 'And Nina put it all together. I'm not used to it yet. It still looks to me like an expensive hotel suite instead of an office.'

'You'd prefer a roll-top desk and banks of clerks sitting on high stools?' Lisle said with a smile.

'I'm not sure I'd go that far, but it does have a certain appeal. Actually, we're looking for more space. A building of our own, possibly in Lenexa or Olathe. Somewhere out south. We've already taken all the available floors in this building. Amazing, isn't it? When Max died, all of Samaritan was in one file drawer in a closet-sized room. It's only been five years and look what it's become.'

'Because of you,' Lisle said.

'Because of a lot of people.'

'But it was your idea. I'm proud of you, Anthony.'

Anthony looked embarrassed at the compliment. 'That means a lot to me. I'm glad you approve. Prof. I always knew you had something in mind for me. Was this it?'

Lisle leaned back in the comfortable chair. 'This, or something. I knew you had it in you to become important and valuable. I didn't know in what way. I thought it might be some area of medicine, since that's my own field.'

'I didn't know that. You never pushed me in that direction,' Anthony said.

'I just pushed you forward.'

'Did you ever!' Anthony said. He took the older man's hand in a rare gesture of affection. 'I've never thanked you and I should have.'

'No, I should thank you for justifying my work and belief,' Lisle said, gently disengaging his hand. 'It's good that we've talked about this now. In a way, it's why I've come. I'm here to say goodbye, Anthony.'

'You're taking a trip?'

'Not exactly. But I hear you are.'

'Yes. I'm going to England next week. To see Blanche. She hasn't been feeling well this winter.'

'And Gilly Powell?'

Anthony felt caught out. He hadn't been going to mention her because of the disturbing conversation they'd had the last time he mentioned her. 'Yes, I'm planning to see her, too.'

'Kismet,' Lisle said under his breath.

'Is there anything you'd like me to bring back for you?'

'No, Anthony. You won't see me when you get back. You won't see me again at all.'

Anthony stared at him. 'What are you talking about? What's wrong? Are you angry about something?'

'No, quite the contrary. I'm proud of what you've become, but you're self-sufficient now. You don't need me anymore. No,' he said, leaning forward, 'that's not meant as a pathetic attention-getter. Just a statement of fact. It's as it should be. You've outgrown your need for me, which is how it's supposed to work.'

'Prof—'

'Don't say anything. I'm not making accusations. I'm not asking anything of you. I'm saying a very fond farewell and explaining it. That's all. My time is done.'

'Prof, is there something wrong with your health? Is that what this is all about? You've got to tell me if that's it. We have access to the best people in the medical field.'

'No, nothing like that. It's just time that I bow out.'

'I don't understand this all or nothing stuff,' Anthony said, angry and frustrated. 'You've been a second dad to me all my life and now we can't even be friends? I don't believe this! I've done something you're mad about. Spit it out. Let's settle it now.'

'Anthony, listen to me. Really listen. I know you've never believed it, but I do see things, know some things that are going to happen. I can't refrain from telling you about them, warn you when necessary. But you don't believe it. It makes you angry.'

'But Prof, that's just one thing we don't see eye to eye on. It doesn't mean—'

'Please, let me finish. I can't keep quiet about what I

see if I'm around, but you don't want to hear it. It's that simple and the solution is for me not to be around.'

Anthony thought for a moment, then grinned. 'I could pretend to believe your predictions.'

Lisle smiled sadly. 'If there's one thing that you're an absolute failure at it's pretending. Anthony, I'm stepping out of your life.'

'What are you going to do? Hide from me?'

'In a way. I'm going to be taken away, but you don't want to hear that kind of talk.'

Anthony threw his hands up. 'I don't get this! And I don't like it.' But a voice in the back of his mind was saying, it's just a momentary mental aberration. He's always been there for me. He always will be. When I get back from England, I'll call him and see if he's over this.

'Someday you'll understand. Maybe,' Lisle said, rising.

'I can't let you walk out of here feeling this way,' Anthony said.

'But you must. Anthony, there is one last thing I must tell you: you'll be betrayed by the woman you trust most. Be careful.'

Anthony felt a *frisson* of something very like fear over-laid with anger. What a hell of a parting statement!

That afternoon Anthony got another shock. 'I'd like two weeks off,' Nina said.

'My God, is *this* the betrayal?' Anthony asked.

'Betrayal? I should hope not!' she said, offended.

'Of course not. I was just thinking about something the Prof said. Nina, you haven't had a day off that I can remember in all these years.'

'Neither have you,' she pointed out.

'Still, you deserve it. But what'll I do without you for two weeks?'

'My mother's agreed to fill in for me and I'll be in touch with her by phone every day.'

'Doesn't sound like much of a vacation.'

'I'll really only be gone for a week as far as you're concerned. The other week you'll be in England anyway.'

'You mean you're taking this vacation right now?'

'All next week and the week after. Is that all right?'

Nina had truly been his right hand since the very day Max Herron died. She was always there, sometimes so obsessively handy that it drove him mad. But he couldn't imagine how he'd get along without her. 'It's all right with me if you're convinced this is a good time,' he said weakly.

'Everything's under control at the moment. We cleared a lot off the agenda at yesterday's meeting. Rhys Jones will be nominally in charge. And should there be an emergency, we can all be in touch by phone.'

'You're right. Yes. All right. You'll leave Friday then. Where are you going?'

'Don't worry. Mother will have a number for me at all times,' she said. 'Just call her if you want me.'

That wasn't the answer to his question, but Nina's phone rang just then. She covered the receiver and said, 'This is the people in Oregon with the windmill idea. Do you want to take it now?'

'I might as well,' Anthony said, heading for his own phone.

The week without Nina was a nightmare. Her mother, Mrs Smith – he never had the nerve to call her by her first name – was terrifyingly efficient. Her schoolmistressy air made him feel he was on trial. He found himself working especially hard to impress her, which he knew was silly, but he couldn't help himself. He was also fascinated by the way she talked. Whenever she spoke there was a faint clicking sound behind her words. He finally decided she had dentures that made the noise. At first this was just an interesting anomaly, but by the end of the week it was driving him wild.

'I'm starting to cringe every time she talks to me,' he confessed to Steven. 'Thank God I'd planned this trip to England on Monday. If I hadn't, I'd be thinking up an emergency just to get away from her. How am I going to tell Nina not to do this to me again? I'm afraid I'll sound like a lunatic, telling her that her mother's teeth make a tiny noise that sounds like a cannon shot to me. That's nuts.'

'You'll think of something,' Steven said placidly. 'You'll be seeing Blanche?'

Anthony ran his hands through his hair. 'Out of the frying pan and into the fire.'

'Do her teeth make noises too?'

'No, but it's unnerving to be around her. The only thing we have in common is biology and my father's betrayal of her. We can't make small talk about that, and it leaves us absolutely nothing to say. But we both doggedly do our duty to each other. We talk about the weather until we're both nearly crazy. And she tells me, in stupefying detail, everything she's done to that house of hers. I know about every damned drain that's ever stopped up and exactly how it was fixed and who fixed it and how long it took and what it cost. Gruesome.'

'Why do you go? She isn't getting any more of a kick out of it than you are, or so it sounds like.'

'I go because she's my mother, and she tolerates it because I'm her son. A sentence we're both serving. Stars in both our crowns. Ugh!' He shuddered dramatically.

Steven laughed. 'But at least you'll get to see your Gilly.'

'I like that,' Anthony said, brightening. 'My Gilly. Sounds good. I can't wait for you to meet her. You'll love her.'

Anthony's flight was leaving at ten on Friday evening. He stayed late at the office, tying up loose ends. His bags were sitting in the outer office so that he could go straight to the airport. He dictated a few letters and was just stacking up the finished files when the phone in the outer office rang.

Anthony was surprised. 'I thought the switchboard cut these phones off at five,' he said.

'Yes, but that's Nina's private line,' Mrs Smith said,

leaping up to answer with an alarmed expression.

He caught the agitated sound of her voice talking to someone. 'Yes, we're just finishing. Yes, of course. One moment.' She came to the doorway. 'I think you better take this. It's Nina.'

Something's wrong. His heart pounding, he went to the outer office and picked up the phone. 'Nina, what is it?'

He heard her draw a deep breath. 'Anthony, it's Dr Lisle. He's had a stroke. I'm afraid it's serious. He's alive but the doctors don't know—'

'Where, Nina?'

'At his ranch.'

'Tell him I'm coming.'

'I don't think he'll know I'm—'

'Just tell him, Nina!' he shouted, hanging up the phone with a bang. 'Mrs Smith, call and cancel my plane reservation and hire a charter for me. I'll head for the airport now while you're arranging it. Find Rory and tell him what's happened. And when it's a decent hour in England, call and explain to my mother and to Gilly Powell.' Mrs Smith was already dialing before he finished. He grabbed his bags and raced down the stairs rather than waiting for an elevator. He was in the air before it occurred to him to wonder what Nina had been doing at the ranch when the Prof had a stroke.

Anthony's rush was abortive. The small plane had engine trouble halfway and had to set down at a tiny industrial airport. Anthony had to rent a car, drive to the next largest town and start over. In the end, it would have been faster to wait until morning and take a commercial flight, as Rory had done. They arrived at the ranch within minutes of each other just before noon the next day.

'There's nobody here,' Anthony said as Rory came in the door.

'I know,' Rory said, 'I stopped in town and asked at the hospital. He was taken there first and flown to Albuquerque. Randy Eagle's picking us up to take us there.' Randy Eagle was a disreputable drinking buddy of

Rory's from way back. 'He said Dad told him the Prof had some kind of seizure yesterday morning. First he knew, that secretary of yours was standing on the porch screaming. What the hell did you send her here for anyway?'

'I didn't send her. I had no idea she was here,' Anthony replied.

Randy Eagle, only slightly drunk, duly arrived in a small plane that looked like parts of several First World War antiques strung together with barbed wire. It was a two-seater and Anthony had to ride crammed in between bags of fertilizer behind the seats. It was the most harrowing hour of his life. He would have gone into shock except that he was too exhausted to notice some of what was going on.

Nina, who by some mysterious means tracked their progress, met them at the doors of the hospital. 'He's stabilized now. I've sent your father to a motel to get some rest. You ought to do the same, Anthony. You look beaten.'

He and Rory were allowed in to see Lisle for five minutes. Lisle was lying shrunken and colorless in an oxygen tent. Only the slight rising and falling of his chest indicated that he was alive. Anthony and Rory sat helplessly for a few minutes before a nurse ran them out. The attending physician was waiting for them.

'He's suffered enormous brain damage. It would be unfair to give you false hope. He won't recover. He'll probably not regain consciousness.'

'How long?' Rory asked what Anthony couldn't.

The doctor shrugged. 'He could suffer another stroke any moment, or he could go on for years. There isn't any way to guess. I'd like to tell you there's something we could try to do that would help him, but there isn't.'

'What now?' Rory asked.

'If he doesn't change for the worse, we can release him tomorrow to an extended care facility.'

'A nursing home?' Anthony said, horrified at the thought.

'Even home care, but it would require round-the-clock nursing. I understand his home is in the country. I doubt you could get reliable full-time staff there.'

'No,' Anthony said firmly. 'Every time someone didn't show up for work the duty would fall to our dad and he's got a ranch to run.'

'Gentlemen, I know you don't like the idea of a nursing home. Most people don't. But it won't matter to the patient. As far as we can tell in cases like this, he has no consciousness of where he is.'

'Doctor, do you think he can hear?' Anthony asked.

'Anything's possible. Just because he's physically unable to indicate a response doesn't mean his senses aren't registering.'

Anthony was allowed to look in on the Prof every two hours for five minutes. Between times Anthony slept on a couch in the waiting room. Nina had disappeared, presumably to catch up on her own rest. In the late afternoon Jeb Wentworth woke Anthony from one of his brief, tortured naps. 'Sorry I wasn't there when you came, son.'

'Dad, I'm glad to see you,' Anthony said, embracing the older man. Anthony explained what the doctor had told him.

Jeb said, 'He always said he was going to end his life walled up. I always thought he meant a jail or something. Didn't make sense, not for an educated man like that.'

'He told me that too. I just thought it was more psychic bullshit.'

Jeb nodded. Not the words he would have used, but the same thought.

'Well, he is walled up now, isn't he? Walled up inside his own helpless body. He was right,' Anthony said. 'I've been thinking – about being walled up. We've got to push the walls back. The doctor said he might have his senses. I'm going to put him somewhere he has medical care, but I'm going to do what I can for his brain, too. Always have scented flowers and music in his room. Have people read to him. That kind of thing.'

'You think he'll know?'

'Maybe not. But it can't hurt and he might know.'

Jeb rubbed his stubbly chin. 'I reckon if it was me I'd rather be left alone, but he always liked a lot of talking and reading and such.'

Anthony thought of something. 'Oh, we've got to get you a power of attorney to run the ranch.'

'No. The ranch is mine, not his.'

'What?'

Haltingly, Jeb explained.

'He *did* know, didn't he?' Anthony said. 'You know, Dad, maybe it wasn't all bullshit. In fact ...' He fell silent a moment, dredging up memories. 'One of the earliest things I remember is that day we got the pigs. Remember?'

Jeb grinned. 'Them damned pigs!'

'I remember the day they were unloaded. I must have been six or seven and I wanted to go see them. The Prof told me I shouldn't. Wouldn't tell me why. Just got that smug, know-it-all look. Said I'd regret it. But I went down and got right in the enclosure with them. Do you remember?'

'Sure I do. That old sow knocked you smack into the shit. I never did smell a boy like you! We had to strip you in the barn and burn your clothes. Even had it in your ears.'

'So, maybe he knew what was going to happen.'

'Listen, son, *everybody* knew what was going to happen. You turn a dumb little kid loose with pigs, you're gonna get a pig-shit covered kid.'

Anthony laughed. 'You're right. It was a bad example. It was only the first one to mind. But maybe he did know things that were going to happen. There were other times. Important things. Storms, even your gallbladder. He said you were going to be very sick, but we weren't to worry that it was life-threatening. It made you so mad when he said that, I remember, but a week later, you were in surgery. Do you suppose he really knew, Dad? He must have.'

'Son, I don't hold with that and neither do you. You're just tired and rattled. That Miss Smith of yours got us nice rooms over to the Holiday Inn. Go on over and get some real sleep with your boots off.'

'Nina. I'd forgotten about her. Dad, what was she doing here?'

'Dunno. Just came to visit.'

'To visit the Prof?'

'I reckon. She sure as heck didn't come to see me.'

'I don't get it. She and the Prof never seemed to have the time of day for each other.'

'Yeah? They seemed right chummy to me. Matter of fact, it seemed to me the Prof was kinda calf-eyed about her. No fool like an old fool, they say.'

Anthony shook his head, as if to clear it. 'Dad, point me toward the motel, would you?'

He asked Nina the next morning.

'Dr Lisle said he had some books he wanted to give me,' she said as if perplexed that he'd even asked. 'I needed some time off and he offered me a place to be in the open air for a change and relax. I didn't see any reason not to come to the ranch. Do you mind?'

'You're free to go anyplace you want. I'm just confused. I didn't think you and the Prof much liked each other.'

'We've worked together a lot over the years. He seemed to be, well, tying up loose ends. He had some books and notes and things he said he wanted me to have.'

'Do *you* think he knew this was going to happen?'

Nina hesitated a long time before answering. 'I didn't at the time. I just thought he was getting ready for a new stage of life. That he was going to take a teaching position or something.'

'Yes. I guess that's what I thought, too. Nina, we need to get some information on nursing homes.'

What Nina had said about Lisle was partly true. She hadn't known what was going to happen to him. But she knew it was going to be something dreadfully final. She didn't believe in what Anthony called 'psychic bullshit' any more than he and Jeb Wentworth did. But she had no trouble accepting that she and Lisle had a bond that was almost mystical, even though she wouldn't have defined it that way. Anthony was the bond. He was the center of both their lives, and that had tied them together.

The evening before his last meeting with Anthony, Lisle had called her. 'Nina, I need to talk to you. Would you be free for a couple days? It's important. It's about Anthony.'

She'd been in two minds. She suspected he found her sexually attractive, and she was repelled at the thought of several days with an old man who wouldn't have appealed to her even in his youth. Could she fend off any amorous approaches without both of them ending up angry? Probably, but it wasn't one of her many fields of expertise. Weighted against that was his mind. He knew Anthony even better than she did in spite of her cannibalistic observations of him. She'd learned Anthony's likes and dislikes, but had no idea what had created them. She needed Lisle's knowledge of Anthony's past. And of his destiny, though that was a word and concept she would have scoffed at if anyone else had expressed it.

'Yes, I can be free,' she'd said and made plans to meet him at the ranch.

He'd been brutally blunt when she arrived and they took a long walk. 'I'm going to retire shortly, Nina,' he'd said grimly. 'It's going to be up to you to protect Anthony.'

Protect him? She'd always thought of herself as fostering his welfare, never as a protector.

'I've tried,' he went on. 'He won't listen and I'm not sure how much difference it would make if he did. There's so damned much I don't know! I've been given small, shiny pieces of the puzzle, but not the whole. You don't know what I'm talking about, do you?'

'Not really,' she admitted.

'Then listen and try to believe me, at least for now. I've got something to hand on to you. A weapon, if you will, but without any instructions. I just have to tell you what I know about it and it'll be up to you to carry and use it.'

She hadn't a clue what he meant, but listened intently just the same.

He took a deep breath. 'I've always known things I had no logical way of knowing. That's one of the reasons I chose psychology as my field – an effort to understand it myself. It didn't help. One of the things I knew was that I wouldn't marry and father children, but I wanted to raise a child. I sensed that if I did, I'd raise an extraordinary child. A child who would make a difference, a large-scale difference. I searched for that child for years and had almost given up finding him. Then, at a house party in England, I saw Blanche and Max meet. There was an instant passionate conflagration between them. That was obvious to anyone, but I sensed something else in it. I sensed the child I'd been looking for. I knew as surely as I knew my name that the first flare of that passion could produce the extraordinary being I was seeking. I had no idea *how* it would happen, but I was certain it would. So I hypnotized Blanche—'

'You *what*?'

'Elementary stuff. A parlor trick, really. All post-grad psych students know how. I just suggested to her that her husband would come to her bed that night, but that he'd look different and she wasn't to be alarmed. It was only what she wanted anyway – to sleep with Max. I think it would have happened without my interference. I was just covering my bases. Then I told Max she wanted him to come to her room that night. He only needed the slightest encouragement. You know the rest.'

'Yes,' Nina said slowly, remembering the story of the hasty marriage, the infant who wasn't expected to live, the adoption arranged by Lisle.

'But then years later it started going wrong. My own fault. I'd always meant to tell Anthony when he was old enough to understand, but I waited too long. He never seemed to be willing to hear what I had to say. He met

Betsy and it was too late to stop it. I hadn't seen that coming. Then Max was suddenly dying and Anthony knew the truth – or at least part of it.'

'Wait. I don't understand. What has meeting Betsy to do with any of this?'

'He's never told you?'

'Told me what?'

'Betsy's youngest boy is Anthony's child.'

'That's impossible. Betsy is his half-sister.'

'Exactly. But he didn't know it because I didn't tell him in time. The boy Martin is a living curse.'

Nina stopped in her tracks, feeling ill. 'Oh no,' she gasped. 'Poor Anthony. That's why they hate each other.'

Lisle held up a hand. 'Anthony isn't sure the child is his. All he knows is that he slept with his sister.'

'Half-sister,' Nina corrected automatically. As if it made a difference.

'But Betsy isn't the danger. Faye is.'

'Faye? In what way?'

'I don't know,' Lisle said, balling his fists. 'That's the damnation of it. But you have to protect him from her.'

'How?' It was a cry from the heart.

Lisle shook his head furiously. 'I've no idea. But it'll be up to you.'

They resumed their walk, both deep in thought.

'When Max died, things changed,' Lisle said. 'It was as if I kept finding bloody puzzle pieces in dark corners of my mind.'

Nina cast him a perplexed look. She still didn't believe in this mystical nonsense, but she no longer entirely disbelieved it.

'The boy Martin, of course. I can hardly think of him without getting sick chills. And Faye. There's something dark and evil about her. But Gilly is a problem, too.'

'Gilly Powell?'

'He's in love with her.'

'Infatuated, at least,' Nina said. She'd recognized this from the first time Gilly came into Anthony's life, but hadn't worried. From everything she heard, Gilly seemed harmless. Domestic, unambitious. Exactly the sort of wife she would have chosen for Anthony when she got around to it. 'Gilly's dangerous to Anthony?' she asked.

'Not deliberately. Dammit! I wish I could explain to you. When I see them in my mind, they're ... they're broken. Both of them. And there's someone else. Someone I feel I'd recognize if the light were a little better. A shadow between them.'

Nina shivered so violently that her teeth clattered.

'You're cold. I'm sorry. The evening air cools quickly out here. Let's go back to the house. I've asked our cook to fix an authentic Mexican meal for us tonight.'

Normalcy was restored.

The rest of the week he'd talked about Anthony's upbringing. Lisle didn't refer to his 'premonitions', which was as far as Nina was willing to go in labeling them. A premonition was socially and intellectually acceptable. Probably not valid, but not as unbelievable and cryptic as talk of fate or second sight.

And then on Friday he was preoccupied. His sentences kept trailing off as though he were listening to some background noise she couldn't hear. At dinner he was placid.

'What shall we do tomorrow?' she asked as they went to the big central room to play a little chess, the usual evening occupation.

'Nothing,' he said calmly. 'I'm done. I've told and showed you everything I can.'

'Are you telling me to go away?' she asked, trying to make it sound like a joke, but genuinely hurt.

'No, of course not.' He put his arm round her and she didn't mind. 'I've just completed my job. That's all I meant.'

Nina went to bed that night puzzled and troubled. She'd listened to everything he'd said all week, could probably repeat most of it, if she had to. But she only had the most tenuous hold on what it was about. It was what she imagined it would be like to be blind. He'd given her gifts, but they were intangible – intellectual gifts; she could sense their texture and temperature and shape, but without sight she didn't have the final vision of what they really were.

She fell into a fitful sleep and awoke late the next morning as suddenly as if someone had fired a gun next to her head. She sat up, disoriented, frightened. Without having any idea why, she knew she had to go to Lisle. Heart pounding, she threw on her robe and ran lightly down the hall to his room. She heard his voice and flung open the door.

He was lying half crossways on the bed, thrashing and muttering.

'Dr Lisle, what's wrong?' she asked, approaching him.

He turned his head and looked at her. Half his face was dead, lifeless, frozen into a one-sided grimace. 'I see it,' he said, although she didn't understand the words at first, so slurred was his speech.

She pulled him back into a more comfortable position and pulled the covers up. 'Don't move. I'll get Mr Wentworth.'

He grabbed her arm in an excruciatingly strong grip. 'I've seen it. All,' he said, the good half of his face twisting in agony. 'Oh, God! Oh, God!'

'Seen what?' she asked, but she knew what he meant. 'The future? Anthony's future?'

'Oh, my God!' he said. 'Steven! Not Steven!'

'What about Steven?' she shouted at him. 'You must tell me,' she insisted, forgetting that she didn't believe in second sight.

'No, no, no! Stop them. Stop it! Auuggghh—'

He stopped breathing for a second and she thought he was dead. She stood incapacitated with horror. Then he took a deep breath. She ran out the front door and started yelling for Jeb Wentworth.

And now, two days later, it was fading and becoming unreal to her. How could she possibly explain to Anthony something she hardly believed herself and knew he didn't want to hear? If only Lisle had been able to tell her what he saw at the end. It was all probably part of the stroke itself, she told herself in her usual practical manner. An hallucination of some kind, brought on by the sudden, violent upheaval in his brain. But maybe not. If only she could have dragged him back to tell her.

Why had he called Steven's name with such anguish and pity?

Chapter Fourteen

'It must have been awful for you, seeing him that way. Not really dead, but not living,' Gilly said, her eyes swimming with tears. 'I'm glad that my mother went suddenly instead of enduring that kind of prolonged death.'

'Rory insisted that the Prof didn't know he was even alive, much less suffering. Maybe he was right,' Anthony said. 'Oddly enough, Nina was my best support in making those three months as pleasant and fulfilling as possible for him. She's all practical efficiency. If you can't label and file it logically, it doesn't exist for her. And yet, she and the Prof came to some understanding at the end. She was with him when he had the stroke even though they never had the time of day for each other before. She visited him a lot while he was in the nursing home, spent hours by his bed.'

They were sitting on wicker chairs in the garden of Gilly's father's home. Brooding blue Welsh hills loomed in the distance, but the Powell garden was a tame oasis of lush green beauty and order. They could hear a chorus of barking approaching. 'Da and the dogs back with the post,' Gilly said unnecessarily. Everywhere Owen Powell went, he was surrounded by a yapping sea of dogs. Anthony could identify only three of them as distinct individuals. Gilly claimed there were only (only!) five, but Anthony would swear there were at least a dozen around the place at all times.

'Some of them aren't really ours,' Gilly had explained casually. 'Dogs like Da.'

The congregation of dogs that kept company with

Owen Powell wasn't the only oddity about him. He was, in fact, a full-blown British eccentric. He dressed like a shabby Lord Byron in peculiar, out-of-date clothing and everything he did was dramatic. He put Anthony in mind of Eugene Gant's father in *Look Homeward, Angel*. He was a loud, bull-necked, long-striding, roaring man. He drank vast amounts of Scotch, but never seemed drunk. Or maybe he was never sober. He could be raging theatrically about the immoral influence of television one moment and weeping at the beauty of a phrase in a poem the next.

Anthony found him fascinating, but exhausting to be around. At first he wondered how Gilly could stand to live with him, but he soon discovered that she was ideally suited to cope. She regarded everything her father did and said with a placid, offhand, almost maternal fondness. 'Now, Da, you're getting yourself in a dither,' she'd say with a soft, Welsh lilt in her voice and hand him a plate of biscuits or the morning paper or anything else at hand to divert his attention.

Owen obviously adored her even when he was raging against her. 'Speak up, girl! Where have you hidden my notes this time? You're trying to ruin me. I'll never get this damned book done if you keep on—'

'Your notes are in a pile on your desk, Da. Do you want sausage or bacon with your breakfast?' she'd reply calmly.

'Neither. I'm going to become a vegetarian!'

'That's nice, Da. Anthony and I will have the pork roast for dinner and I'll fix you some rice, shall I? The dogs can have the leftovers.'

'Rice? Rice! That's for coolies. Will you be trying to starve me to death while you fatten up those mongrels?'

'Now, Da,' she said, kissing him on the forehead and drifting off, humming lightly.

Owen looked after her, grinning.

There was a welcome respite from him every afternoon when he and the dogs walked to town to get the mail. It always took him a good hour or two and he came back

220

smelling of booze and regaling them with whatever news he'd picked up at the pub. His absence provided Gilly and Anthony with their only opportunities to talk quietly and privately.

'I'm sorry I wasn't able to get here in June,' Anthony said as the sound of barking grew closer.

'I'm sorry, too. The garden was at its best then,' she said. 'There are some nice things in September, but nothing like June.'

'I was coming to see you, not the garden.'

She looked sideways at him and smiled. 'But I *am* my garden.'

He could only stay five days as the time had been stolen from an already overloaded schedule. And now that he was finally there, he felt he'd been there for ever. He and Gilly were so compatible, so at ease with each other. As if he'd known her always.

And yet at other times he was aware of time racing by too quickly. They'd barely exchanged a few stolen kisses; there was practically no privacy. Owen Powell didn't seem to regard the difference between night and day as an important one. Nor did he have much concept of privacy. Sometimes he'd be clattering away at his old manual typewriter at four in the morning. Other times he'd stroll right into the small guest bedroom. 'Sorry, but those damned dogs have stolen my slippers again,' he'd say, walking past Anthony to search under the bed. There was no question of Anthony stealing to Gilly's room or she to his. The old boy and his army of miscellaneous canines seemed to turn up everywhere at all hours.

Yet, in an odd way, it was all right. This intense, compacted courtship was as stately and old-fashioned as their correspondence and Anthony rather liked that. Still, he had a proposal to make and he didn't want it interrupted by Owen and the dogs.

'Gilly, can we leave for the train early?' he asked her the evening before his departure.

'Of course. We can drive to Stonehenge, and I can leave you in Salisbury.'

'Steven and I "did" England years ago,' Anthony said the next morning when they got on their way. 'But we didn't go to Stonehenge.'

'That's a pity. I love it there. Of course, if it were up to me, I'd plant some nice perennial beds around those bleak rocks,' Gilly said with a laugh. 'Just to soften their edges a bit.'

Anthony's first view was the best. It was a gloomy, over-cast day and as they came over the last low rise the stones looked at first as though they were part of the gray sky, merely an unusual cloud configuration close to the ground, then the realization of what he was seeing struck him. 'Stop. Pull over,' he said.

Gilly did as he asked and smiled at him. 'I felt the same way the first time. I wanted to approach them slowly, with proper reverence. They are dear old things, aren't they?'

Anthony didn't speak for a moment. Then, finally, he said, 'But they're swarming with tourists.'

'Yes, they keep talking about roping them off so people can't touch them, but I hope it never happens. You have to put your hands on them and lean your cheek against them to hear what they have to say.'

They drove closer and stopped in a car park before walking a long path to the ruins. Fortunately, it started to rain in earnest as they got out and many of the tourists fled for cover. There were perhaps a dozen left to exam-ine the rocks with Gilly and Anthony. He liked the rain because it gave them an excuse to huddle together under the protection of their umbrella. He put his arm round her and could smell the sweet lavender scent of her hair.

'Magnificent,' he whispered.

She slipped her arm round his waist. 'When I'm here,' she said, 'I can sense the people who labored to build it. But I can't get quite close enough to them to ask why they did it. It would have been such a huge labor that there must have been a terribly important reason. The rock came from Wales, you know.'

They walked round the stones for a while, touching and staring, then went to stand outside the circle and look back. 'I have something important on my mind, too,' Anthony said.

She looked up at him, a knowing look in her eye. 'Do you?'

'I want to marry you.'

'Good,' she replied without hesitation. 'Yes. Yes, Anthony.'

It seemed too easy to be true. 'Now?' he asked.

She laughed. 'This minute? Standing here in the rain? Very well. I, Gilly, take thee, Anthony—'

'You're making fun of me?' he asked, cocking an eyebrow.

'Never, never.'

He kissed her long and hard and, in the process, dropped the umbrella. When she finally pulled back, smiling and breathless, fine red tendrils of hair were sticking to her wet forehead. 'Oh, Anthony Wentworth, you're a lovely, lovely man.'

'You still haven't answered me,' he said, wondering how long that drop of rain was going to hang from the tip of her nose before she noticed.

'I must look like a wet rat,' she said. 'Let's go back to the car.'

They ran. Halfway back, Gilly turned a giant circle, hands in the air, face tilted up to the rain. He stood watching her, thinking how ageless and childish she looked. She could have been the daughter of one of the ancient men who built Stonehenge. There was a primitive purity in her merriment that made a sob of joy rise in his throat. A sudden thought came to him as clearly as if somebody had actually spoken it.

I'll never be this happy again!

Pinning her down to a date wasn't easy. 'I promised to stay with Da to see this book through,' she said.

'He could do it without you. He always did before.'

'Yes, but I promised. And he's having trouble with this one. Don't be impatient, Anthony. We have the rest of our lives. He needs me.'

'*I* need you.'

'And you shall have me.'

'All right. When? How long until he's done with this damned book?'

'Next summer.'

'Next summer?' Anthony groaned. 'That's a million years from now.'

'Only half a million. Anthony, why don't you come over after Christmas. We could meet in London. We should – you know.'

His perplexity showed in his face. 'Should what?'

'Uh, be together.'

The light suddenly dawned. He took her face in his hands. 'You are the most wonderful Edwardian lady, Gilly. I don't need any proof that you'd be a good wife.'

She looked down, blushing. 'But Anthony, I don't know – I mean, I never ... well, I might not be any good at it, you know.'

'I sort of hope you're not,' he said, a dim memory of Betsy's shocking sexual expertise stirring in the back of his mind. 'I'll come back for New Year. But just to bring you a ring,' he said.

Pressure of work at Samaritan, which Anthony suspected Nina was exaggerating somewhat, kept Anthony from returning to Gilly until mid-February of the next year. He was relieved to be away from Samaritan for a while. The general upheaval in the US had infected the organization to some extent and he'd taken an unpopular stand that had raised hackles at the last board meeting before his departure.

'I've been getting suggestions that Samaritan take some sort of official stand on this whole Watergate business,' he said briskly as soon as the meeting was under-way, 'and I want to remind you that Samaritan is not and

224

never will be a political body. No matter what's going on in government, Samaritan has no view and will neither express nor in any way act on any view.'

'Come on, Anthony, you know Nixon is a crook!' Wayne said, leaping to his feet.

Anthony gave him a surprised, offended look. 'Wayne, you're not a member of this board and have no speaking privilege at this meeting. You're an observer, here only to make a report when I ask you to.'

Wayne's face flushed. 'Yes, sir,' he said meekly and sat down as stiffly as a knight in armor.

'But Anthony, the man's pathetic,' Rhys said. 'Have you seen him on the news? He looks beaten. Don't you think—'

Anthony was nearly as severe with Rhys. 'What I think of Nixon – or what you or Wayne think, for that matter – isn't a subject for this board or this organization. That's exactly the point I'm making. I've tried to be tolerant of everyone's enthusiasms. I've let portable televisions be put in the coffee lounges, even though we're probably losing hundreds of hours of work to people slipping in there to watch the hearings. I've endured tirades on both sides when I was trying to get money out of contributors. But I will not have Samaritan taking an official view. Do you all understand?'

'You shocked them,' Steven said later as the two of them sat impatiently in a long line at a gas station.

They were due at a fund-raising dinner, and Anthony was getting worried that they'd be late. He tapped his palms on the steering wheel and glared at the car in front of them with the odd-numbered plates that wasn't supposed to be here on an even-numbered day. 'What was shocking? You don't see the Red Cross or United Way issuing statements about politics. Why in the world should we?'

'That's not what I mean. You let Samaritan's board function with a minimum of interference most of the time. It's rare that you jerk their reins and remind them that

225

you're in charge. That's what shocked them. They probably should be reminded more often.'

'Sometimes I wish I could forget I'm in charge,' Anthony said wistfully. 'If I'd had any idea when we started this what a huge responsibility it would become –'

'– you'd have done it anyway,' Steven finished.

'God help me, I probably would have. But I'd have set it up so I had one month a year in a mental institute to get my brain unscrambled. Some of the things they come up with!'

'The bodyguard idea?' Steven asked.

Patty Hearst had been kidnapped two weeks earlier and Nina had suggested that Anthony have full time bodyguards to keep anyone from snatching him. He'd laughed it off when she first suggested it, but was appalled when she brought it up at the meeting and several others had taken up the standard. 'Nobody would want me,' he'd objected. 'I'm not that rich.'

'Maybe not in your own right, but you have control over a great deal of money that some bunch of nuts might want to get their hands on,' Faye's husband Charlie Brent said.

Anthony stared at him in amazement that he'd go along with this crazy idea. 'That could be so, Charlie, but I'm not having a couple of goons follow me around and that's that. No. I won't have bodyguards. That's final.'

'Bodyguards, for God's sake!' he snorted now to Steven as the gas station line inched forward.

'You need a vacation,' Steven said.

'Do I ever!'

'You're an island of grace and beauty,' Anthony whispered to Gilly.

Gilly giggled. 'How poetic.'

Someone behind them hissed, 'Shush.'

'Are you enjoying the play?' Anthony asked.

Gilly whispered, 'I've seen it before.'

'Let's go,' he said. She was already shrugging into her coat.

They slipped out of the Samuel Beckett play and got a cab to take them on a roundabout route back to the elegant little hotel that had once been a royal mistress's town house. Anthony had taken two suites that had a private staircase between. He'd made a point of showing it to Gilly and told her the amusing story of the time the King had been locked in from both ends. Then he moved along briskly to explain that Rhys, who had once stayed here, explored it himself and nearly met the same fate. Not very subtle, but he just wanted to make sure she knew about it without any pressure to avail herself of it.

After getting her checked in, he'd taken her to dinner and presented her with the ring he'd picked out after having looked at several hundred. It was an oval shaped emerald with a half-circle of diamonds on one side. 'The wedding ring is the other half circle,' he explained. 'I hope you don't mind that it's not a big, flashy diamond ring. I kept seeing green with your red hair.'

'I think it's the most beautiful thing I've ever seen,' she said, holding her hand out and admiring the look. 'It's perfect.'

'It's old-fashioned. Like you.'

'Coming from anyone else, I'd take that as an insult.' She leaned forward for a chaste peck of a kiss over the table, which stopped the English waiter who had been approaching them dead in his tracks.

They'd gone on to the first half of the play, then for a cab ride along the Thames, frigid and sparkling under a full moon. At eleven, they returned to the hotel. Anthony took Gilly to the door of her suite, but no further. They made awkward, uncomfortable small talk about their plans for the next day. They were going to visit Blanche and tell her about their engagement. Gilly asked what she should wear to meet his mother, which was silly because he didn't care in the least, and she only had the choice of what she'd brought along in her small suitcase.

'We'll leave around ten?' Anthony said, as if they were planning a business meeting.

'That will be fine. Fine. I'll be ready,' she said.

They leaned toward each other to kiss goodnight, missed each other's lips, tried again. 'Well, goodnight then,' Anthony said, feeling like a full-blown fool.

He went down to his room, cursing his awkwardness. He'd meant to make her feel comfortable; instead, he'd created a gauche, artificial mood that had temporarily turned them to strangers. He stripped, turned off the lights and got into bed. Tomorrow would be better. They'd visit Blanche – talk about artificial situations – make their escape from her, then maybe they'd go to Harrods or the Tower or something fun.

He was almost asleep when he heard the door to the stairway open slowly. 'Anthony?' Gilly said softly.

'Gilly!'

'Thank God!' she said with a breathy laugh. 'I had the most horrible feeling I might be sneaking into someone else's room. Where are you?'

'Over here,' he said, lifting the sheets to make room for her.

She slid into the bed and his arms.

His first thought was delighted amazement at how warm and soft she was. And then at how perfectly her full breasts fitted the palms of his hands. Gilly was eager, but shy. 'You'll have to show me what to do,' she said.

'You don't have to do anything unless you want to.'

'But surely—'

'Shhh.' He kissed her.

'We've got to go see your mother in a few hours,' Gilly said as light began to fill the room. 'How can I face her? Oh, Anthony, if I'd known how much I was going to like this, I'd have never let you out of my sight. Now I don't know how I'll behave myself for long enough to meet Blanche. Do we have to stay long?'

'No. Thirty seconds or so.'

She laughed and rolled over, snuggling against him. 'We ought to make it at least a minute.'

'Why don't I call her and say we'll come tomorrow instead?'

'I won't want to go tomorrow either. Let's get it over with, then we can stay here until an hour before your plane leaves. Oh, Anthony,' she said, sitting up, looking shocked. 'I'm a wanton. I probably always have been and didn't know it. Is that possible?'

'She doesn't approve of me,' Gilly said as they drove away from Leland House. Blanche had received them with aloof courtesy, accepted their announcement with ennui and spent half an hour complaining about her domestic staff.

'No, it's *me* she doesn't approve of. Here I am, this hulking American stranger who was dumped in her lap and identified as her son. It was a shock.'

'No more for her than for you.'

'Oh yes. Much more. I was proof of her husband's decades-long betrayal and deceit. And by the time she knew, he was gone. She couldn't bring him back and demand an explanation or even an apology.'

Gilly glanced sideways at him. 'You're very charitable towards her.'

'It's the best I can do, since I can't like her.'

'Anthony, that breaks my heart. You should have had a mother to love.'

He grinned at her. 'Don't pity me, love. I've had a great life. I grew up with Dad and the Prof and nobody could have asked for better family. I've got more money than I know what to do with. I've got a business I'm proud of and enjoy. I've got Steven and Nina and Rhys and, most important, I've got you. There's absolutely nothing else in the world I want. You can't feel sorry for someone as extravagantly blessed as I am.'

'Tell me about them, your Steven and Nina.'

'I can tell you about Nina easily: she's the perfect secretary. She doesn't have any life apart from that role. She works like a Trojan, never gets rattled, organizes me to within an inch of my life. But Steven's harder to explain. He's very complex. I've known him for years, but I don't understand him at all. He's a good man. Thoroughly, utterly good, but the goodness seems to exact a terrible price. I don't know why. Even when he's happy and laughing about something, I have the feeling there's a barrier, a sorrow or grief of some kind, between him and the world.'

'He sounds grim to me.'

'That's because I'm not expressing myself well. He's charming and witty. People are drawn to him like a magnet. He's bright and smart and he's my best friend.'

'Is he married?'

'No, even though he's so good-looking that women fall at his feet in droves.'

Gilly was silent for a minute, then said, 'Do you think ...'

Anthony knew what she was thinking. 'No, I'm sure he's not. I was in a bar with him once when a man made a pass at him. He reeled back like Queen Victoria meeting a flasher. It's the only time I've seen him completely flustered.'

'Will he mind about me? Since you're such close friends, will he feel I'm taking you away from him?'

'I can't imagine that he would,' Anthony said with false confidence. He'd actually wondered why Steven hadn't shown more interest in knowing about Gilly. He'd always assumed it was because he, Anthony, tended to go on about her to such a boring extent. But maybe there was the slightest element of jealousy. He'd have to make sure his marriage didn't jeopardize his friendship. Steven really was as vital to him as Gilly.

'How's your father's book coming along?' he asked to change the subject.

'Slowly. I sometimes think it's deliberate. To keep me there. But Da can't fool me. I know all his tricks. I've given him a deadline. The first of June.'

'Is that when we can get married?' Much as he hated the fact that her loyalty to her father was delaying them, he valued that loyalty and knew it would soon be transferred to him.

'Yes. Shall we make plans? Where, when, who?'

'Do you want a big wedding?' He'd never given any thought to an actual ceremony.

'I just want you and a big bunch of tuberoses.'

'I assume that's a flower?'

'No, it's a baseball team!' she said with a laugh.

'You really don't want a big-deal wedding?'

'No, but it's up to you, too. To tell you the truth, if I had my way, it would just be us, and Da, and Uncle Rhys and maybe the postmistress in the village church. And your friend Steven, of course. And I wouldn't wear white. I look dreadful in white. I'd wear green like my ring.'

'Then that's how it'll be.'

'Anthony, really? That would really be all right with you?'

He negotiated a tricky turn, then pulled off into a layby in the road. He took her face in his hands and said, 'Anything you want is all right with me, but especially this. I have to spend so much of my time being the public Anthony Wentworth, I want my wedding to be private and personal.'

She put her small hands over his. 'Oh, Anthony, what would we have done if we hadn't found each other?'

'It couldn't have happened. If I'd been an Eskimo and you'd been a harem girl, we'd have found each other. It was fated.'

Chapter Fifteen

'You've missed a comma here, Wayne,' Steven said, making a pencil check on the report he was proofreading.

Wayne leaned across the desk, turned the paper and looked. 'God, you're right! I've had three secretaries check this and they missed it too. Thanks. I'd hate to have given it to Anthony this way.'

'I don't think Anthony would have thrown you out for a comma.'

'No, but I'd have known I'd let him down. It has to be perfect.'

'He doesn't demand perfection, you know.'

'Yeah, but he deserves it. He gives so much to Samaritan, well, he ought to get as much back from us, I think.'

Wayne's devotion and enthusiasm had been a surprise to Steven. On the whole, a pleasant surprise. Considering that he was Betsy's oldest boy, Steven had had grave doubts about his character when he came to Samaritan. But he'd worked out well. He was bright, an obsessively hard worker, and imaginative. Most important, he was absolutely dedicated to Anthony. On the other hand, Wayne's devotion was only to Anthony and Samaritan not to the good works that were the object of both. That troubled Steven.

Then, too, rumor had it that he was a first-rate womanizer in his limited free time, but Steven tried to ignore that. Anthony's policy was that the organization had no right to interfere in its employees' personal lives, but neither did the employees' personal lives have any right to reflect badly on Samaritan. In other words, do what you want away from the office, but if you create an open scandal, you're out.

Steven wasn't sure he agreed with that, but he recognized that Samaritan was more than a cause, it was a modern business that had to be practical.

'Are you ready to go to Wales for the wedding?' Wayne asked. There was a boyish note of envy in his voice.

'Day after tomorrow,' Steven answered.

'Steven, do you think that this Powell person is good enough for Anthony?'

Steven almost laughed, but restrained himself with effort. 'This Powell person' indeed! 'I don't know Gilly Powell, Wayne. Never met her. But Anthony loves her. That's good enough for me.'

'I know,' Wayne said, failing to see the irony in Steven's reply. 'He talks about her a lot, but frankly I'm not comfortable with what I hear.'

At this Steven did laugh. '*You're* not comfortable? Wayne, it has nothing to do with you.'

'Steven, I'm serious. I know Anthony's trying to tell us what's so great about her, but it sounds to me like she's just a sort of housewifish frump. All this stuff about gardening and being so old-fashioned and quiet and all.'

'What if she is a frump? Anthony's marrying her, not you.'

'But Anthony *is* Samaritan. It's his life. He needs a wife who's part of it. To contribute. His wife needs to have money, social position, style.'

'She's Rhys Jones's niece, Wayne. You couldn't ask for better social credentials than that.' He realized as soon as the words were out of his mouth that they'd been a mistake. None of Betsy's boys had forgiven Rhys his unwitting part in their father's death.

'Rhys Jones,' Wayne sneered. 'Great credentials. A murderer for an uncle.'

'Let's not get into that again. Is that what you imagine you dislike about Gilly? That she's Rhys's niece?'

'It's a bad match, Steven. I don't like anything about it.'

'At the risk of being repetitive, it doesn't concern you, Wayne. Anthony's not asking your opinion or anybody else's. And you'd be making a huge mistake to let him know how you feel.'

'Yeah, I know. You won't tell him, will you?'

'I'm not a gossip.'

'No, I know you're not. Sorry.'

'Mr Packwood?' Steven's secretary said from the door. 'I'm sorry to disturb you. There's a woman on the phone who insists on speaking with you. I told her you were in conference, but—'

'Who is she?'

'The name she gave was Ellen MacLaughton.'

The mother of his son!

'Put her through,' Steven said. 'Will you excuse me, Wayne?'

Wayne, who'd planned to fish another report out of his briefcase while Steven talked, nodded and gathered up his work.

Steven waited until Wayne was out of earshot. He needed a few seconds to get a grip on himself. He took a deep breath and picked up the phone. 'Ellen?'

'Oh, Steven, I'm sorry I had to make such a flap—'

'Gary. Is this about Gary?'

'Don't panic. He had to have his tonsils out and there have been some complications. The doctor swears he's not in danger but I'm worried.'

'Where? Where are you?'

'California.'

'I've looked everywhere for you. Give me the city and hospital name.'

'Prospect, California. There's only the one hospital. Come to Sacramento. I'll have someone pick you up. Steven, I'm sorry. I didn't mean to alarm you. It's just that—'

'Ellen, hang up. I need to get a plane.'

Anthony was disappointed, but understood that Steven's son had to be his first priority. 'Steven, don't worry. From what you say she said it can't be too bad. If the doctor isn't worried—'

'Ellen wouldn't break down and call me unless she thought he was in danger of dying.'

'How long has it been since you've seen him?'

'I've never seen my son.'

'What? Never?'

'Not in person. Ellen sends pictures sometimes. But I haven't heard from her in two years. I hired detectives to find her, but they couldn't.'

'How old is he now?'

'Eighteen next Christmas.'

'What about her family? Wouldn't they help you?'

'There was only her father and he died some time ago. He was a writer and his literary estate is handled by a New York agent who refuses to reveal where he sends her checks. At least her father's books are still selling. You see them everywhere. I assume she's well enough off to take care of Gary. I send money to the executor as well. They're cashed by him and I have to assume he's writing checks back to her. But then maybe I'm just making payments on some agent's house on Long Island. I don't know.'

'God, Steven. What a messy thing. You should have told me sooner.'

'Why? There's nothing you can do.'

'I could have sympathized.'

'Thanks, Anthony,' Steven said with a weak smile.

He was met by a disreputable-looking man in overalls. 'You Packwood? I got the truck outside.'

'Are you a friend of Ellen's?' Steven asked as they reached the parking lot and climbed into a beat-up pickup truck.

'Naw, not to say friends. Do a little heavy work fer her sometimes,' the man replied. He didn't give Steven any more information, not even his name. He turned on the radio to its highest decibel. An hour later they arrived in a town that was little more than a cluster of shops at a crossroads. A mile beyond, there was a single-story building called simply 'Hospital'. The driver pulled up at the front door.

A woman pushed open the doors and ran toward him. 'Steven! It's all right. He's fine now. I'm so sorry I dragged you clear out—'

'Ellen?' he asked, surprised. The girl he'd known was slim, pale, arty and ethereal-looking. This was a lovely woman with a healthily rounded figure, tanned skin and a thick braid of dark hair circling her head like a tiara. She was wearing jeans, well-worn cowboy boots, and a faded plaid shirt.

'Have I changed so much?' she asked.

'I wouldn't have known you,' he said. 'Gary? How is he?'

'He's all right. I've made a fool of myself. It was a reaction to the anesthetic. I think there was a medical crisis, but by the time I knew about it, it was past. But Steven, when they brought him out of surgery, he looked so pale – as if he didn't *have* any blood. I was tired and just got hysterical. I feel terrible that I upset you.'

She led him into the hospital and down the single hallway to a room at the end. There, a slight seventeen-year-old boy who was almost a man, with straight, dark hair lay sleeping in a bed. He had round, pink cheeks. 'I hate for you to see him like this the first time. His face isn't usually so fat,' Ellen whispered.

'He's beautiful,' Steven said, his voice threatening to crack. 'You're sure he's all right?'

She nodded and tugged at his arm, indicating a man standing in the hallway. She pulled the door partially closed behind him and introduced Steven to the doctor who reassured him that Gary was fine. 'He's a bit old for this operation. It's easier when they're little, which is what I've been telling Ellie for years. But she wouldn't listen. She isn't one for listening much, but you know that.'

Steven felt an odd pang in his stomach. This man was obviously an old friend of Ellen's and he, the father of their child, was a stranger.

'You can take him home tomorrow if he gets plenty of sleep today,' the doctor was going on. He then proceeded to give Ellen instructions on food and post operative care.

Steven wandered down the hall and sat down heavily on a chrome and plastic sofa by the front door. There had been too many sensations too quickly to absorb. He felt exhausted by emotion. Mostly, now, he felt relief, but also an overwhelming perplexity. He'd known Gary's age, of course, and the pictures had shown him the boy growing up, so why was he so dumbfounded to discover that the baby he'd never known was very nearly a grown man?

'Steven?' Ellen said softly. 'Are you hungry?'

'I – no, I don't think so.'

'Well, I am. Let's get something to eat. There's a cafe in town.'

Ellen led him to her vehicle, a newish but plain brown van. There were hay bales behind the back seat. 'Just stay here and rest,' she said as she pulled up in front of a tacky-looking cafe with gas pumps out front. 'I'll get you a sand-wich.' She came back with a brown bag. 'There's a pretty spot to watch the sunset just up the hill. We'll eat there,' she said, backing out with brisk expertise. They followed a winding side road and pulled off into a gravel area that looked over the valley where the town and hos-pital lay.

She took the bag back from Steven and brought out square paper cartons of orange juice and waxed-paper-wrapped sandwiches. 'What is this?' Steven asked, sur-prised.

'Alfalfa sprouts and goat cheese on wholewheat,' she said, as if it were the most obvious thing in the world.

'And you eat it? Deliberately?'

'It's good for you. Try it, you'll like it.'

He didn't, but he discovered that he was hungry enough to eat almost half of it anyway. When they'd finished, Ellen said, 'Steven, I've got so much to say to you.'

'Oh?' he replied, biting back a more sarcastic reply.

'When this happened, it opened my eyes to a lot of things about myself and I don't like any of them. When I thought Gary might actually die – well, it just turned me inside out. I suddenly realized I couldn't have lived with myself if he'd died and you'd never gotten to know him. It would have been due entirely to my own selfishness. I was so young and wrongheaded when he was born, and I guess I'd grown up without ever bothering to go back and re-examine what I'd been doing all these years. I was punishing you for not loving me.'

'I'd have married you, Ellen. I begged you to marry me.'

'I know. But that made it worse, don't you see? You were willing to "sacrifice" yourself and marry me, as if I were some kind of nasty responsibility. That was worse than not loving me. So I guess I thought, in some stupid way, that I could *make* you love me by withholding Gary. It was stupid, and wrong.' She glanced up at him, trying to gauge his reaction, but Steven's features were frozen.

'I can't begin to apologize or to make it up to you. What I've done all this time has been enormously wicked.'

Steven cut off her apologies. She was right: what she'd done couldn't be made up for and certainly not with mere polite words. 'What have you told him about me?' he asked.

'That you're wonderful,' she said softly, embarrassed.

'No, I mean why does he think he's never met me. His own father,' Steven added, his anger shading the words.

'He's never asked. I didn't tell him anything. It's just been us, Steven. He didn't miss you because he never knew you.'

'Surely he's wondered?'

'I don't think so. He's a very unusual boy. Very accepting. Very forgiving. Very good. Like you, Steven. So much like you that it's eerie.'

Steven sighed with the pain of the lost years. 'He's almost grown up now.'

'But you must get to know him.'

'What makes you think he wants to know me after all this time?'

'He will. Believe me, he will. He's a loving, good boy. I thought maybe you'd stay with us for a while. A few days ...' Seeing his wary expression, she added, 'With him. Just you and him. I could go away if you'd rather be alone with him.'

Steven stared out over the valley for a long moment. Finally he said, 'Yes, I think I would rather.'

By morning, Steven had relented. There was no point in running her out of her own house. That would be pointless retaliation. Besides, he had a horror of finding himself stuck with a youngster who resented and disliked him in spite of Ellen's protestations to the contrary.

He met his son in the parking lot of the hospital the next day. He hadn't gone in with Ellen to bring him out, thinking it could be very awkward for everyone. Gary came across the parking lot slowly. Steven went to meet him. 'Gary, this is your father,' Ellen said, smiling warmly. 'I think you should probably call him Steven. Would that be all right?'

Steven nodded stiffly.

Gary smiled sincerely but very carefully, and said in a croaking voice, 'I'm glad to meet you, sir. You look just like I imagined.' It was too much. He started coughing. It made Steven hurt to watch.

'Don't talk. We've got all the time in the world,' Steven said. 'Here, you ride in the back so you can lie down.'

They got into the van and rode without speaking back up the road Ellen had taken the night before for their picnic supper. They passed the point where they'd stopped and kept climbing slowly as they wound through narrow, unpaved roads. Eventually Ellen turned off the road onto a driveway that was little more than a rutted track. She drove very slowly, to keep from jarring Gary.

Steven was surprised at the house. It was very rustic, but quite large, with a two-story central section and two single-story wings going back from each side to an apparent drop-off. There was also a barn and chicken coops and several other outbuildings as well as wooden enclosures. 'We raise goats and bees and sell the cheese and honey,' Ellen explained.

'Don't you have enough money?' Steven asked, thinking of all the cash he'd sent off into the unknown for her.

'We have more than we know what to do with, thanks to you and Dad's royalties. But I put almost all that away. We work because it's necessary to work, to have a reason for getting up every day. I only dip into the savings for Gary's schooling and emergencies. Like when the septic tank collapsed last year.'

'Phew!' Gary said from the back seat.

Ellen laughed. 'The average person might think goats smell pretty bad, but until you've had a septic tank open to the sky, you haven't smelled real stink. Honey, you feel well enough to get out?'

'Sure, Mom,' Gary said, his voice reedy and tired.

He slept most of the day and Ellen got busy catching up on her chores, so Steven had time to explore the house and grounds. Their home was unique and wonderful. Built and decorated in old Spanish mission-style, it was open, clean and simple. Most of the rooms had rough stucco walls with niches for vases and handmade rugs hanging everywhere. He discovered the source of the rugs when he came across a room at the end of one of the wings. It was practically filled with an enormous loom. The floors throughout were polished planks. The mission style had been abandoned across the back of the house, however. Instead of narrow slits in the thick walls, it was almost completely windows. Great sheets of glass from floor to ceiling gave out upon a breathtaking view of an untouched valley below and rugged hills across.

I could live here and be happy, Steven caught himself thinking and immediately quashed the thought. But it was the most peaceful place he'd ever been.

He set out to explore the outbuildings. One had big copper vats and wooden shelves filled with wooden boxes. Bits of wool stuck out of some of them and bits of dried plant materials from others. 'This is my dyeing shed,' Ellen said from behind him at the doorway.

'You make your own yarn for your weaving?' he asked.

'Most of it. I had sheep for a while, but they were a terrible nuisance and as stupid as breadsticks. I came to hate the silly things. Now I buy the raw wool and spin and dye it.'

'Do you sell the rugs?'

'I guess I'm going to have to someday. I'm about to run out of walls and floors. Come meet the goats. They're not a lot smarter than sheep, but at least they're more self-reliant.'

She gave him a tour of the barn, the chicken coop and the neat ranks of beehives. 'You're pretty self-reliant yourself,' Steven said as they started back to the house.

'Thank you. We are. But I don't know how I'll manage by myself when Gary goes to college next year. It's the only real disagreement we've ever had. He doesn't want to go. He's happy here and there's a part of me who wants to keep him, but I can't. He has to see some of the rest of the world. I'd be happy if he chose to live this kind of life, as I did, but he has to choose it from a range of possibilities, not because it's the only thing he's known.'

'Where has he gone to school so far?'

'The valley school, but he'd pretty well learned everything they had to offer by the time he was thirteen. I still send him, but I teach him myself and he takes correspondence courses from USC.'

'Is that where he's going to college?' *What a fool I feel asking questions like this about my own son*, Steven thought.

Ellen stopped at the boot scraper by the side door and started getting the muck off her boots. 'That's part of the disagreement. I want him to go to a big state university or an Ivy League school, just to broaden his horizons. He has his eye on a theological seminary about fifty miles from here.'

'A theological seminary? He wants to be a minister?'

'No, he just wants to furnish his mind,' she said. 'Get that mud off your shoes before you come in. I killed a chicken this morning,' she said over her shoulder. 'How do you like it cooked?'

The house had electricity, but few uses for it. There was no television or radio, except for the dusty short-wave for emergencies. There were a few electric lights, and a great many more kerosene lamps. But there didn't seem to be any of what Steven was looking for. 'Do you have a phone hidden somewhere?' he finally asked Ellen in the late afternoon.

She was stirring the chicken stew that was simmering on the vast, black wood stove. 'Only in town. Do you want me to drive you in?'

'I can find it, if you don't mind if I use your van.'

'Of course not. Anything here is yours to use.'

He drove into town, found a general store with a pay phone at the back and called Samaritan. 'Nina, this is Steven.'

'Steven! Is everything all right? Anthony's been calling every hour.'

'Fine. Everything's fine. Look, Nina, since I was going to be gone with Anthony anyway, can you do without me there for a while? Maybe a week or so?'

'Of course. You're staying with Ellen?'

'With Gary,' he corrected her.

She was eager to extract more personal information from him, but he didn't want to share it. He briskly sorted out business – a report that Rory was to look over before final typing, some calls his secretary needed to make for him. He tried to get away quickly, but she said, 'Wait!

Where are you? How do I reach you if I need to?'

'You can't. I'll call back in a day or two. Goodbye, Nina.'

He strolled around the general store. The goods in the front section were meant to snag tourists passing through. There were tee shirts, cedar knick-knacks and ceramic mugs. But the back of the store, where the locals shopped, had practical things. Steven debated with himself. To buy appropriate clothes would be an acknowledgement that he intended to stay. But on the purely practical side, he'd come away with only the emergency suitcase he kept at the office: a clean shirt, clean underwear and shaving tackle. No, he couldn't stay even a day more wearing a suit. He bought two pairs of jeans, three chambray work shirts, a pair of sturdy boots, underwear, socks and, because it struck his fancy, an old-fashioned red flannel nightshirt.

When he got back to the house dinner was ready. He changed into his new, more appropriate clothes and joined Ellen and Gary at the table. Ellen had fixed a pureed potato soup for Gary, which he sipped carefully but managed to put away a good deal of. She and Steven had chicken stew and dumplings. There were a lot of green and brown bits in it that Steven couldn't identify and decided it was wiser not to ask about. They tasted good.

Gary had come down to dinner in a red nightshirt like the one Steven had just bought in town. Ellen had changed from her work clothes into a pink cotton caftan caught round her waist with a brightly beaded belt. She'd even put on a touch of lipstick for the occasion. Steven was struck with how pretty and wholesome she looked. But his main interest was Gary. The boy, in the way of healthy youth, had recovered amazingly. The swelling in his face and neck had gone down. He had a lean, almost ascetic face. His outdoor life had made him rugged; his inborn nature had overlaid the ruggedness with something very gentle. 'You're feeling better tonight?' Steven said to him.

'Thank you, sir, yes.'

Steven held his hands up. 'Please, no more "sir" stuff. Is your throat still sore?'

'A little, but with God's grace, I expect it'll be nearly normal by tomorrow.'

Steven was surprised. Young people these days seemed to feel that mentioning God was tantamount to obscenity. It didn't seem like an attitude he would have got from Ellen. When he'd known her years ago, she was a belligerent atheist, but she'd changed in many ways. Maybe that was one of them.

'Do you go to church in the valley?' he asked Gary.

'No. But I attend services every day.'

'Don't be obscure, dear,' Ellen said, dishing up some more stew and dumplings for Steven. 'Gary has his own services. Out in the woods.'

'What religion are you?' he asked generally of both of them.

'I'm not anything and Gary is his own, aren't you?'

'Not quite. That makes me sound like some sect. Actually, I consider myself part of the universe, si— Steven. We all are, of course, but some of us are more acutely aware of it. It isn't so much religion as a sense of oneness with the Creator. But I have so much to learn.'

'That's why you want to study theology?'

'Mom told you? Yes, from my reading I believe all religions started with that sense of oneness, but the trappings and ceremony, not to mention historical circumstance, have obscured the original inspiration. What I want to do is study the organized religions, try to dig back to their origins and learn from them as they were originally intended.'

'To what purpose?' Steven asked bluntly.

Most people to whom Gary expounded his theory, including his mother, didn't want to hear any more than they had to. He'd never been asked this question. 'I'm not sure. For my own fulfillment, primarily. But also I hope to gain an understanding that I can share with others.'

'To proselytize?'

'No! Well, maybe. I think proselytizing serves a valid purpose, don't you? Most people are unaware that we are all seekers of truth. To have it handed to them whole is to serve them and God at once.'

'What do you know about most people, Gary? How many people do you know? Your mother, your neighbors, the predigested historical figures in your books. But what do you know, really know first hand, about stupid people, or wicked people, or people trapped in poverty – or wealth, for that matter?'

'Well—'

'Do you read newspapers, watch the national news? Have you ever met a Hindu? Or an old person in a nursing home? Or a crippled person? You've read a lot, but have you any real knowledge of how others live their daily lives? Their circumstances influence their thinking the same way your circumstances have shaped your attitudes.'

'But, sir, our isolation is what's allowed me the freedom for contemplation.'

Ellen started silently clearing their plates. Steven and Gary were both leaning forward across the table, their gazes locked – in interest, not antipathy.

'That's only partly true,' Steven said. 'Isolation encourages contemplation, but you can be contemplative in a New York subway, if you're inclined. Gary, I don't think you can understand or formulate anything that's theologically sound for anyone but yourself unless you have knowledge and experience with the rest of the world.'

Ellen passed behind Steven, put her hand on his shoulder for a second and squeezed it gratefully.

'So you agree with Mom?' Gary said. There was no resentment in the question.

'I agree with her, but for different reasons.'

'You've studied religion?'

'I studied to be a priest,' Steven said.

'Why aren't you then? A priest?'

246

Steven sighed. 'For a million reasons, but mainly because I turned to it for the wrong reasons. Maybe we'll talk about it someday, but right now we're talking about you. Tell me, what do you feel is the role of good works?'

'Excuse me, guys,' Ellen said. 'This could go on for ever. There's a poppy seed cake on the counter. Help yourselves if you want. I'm going to my weaving.'

They talked well into the night. They thrashed out the major tenets of the world's religions. Gary was exhausted, but refused to go to bed. 'I've never known anyone like you,' he said admiringly at one point. Steven finally insisted Gary go to bed at five in the morning and he himself lay wide awake for another hour thinking about this bright, intense boy who was his own child.

When Steven woke the next day it was noon. He helped himself to a slice of last night's cake, and eating it out of his hand went looking for Ellen. He found her in her dyeing shed, stirring a steaming pot with a wooden broom handle. 'Oh, you're finally up. Did you sleep well?'

'Did I ever. That's the most comfortable bed I've ever run across.'

'It's a goosedown mattress strung on a rope frame. That one in the guest room was an experiment that was so successful that they're all we have now. I'm not entirely opposed to everything modern, but I do think modern mattresses are the worst thing ever invented. Except maybe modern jeans. They're so stiff. Take those you're wearing off and put them in that pot over there. I'll soften them up for you.'

'What? Right now?'

'Of course. Who's to see?'

'I think I'll keep my pants on, if you don't mind,' he said with a laugh.

'Prude,' she said, smiling. 'Then make yourself useful. Pull that vat over and turn on the hose, would you?'

He helped her get her newly dyed material into the first rinse and soaked himself almost to the shoulders trying to help her wring it out. 'Don't you think a trip to a yarn store would be easier than this,' he said when they were finally done.

'Easier, but not half as much fun.'

'We're having fun? I didn't realize.'

'What a city slicker you are,' she said, taking his soggy arm and steering him toward the house. 'There's a nice flat rock out behind. It's always in the sun. You'll dry out there.'

The rock was a large slab about the size of a garage floor hanging partially out over the valley. Steven flopped down on his back, spreading his arms. 'Warm,' he said happily.

'That's the dangerous thing about it. I'm always afraid I'll fall asleep and roll off. Steven, about Gary, what do you think?'

She'd settled down crosslegged next to him. He rolled onto his side, propped his head on his hand and thought for a moment before replying. 'You've raised an incredible boy. He's very bright. Very sincere. And terribly naive.'

'Yes, and that's my fault. I love it in him. I've preserved it, always thinking there was plenty of time for him to learn about life outside our tiny circle. Now it's past time and he doesn't want to go.' She was nervously plaiting some long strands of grass that had grown up in a crack in the rock.

'Maybe that's not so bad,' Steven said. 'I've never known anyone so content. What a gift to have given him.'

'But you heard him – even his own ambitions, which aren't mine, can't be fulfilled here.'

'I think he knows that now.'

'If he does, it's thanks to you. You did a good day's fathering, Steven Packwood. Aren't you astonished at how alike the two of you are?'

'I do see myself in him. The hair, his chin.'

'I mean inside.'

'We're nothing alike, Ellen.'

'But you are. Your concern with right and wrong—'

248

'We might be interested in the same questions, but he'll find the answers. I never have. Even now, he's sure of the things he's sure of. And the rest, he knows exactly what he's asking. I haven't a clue.'

He'd rolled back and closed his eyes. He felt the shadow on his face a moment before the soft touch of her lips on his. He slowly put his arms round her, feeling the heat of the sun on her shirt and the firm muscles underneath. She was the first to pull away. 'That was just a thank you,' she said wistfully. 'You taste like poppy seed cake. I'm going to go see how Gary's doing.'

She got up gracefully and walked away. Steven watched her, thinking what a lovely shape she had. He ought to be in love with her; why wasn't he? If he stayed longer, would this sense of comfort and ease turn into love?

That night, Steven was awakened by her scent. A fresh, outdoor flower smell. He opened his eyes. Ellen was sitting on the edge of his bed. The moonlight from the window made her high-necked white granny gown seem to phosphoresce. Her hair was loose and fell in glossy combed-out braid kinks to her hips. He sat up and stared at her for a long moment.

She put her hand to his cheek. 'Steven, please let me stay. Just for a while. I want to be near you. You don't have to love me or even pretend. But I need you tonight.'

He knew it needn't go any further and shouldn't go further. If he asked her to leave, she'd leave. With the burden of guilt she bore, she wouldn't reproach him, not even subtly. But he also knew, as he inhaled her scent and felt the warmth of her hip against his thigh, that he wouldn't resist her. Couldn't resist her.

He took her hand, kissed the palm and reached out to embrace her. 'Ellen.' It was almost a sob.

He stayed three weeks. Twice a week he called in to the office, calmly put off Nina's frantic demands to know when he was coming back and where he was. But in his own mind, he wasn't so calm; he knew he had to make a decision soon. Would he stay here, sink into this simple,

249

peaceful life? It was tempting. Ellen was a comfortable, gentle lover, nurturing him as she nurtured her bees and goats and chickens with a relaxed, offhand sense that it was all very natural. She made no demands of him. Most important, he could spend time with Gary, talking, arguing amiably about theory, walking the hills and seeing nature through Gary's appreciative eyes.

On the other hand, could he give up Samaritan? Life at Ellen's farm was peaceful, but he was useless. Selfish. And Gary, at his urging, would soon leave the farm. At Samaritan he was doing good. He was worthwhile there, putting his life to use. Just as important, there was Anthony, whose friendship meant more to him than he could define or explain. Anthony exuded an air of power, of purpose, of virtue in its most practical sense that enveloped and drove Steven.

He tried to talk about it to Ellen. 'I want both and I can't have both,' he said.

'Come to bed,' she said.

'No, Ellen. I want to talk, maybe just hearing myself explain will make it clear to my own mind.'

She reached out to him, ran her hands up inside the back of his shirt and began gently caressing his back. He felt his body responding, as it always did, to her touch.

And that was when he suddenly understood. It was so simple he felt like a fool for not having seen it from the first. Ellen's appeal was to his weaknesses, the rampant sexuality that he'd always fought to control, his tendency toward intellectual laziness, his fear of facing his own conscience.

But his relationship with Anthony was based on his strengths, his virtues. That was an important key to why he loved Anthony and Samaritan. Ellen expected nothing of him and, with her, he *was* nothing. But Anthony expected him to be a hard worker, a virtuous man, a loyal friend. And with Anthony he was all those things. He was somebody – to himself and to others.

★ ★ ★

He dressed quietly in his city clothes, took only the bag he'd arrived with and left on foot at dawn. Before going, he wrote Gary a note, giving him his phone numbers and addresses at home and at Samaritan.

> It would be wrong of me to stay here now. I have to go while I still can [he wrote]. But I'm always available to you. More than that, I'm eager to hear from you and to be a part of your life now that I've found you. You're a good son. Please give me the chance to be a good father.
>
> With love,
> Steven

PART FOUR

1974-1980

Gilly

'King Arthur loved Sir Lancelot, and Queen Guinevere took kindly notice of him ... At this time Queen Guinevere loved Lancelot for his bravery, for his courtesy, for his fame, and for his lack of cleverness. She did not as yet want to change him, push back his untamed lock of hair, whip him with doubt and confusion and jealousy to keep her image glowing in his brain. She did not yet love him enough to be cruel to him.'

The Acts of King Arthur and His Noble Knights,
John Steinbeck

Chapter Sixteen

Steven and Gilly didn't deliberately avoid each other. Each, in fact, was mildly curious, if slightly antagonistic, about the other. But circumstances were such that they didn't actually make each other's acquaintance until the year after Gilly and Anthony married.

Anthony and Gilly had taken several unexpected trips after their wedding in June, one to visit her father in August when he claimed, melodramatically, and quite erroneously, to be having a heart attack; another in October to visit Blanche when she suddenly developed pneumonia and very nearly did die. In November Anthony decided they needed a pleasant vacation and took his bride to Bermuda.

During these months, Steven had been working harder than ever. Assiduous to the point of exhaustion, he'd courted contributors, prepared reports, grilled potential recipients of Samaritan's bounty and, between times, had taken his son Gary to visit a dazzling range of colleges.

'You're working too hard,' Anthony told him a few days before leaving for Bermuda. 'Back off and come meet Gilly. Dinner?'

'Can't. Thanks anyway. I have to work on some figures with Rory for a project I'm proposing. Something's not adding up right.'

'Gilly's dying to meet you,' Anthony said, not quite truthfully. Gilly had showed a disappointing lack of interest in meeting Steven. She seemed to feel that Steven was important to Anthony at work; she was important at home; and the division was, if anything, slightly unfair to her. Not that she complained; she was merely unable to disguise her boredom when Steven was mentioned.

But Anthony wanted them to be friends, and the first step in the process was getting them together.

As usual, there would be a meeting of the board of Samaritan in the New Year. Samaritan had two kinds of board members. There was a handful of full-time working members – Anthony, Rhys, Steven, Rory, Charlie, Faye and now Wayne – who met every week. They were augmented by prominent businessmen who lent their social, business and financial expertise and connections at a monthly meeting. Anthony felt it was important to make these others feel as close and involved in Samaritan as possible, even though they were not part of the daily workings. Hence, twice a year there was a week-away-from-the-office board meeting when the organization's work for the past half year was reviewed and goals were set for the next half. These meetings provided an opportunity for the twenty or so top people in the organization to socialize and relax together, and they were also a perk. A noble excuse for getting out of the Midwest for a week during the hottest and coldest parts of the year. The mid-winter meeting was usually held in some warm resort in the south, but this year Gilly had asked that it be held at Birches, the Connecticut estate Anthony had inherited from Max.

'But it's cold and bleak there in the winter,' Anthony had objected. 'They're used to being near a beach. They'll revolt.'

'Trust me, Anthony. If the house has half the potential you and Nina have led me to believe, it can be a lovely place to have your meeting. Let me try. If I'm wrong, I'll never suggest it again.' Anthony wouldn't have denied her anything and so, anticipating grumbles and complaints, he agreed. Gilly went a week ahead of him. 'Just to get a few things done,' she said, rubbing her hands in domestic anticipation.

When Anthony arrived, he was astonished. The house had always seemed merely a setting. A big place, convenient for business entertaining, pleasant in the summer; a big house with a few distasteful associations. But when he walked in the door that day, he was amazed at what Gilly had done with it. She'd made it a warm, welcoming home. The air smelled of cinnamon, oranges and the crackling fires that burned in every fireplace. There were handmade quilts on every bed, big fluffy towels in the bathrooms, bird feeders at many windows with winter birds flocking as if they were being paid. There were colorful afghans everywhere that invited visitors to take off their shoes and worries and cuddle up. Winter arrangements of poinsettias brightened dark corners. Fat, scented candles burned in bathrooms and on mantels and end tables.

She'd thought of everything to make people feel at home. The back hall off the kitchen contained a large assortment of all the warm outdoor clothing anyone might need: boots, mittens, woolly hats and heavy coats, and even some cross-country skis and poles, should anyone want to venture out for real exercise.

'This is wonderful, Gilly,' Anthony said. 'I expected this house to be dank and cold. You've worked a miracle.'

'It's been fun,' she said, snuggling against him. 'Come sit by the fire with me. I've got a stew cooking for our dinner.'

'Gilly, you're not thinking of doing the cooking yourself?'

'No, I've hired cooks, but not for tonight. It's just us tonight. The help arrives in the morning. Including Nina, who was determined to be here tonight. I nearly had to threaten to bar the door against her.'

'Is she making things difficult for you?'

'Not deliberately, She's just being herself. We've had a few subtle, feminine tiffs over areas of authority, but I can stand up for myself. Take off your shoes. Sit down. I'll be right back.'

She brought him a steaming drink made with wine and

spices and honey. He leaned back, stretched his stockinged feet toward the fire and sipped. 'Mmmm, good,' he said, putting his arm round her.

She had indeed worked a miracle, one that he couldn't fully explain to her. He'd spent a fair amount of time in this house over the years, but had never been able to erase the memory of meeting Betsy here. That encounter, a burden of shame and guilt, had haunted this house for him. And now Gilly, with her charming domesticity, had unknowingly banished the hateful ghosts. Gilly had made the house his – and hers. It was a fine and remarkable gift.

She was a gift.

The response as guests began arriving was gratifying. The revolt Anthony had predicted hadn't materialized, though there had been a lot of head shaking and mock shivering at the mention of going east instead of south for the meeting. Nina arrived the day after Anthony and the day before the rest of them were due. Even she, who was usually fairly oblivious of her surroundings, was impressed with the house and graciously gave Gilly her due. 'It's remarkable. I wouldn't have believed it was the same place. But I'm concerned about meeting space. I do wish you'd let me—'

'It's been taken care of, Nina,' Gilly said. 'Come see.'

The house had been built with a modest ballroom, which Max and Blanche hadn't needed. It had been closed off and ignored since Anthony inherited it. Gilly had seen that the room was cleared, cleaned and set up for their meetings. Around the walls were credenzas with the paraphernalia of business. Typewriters, a copying machine, notebooks, pens, a phone.

But it was the object in the center of the room that drew the eye. It was a huge, fully extended dining table that could comfortably seat twenty-six. Slightly oval, it was a work of art in mahogany with a wide parquetry border all round the circumference that was vaguely Celtic in design.

'Good God!' Nina said, gingerly approaching it.

'My father gave it to us as a wedding gift,' Gilly said, smiling at Nina's surprise.

Anthony had come in behind them. 'We have no idea where he got it,' he said. 'We suspect that even as we speak the National Trust is probably riffling their records trying to figure out how they misplaced something this big. Isn't it something!'

'Magnificent,' Nina said, gently running her hand along one edge. 'It must be very old.'

'The top surface is, but the legs are newer. Gilly had an antique dealer out to look at it. After she revived him from a deep faint, he went away babbling hysterically and never really told her anything except that the legs are Sheraton. Unfortunately, we couldn't find enough matching chairs to go round it, but I don't suppose anyone will notice.'

When Anthony awoke the next morning, the bustle had began. An army of maids were doing a last minute dust-polish-vacuum. Smells of cooking were wafting up from the enormous kitchen that had been designed for entertaining. Workmen somewhere outside were attacking a newly fallen limb with chain saws. He could hear Nina outside his door giving orders to the new secretarial assistant she was breaking in. ('She doesn't break them in, she breaks them down,' Steven had said of her previous victims.) Anthony stretched luxuriously, enjoying the sense of other people working, then got up and showered, shaved and dressed. He hoped Steven would get here soon. He needed a dose of his wry wit.

As Anthony came down the steps, he met his brother Rory coming up.

'Glad you're doing this,' Rory said gruffly. 'The travel expenses were down thirty per cent. Would have been more if you'd let me charter that bus to bring them all from the airport.'

'We've been over that. It would have meant everybody had to arrive at the same time and it would have inconvenienced several of them.'

'What the hell if they are inconvenienced? They work for you, don't they?'

'Rory, you should have been a prison warden,' Anthony said.

Rory's lips twitched in an almost smile. 'Now, about the food, I gave Gilly a budget—'

'I'll bear the cost of the food. I told you that.'

'And I told you it's a legitimate business expense. There's no reason you should. If you're intending to take it as a personal tax deduction, I should warn you—'

'Rory, come in and relax. I'm paying for the food and I have no intention of tangling with the IRS about it. End of discussion.'

Later, when he ran into Gilly, who was refreshing the hothouse flower arrangements in the ballroom, now renamed the boardroom, he said, 'If you'd known about Rory, would you have still married me?'

She pulled a fading rose out of an arrangement. 'Let's just say I might have thought about it a little longer.' She smiled at him. 'He's always set things up with the hotels you stayed in, hasn't he? He has the silly impression that I'm another hotel manager who needs to be whipped into shape.'

'I'm so sorry.'

'Don't be. I'm not fragile. You've met my father. If I can cope with him, I can cope with anybody. That includes Rory. And even Wayne Graves.'

'Wayne? Has Wayne given you trouble?'

'Not yet, but he doesn't like me.'

'What? Has he said anything—'

'Hold it! Don't go all chivalrous. I shouldn't have mentioned it. Wayne has never said or done anything offensive. I just sense that he'd like to.'

'I'm sure you're mistaken.'

'Perhaps I am,' she said, giving him a quick kiss. 'Now, I've got a lot to do. You hang around the front door and greet arrivals.'

Rhys was the next to arrive. He was awed by the state

of the house and went into raptures over the strange table. Faye and Charlie came an hour later and were followed by a flock of executive secretaries kept in formation by a handful of Rory's financial people. Wayne arrived just behind them with his brother Harry in tow. 'Anthony, I hope you don't mind, but Harry's interested in joining us when he graduates this spring. He won't come to the meetings, of course, but I thought ...'

This was improper procedure, even though Anthony was pleased that another of his nephews had an interest in Samaritan. Wayne had only been appointed to the board of directors a month earlier. Several of the other directors had been inclined to reject Anthony's suggested promotion on the grounds of Wayne's youth and brashness. Still, even those who most disliked him had to admit that he was a hard worker and had excellent connections with a whole new generation of potential contributors.

'Glad to see you again, Harry. I don't believe you've met my wife, Gilly. Gilly, if you can find somewhere to squeeze Harry in, I'd like a quick word with Wayne.'

'I'm in trouble, aren't I?' Wayne said when the others were barely out of earshot.

'It was rude of you to invite a guest without asking your hostess.'

'I tried to call Nina yesterday, but I couldn't get—'

'Nina isn't your hostess. Gilly is.'

'But I thought since it was business—'

'This is Gilly's home.'

'Yes, of course. I really am sorry. What a social klutz!'

'Wayne, if this were a purely social week, I'd be very happy to have Harry here, but it is, as you pointed out, business.'

'I'll tell him he has to leave. Anthony, I'm sorry I screwed up this way.'

'I'll take care of it.'

Harry was easily the most likeable of Betsy's boys. Short and chunky, he looked as cuddly as a teddy bear and had a warm, easy personality to go with his appearance. Now he was embarrassed, but understanding. 'I told Wayne it wasn't right for me to come, but he kept harping on me, saying how much I'd like everybody. I shouldn't have let him talk me into it. I'll get my things out right now.'

'There's not that much of a hurry,' Anthony said. 'Are you really interested in Samaritan, or was that part of Wayne's sales pitch?'

'Oh, I certainly am.'

'I'm glad to hear it. Let's do this: you stay today while everybody's arriving. You can leave in the morning. Then write and tell me about how you see Samaritan and what role you might have. Send along transcripts and all that. I'll take a look at it all.'

'Thank you. I don't want any special consideration.'

'You won't get any,' Anthony assured him.

'You jerk! You made an ass of me,' Harry said later to Wayne.

Wayne paced the room. 'It would have been all right with Anthony. It was that bitch Gilly who made him throw you out.'

'He didn't throw me out. He just gave me the opportunity to slink away unharmed, which is more than I deserved. And you're wrong about his wife. She was real nice. Anyway, he hauled you offside before she could talk to him.'

Wayne put his hands to his head dramatically. '"She was real nice"? Jesus, Harry, have you fallen for her too?'

'I haven't fallen for anybody. But she seemed like a nice lady.'

'Have you forgotten that she's Rhys Jones's niece?'

'Can it, Wayne. Who gives a shit?'

'You should, for one. That old bastard killed your father, in case it's slipped your mind.'

'Don't you ever get tired of harping on that?'

'Tired of it? We're talking about our father being murdered!'

'Killed,' Harry corrected.

262

'Yeah, killed by Rhys Jones. Whose niece has gotten herself in bed with Anthony.'

'Wayne, you wear me out. Let's go look at the stables.'

'There aren't horses anymore, I asked.'

'Let's go anyway. Once we get there, there'll at least be a horse's ass.'

Gilly slipped away to her room to take a little break from smiling. She was pleased at the way it was going so far. This house was perfect for entertaining. That was what it was built for. But it had apparently always been left in the hands of decorators, a breed of individuals she didn't approve of. They never had any aim except to impress, and often shock, people with their own precious cleverness. All too frequently, cleverness amounted only to outlandishness – colors and textures that jarred the soul, sculptures that were downright ugly and sometimes dangerous to get near, vast blank spaces setting off a single object which usually didn't deserve the attention.

To decorate a home you needed first to know what the people who lived in it needed and then make sure every item in it conformed to those needs. A home could be warm and cozy, as this one was now, or simple and natural to blur the edges between indoors and outdoors. Or a home could encourage harmonious family living. That's what she'd do with the Kansas City house when they started having children. Adequate child-scaled furnishings mixed with the adult tables and chairs, plenty of low table space for games and jigsaw puzzles, accessible drawers for crayons and toys. When they started having children.

She'd been disappointed again this month. But then, they'd only been married a little over half a year. It wasn't unusual to take longer than that to get pregnant. It didn't necessarily mean there was a problem. There couldn't be. It was too important to them both to have children. Gilly herself was born to mother, but more vital was Anthony's feeling about family. You'd have thought having two families, his biological one and his adopted one, would have been more than enough for anyone, but Anthony had a need to be surrounded by 'his own'. Witness the fact that he'd made that dreadful nephew of his, Wayne Graves, a board member. Anthony said it was because he was so clever and hardworking and loyal. Well, maybe so, but there were a lot of young men that qualified on that score. Wayne Graves was pushy, arrogant and had a lecherous look that Gilly distrusted. Anthony was a good enough judge of character to recognize all this in Wayne if he hadn't been blinded by their blood connection.

Still, Gilly had no intention of interfering in Samaritan. If Anthony needed her as hostess or window-dressing, she was more than happy to comply, but she had little interest in the organization itself aside from the fact that it was worthwhile, and Anthony's obsession with it illustrated his fine, strong character.

But whether she liked Wayne or not, it was crucial for her to get along with him. She wouldn't have any part in a feud, however subterranean, that upset Anthony. Now there was another nephew on the scene. Harry Graves. Then there was also this Steven person to cope with yet. It was truly critical that she make friends with him – if he ever showed up. The butler had passed her a message about a delayed plane and Anthony was fretting about his friend.

A crisis in the kitchen took her out of her reverie and back to the front line of hostessing.

The first duty of a hostess, Gilly felt, was to make her guests feel comfortable and relaxed, and they couldn't feel that way if the hostess was in a dither. So Gilly ruthlessly repressed the memory of the scene that had just occurred in the kitchen – smoke and tears, a bad combination – and was smiling and calm when the first of her guests began to gather in the huge living room. A groaning buffet table was being set up in the next room, but she resisted the temptation to so much as look over her shoulder to see how it was going. When the guests had all come down and the dinner was in full swing, Gilly stepped into the front hall to catch her breath and relax for a moment. 'You must be Gilly,' a voice from above said.

She glanced up at the man coming down the stairs. 'You must be Steven Packwood.'

'I'm sorry I was late arriving.'

'I'm sorry I missed you. Anthony told me you'd arrived, but we had a ham turning to cinders in the kitchen and a caterer's girl having hysterics.'

They stood for a moment, assessing each other. He was every bit as good-looking as everyone had told her, but Gilly was wary of men like this who were too good-looking. They tended to be even more arrogant and self-centered than beautiful women. They were also often quite stupid, having always been able to dazzle people with their appearance without the need of substance behind it.

'Have I got egg on my tie?' he said, smiling.

'What? Oh, I'm sorry. I was just trying to weave together the friend Anthony had talked so much about with the reality of the person. What a silly thing to say,' she added, unaccountably flustered.

'Not at all. So am I,' he said frankly.

'And what do you think? Do I match my description?'

'Entirely. You're quite beautiful.'

Gilly didn't know what she had wanted him to say, but this wasn't it. The way her thoughts had been running, it was nearly an insult.

'Thank you,' she replied stiffly.

He caught the blast of ice and wondered what the hell he was supposed to say to her. Beautiful women always liked being admired, didn't they? 'You've done wonders with this house,' he said, casting wildly for suitable small talk.

'Do you think so?'

Steven bit back the impulse to say, 'I wouldn't have said so otherwise,' and replied, 'Yes, it seems like a different place entirely.'

'You've been here many times before?'

'Since my childhood.'

Well that puts me, the newcomer, in my place, Gilly thought and suddenly recognized that she was being over-sensitive. He might not have meant that at all.

'Ah, you've found each other,' Anthony said from the doorway. He strode forward and put an arm round each of them, forcibly drawing them closer than they had any desire to be. 'This is great. I can't believe you two have never met before.'

'I was telling your wife how nice the house looks,' Steven said.

'Hasn't she done wonders for this place? She's a marvelously talented woman, besides being gorgeous.'

Gilly wanted to wriggle away. She was hating this, him bragging about her, especially about her looks, as if he could convince his friend that she was worthwhile. As if he *had* to. 'If you two would excuse me, I need to check with the caterers,' she said, making her escape. She noticed Anthony's disappointed look, but couldn't help herself. She'd meant to get along with his friend, but had felt massively uncomfortable around him. Perhaps if she got a fresh start at it later?

She kept a surreptitious eye on Steven Packwood for the rest of the evening and found him too polite, too charming, too good-looking, too perfectly dressed. She also noticed, and disliked, how attractive the rest of them found him. Nina, previously all business and efficiency, absolutely fawned on him. Wayne trailed him around like a puppy, hanging on his every word. Even her Uncle Rhys treated him as a respected elder, though Rhys was the older. Worst of all, Anthony was at Steven's side more than he was at hers. At least with Anthony, Steven reciprocated the attention and affection. That was one point, one very small point, in his favor.

She started observing how people treated Anthony and how they treated Steven and she didn't like the difference. Everyone was friendly to Anthony, in a sense they were too warmly friendly. It was very casual, not respectful enough for her taste. But they treated Steven with a hint of deference. Just a hint, but it was there.

'You look tired, honey,' Anthony said when she finally came to bed late that night.

'A little,' she said, turning her back so he could undo the zipper of her dress.

'It was a lovely party, Gilly,' he said, kissing her shoulder as she slipped the dress off. 'And you'll get to rest tomorrow when we start our meetings.'

She turned and smiled. 'Just who do you think is going to be running around behind the scenes making sure you have plenty of coffee and meals ready when you take breaks?'

'But you hire people for that,' he said, perplexed. 'What would you have to do?'

'Oh, Anthony, you are *so* naive,' she said, kissing his nose. 'May I sit in on some of the meeting if I get some time?'

'Sure. But you can't talk.'

'What would I have to say?' she said.

Anthony wasn't the world's most perceptive person, but he recognized thin ice when he was hurtling across it. Trying to change the subject, and making a poor choice, he said, 'I'm glad you finally met Steven. You liked him, didn't you?'

Gilly just smiled and headed for the bathroom. He heard the tiny clink of her hairpins as she removed them and dropped them into the little silver bowl he'd given her to hold them. Then she brushed her teeth, seemingly for ever.

'You do like him, don't you?' he pursued the subject when she finally emerged, wearing a sheer pink nightgown, her hair loose.

'I hardly got to know him,' she hedged.

'Gilly, you didn't like Steven! Why on earth not?'

'If you must know, I didn't like the way everybody kowtowed to him, including you.'

'What are you talking about?'

She got into bed and snuggled against him. 'Anthony, everybody's very nice to you, but they treat him differently. More respectfully. I didn't like it.'

Anthony put his arm round her. 'Gilly, everybody knows me. They're just more comfortable with me.'

'But they ought to know him just as well. He's been with Samaritan as long as you, hasn't he?'

'Sure, but Steven's hard to know. Nobody, not even me, understands him. You can never tell what he's thinking. I can, better than most, but even I'm surprised sometimes. Gilly, I want you to like him. It's important to me. Just take some time, get to know him better. Do that for me, will you?'

Gilly would normally have agreed mildly to his request. But she was very tired and feeling pressured. She said snappishly, 'Why does it matter if I like him? Isn't everybody else adoring him enough? Including you.'

Anthony pulled back so he could look in her face. 'Gilly, if I didn't know better, I'd think you were jealous! You're not a jealous person normally.'

'That shows how little you know me. I'm a very jealous person.'

'Honey, there's nothing to be jealous of. Steven and I aren't in competition.'

'But I am,' she admitted. 'I don't want you to love anyone but me.'

He hugged her fiercely. 'That's silly. Flattering, but silly.'

She buried her face in his chest. 'Oh, Anthony. I'm sorry. I'm just rattled by trying to make this meeting so perfect. I got off on the wrong foot. I'm going to like your friend Steven. I know I am. Please forgive me for saying such awful things.'

In spite of Anthony's obvious lack of enthusiasm about having her sit in on the board meeting, Gilly decided she would do just that. She'd got up feeling nasty and guilty about her jealous outburst regarding Steven. Surely it had been her own strained nerves that led her to such unhappy observations. Watching the board meeting for an hour or so would give her a fresh opportunity to watch them all in action without being expected (or even allowed) to take part.

She gave them an hour to become immersed in their business, before quietly slipping into the room. Anthony saw her, but she made a shushing motion with her finger to her lips, and he let his attention go back to Rory's financial presentation. Within a few minutes she was sorry to see that he'd apparently forgotten she was there. After a while, however, she became interested in what was going on; not so much the content of the discussions, but the social dynamics of them. Nobody was the least shy about disagreeing with anybody else, nor was anyone blasé. While it was all very civilized and business-like, there was a constant shifting of loyalties within the group. They were going over expenditures category by category and that was where the disagreements came into play.

Rory felt that money spent on medical research was too high. 'There are plenty of other organizations in this area. There's duplication of funding and effort though we try to avoid it.' Faye agreed with him with some vehemence, so did Charlie. But Rhys, Wayne and two other directors disputed this and gave impassioned arguments for their views. Anthony stayed out of the dispute and simply moderated. Steven also kept his views to himself.

Rory also criticized the amount of money and time spent on helping a failing community hospital. This time Faye disagreed with him. 'There is a definite need which no one else is able or willing to fill,' she said.

Charlie took up Rory's view. 'But there should be a lot of others involved. The AMA could have taken a stand and didn't. The city council should have given the necessary tax breaks and didn't.'

Steven said, 'Saying they should have isn't productive. The fact is they didn't and wouldn't.'

'Steven's right,' Faye said. 'Wishing won't make anything so.'

'But actions can,' Rhys said. 'If we'd spent more effort educating and informing the other groups that had it within their power to help, there might not have been the need for the money we provided.'

'That's true on a lot of fronts,' Wayne said. From the way a few of the directors glanced at each other, Gilly judged this was something of a hobby horse of his. 'If we could just lobby—'

Anthony cut him off. 'As a non-profit organization, we're expressly forbidden by law from lobbying. You know that.'

'Bad choice of word,' Wayne said. 'Not lobbying, informing, educating,' he said, using Rhys's words, but failing to give credit. 'We need to do more of it. Let the politicians and power groups know just what's at stake.'

'Sounds like lobbying to me,' Anthony said, frowning.

'Not legally,' Wayne argued.

'Wayne, we observe the spirit as well as the letter of the law. To do otherwise is to court legal action and possible disaster for Samaritan.'

'Still—'

'I'm not through speaking,' Anthony said firmly. 'As you know, I consulted with a number of attorneys when I set this foundation up and drew up guidelines for our range of activities based on their advice. Our educational services are provided to the public, not to politicians or power groups who can influence legislation. If you want to dispute those guidelines, you'll have to present detailed arguments in writing. If you want to research the question in your own time and on your own money, I'll consider entertaining your suggestions within the agenda at some future date. But I warn you, I'm unlikely to approve any change.' He didn't need to remind them that he, not they, had the power to make the decision.

Gilly was stunned. She'd never seen this aspect of Anthony, though she realized she should have suspected it. A man doesn't run a business or foundation as large as Samaritan without being able to take full control when necessary. Still, it was heady stuff, seeing him in action this way. She glanced at Wayne, waiting to see his reaction, hoping he'd continue to argue and thereby get himself into more trouble with Anthony.

Instead, he grinned and saluted. 'You win, boss,' he said with a laugh that combined respect and resignation.

The tension was broken.

'Rory, continue,' Anthony said.

Gilly watched for a little longer, then slipped from her seat at the back of the room and drifted over to check that there was still plenty of fresh coffee. Steven came up as she was quietly stacking a few dirty cups on a tray to take back to the kitchens with her. 'Let me help with that,' he said, taking the tray from her.

'Aren't you needed in there?' she said as she closed the door behind him.

'The next item on the agenda is a pet project of Faye's that went way over budget. Rory will be rude. Faye will be livid with outraged dignity. Charlie and three of the honoraries will take her part, four will take Rory's. Anthony will let them all rave for a decent interval, then come down on everybody, summarize the flaws all around and ruthlessly move on.'

'And how long will it take?' she asked, smiling.

'Just long enough to have one cigarette with you,' he said, setting the tray down on the kitchen counter. The caterer's assistant in charge of washing up took it from him. She dropped a dishtowel, which he stooped to retrieve for her, inadvertently reducing her to blushing confusion. Gilly was reminded of Anthony telling her about Steven's 'automatic niceness', as he called it.

'I don't smoke, but I'll sit with you,' she said, leading him to the main living room. 'Can you always predict what's going to happen in the meetings?' she asked.

He lit a cigarette and stood, stretching, in front of the fireplace. 'Not always. But usually with Wayne and

271

Faye. But sometimes there are surprises.'

'Was what happened to Wayne just now a surprise?'

'It certainly was for him. I knew it was coming sooner or later. Anthony likes to give people lots and lots of rope, but he never loses his grip on the end of it. He doesn't mind reeling them in when it's time.'

'He was wonderful,' Gilly said simply.

'He always is. I'm glad you know it.'

'Why would I have married him otherwise?'

Steven shrugged. 'I've never had the faintest idea of what women see in men or want from them,' he said with such wounded perplexity that Gilly sensed it was the absolute truth.

'I think I could like you, Steven,' she said, matching his honesty.

'I'm afraid you're going to have to,' he replied, smiling. 'We're lashed to the same oar.'

Chapter Seventeen

Gilly's winter reception at Birches was such a huge success that Anthony decided in future both of the annual meetings would be held there as long as she was willing to tolerate the invasion. Gilly happily agreed, assuming that before long she would have babies to occupy her time and wouldn't wish to hostess the meeting. In the meantime, she enjoyed the role. But as time passed, getting pregnant seemed less and less likely. Month after disappointing month passed. After a year of trying, Gilly started visiting a round of gynecologists, who all told her the same thing: she'd never have a child of her own. Faulty fallopian tubes, they said. She underwent several painful, humiliating medical processes to correct the problem, but they were expensive failures. By their third wedding anniversary, she finally admitted to herself that she'd never give Anthony a son of his own.

She hated this knowledge. Mothering was what she was *for*. She agonized for herself and for Anthony, never realizing that he was upset for her sake much more than he was for his own. Several times he almost blurted out that he suspected he already had a son, Martin Graves, but stopped himself in time, recognizing that this would cause her further distress.

She brought up adoption, but Anthony showed no enthusiasm and she felt little herself. She didn't just want to have children; she wanted to swell with pregnancy, experience childbirth, feel a nursing infant suck at her breast. She wanted it to be Anthony's baby and hers, to have her eyes, his hair. Adoption would have given her children to raise, but this was not the whole of what she wanted.

She tried to resign herself to childlessness and gave her efforts, instead, to being the best wife possible. She planned ever better meetings for Anthony's board. Twice a year she was in her glory. She planned social activities for the summer and winter meetings, hiring swimmers for a synchronized swimming demonstration one summer in the refurbished pool, arranging horseback riding, moonlit dinner dances and leisurely croquet games. One winter she arranged for a hayride and another time forced everybody outside for a snowball fight that was talked about for years.

Between times she gardened with a vengeance. She personally kept up both the Kansas City and Connecticut estates' gardens, traveling back and forth once a month throughout the year. Anthony insisted that she have help with the heavy work, but Gilly turned over the compost piles, raised the seedlings, and put every new plant in place precisely where she wanted it. She regarded hired gardeners in the same light as professional decorators. Every Christmas their mail was thick with seed catalogs which she lovingly put away until after the winter board meeting. As soon as the meeting was done, sometimes even before the last guests had gone, she settled in to study her new catalogs.

That's what she was doing after this, her third, winter board meeting. As usual, she and Anthony had stayed on in Connecticut for a week and this year Steven had agreed to be their house guest. Over the years he and Gilly had grown friendly. Gilly was about the only person in Samaritan who was not awed or intimidated by his brooding intensity. She even made fun of him. 'Uh-ho, Steven's dreaded conscience has kicked in,' she'd laugh when he suddenly went silent and thoughtful. And he'd laugh at himself, something he'd never done much before knowing her.

She understood now that, far from being self-satisfied, he was deeply troubled by his failure to live up to incomprehensible standards he set for himself. The other factor that won her over to him was his clear adoration of Anthony; that, above all, formed a bond between them. They both respected Anthony's simple clear-sightedness, his ability to make good, brisk decisions without agonizing. Gilly could lose a week's sleep over whether the paint for a wall ought to be a mauve-pink or a salmon-pink. And Steven, she claimed, was eternally troubled over how many angels could dance on the head of a pin. They admired Anthony's ability, when wrong, to apologize sincerely without wallowing – something Steven was particularly prone to do. And Steven often expressed to Gilly his envy of both Anthony's and Gilly's ability to stop worrying about things they could do nothing about. Even Anthony's one great failing, his inability to see the flaws in his family, was endearing to them, although it sometimes drove them mad.

Gilly got up and showed a catalog page to Anthony. 'What would you think about a bank of this hemerocallis to the south of the gazebo?'

Anthony put down his newspaper and glanced at the page, not sure which picture she meant. 'At this place or the Kansas City house?'

'Oh, Anthony, I despair of you. We don't *have* a gazebo here.'

'We don't? What's that wooden thing behind the stables?'

'That's a tool shed, you dolt,' she said, kissing the top of his head. 'Steven, what do you think?'

She showed the picture to him. Steven abandoned the book he was reading and appeared seriously to consider what she was showing him. 'Too much orange,' he declared. He didn't know or care anything more about plants than Anthony did and wouldn't recognize a gazebo if it sneaked up and bit his ankle, but he had more skill at pretense, which Gilly saw through but found charming.

'I think the two of you could live on the moon and be happy,' she said with mock disgust.

'Is anybody hungry?' Anthony asked. 'How about buzzing over to that new McDonald's?' Gilly rolled her eyes.

'We could bring you back something if you don't want to go,' he offered.

'If there's anything worse than a Big Mac, it's a cold Big Mac. You two go. I'll fix myself a sandwich here.'

Anthony and Steven put on their coats and boots and set out in the small pickup truck Anthony had bought to keep in the country because it reminded him of his boyhood on the ranch. He wasn't entirely happy with it, however, because it wasn't beat-up enough. 'I'd like to put a gun rack in the back window, but I'm afraid the neighbors would take up a petition,' he said as they started out.

'How are your plans for your trip coming along?' Steven asked. Anthony had taken off no time at all the previous year and Gilly had insisted on a vacation to Portugal the coming month. There were some gardens she wanted to see and she said he needed a rest.

'My plans? Are you kidding? Gilly plans and I do what I'm told. I wish you'd change your mind and come along.'

'The last thing the two of you need along on a second honeymoon is an extra body.'

'Don't be silly. You'd give Gilly another person to carry packages and plants. The last trip we went on, I rode home with a tree in my lap. The stewardess was nice about it. Offered the thing a glass of water.'

When they were slowly sipping their second cups of coffee, Steven said, 'Are you putting Rhys in charge again while you're gone?'

'Wayne's been nagging you to nag me?' Anthony asked

'Of course. He's obsessed.'

'Am I wrong to trust Rhys?'

'No. He's a good man. Not inspired, can't quite see the whole picture for his interest in the arts, but when he's in charge he works himself to the bone, and with Nina to watchdog him, he does a fine job.'

'So what's Wayne's problem with him?'

'You know the answer to that. The golf incident.'

'Steven, that was six years ago and it was an accident!'

'Wayne was at a very impressionable age. Instead of getting it all into perspective, he's exaggerated it in his own mind. He's forgotten what a bastard Ned was and has made him a sainted father in his memory.'

'Is that all there is to his dislike of Rhys?'

Steven paused, then decided he owed Anthony the truth. 'Not entirely. He thinks you favor Rhys because he's Gilly's uncle. He seems to think she pushes you into it.'

'That's crazy. Gilly never interferes in Samaritan.'

'Everybody but Wayne realizes that. Don't worry about him. He grouses behind the scenes but still believes you can do no wrong. You're a combination of Ned and God in his mind.'

'What a combination!' Anthony said, laughing. 'God can't be happy with the pairing. Well, Wayne's going to have to accept it. I've decided to give Rhys a power of attorney as well as informal authority this time.'

'How come?'

'Because the last time Gilly and I tried to get away I was tied to the phone the whole time. Rhys was making good decisions, but had to keep getting my official approval every time somebody wanted a damned box of paperclips. It cost a fortune in long distance, nearly ruined our trip, and made it twice as much work for him. Remember that child who needed the dialysis machine and nearly died because of our delay? We can't have something like that happen again.'

'You're right. But a power of attorney is a powerful document.'

'I've talked to Athalon about drawing it up. It'll be limited to the affairs of Samaritan and also limited to the length of time I plan to be gone. Rhys wouldn't abuse it.'

'I know he wouldn't. Anthony, look at those bird feeders in the window of the hardware store over there. I don't think Gilly's got one like that. Want to pick up one for her?'

'Sure. Better that than taking back cold french fries.'

Anthony's plans for escaping Samaritan for a month went badly awry at the last moment. He went into the offices the morning of their planned departure to sign over authority to Rhys and clear up a few odds and ends, but was met by a distraught Nina. 'I just got a call from Mrs Jones. Rhys is in the hospital. He complained of stomach pains all night and they think they're going to have to take out his appendix.'

'Hell! What do I do now? Where's Steven?'

'His secretary is looking for him.'

Faye came into the office just then with an armload of papers. 'Anthony, Rory's giving me trouble over some expense reports. Could you ask him— What's wrong? You look mad.'

Anthony repeated the message Nina had given him. 'I've promised Gilly a real trip – no phones, no business, no interruptions.'

'Then I won't bother you with my problem. Just let me know if I can be of any help,' she said, slipping away.

Steven arrived a few minutes later, looking as upset as Anthony. 'I just got a call from Ellen. A bunch of hippies staged a protest in town and the police scooped them all up, including Gary because he looked like them. He'd just gone in to get some goat medicine and the police won't turn him loose.'

'Everybody's falling apart on me! Shit!' He explained about Rhys.

'Can you delay your trip for a couple days?'

'God, no! I wouldn't dare. Gilly's made a million plans. She's counting on this and she deserves it. I've made her a promise and I'm going to keep it. I'll figure something out.'

'I can't let you down like this. I'll take charge and I'll work out something—'

'Steven, go bail your son out. Get out of here. You're in my way.' He had to practically shove him out the door by brute force.

The light on his phone blinked. Nina wouldn't put anyone through lightly while this was going on. He knew it must be Gilly. Putting on a bright, unconcerned voice, he said, 'Hi, honey.'

'What are you still there for?' she asked. 'Aren't you coming home?'

'What's the rush? The plane doesn't leave for four hours.'

'Anthony? There's something wrong, isn't there? We're not going to get to go.' Her voice trembled with disappointment.

'We *are* going. It's just a little hitch. I'll have it settled in half an hour.'

He hung up and buzzed Nina. 'Find Faye. I want to talk to her.'

Twenty minutes later the power of attorney had been signed over to Faye. Anthony was extremely uncomfortable with it. Not because he doubted Faye's abilities and integrity, but because it had all been done in such a rush without time to think things out and weigh alternatives. He knew that Steven, if consulted, would have argued strongly against the appointment. But Steven would have insisted on tearing himself in half between his son and Anthony.

He hated being rushed. And he hated ignoring Steven's advice, even when Steven hadn't been offered the chance to express it. But it was necessary, unavoidable and *done*.

Gathering up a few reports he hoped to sneak past Gilly and read during their trip, he got ready to leave. 'Nina,' he said, handing her a handwritten list. 'Here are the few itinerary items Gilly was willing to share with me. I don't know where we'll be the rest of the time.'

'Couldn't you call in and let me know each time you reach a new destination?'

'No, I can't. I don't want to. I'm entitled to a month off.'

'You've given authority to Faye?' she said with forced blandness.

'Yes, I have. I don't suppose you trust her either.'

It was a challenge, but Nina never wilted before one. 'No, not for a minute. I think—'

He put his hands up. 'Pardon me, Nina, but I don't want

to know what you think just now. I don't want any more opinions. I'm going on vacation and *I'm going to have a good time, dammit*!' He ended with a growl. 'Don't you dare call me for anything short of a fully-fledged disaster.'

'If you say so,' Nina grumbled, flipping angrily through a stack of file cards as if it were interfering with her work.

It was a second honeymoon, but far better than the first. They knew each other well now. Nobody was straining to impress anyone. The boundaries and rules had been set long ago. Gilly knew just how far Anthony could be pushed on shopping before he rebelled. He knew her 'tilt' point on golfing. She didn't make him tour gardens and he'd given up nagging her anymore to try scuba diving.

She'd set aside three or four days each week for planned tours or activities, the rest of the week to be spent just sleeping, eating, making love, and watching sunsets from balconies. After the first week, Anthony imagined that he could actually feel himself getting younger. They enjoyed the kind of restful happiness that only a judicial mix of wealth and love could create.

They celebrated his thirty-first birthday by drinking far too much wine and eating too much cake in bed during a long, rainy day. 'You know, young people used to adopt the motto that you can't trust anyone over thirty,' he said late that night, only slurring his words a little. 'It sounded pretty good to me then. Now, however,' he said, making a dramatic gesture that almost unbalanced him, 'I've decided thirty is pretty good and here I am thirty-one. I know a hell of a lot.'

'What do you know?' Gilly said sleepily. She licked some white icing off his ear. She'd put it there a little earlier for some reason that now eluded her.

'I know I love you.'

'But you knew that before you were thirty.'

'True, true,' he said. 'Are you happy, Gilly?'

'So very happy.'

'Is there anything you want?'

'No, except—'

'Except what?'

'Only, it would have been nice if Steven were here.'

'Here!'

'Not in bed with us, silly. I mean on the trip. Wouldn't you have loved to have seen him on one of those little donkeys we rode up the hills.'

The image struck Anthony as unbearably funny. 'That would have been great and he'd have gone crazy at the sight of you.'

'Me? Why?'

'Trying to stay on the donkey, hold down your skirt against the wind, hang onto your hat and purse and give orders in mangled Portuguese at the same time.'

'It wasn't *that* funny.'

'It was and I'm afraid it'll lose a lot in the telling.'

'And I suppose you'll tell him about me falling off the dock that time, too?'

'Wouldn't pass up the opportunity for all the money in the world.'

'Then he's going to hear all about what you looked like when you discovered you'd been eating squid and didn't know it.'

'You wouldn't.'

'I would. I might even make up some details to make it a better story,' she said smugly.

Anthony was suddenly sober. 'I miss him too.'

The next day they set out for a small village that had a public garden Gilly was dying to see. It was one of the few places on the list Anthony had given Nina, so he wasn't entirely surprised when they checked into their hotel and the manager said, 'Mr Wentworth, a messages for you. She come by telephone. Much ringing.' He handed Anthony a veritable sheaf of fluttery pieces of paper.

'Anthony, what's wrong? Is it Blanche?' Gilly asked.

'I don't know. They're from Nina.' He was concerned. She'd understood how important it was that he was not to be disturbed. To have left all these urgent messages, it must be something very bad. 'I have to call her.'

'I know. Of course you do.'

Gilly and an army of bellhops – barefooted village boys – took their belongings upstairs while Anthony commandeered the manager to help him get a telephone line to Kansas City. It was a good half-hour of multi-lingual wrangling before he finally heard Nina's faint voice.

'Nina! Anthony here. What's wrong?'

'Thank God! Anthony you have to come back this minute. It's terrible. It's Faye—' There was a drawn-out crackle of static.

'Nina? Nina! I can't hear you. Shout.'

'Faye's taken over. She's fired Rory, thrown out the board of directors and put in a dreadful man, a Joseph Fiore, as her second-in-command. He's cleaning Samaritan out.'

'She can't do that,' Anthony said, wondering if Nina had gone crazy.

'She can and is. She's flapping that damned power of attorney in everybody's face. Athalon's frantic because he wrote it, not knowing you'd scratch out Rhys's name and put hers in. She's filed for divorce from poor Charlie, says she's going to marry this Fiore scum. Anthony, you have to come back. Right now.'

'Athalon can't find a way to stop her while I'm getting there?'

'No, you'd have to sign a retraction document and it can't get back to Kansas City any faster than you can.'

'Where's Steven?'

'On his way. This all broke loose yesterday. I called him right away when I couldn't get you, but he has no legal authority to contradict her. Only you can do that.'

'Shit! This is all my fault,' Anthony said. 'I trusted her. I trusted her!' It was a cry of anguish.

'Fault doesn't matter. Fixing it does, if it's not already too late,' Nina said brutally. 'I have a chartered plane waiting at an airport that I believe is about thirty miles from you. It will take you to Lisbon. I'll have a car sent for you and do what I can here in the meantime.'

There was another crackle of static and then a long hum. Anthony hung up the phone. Gilly was standing by him. She put her hand on his shoulder. 'I heard,' she said. 'Nina was talking loud enough for everybody in town to hear. I'll get the bags back down.'

'Honey, I'm sorry to do this to you.'

'Anthony, you dolt. I know what's important and what's not. Besides, this way you'll feel guilty and have to bring me back when this is all settled.' Then she added in her practical way, 'You better go to the bathroom before we leave. You never know when you'll get another chance.'

'You know, the Prof told me,' Anthony said.

'Told you what?'

'That I'd be betrayed by the woman I trusted most. I thought he meant you or Nina and that was so clearly ridiculous that I didn't pay any attention. But I've never forgotten. It was nearly the last thing he ever said to me. He was right.'

'Have you got those documents retyped for me?' Faye asked.

'Not quite yet,' Nina said. 'I'll have them done this evening. I'm very sorry, but my typewriter broke down and I couldn't find another with the same typeface, so I had to start over,' Nina lied. The completed documents were in the bottom drawer of her desk.

Faye had annexed Nina's skills just as she'd taken over everything else of Anthony's at Samaritan. Nina had been walking a fine line, trying to pretend to co-operate with Faye so she herself wouldn't be tossed out on her ear and lose her inside position. At the same time, she was subtly thwarting her as much as possible.

'I don't have time to wait. I have a dinner engagement.'

'I'll stay until they're done and bring them to you this evening, if that would be all right?' Nina offered innocently.

'Oh, very well, but you're going to have to do better in future, Nina, if you're going to stay with me.'

What a laugh, Nina thought bitterly, in another day or two at this rate Samaritan would be dismantled entirely. The documents Faye was waiting for were the dissolution papers. She'd planned it well, Nina had to give her that. For the first two weeks Anthony was gone Faye had gone along as innocently as a baby, but planning furiously behind the scenes. Then a couple days ago, she'd called a board meeting and announced that the directors were all being dismissed, Rory fired, all funding canceled and the organization would be dissolved. Thank God she'd overlooked one thing – a press announcement. If she'd thought of that, the whole thing would be public knowledge and Samaritan really would be wrecked.

It still might be. If Faye got an opportunity to sign and notarize the dissolution papers before Anthony returned, it would all be over. Anthony's dream would be flushed away by this vindictive bitch, Nina thought. Faye had arranged a meeting with Athalon for ten o'clock the next morning; the flight Nina hoped Anthony could catch was due in at eight. There was only a two-hour margin of error. Anything could go wrong. If he missed the plane, if it was late, if traffic was unusually bad – the possibilities made Nina's stomach hurt.

She had to get that damned power of attorney away from Faye. But of course Faye was hanging on to it for dear life, never letting it leave her side. She carried it around with a bunch of other papers in a lizard-skin briefcase that was never out of her hand. She'd made and handed out a bunch of copies, but they weren't valid legal documents, Nina didn't think. She'd have to check with Athalon, but if she could get the original away from Faye, there'd be a delay while the legality of a copy was argued out. And that delay might be what Anthony needed.

'Faye, give me your address. You've moved, haven't you? I'll run the documents by at ten. Would that be a good time?'

'Oh, all right, but make sure you're prompt,' Faye said. She scribbled an address and swept out of the office, the lizard-skin briefcase tightly in hand.

Nina picked up the phone and dialed. 'Mother? I need

your help. I'll pick you up in fifteen minutes.'

Mother and daughter arrived at the door of Faye's apartment at ten on the dot. Faye opened the door just a crack, apparently hoping Nina would hand her the documents and go away.

'Faye, dear,' Lillian Smith said, pushing ever so gently at the door. 'Nina mentioned that she was dropping by and I begged her to let me come along. I haven't seen you for ages, although I correspond with your mother frequently. I know it's late, but we'll only stay a few minutes.' She pushed her way past Faye. 'Oh, what a very lovely place this is. Small, of course, but I understand it's only for a short time.'

Faye looked angry, but she'd been in awe of Mrs Smith all her life and old habits die hard. 'Would you like some tea?' she asked resentfully.

'I'd adore that,' Lillian said, ensconcing herself firmly in the deep armchair.

Nina was visually scouring the apartment. She finally spotted the lizard-skin briefcase sitting on a small table just next to the door to the kitchen. She couldn't touch it, much less rummage through it without being seen while Faye was so close. She held up two fingers – plan number two – to her mother. Plan one would have been to ask to use the bathroom in case the papers were in the adjoining bedroom.

Faye came back with a tray with teacups. 'I'm sorry I can't ask you to stay long. I'm exhausted,' she said, setting the tray down with a thump.

'I don't suppose you have any lemon, do you, dear?' Lillian asked.

Faye started to rise from the seat she'd taken on the sofa. Nina leaped up. 'Sit down, Faye. I'll find one. Mother's so anxious to visit with you.' She crossed in front of Faye, glanced back to confirm that she wasn't being watched, and scooped the briefcase up as she passed. She set it on the kitchen counter and got a lemon out of the refrigerator.

As she came back to the living room, she smiled a little.

Her mother, bless her for her brains and cunning, had positioned herself in a different chair, one facing the kitchen doorway. '... so, I told Blanche that maybe next year I could get over for a visit. What do you think is the best time of the year to go? You've been to see her a number of times, haven't you? Oh – Oh, no. OH MY GOD!' she ended on a hideous shriek, clutching her chest.

Faye jumped up. 'What's wrong, Mrs Smith, what's the matter?'

'Oh, God, it's her heart!' Nina screamed. 'I knew this would happen if she didn't take her medicine.'

'I'll call an ambulance,' Faye said.

'No, she's got her pills on her someplace. Find them, I'll get her some water!'

Faye had to lean over Lillian Smith to go through her pockets and purse, which she was clutching in her lap. That put her back to the kitchen. Lillian thrashed around in agony, making it even harder for Faye to search.

Nina ran into the kitchen, flung open the briefcase, now handy on the counter and started frantically flipping through the contents. There! A file folder marked 'POA'. Thank God Faye was well organized. Nina jerked the paper out, smashed it into a ball and stuffed it into her bra.

'Mrs Smith, you must tell me where your pills are!' Faye was shrieking from the other room.

Nina set the briefcase back on the table where it had originally been, ran a glass of water and tore back into the living room. 'Oh, God, how stupid of me! I've got them,' Nina said, pulling an unmarked bottle full of plain aspirin out of the pocket of her dress. She stuffed one into her mother's mouth. Lillian was now lolling back in the chair, seemingly semiconscious. Nina forced her to take a sip of water.

'I'm calling an ambulance,' Faye said.

'No, wait a moment. Mother hates a fuss. I think she'll be all right now.'

On cue, Lillian opened her eyes and said weakly, 'Nina? Faye? Oh, I'm so sorry.'

They nursed her along for a few more minutes, giving

her sips of water and watching her recover. 'I'm taking you straight to the hospital, Mother. You scared me to death that time. Faye, will you help me get her to the car?'

They lifted her slowly, Lillian letting her knees go weak and rubbery. Nina hoped Faye couldn't hear the paper in her underwear crackling as she moved. It was hard to keep an invalid's slow pace when she wanted to run like hell. Finally they got Lillian into Nina's car.

'I'm so sorry, Faye dear. Please don't tell your mother about this. She'd worry about me,' Lillian said in a soft, quavering voice.

Nina started the car and sped off before Faye could reply. She turned right three blocks later, pulled over to the curb and stopped the car. She leaned over and hugged her mother fiercely. 'You were wonderful!'

Lillian shook her off, and raised her hands, trying to sort out her mussed hair. 'That's the most embarrassing thing I've ever had to do,' she said stiffly. Then she turned her face to Nina and smiled broadly. 'But I was wonderful, wasn't I?'

Chapter Eighteen

Nina started trying to reach Athalon at dawn. His wife, sleepy and angry, curtly told her John had gone to St Louis to take a deposition the evening before and she believed he was coming straight to the meeting from the airport. Nina didn't know whether she had solved the problem by stealing the power of attorney or not. And she wouldn't know until the showdown point. Faye was to meet Athalon at ten o'clock in the small meeting room just off Anthony's office. Nina had a few people there waiting. Steven, grim and silent with helplessness, was present, as were Rory, Wayne, and Charlie Brent.

Wayne kept pacing and muttering. While he was even worse than Anthony when it came to blind family loyalty, he'd been forced to choose between his loyalty to his Aunt Faye and his devotion to Anthony. There was no question which side he had to come down on. Faye had played a complicated, nasty trick that threatened the very essence of Anthony's greatness. She had to be stopped. But Wayne had consulted with several lawyer friends who told him that there was nothing he could do. He didn't know exactly what he was doing here, but Nina had called him at eleven the night before and demanded his attendance, dropping veiled hints that something interesting might happen.

Charlie Brent looked like he'd been run over by a truck. He was pale, nervous and had dark circles under his eyes. Nina felt a twinge – only a twinge – of guilt at having him there. But she needed interested witnesses, in case it went her way. And she wanted to make certain that Charlie, for his own sake, knew just what was going on. She suspected he was so besotted with Faye that he'd go crawling back to her if she so much as crooked her little finger. If they managed to save the organization, Charlie would want to remain a part of it. That meant his break with Faye had to be absolute and complete.

Nina got them settled with coffee and called the airport to see if Anthony's flight was in. She got an idiot clerk on the phone who couldn't figure out what plane she was talking about. There wasn't time to wait for someone more knowledgeable. She hung up and went back to the meeting room.

Faye swept in at five minutes to ten. She took a quick glance at the group that was assembled, and laughed. 'You must think I'm going to waste time throwing you out. It would give you, perhaps, a fifteen-minute reprieve. Well, it's no go, folks. If you want to stay and watch the end of your precious Samaritan, I don't care. In fact, it'll make it a bit more fun for me.'

Steven leaned forward. 'Faye, what the hell are you doing this for?'

'Come on, you may be an awfully lofty thinker, but you're not stupid. You know why.'

'I want to hear you say it just the same.'

Faye's sweet face turned ugly. 'Revenge, asshole. Revenge, money, power. All those things a goddamned monk like you pretends you don't understand.'

The door opened and John Athalon came in, scowling. Nina leaped up to meet him. 'John—'

'Later, Nina.'

'I just want a word—'

'It'll have to wait. I want to get this over with. I have another appointment.'

Nina stared at him in amazement. He was obviously angry, but why was he taking it out on her? Had he gone over to Faye's side? Was he trying to rush them on her behalf? He knew she'd contacted Anthony and that he was on the way. Why wasn't he helping her stall Faye?

Faye sat down and took the dissolution papers from her briefcase. She spread them out for Athalon's perusal. He glanced at them, not even reading them carefully. 'This looks fine,' he said. 'Sign them and we'll have Nina notarize them. You are a notary, aren't you Nina?'

Nina nodded, stunned.

Faye signed with a flourish, glancing round the table with a victorious smile when she finished. She shoved the papers across the table toward Nina.

'We'll need a copy of the power of attorney,' Athalon said.

'You have a copy,' she snapped.

'You mean this?' He took a paper out of his own brief-case.

Faye glanced at it. 'Yes, of course.'

Athalon was all innocence. 'But this isn't valid. It's a copy of an original that hasn't been filed with the court.'

'Filed?'

'Filed. Registered with the county court as a binding legal document. Surely you filed the original after you made this copy.'

'Me? That's not my job. You're the lawyer.'

'Yes, but I'm not *your* lawyer. It wasn't my responsibility.'

The atmosphere of the room had changed. Hope was in the air. Nina sighed with relief. Athalon had known all along what he was doing. He hadn't stopped her, but he had slowed her down. Wayne was smiling tentatively. Steven's eyes glittered. Rory was leaning back in his chair, hands in the pockets and a satisfied smirk on his face. Even Charlie had perked up and was leaning forward.

'Then I'll file the fucking thing,' Faye said. 'It shouldn't take more than an hour, should it?'

'Depends on traffic,' Athalon said.

Faye opened her briefcase, pulled out the file marked 'POA' and whipped it open. She goggled at the empty folder. Frantic, she dumped the contents of the briefcase on the conference table. 'It's here. It just got out of—'

She looked up slowly at Nina, realization dawning. 'You bitch,' she said slowly, poisonously. 'You lying, thieving bitch!'

The men were perplexed, having no idea what had gone on between them.

Faye whirled on Athalon. 'She stole it. She brought that old prune of a mother over who faked a heart attack, and Nina stole the power of attorney. I want her arrested for theft. Right now. I'm calling security!'

She spoke while running for the door, which was flung open in her face. Anthony stood there, rumpled and frazzled with lack of sleep, his face white, reaching for the doorknob.

'Thank God!' Nina said, sinking into a chair and quickly pulling out a handkerchief to blot away the tears of relief that were starting in her eyes. She'd never cried in front of anyone and wasn't about to break the tradition now.

'I've already called security, Faye,' Anthony said coldly. 'They're here to escort you out of the building. You are never to enter it again.' He grabbed her arm in a grip that must have hurt, but she was too furious to notice pain. 'I never want to see you or hear from you again, Faye. Ever. Do you understand that?'

She drew back and spat in his face.

Anthony looked for a moment as if he were going to strike her, but instead he roughly shoved her out of the door and into the grip of a security officer who'd been standing just outside. Wiping his face with his sleeve, he said, 'Put her out. She's to take nothing with her. Not so much as a scrap of paper. Frisk her if you have any doubts.'

Faye was screaming a stream of obscene abuse. Anthony slammed the door in her face and stood resting his hands against it for a long moment before turning back to the rest of them. 'John, have you prepared a retraction document or reversal or whatever it's called?'

Athalon was grinning from ear to ear. 'I have, but there's

no need for it. The original has disappeared.'

'Disappeared? What do you mean?'

'Faye claims it was stolen. I don't know the truth.' He looked at Nina and said firmly, 'And I don't *want* to know the truth.'

Anthony looked from one to the other of them. 'You'll all explain this later, I assume. In the meantime, Rory—'

Rory was on his feet, making notes on a pad in his hand. 'I'll get to the bank right now and—'

'— put a stop payment on everything,' Anthony finished. 'You'll have to be there every morning for at least the next couple weeks until all the checks have cleared and you've passed approval on the legitimate ones.'

'Fiore's taken a lot of the records. It would be better to close all current accounts and open new ones.'

'No, the payees might find out there's been some hanky-panky with the accounts and ask awkward questions. Start new accounts for everything written from here on, but keep the old ones open and monitor them. Did he fire your whole staff?'

'All but the secretaries.'

'How many of them can you get back by this afternoon?'

'Most. Maybe all.'

'Work on that as soon as you're through at the bank.'

As Rory left, Nina said, 'Anthony, hold it. Aren't you going to do anything about Faye?'

Athalon spoke before Anthony could answer. 'I'd strongly advise against going after her.'

'Why?' Nina demanded. 'She tried to destroy Samaritan. She can't be allowed to get away with it just because she wasn't entirely successful. She and Fiore are embezzlers.'

'Nina's right!' Wayne said loudly.

'I'm sorry, but she isn't,' Athalon said calmly. 'What Faye tried was immoral, but not illegal. She had a power of attorney that allowed her to dismantle the organization. That wasn't what it was intended for, but she had the legal right.'

'But you said yourself that it wasn't legal since it hadn't been filed,' Wayne argued.

'I wasn't entirely truthful,' Athalon said.

'Jesus! You really put yourself on the line to get a little time, didn't you?' Wayne said.

'Yes, and if it all came to court I could be sued for malpractice and probably disbarred for knowingly giving erroneous information. Nina could be put through hell for burglary. Anthony would look like a complete fool for having given Faye the authority. Even the greenest new attorney could keep us all in court on one charge or another for years and years. There are a stupendous number of technicalities and countersuits possible here.'

'And being in the courts would mean being in the press,' Anthony said.

Athalon nodded. They all subsided.

Anthony went on, 'An organization that solicits and manages enormous amounts of other people's money must be above reproach in the way they are seen to handle it. We might gain some sympathy over being tricked this way, but we – I, more accurately – would be shown up as every bit as stupid as I was. Nobody would ever trust us with a dime again. We must not wash our dirty linen in public and endanger the welfare of Samaritan.'

'But the money they took out,' Wayne said, not willing to see Faye let off so easily.

'It was my fault,' Anthony said. 'When Rory gets a total for me, I'll find a way to make it up out of my own income and savings. Samaritan will *not* suffer because of my blind stupidity.'

'This is terrible,' Charlie said, almost in tears. 'It's my fault. If I'd been a good husband—'

'Charlie, shut up,' Anthony said, but not nastily. 'Faye's an evil person. Steven's always known that, but you and I and Wayne had to see it for ourselves to believe it. We've all been fooled for years and we've all had our eyes opened.'

'Still, I'm helping you make up the loss,' Charlie said.

'So am I,' Wayne echoed.

'No, it's my doing. If I'd accepted the responsibility in the first place, Anthony wouldn't have been forced to turn to Faye,' Steven said.

'Oh, for Christ's sake!' Anthony shouted. 'Will you all stop trying to hog the guilt? What's the matter with you?' He stopped, put the heels of his hands to his eyes for a second, then went on more calmly, 'You all contribute enough already and I'm the one who let this happen,' he said. He was sagging with exhaustion.

'How long since you've slept?' Steven asked.

'Oh, I don't know. A year or so, I think,' Anthony said.

'We can clean this up without you,' Athalon said. 'Go home and get some sleep.'

'I can't. I leaped off the plane and abandoned Gilly. I've got to go fetch her and her three tons of luggage. She and all her plant cuttings are probably impounded by now.'

'I'll go for her,' Steven said. 'And I'll drop you along the way.'

Catastrophe had been averted.

The massive checks that would have wiped Samaritan out were to have cleared the day Anthony returned. Owing to Rory's stop payment orders, and some helpful delay on the part of the bank, they didn't go through. There was no trouble with the bank; the president was one of the unpaid directors who'd been dumped. He understood the nature and consequences of Faye's attempted coup. Likewise, the vast stock and bond holdings that were in the first stages of ownership transfer were retrieved.

Samaritan lost only half a million dollars. The reinstated board of directors insisted vehemently that Anthony not make it up out of his own earnings from Herron Paper Products. 'It was my fault,' he argued. 'Samaritan is my responsibility and it was my own lack of wisdom that caused the loss.'

But even Rory, the supreme corporate miser, agreed with the others. 'Our other salaries run to practically a million a year. You should have been taking a salary all these years. You do a huge amount of work. Even a nominal salary for the last ten years would have nearly equaled the loss. Besides, you put in the hundreds of millions that started this.' The other employee-directors concurred with this argument and the unpaid directors managed to make clear, without ever saying so outright, that making up the loss would be regarded as show-off martyrdom.

Anthony bowed to the pressure, but a month later sold the house in Bermuda he'd inherited from Max and quietly turned the funds over as a private donor without any fanfare. It passed into the treasury without any hoopla, and eased his own conscience somewhat.

The experience shook his faith in his judgment. He took to working even longer hours than before and asked Nina and Rory to put together a concise overview of the entire list of assets and holdings of the corporation as well as a ten-year corporate history. He studied the resulting report until he had it committed to memory. The decision had been made at the beginning that money raised from donations would be immediately divided into three parts: forty per cent went to actual funding of projects, another forty per cent went to investments whose dividends would go toward projects, and the remaining twenty per cent toward the operation of Samaritan – salaries, travel, rent, supplies, etc. Rory had kept the average expenditure under eighteen per cent most years and the remaining money went into investments.

The original plan was to continue the forty per cent reinvestment plan until the assets equaled one billion dollars, at which point the reinvestment program would be reduced to twenty-five per cent of money raised. In the beginning this seemed such a vast sum that Anthony never even considered it as a real possibility. But in ten years, they had nearly reached the halfway point to that goal.

The investment total was in excess of $400 million now, meaning an average dividend of nearly $30 million that could be spent to the benefit of the unfortunate. In addition, donated funds kept coming in and the forty per cent share of those added significantly to the amount Samaritan was able to disburse annually.

And all of it could have been destroyed in a few more days if Anthony hadn't given Nina that one telephone number where she was finally able to reach him. The thought haunted him. Anthony had never given worry and guilt much room in his life, he let Steven take care of those activities. But now he could hardly sleep at night.

He kept thinking back to the very first time he and Steven had talked to Nina about Samaritan. She had said then that he must keep control himself. And for all these years he had done so, not minding the work and responsibility. But this incident with Faye, combined with another birthday, had made him start thinking about the future – the long-term future, his own mortality. Someday he'd die. Before that, he'd get old and tired and wishful of retirement. And to whom would he hand over Samaritan? Steven would be his first choice, but besides Steven's own objections, there was the fact that Steven was even older than he was.

No, Samaritan would have to pass on to a new generation. Samaritan was founded on Max Herron's money. It ought to be in the hands of Max Herron's family. But Anthony and Gilly would have no children. Originally he'd been disappointed, but not crushed by this fact. He and Gilly were so complete with each other that he didn't feel any obsessive need for children.

Wayne was his next thought. Wayne knew Samaritan inside and out. He had an eerie gift for investments and was being groomed to take over that area. He'd do it superbly. But Wayne's fervor was for the stock market, not doing good. He recognized, in a business sense, that Samaritan existed for the purpose of giving away money, but he didn't get excited about finding worthy recipients.

He, like Rory, did his own job exceptionally well, but regarded the beneficiaries of Samaritan's efforts as almost a necessary evil. No, it couldn't be Wayne.

Nor was Wayne's brother Harry a reasonable choice. Harry had joined Samaritan after that first board meeting in Connecticut and had proved well worth his salary. He was great at fund-raising, being a charming, attractive, outgoing young man. He had an excellent sense of just who had spare cash and the best methods of extracting it. Like Wayne, he was being unofficially groomed to take over that area of operation someday. But, like Wayne, his interest was limited to his area of expertise.

Neither of the Graves boys, or any of the younger members of the organization, seemed to feel the same pleasure as Anthony did when someone genuinely in need of help came to them. To fund medical research that could relieve suffering, to provide fast, sensitive, sensible disaster relief, to enrich people's lives with vital information – this caused a heady sense of deep spiritual satisfaction to Anthony, Steven and Rhys. This was, as far as they were concerned, the pay-off for their efforts. To the younger men, it was simply an end result of a process, a process which was itself the pleasure.

The one thing Anthony tried very hard not to think about was Martin Graves. He was not only a Herron, but Anthony's own son – maybe. He was the logical successor. But when his mind lit on Martin, Anthony told himself several things in brisk succession: the boy was only twelve or thirteen; he might not be his; he would certainly have absorbed Betsy's attitudes; and, most important, elevating him to successor at some later date would mean admitting to Gilly, if not the world, that he'd fathered a bastard on his own half-sister, which was a thought that still made him feel dirty and sick.

And so, for all his worry, the question went unresolved as other matters demanded his attention. He had just begun to consider Charlie Brent as a possible choice when Charlie himself came to him one evening. Faye had disappeared after her plan for wrecking Samaritan had gone awry. Nobody had seen or heard from her. But she had finally contacted Charlie.

'This is awfully awkward,' Charlie said, fidgeting with the pipe he always had in his hand. He had turned up at Anthony's home, without warning, one night a week after Faye had lost her bid to destroy Samaritan.

Anthony poured them both some brandy. 'We're old friends, Charlie. Nothing should be awkward between us.'

'It's about Faye.'

'Ah. Well, she is awkward to everybody. But her actions aren't your fault. I thought that had been made clear a long time ago. She—'

'She wants me back,' Charlie said.

Anthony swallowed the scathing words he'd been ready to turn loose. 'And?'

'And I think we're getting back together.'

'Oh, I see.' Anthony wanted to grab him by the throat and shake sense into him.

'Anthony, I know I'm an ass,' Charlie said, near tears. 'But I love her. God only knows why! I always have and I guess I always will. She says that Fiore put her up to it. She was just dazzled by him. It was weak and stupid of her, but she's seen now what a dreadful person he really is. She's terribly embarrassed and contrite. And I believe her. I have to.'

'Charlie, you don't owe me any explanation,' Anthony said. This was the most awful bullshit he'd ever heard. He couldn't believe anyone with an IQ higher than a kitchen appliance would believe it, and yet Charlie obviously did. Charlie was bright and hardworking, a highly moral man, much too good for Faye. That was so obvious to everyone who knew them; why couldn't Charlie himself see it?

'But I do need to explain. Not just as a friend, but as a board member.' He paused, waiting for Anthony to react, but Anthony remained determinedly bland of expression. 'You see, I know I should have quit the board as soon as we knew what she was up to. But she'd dumped me too, and so I stayed. And I'd like to continue to serve.' It was a plea.

'I don't know—'

'I know what you're thinking. I know. It would look bad, after what she tried to do, but being on this board means everything to me. It's the only worthwhile thing I do. Anthony, don't say anything. I'm not asking for a decision now. Just think about it. Ask the rest of the board. I just wanted to let you know how desperately I want to stay on, but if you feel I shouldn't, I'll understand.'

'I'll talk to the board. I can't promise anything.'

Anthony did leave it up to the others, but managed to make clear his own feelings, which were that Charlie, though a fool where Faye was concerned, was a valuable asset to Samaritan, and should be kept on.

Wayne, who'd grown very fond of Charlie, agreed whole-heartedly. But Rory, and many of the others, had grave doubts.

'Are you afraid she'll influence his behavior?' Anthony asked.

'No, it's the look of the thing that bothers me,' Rory said.

'I agree,' Nina piped up. 'While our recent problem isn't, thank heaven, public knowledge, there are a great many people who know what almost happened. I think keeping Charlie on if he goes back to Faye will alarm those people.'

'But Charlie had nothing to do with her actions,' Wayne said angrily.

'I know he didn't, but it's a matter of appearances,' Nina insisted.

'The hell with appearances!' Wayne said.

Anthony stepped into the argument at this point. 'Wayne, you know better than to say that, even in anger. Appearances mean a great deal to us. You may not like it, but it's a fact. If people think we're acting foolishly, they won't contribute funds to fools.'

'I know that. I'm sorry,' Wayne said.

Anthony looked round the table. 'Could we agree to a compromise? Let Charlie remain as a director, so long as Faye is never included in any Samaritan social event and is never seen with him at any business-related gathering. And with this further proviso: if she creates any more trouble for us, no matter how slight, or if she shows up anywhere, I will personally dismiss Charlie. Would that satisfy everyone?'

With some reluctance, they all agreed. The only person, oddly enough, who opposed the idea was Wayne. 'We are all individuals, responsible for our own actions. I don't see why Charlie should be considered responsible for Faye's.'

'Because we are making that a condition of his remaining on the board,' Anthony said, firmly closing the discussion.

He thought, and devoutly hoped, that this would be the end of Faye's involvement in his life and Samaritan's.

Chapter Nineteen

'What's on the agenda this morning?' Anthony asked Nina brightly several months later. He'd taken the need for increased vigilance over Samaritan's affairs very seriously, putting in extra hours and interesting himself (some called it meddling) in all areas of the organization's affairs.

'I have two people who both insist on seeing you,' she sniffed. 'One is a young man that personnel has sent up. They say he's intelligent and highly qualified, but refuses to take a salary. They don't know what to do with him.'

Anthony smiled. 'What a refreshing attitude.' Most of the young people who applied to work for Samaritan were of three classes: those who simply wanted a job, any job, and had failed to qualify for the fast food business. They were turned away in droves. The second were the hippies in search of a cause to which to attach themselves. Flower children looking for a garden in which to grow. They were, for the most part, highly idealistic, entirely impractical and usually stoned. They, too, were turned away. The third group were the establishment crowd, the young men (and young women, in increasing numbers) that a later generation would call 'yuppies'. Though the term wasn't common yet, the attitude was as old as money. These young people thought well of themselves, intended that the world should think well of them, and saw Samaritan as a stage upon which to use their skills. And for the most part those skills were considerable. They were bright and ambitious. They were Wayne and his ilk. They wanted to be paid handsomely, and in order to attract and keep these skilled drones, Samaritan had to pay.

'Who's the second one, Nina?'

'A nun – sort of.'

'How can you be sort of a nun? I thought it was like pregnancy. You are or you aren't.'

'Well, she calls herself Sister, but she's not Catholic. She's determined to see you and refuses to go through the proper channels.'

'Then she shall see me,' Anthony said cheerfully. He liked the idea, actually. Most of the people who reached his office had been filtered through so many layers of interviews that he got a 'white bread' view of what was actually going on.

Anthony went through some paperwork and was almost caught up when Nina came to the door. 'Mr Don Shermerhorn,' she announced.

Anthony liked the young man on sight. He had an open, engaging smile, a loose stride and looked like a person who didn't care much about clothes himself but knew other people did. He took Anthony's hand in a firm, work-roughened grip. 'I'm afraid your people think I'm a dangerous maniac, out to destroy the capitalist system.'

'Are you?' Anthony said, gesturing for the young man to take a chair.

'No. As I've explained downstairs, I'm impressed with Samaritan. I think it does valuable work. I want to be part of it and I think I can contribute. I'm not ambitious for myself, but I could be very ambitious for Samaritan.'

'How would you support yourself without an income?'

'I have friends and family. And I've never had an income as such, so I'd hardly miss it,' he said, seemingly perplexed that Anthony would interest himself in this aspect of the proposal. Nobody down in personnel had shown much concern for his welfare, only their own.

'What is your background?' Anthony asked.

'I grew up in a medical mission in Egypt. I was sent to Oxford for a couple years to become "civilized". I have very little formal medical training, but an enormous amount of practical experience. And I've educated myself as thoroughly as possible. Much of your work at Samaritan is medical – research funding and such.'

'And we have our own experts,' Anthony put in. Much as he liked this young man, he couldn't have him thinking that a self-educated pseudo-doctor was going to get anywhere with their medical experts.

'I know, but most of your medical-related funding is for standard diseases, including cancer and heart disease. What is often neglected, and what I know about, are the deficiency diseases. Beri-beri, yaws, and all the less identifiable results of poor nutrition. Lack of proper diet in the poor causes many of the problems that keep them poor. Lethargy, pain, deficient motor co-ordination, bad eyesight – all of these contribute to what the world sees as a lack of ambition and lack of intelligence.'

'And what do you propose that Samaritan do about this?' Anthony asked.

'I don't know,' Don Shermerhorn said frankly. 'I'm familiar with the problem, I think the solution lies within Samaritan, but I don't know just where or how. That's why I want to work here, to learn how Samaritan operates. Just what it's capable of doing.'

Anthony was impressed. Here was someone with a genuine fire to do good, coupled with a practical attitude. A rare thing, indeed. 'Very well. We'll take you on. But you must take a salary, however minimal, in order to keep the books straight – insurance, withholding taxes, all that necessary paperwork would be hopelessly snarled with one unpaid employee. It's a contradiction in terms.'

'Okay, but give me the least you can and also give me the hardest job you can find.'

'I'll do better than that. I'll give you the hardest boss.' He pressed a button on his desk. 'Nina, ask Rory to come up.'

The second visitor that morning was just as fervent as Don

Shermerhorn, but a good deal less practical. 'Mr Wentworth, Sister Doreen to see you,' Nina announced. 'I'll just stay and take notes, shall I?' she said.

Anthony stared at her. Nina, an executive secretary, was much above mere note-taking. She had her own staff of downtrodden secretaries who were saddled with such jobs. If Nina wanted to be here, he'd better let her.

Sister Doreen was a skinny, frumpy, middle-aged woman with severe hair and unfortunate dentures. 'Mr Wentworth, I'm so glad to meet you – at last,' she added, casting a disapproving glance at Nina. 'I won't take more of your time than necessary,' she said, throwing herself into the visitor's chair. 'I run an orphanage for Asian babies. Korean, Malayan, Chinese, Cambodian. Six months ago our home burned. Thank the Lord no one was harmed, but we have no facilities.'

'Where are the children now?' Anthony asked.

'Farmed out to local people. I have seven of them myself.'

'What about insurance?'

'That's the problem. We didn't have any. We couldn't afford it. It came down to paying the premium or buying milk for the babies and there was no question of where to spend our small funds.'

'Mrs – uh, Sister Doreen, I'm not sure why you had to see me about this. We have a whole department that processes requests for financial aid. They're very fair, compassionate people.'

'But you see, that's it. We don't need money. We have a benefactor. We've been offered fifty thousand dollars to build a new facility and another fifty thousand to operate it. But there's one difficulty. Our benefactor, apparently feeling that our failure to keep up our insurance premiums showed lack of good monetary judgment, insists that Samaritan administer the money for us.'

'Why doesn't the benefactor administer it himself?'

'I suppose he's too busy. We can hardly complain, ever mindful of looking gift horses in the mouth.'

'Who is your benefactor?'

'We don't know. He, or she, prefers to remain anonymous.'

'I see. Well, Sister Doreen, I don't see any particular problem with this. We have staff experienced in contracting for building. You will, of course, have to fill out the proper application and naturally we'll investigate you.'

'Oh, you'll find we're quite legitimate.'

'I'm sure we will. Why don't you contact me again a week from now?'

As soon as Nina had shown Sister Doreen out, she returned. 'I don't like it.'

'Her or the proposal?' Anthony asked.

'Oh, she's all right. But there's something wrong with this.'

'Why do you say that?'

'It's just a feeling.'

Anthony goggled at her. This was so unlike Nina. Emotions were never part of her considerations. 'A feeling?' he asked.

'With your permission, I'll oversee the investigation myself. May I hire a detective?'

'A detective! My God! What's wrong with our own staff?'

'Nothing, and if you'd rather they—'

'No, no. If you feel this strongly about it, you have a free hand.' He watched her leave, wondering what in the world had come over her. Could it be hormonal? he wondered. Whatever the reason for Nina's suspicions, he owed it to her to let her take the bit in her teeth. Her judgments, however heartless, were usually reliable.

But the request itself wasn't all that strange. Samaritan administered a dozen or more anonymous bequests a year. They had one paid director who was specifically in charge of these activities. Usually they were just like this situation, someone wishing to benefit a worthy, slightly incompetent, cause. Often, too, they were to benefit minors. And although the benefactor might be anonymous to the recipient, he or she was known to Samaritan. Still, that shouldn't make any difference.

Anthony put it out of his mind until the directors' meeting a week later. Nina handed him a slim folder of papers. 'This is the report on Sister Doreen and the AAA.'

'You look glum,' Anthony said, skimming through the papers in the folder. The Asian Adoption Agency was legitimate. They'd been in operation since the Second World War and had grown in responsibility during the Korean War. They placed an average of a hundred babies a year with American families. They had no religious affiliation, though they had often accepted donations of time and money from several nearby Methodist churches. The first administrator had been a British nurse, hence the appellation 'Sister' which had carried on through subsequent administrators as a quirky tradition.

Their finances, up until the fire, had always been precarious, but they'd managed to keep going. The legality of the adoptions was above reproach. The medical care of the children, thanks to volunteer nurses and doctors, superlative. It appeared that, with a new physical facility and the one large gift, they ought to be back on their feet.

'So what's wrong with this?' Anthony asked Nina.

'I don't know, but there's something the matter. I'm sure of it. Could you put them off another week?'

'Meantime, Nina, these babies are farmed out all over the countryside.'

'I don't like that either. But there's something fishy about this.'

'Nina, if you're that sure, I'll give it another week. But if you can't come up with a reason to refuse this by then, I'm going to recommend that we participate. Call Sister Doreen. Tell her we are very sorry, but we must delay one more week for a final answer.'

Anthony was concerned, not only for the babies, but about Nina. This behavior was so foreign to her; hunches, feelings, and unfounded suspicions never seemed to play a part in her work. That was one of the things that made her so valuable; while everyone else went on emotional binges, Nina stayed aloof and exasperatingly responsible. For that very reason, this anomaly was worth heeding.

As he walked into the monthly full board meeting, he felt, as always, a lifting of his spirits. This was the heart of Samaritan, where the past and future were constantly evaluated, where proposed projects were held up to a harsh light and examined. It was also a place where a fair amount of gossip went on unless Anthony kept them strictly to business. Of course, usually the gossip had to do with business, however tangentially – who'd lost money, who'd made it, who'd inherited it recently – so Anthony often let them ramble on for a while.

Everyone was assembled as he entered the room. Coffee was being poured and stately scuffles were going on over the best sweet rolls. '... so I told him, you'd better get the auditors in as fast as you can. A leak like that can turn into a flood overnight,' their resident banker was telling Charlie Brent.

'Fiore's probably behind it,' Charlie groused.

'Is Fiore's bank in trouble?' Anthony asked, stirring a second packet of sugar into his coffee.

The banker, Jonathan Mersey, turned. 'Anthony! Didn't see you come in. How's Gilly? Francie sends her best. No, not big trouble. I was just telling Charlie that a friend of mine is on their board of directors and says there's money missing from their teller windows. You know, a bank never likes to admit anybody could, much less is, stealing from them from the inside. Wrecks the depositors' faith. But this started out nickel and dime stuff, and my friend's concerned that their own people aren't doing enough to find the guilty teller. Big place, of course. A good dozen or more suspects. And you can't fire them all to get the one out.'

Nina nudged Anthony and glanced pointedly at her watch. He took the hint and called the meeting to order.

'The first thing we need to sort out is this clinic in Alabama. Can the situation be saved or must we withdraw the funding?'

'I must have missed something,' one of the directors said.

'That's right. You weren't here at the last meeting. To summarize,' Anthony said, 'we funded a small, non-profit maternity clinic in a poor rural district of Alabama. They have the best intentions in the world, but the worst luck and management. Instead of putting the money into a bank, they were persuaded to give it to a phony investment counselor who made grandiose claims then left town with most of it. Most of the staff quit when a case of chickenpox was misdiagnosed as measles. Their last shipment of calcium tablets got lost in the mail – it's a long litany of good-hearted errors and plain bad luck. They seem to be hopeless.'

'Why don't you send them that Shermerhorn boy you stuck me with last week,' Rory suggested hopefully.

'Do you think he could straighten them out?' Anthony asked.

'He couldn't make things worse,' Rory said. 'Nobody could.'

Coming from Rory, this was a recommendation. 'Good. We'll send him. Now, this application from the musicians. Rhys, would you give us your opinion?'

Anthony and Steven had planned on a rare afternoon of tennis, but rain had driven them home to Anthony's house. Gilly met them at the door. She was wearing jeans shorts with a stained tee shirt, and had her hair pulled back in a ponytail. 'I thought I heard the car. I'm glad you two are here. I could use some help.' She trotted off to the kitchen, expecting them to follow, as they did.

'What in the world are you doing?' Anthony asked. There were tomatoes everywhere. Baskets full of them sat on the table, the counters and the floor. Even though the air conditioner was running full blast, the air in the room was thick with steam and spices.

She was dropping tomatoes into a vat of boiling water, swirling them round and taking them back out to stack neatly by the sink. 'Making sauce, of course,' she said.

In past years she'd occasionally mentioned making tomato sauce, but Anthony had never actually seen the process, nor guessed that it was such a grand-scale operation. 'What can we do?' he asked.

She glanced at them. 'Not in those clothes.'

Anthony found ratty clothes for himself and Steven and they returned. 'Now, I'll do the blanching,' Gilly said. 'Steven, you peel and de-seed, then Anthony can take charge of the blender. I'll take care of the spices as they go into the pot.'

'Peeling makes sense to me,' Steven said, 'but what's de-seeding?'

'I swear if it doesn't come from styrofoam, you two don't know what to do with it. Look.' She picked up a blanched tomato, ripped the loosened skin off – which went to a colander for later transport to the compost pile – and cut the slippery, nude tomato in half. Then she took each half in one hand and squeezed it like a sponge over another sieve.

Steven stepped back in horror. 'That's the most revolting thing I've ever seen.'

She giggled. 'It's not revolting. It's food. Try it.' She cut another tomato and handed the halves to Steven.

'Oh God! They're slimy and warm besides. That's even worse. This must be what it feels like to deliver a calf.'

'Steven! Don't be nasty!'

Anthony was leaning over the sink, laughing.

'You think it's funny?' Steven said to him. He lifted up Anthony's shirt and slapped a handful of warm tomato pulp on his back. Anthony yelped and spun round.

'If you two can't behave, I'll send you outside!' Gilly said primly.

'We'll behave,' Anthony said, lobbing the tomato pulp back at Steven when she turned her back.

'I saw that,' she said, without looking. 'Anthony, you boil the bottles and lids, since you can't be trusted to play nicely.'

By the end of the afternoon, they'd put up thirty quarts of tomato sauce. The three of them were covered with pulp and sweat and reeked of garlic and basil. The fat, sparkling jars sat in neatly labelled ranks on the kitchen table, a clean tea towel under them. Gilly's face was flushed and there were smudges of sauce on her shirt, her face and her hair. 'Steven, you mop the floor,' she said. 'I'll do the counters and set the pots to soak and Anthony can take all the garbage to the compost.'

'I see where I rank in your affections,' Anthony said.

'In my kitchen, I'm management,' Gilly said. 'Go.'

They cleaned up the kitchen and themselves and, as the sun set, they sat at the table on the patio and ate spaghetti with fresh sauce. Gilly had made the pasta and put home-grown mint in the iced tea. She'd scissored snips of cornflower petals over a simple green salad, making it look like something exotic. When she'd gone into the kitchen to bring out dessert, Steven said, 'Don't ever tell her, but I can't remember being more satisfied with a day and a meal.'

Anthony leaned back and smiled. 'She knows. She can read us both like books. Pretty simple books, at that. You know, you and I think we're dealing with the business of the world every day, but *this* is the legitimate business of life. Food, love, fresh air, a beautiful woman.'

'You know how lucky you are,' Steven said.

'So lucky it frightens me sometimes. Nobody deserves what I have.'

Nina had attended secretarial school with a young woman named Lottie Mayhew. She and Lottie had kept in touch in a passionless way that suited them both. They lunched once or twice a year and dutifully recognized each other's birthdays with innocuous greeting cards.

Lottie had a responsible position at Joseph Fiore's bank.

After the board meeting. Nina called her and arranged a lunch for the next day.

'Lottie, could you do me a favor?' Nina asked as they were leaving the restaurant, replete on salads and unsweetened tea. They both believed that a high-level secretary had to keep trim and neat.

'I'll certainly try, Nina.'

'I want to follow some money around your bank. If it's even there, and it might not be. I don't want to know amounts or accounts numbers, nothing that would violate the confidence your employers have in you. Here's what I'd like to know ...'

'My darlings, you look gorgeous,' Gilly said, studying Anthony and Steven.

'Like gorgeous penguins,' Steven said. 'I hate this tux.'

'Just the same, you're going to wear it. You two dress up all the time for other people. Just for tonight, I want you dressed up for me.'

'Where are we going?' Anthony asked.

'A hideously expensive new restaurant downtown. Be prepared to spend a fortune on me.'

'It's only fair. It's not everyday a person turns thirty,' Steven said.

She grabbed his arm and shook it. 'Twenty-nine and you know it.'

The phone rang. 'Ignore it, please,' Gilly said.

'I can't,' Anthony said with an apologetic shrug.

When Anthony rejoined them, he looked upset. 'That was Nina. She wants to come see me.'

'Anthony, I don't believe that for a moment. You're just trying to get out of dinner,' Gilly said. 'She has you all day. I've got you now.'

Anthony accepted the drink she handed him. 'Sorry, hon. I think it may be important. You and Steven go ahead. I'll catch up if I can.'

Nina arrived minutes after Steven and Gilly left.

Knowing full well that anything important would take a while, Anthony had quickly changed into casual clothes and ordered a pizza. 'All right, what's it all about?' he asked Nina as she bustled past him with an armload of papers.

'The AAA. The Asian Adoption Agency. It's all a fake.'

'Nina, sit down. A fake? We checked them out.'

'I don't mean the agency. I mean the benefactor.'

He sat down opposite her. 'Tell me what you've got.'

Nina started shuffling her papers, found a sheet of notes. 'It's very complex and there are big gaps in what I know, but here goes. It all came out of Fiore's bank.'

Anthony felt himself tensing up. 'Yes?'

'One of their tellers has a child from the Sister Doreen's adoption agency. He had an account, newly opened, into which the money disappearing from the bank seems to have gone. My friend tells me he's the most upright, honest person in the bank and would never have stolen so much as a penny.'

'But it looks like he did.'

'What probably happened is that the account was set up without his knowledge and someone else put it in there. My friend says there are several ways this could have been done, but I don't know enough about banking to quite grasp which is most likely. Anyway, he had this account full of stolen money. Then there was a transfer of these funds to another account within the bank. Another new account. A trust account to be held for the adoption agency, which could be withdrawn only by Samaritan.'

'I see – I think. Samaritan was to accept this money, which was stolen funds.'

'At which point, someone would have blown the whistle. It would have looked like Samaritan was in on it. That we, working with the adoption agency, had encouraged, maybe even planted, this teller in order to embezzle from the bank.'

'Jesus! That bastard Fiore.'

'There's something else. My friend was asked to drop some paperwork off at Fiore's house the day before yesterday. Faye was there, in a dressing gown.'

'Shit! She hasn't given up. Poor Charlie.'

The doorbell rang and Anthony went to fetch his pizza. When he returned, wafting the scent of oregano and hot cardboard, he said, 'This is rotten. Fiore's behind this. Fiore and Faye. They were trying to get me, but they were perfectly ready to let this poor teller go to jail in the process and deprive Sister Doreen of the money the orphans desperately need.'

'They were just the bait,' Nina said. 'You and Samaritan were the fish they were trying to catch.'

'Can we turn it on them?'

'I asked Lottie about that. She thinks so, but only if we have the authorities inside the doors first thing in the morning. Apparently there are some loose ends they haven't tied up. Signature cards not yet signed, that sort of thing. It seems that they think they've got control of the time schedule and can take care of the last details whenever they like.'

'What else does this Lottie say?'

'Please, don't use her name. I shouldn't have mentioned it.'

'What does this unnamed person say?'

'That Fiore's despised within the bank. The employees all hate him. The directors don't talk to the hired help, of course, but they come out of every board meeting white and tense and talking to each other in little discontented knots. My friend says there have been several attempts to get him out, but they've failed so far. They need something specific to hang on him. And this could be it.'

'Can we rat on him without sacrificing the teller?'

'If we move instantly, probably.'

'Jonathan Mersey has a friend on that board.'

'I know. It was hearing him talk about it this morning that got my mind on Fiore.'

'Mersey can tell us who we ought to talk to. Nina, run him down while I eat, will you? Get him over here. Do you think Faye's involved – officially?'

'She's certainly involved. And certainly not officially.'

'That's my guess, too. Poor old Charlie.'

'Gilly, you chose well. Nice place for a birthday dinner,' Steven said. 'Too bad Anthony didn't make it.'

'I knew he wasn't going to. He had on his jeans and ordered a pizza within a minute of our leaving, I'll bet you anything. But I had wonderful company.' She set her cup down and put her hand over his.

Steven had to fight to keep from pulling away from her. He disliked it when she touched him. It roused strong feelings that he knew he shouldn't have.

'You're really very dear,' she went on, leaning forward to give him a sisterly kiss on the cheek.

He was suddenly swamped with a wave of emotions: tenderness, lust, guilt and regret. He very nearly grabbed her and drew her into his arms. Good God! Had he lost his mind? This was Gilly! *Gilly*. His friend, his best friend's wife. It was as though, walking along a plain of platonic love, he'd inexplicably dropped into a yawning chasm of desire.

'Steven? What's wrong,' she said as he suddenly drew back.

'Ah, nothing. Just a little, ah, indigestion.'

'Darling. I'm so sorry. I've got some antacid in my purse.'

'No, that's fine.'

'Don't be a macho poop,' she said, rummaging in the tiny bag she carried. 'It's right here. Waiter, another glass of water.'

'Gilly, stop fussing,' he said angrily.

She thought he was angry at her. Her eyes began to fill. 'I'm sorry, Steven.'

He took a deep breath, tried to get a grip on himself. 'Gilly, dear, I'm being awful. Forgive me?' She'd be

316

appalled if she had the slightest idea what was going through his head.

She sniffed delicately. 'You could never do anything to require forgiveness. You just feel bad and it's dreadful of me to keep you here. Let's go.' She took his arm, inviting him to lean on her, which horrified him into speechlessness.

As they left the restaurant, they were observed by someone keenly interesting in all the patting, touching, kissing and meaningful looks.

A few minutes later, Joseph Fiore arrived. 'Faye, you're early.'

'I told Charlie I had an appointment to go to. He was threatening to come along. I had to get away. And I've been most entertained while I waited for you. Most entertained.'

He pulled out a chair, brushed aside a hovering waiter, and sat down heavily. 'I've been on the phone. Wentworth's asked for another week to consider AAA. It worries me.'

'Don't let it. Charlie says they're swamped with work and this sort of piddling thing's bound to be pretty far down their list. It's just as well. We aren't quite ready, are we?'

'All but the signature cards. I've invented a lot of paperwork to be signed tomorrow. I'll slip the signature card in on the teller while I'm chewing him out about his slowness.'

'This is going to work, isn't it?'

'Of course it is.'

'If it doesn't, we're through.'

He reached under the table, laid a meaty hand on her thigh and squeezed so hard she winced. 'Don't you talk that way, you bitch. I've taken all the risk. You try to bale out on me and you'll be sorry. Do you understand?' He squeezed harder.

Before the bank opened the next morning, a group of

people had assembled and demanded entrance. This group included a representative of the bank's bonding company, two men from the Federal Deposit Insurance Corporation, an FBI agent, two independent auditors and half of the board of directors. Fiore was controlled, but furious and outraged at the invasion. As the next two days ground slowly past, and more and more details of the scheme to steal from the bank in order to discredit Samaritan came to light, he became progressively less controlled. The inherent brutality and coarseness in his nature, which was usually disguised by his moneyed sleekness, began to come out. Several dignified elderly directors found themselves shocked to the core by his language and insinuations concerning their motives.

The teller who was to have been the fall guy was so distressed that he had to be sedated until he realized that the authorities recognized that he was probably the victim, not the perpetrator, of the plan. Nina's friend Lottie went about her work tense and pale for fear of what she had helped unleash. The directors tut-tutted and wrung their hands with worry over how this might ultimately reflect on their own reputations within the business community.

And in the bowels of the vast bank, the financial experts beavered away, tracking transfers of funds with a combination of disapproval and admiration. It had been a fantastically elaborate plan, showing enormous intelligence and cunning. If Fiore had been given just a few more hours to polish up the details, and if the experts hadn't known just what they were looking for, it would probably have succeeded brilliantly.

At the end of the second day, Fiore was arrested. He blamed Faye Brent for everything. The authorities conferred among themselves and came to the conclusion that while Mrs Charles Brent might have a moral involvement, she was not legally involved to the point that criminal prosecution was possible.

Samaritan watched from the sidelines.

Their own link with the crime, and it was a tenuous link, was Charlie Brent.

'I've been such a fool,' he said to Anthony the night of Fiore's arrest. He'd come to Anthony and Gilly's home. 'I don't know why you didn't just have me locked up until I came to my senses.'

'Are you talking about Faye?' Gilly asked softly. She didn't know Charlie well, but had always liked him. But now his boyish good looks were ravaged with disappointment and humiliation. She didn't begin to grasp what Anthony had told her about what had happened, but she knew it was nasty and it wasn't Charlie's fault. The man was miserable and she felt very sorry for him.

'I can hardly stand to hear her name now. How could I have been so blind to what she was?' he asked Anthony.

'At the risk of being awfully trite, love *is* blind, Charlie,' Anthony said sympathetically.

Charlie signed deeply, wincing as if even breathing hurt. 'I've come to resign from Samaritan, Anthony.'

'No! You can't do that,' Gilly said.

Both men looked at her with surprise.

'It means so much to you and you didn't do anything wrong.'

'Gilly, Charlie has to resign,' Anthony said. 'Don't make it any harder for him.'

'I don't understand why,' Gilly said, hurt at Anthony's curtness, but unwilling to give up so easily.

'But I do,' Charlie said, grateful for her defense of him. 'We had a bargain. I don't go back on bargains. Besides, I need to get away. I need a fresh start on something.'

Almost everyone understood and accepted Charlie's resignation. Many were sympathetic, some were slightly contemptuous of his foolishness. The only one who objected was, predictably, Wayne Graves. Learning that Charlie had visited Anthony's home to resign, he developed a complex argument that it was somehow all Gilly's fault. He couldn't believe that Anthony, whom he worshipped, could let Charlie, whom he loved, resign. There had to be another explanation and it had to be Gilly. He explained this theory to practically everyone except Anthony and finally got himself so worked up with frustrated indignation that he, too, resigned.

He meant it as a gesture, but Anthony, who wasn't at home with subtleties, didn't understand that he was supposed to talk him out of it. 'I'm sorry to hear that, Wayne. But I know how loyal you are to Charlie and I respect that. If you change your mind, you know we'll always welcome you back,' he said.

Wayne suddenly found himself out of work and Anthony was left bleakly thinking that Wayne had judged him to be in the wrong and rejected him. That was deeply painful to consider.

'Nina, come out to lunch,' Anthony said. 'There's something I want to talk to you about.'

Nina was stunned, but made reservations for a nice restaurant. She was more stunned when she found herself eating at a McDonald's.

'Nina, I'm sick at heart. I feel old and tired. I've been thinking, when things settle down, I'd like to get away with Gilly. Somewhere that nobody but you could find us. I mean *nobody*.'

'You want a hide-out,' Nina said, nodding.

Anthony laughed, for the first time in days. 'I hadn't thought about it in those terms, but yes. I want a hide-out. Not a resort where I might run into anybody I know. Someplace of my own. Remote. Primitive. No reservations. I keep thinking about the ranch, but too many people know about it. I want to be able to disappear every now and then. I don't know if I'd even do it, I just want to know I could.'

'Another ranch, perhaps?'

'That would be great.'

'Would you want to buy it in another name?'

'Is that possible?'

'I don't know. I'll find out. How about Wyoming?'

'Nina, you're wonderful. What could I have done all these years without you?'

He was then treated to a once-in-a-lifetime sight: Nina blushed.

Chapter Twenty

Nina really got her teeth into the thing. The challenge and secrecy of it appealed to her. She had to share her Great Man with the world, but in this she had him to herself. She created documentation for Anthony Smith, a largely absentee rancher, and after several months of searching found an enormous cattle ranch in the Kansas Flint Hills. It was breathtakingly empty land and had the advantage of less severe winters than the Montana and Wyoming lands she'd first investigated. It was also easier to get to, being about a three-hour drive to Kansas City, so Anthony could easily move back and forth between the real world and his secret world.

Anthony didn't intend to keep the knowledge of the ranch as exclusive as Nina assumed, but in the end neither Gilly nor Steven knew about it. Or rather, Gilly knew such a place existed, but had no interest in it. When Anthony went to look at the property the next April in preparation for purchase, Gilly was involved in her spring planting and couldn't go along. 'I think it's nice for you to have a place to get away from your work. I have my gardens; you need a tranquil spot, too,' she said. He'd found her up to her elbows in damp vermiculite in the new greenhouse.

'Don't you want to look at it?' he asked.

'Later, perhaps. My seedlings are at a critical stage. They need a fine misting every few hours. I'm afraid the gardeners might forget. You go along.'

Steven was visiting his parents when the Flint Hills ranch sale went through. Anthony meant to tell him about it when he returned, but something else came up. A freak spring forest fire had wiped out thousands of acres of trees earmarked for Herron Paper. Steven's brother Bob had taken the lion's share of responsibility for Herron Paper, leaving Anthony and Steven free to devote their time to Samaritan. But Anthony had always kept a hand in, working at least one day every week, and often two, in the company offices. In this instance, however, Bob Packwood's wife was having a baby prematurely at the same time his eldest daughter was having her tonsils out and family duty called to him more stridently than business. Anthony and Steven visited the afflicted lands, consulted with the suppliers, scrambled for an alternative supply of wood pulp, rearranged the shipping schedules accordingly and crawled over the standing and special orders, trying to find a way to make up for the loss.

As they were winding this up, Anthony got a call from England. Blanche had died. Faye and Betsy had been with her and with almost indecent haste had already buried her. Anthony went to England, visited the grave, and tried to find genuine regret in his heart, but couldn't. He put Leland House into the hands of estate agents before returning to Kansas City.

Somewhere along the way, Anthony put his secret ranch in the back of his mind and left it there. Once or twice, when Nina handed him papers or checks related to it that needed signing, he'd remember and mean to tell Steven next time they got together, but other thoughts always intruded and took precedence.

In May an American Airlines DC-10, taking off from O'Hare, lost an engine and 273 people died, among them two of Samaritan's employees, a young husband and wife from the investment department. At the funeral, Anthony gave a short eulogy. As he was speaking, Gilly moved closer to Steven, tapped his arm and whispered a question. 'Handkerchief?'

Gilly was a weeper who was never equipped for tears. Steven suddenly found this heartbreakingly endearing. He could also sense the nearness of her body to his, as though she was radiating heat. No, not heat, just 'being'. And there was no way to escape except inching away and all but sitting in Rhys's lap. He'd avoided being alone with her ever since the night they'd ended up in the restaurant together. He'd thought for a while that he was cured, that he was over the temporary madness that had made him want to have her. And yet, today, even in the midst of a solemn ceremony, he was so sensitive to her physical presence that he was short of breath.

He sought out Anthony after the service. 'Could you do without me for a week or so? I'd like to take a little time off.'

'Of course. Is there something wrong?'

'No, nothing at all,' Steven replied, adding to himself, *nothing except that I can't be in the same room with your wife without wanting to grab her.* 'I just need a rest.'

'Where are you going?'

'I don't know. Colorado, maybe. There's a resort I went to with my parents once when I was a kid. I'll let Nina know where to find me when I discover where I am.'

It was his inadvertent celibacy, Steven told himself as he approached the Stanley Hotel in Estes Park. That was the problem. There had been such a press of business that he hadn't been with a woman for a long time. He'd finally almost accepted that he needed sex as much as he needed food. Not as often, but just as intensely. In his youth, when he was trying to be a priest, he told himself his physical hunger for the opposite sex was a failing he must overcome, like a drug. Later, when he'd rejoined the world, and its women, he told himself that his sexual appetite was merely a weakness, a minor flaw but one that must be cured if he were to focus his energies on important things.

That attitude had in turn been amended. It was an age of easy sex, casual relationships, of newly liberated women availing themselves of the same unconstrained liberties that had formerly been the exclusive privilege of men. And Steven was a good-looking man who attracted these women like a magnet. So long as they understood there was no possibility of a long-term relationship, Steven was happy to avail himself of their new freedom.

And yet the thrill of liberation had faded for him. The next to last time he'd awakened in the morning in bed with a strange, albeit very attractive, woman, he'd felt vaguely disgusted with himself. The last time, he'd been nearly frantic with loathing for her.

It came to him unexpectedly as he was signing in at the hotel. What he needed, he abruptly realized with a shock, was a wife.

A wife!

It was an amazing concept, made all the more amazing by the fact that he hadn't considered it before. He'd tried to get Ellen to marry him all those years ago and he'd never got entirely out of the habit of thinking that some distant someday they'd eventually marry in order to legitimize Gary. But Gary was nearly twenty-three years old now, a grown man with no need of legitimacy. And Steven himself had just turned forty.

Forty! Too old to be drifting aimlessly, having meaningless one-night stands with brash young women who put a notch in their birth control pill dispensers and moved on. Pretty soon he'd be pathetic, look like one of those recently divorced leisure-suited fifty-year-old stockbrokers who panted around the smorgasbord of liberated young women, desperately wanting a taste of the action before it was too late.

She appeared as if on special rush order. Steven later wondered, half seriously, if God had had her waiting in the wings, ready for her cue. Much later, of course, he knew how sinfully wrong that assessment was.

He'd tried a swim in the frigid swimming pool and come out realizing that was one more thing he was too old for. He was so cold his teeth hurt and his joints felt frozen.

He was heading for his room with undignified haste, thinking only of a hot shower, when he saw Gilly two doors down the hallway.

'Gilly?' he called.

Had she and Anthony decided to join him? That was all he needed!

The woman turned. It wasn't Gilly, of course. But there was a resemblance. The same ripe, womanly figure, and knot of glossy red hair, although this woman's was darker. And the faces weren't alike. Gilly's features were generous, softly voluptuous. This woman's were fragile, pixie-ish.

'I'm sorry for bellowing at you that way. You look like someone I know,' Steven said.

'I'll forgive you if you help me with this key,' she said. 'I'm pretty much of a fool with mechanical things, but you'd think a key ...'

He couldn't make it work either, so he invited her to call the front desk from his room. Steven excused himself to dress in the bathroom while she made the call. 'They're sending someone up,' she said when he emerged. 'I'll just wait in the hall.'

'There's no need. I'm very well behaved.'

She laughed. 'I believe you. I just felt I was imposing.'

'I'm almost incapable of being imposed upon. I'm Steven Packwood, at your service.'

She took his hand in a firm grip. 'Dianna Jarvis.'

While they waited for the bellhop to bring a new key, he learned that she was single, a buyer for an exclusive gift shop on the Plaza and on a short vacation to indulge in some horseback riding. By the time the new key arrived, they'd expressed surprise at the coincidence of living only a block away and meeting in Colorado and had planned to go horseback riding for the afternoon. By that evening, when they had dinner together, Steven had himself half convinced he was in love with her – or could be.

He and Dianna Jarvis had a lot in common. She'd

grown up Catholic, fairly wealthy, though not nearly so pretentiously moneyed as he, and was the eldest of three children. Like him, she had a younger sibling with severe psychological problems who'd been a financial and emotional strain on the family. The girl had committed suicide the year before.

'No! How awful for all of you,' Steven said.

'Not really so awful as you'd think. I loved Lois, but she'd destroyed our family. She didn't mean to, but she had, and she knew it was because of her. My parents had just gotten divorced, my middle sister is an alcoholic and Lois was getting worse and worse. I was considered the sensible one who could cope and I was at my breaking point, too. Suicide was an open door with peace behind it. She probably hoped we'd all get well somehow without her. Maybe we will. I'd have made the same choice. Oh – I can't believe I'm telling you this. I've never talked about it to anyone.'

'But suicide's never the answer to anything,' Steven said.

'I know it's not supposed to be. But maybe it is. At least sometimes. What a dismal date I am! Tell me more about yourself, Steven. Did you say you were involved with Samaritan? It's a fine organization. I've done volunteer work for them. Quite a bit, actually. Every Saturday I go down to the house you operate for battered women and take care of some of the children so the mothers can get out on their own for a while.'

He liked that tenuous connection between them and admired her generosity with her time and affection.

Dianna only had three days of vacation and they spent almost every minute together. Except at night. At the close of each day, Steven walked her to her door and kissed her goodnight and went to his own room. He wasn't sure why it was so important to do it this way, but it was. This was something serious; how serious he wasn't sure yet. But he didn't want to risk blighting it by hastiness.

When he offered to drive her to Denver to the airport, he very nearly packed his own bags to go along, but forced himself to stay behind, to think it out and try honestly to assess his own feelings and motives. In spite of this resolve, he found himself singing out loud to the radio as he drove back to Estes Park, as carefree as a schoolboy, a feeling as rare as it was heady.

The next morning, he rose early, full of energy and not sure what to do with himself. He went down to breakfast and was reading the morning paper when someone sat down as his table.

'Why, Steven. It *is* you. What a pleasant surprise.'

Steven nearly leaped out of his chair with surprise. 'Faye! What are you doing here?'

'I came up to look at some property. A little house up in the mountains. Somewhere to get away.'

'Get away from what?' he asked, thinking what a good thing it would be for the rest of the world if Faye were isolated.

'Everything. Mostly myself. No, don't leave. Please sit with me.'

'Faye, we don't have anything to talk about.'

'Then just listen for a minute. Steven, we've known each other all our lives. In honor of that, if nothing else, just listen to me.'

Steven glanced pointedly at his watch and subsided. 'What about?'

'About what an unmitigated bitch I've been.'

'Agreed.'

'Don't be sarcastic. I mean it.'

He studied her as he talked. She was just a month older than he was, and she still had the wholesome, girlish look she'd always had. But the fair hair looked a little dull now. He suspected there would be gray in it if it weren't expensively treated. And the most exclusive cosmetic saloons couldn't quite disguise the tiny lines of age starting round her eyes and mouth and neck.

'Please don't glare at me like that until you've heard

me out, ' Faye was going on. 'Then, if you still hate me, you're welcome to it. I can't explain what I did. Not to you or Anthony or even to myself. I must have gone utterly mad. It was dreadful. Inexcusable. I can't even, in the depths of my heart, blame it on Joe Fiore. He was wicked, through and through, and I was – I was mesmerized by his very wickedness, I suppose. But I'm not trying to make excuses. There is no excuse.'

'Why are you saying all this bullshit?'

'Because it's true. Swear to God. Cross my heart,' she said with a tearful smile. 'Remember when we used to say that when we were kids in the summer at Birches?'

'Yes, and you were usually lying then, too,' he said, but he was softening a little. He didn't believe her, but at least this was an entertaining act.

'Steven, I've lost everything. Everybody. Charlie's left me, Wayne won't speak to me. I wouldn't dream of inflicting myself on Anthony. He'd spit on me and I wouldn't blame him. Mother and Max are both dead. But you – Steven, you're part of my whole life. You're all I have left of me when I was a nice person. Please don't run off. I'm at rock bottom and I'm so glad to see you.'

'You should have been an actress. You're damned good.'

'You're right not to believe me. I'm telling you the God's truth, but I can see why you doubt it. Will you help me with something anyway?'

'Probably not. But give it a try.'

'I'm supposed to look at a house up in the mountains. I'd like you to come along and give me your opinion. I've sold the house in Kansas City and I'm going to stay out here.'

'With that as an enticement, I guess I could go look,' Steven said, thinking he had nothing else to do today with Dianna gone. Besides, he was curious to know what she was really up to.

They drove in Faye's modest rented car, a plain, dark blue, stick shift Ford. That impressed him more than anything she'd said, the fact that, without knowing she'd run into any acquaintance to impress with her martyrdom, she'd rented a non-flashy car. Perhaps there was a grain of truth in her reformation – but only a grain.

'Do you hear anything from Charlie?' she asked wistfully as she slowed almost to a crawl and cautiously wound her way through the switchback roads up a steep slope. 'I feel the worst about Charlie. Charlie trusted me and I betrayed that trust.'

'So did Anthony, and Wayne.'

'That's true, I'm sorry to say. But you didn't trust me.'

'I haven't trusted you since we were eleven and you bullied me into exploring that abandoned well. You said you'd throw me a rope to climb out with, but you left me there for four hours.'

'I didn't!'

'You did.'

'Come on, Steven. Kids do stuff like that.'

'Oh, the trick wasn't what got to me. It was when they finally found me and brought me back to the house, half frozen and scared witless, and you threw yourself on me, crying and saying to everybody how you'd begged me to take you along to play that day. You were so convincing that I almost believed it had happened that way. No, Faye. I haven't trusted you for a long, long time.'

The house was lovely, very new with lots of glassed views. Faye had a key and let them in. Though there was no furniture, the current owners having already moved, it was clean and welcoming. There was a big fireplace in a living room that was like a huge den. Along two walls were floor to ceiling bookcases. 'This would be a wonderful place for me to work,' Faye said.

'Work at what?'

'Writing. Didn't I tell you? I'm going to try my hand at children's books. It's something I've always wanted to do.'

Steven laughed. 'No, Faye, that's taking it too far. Anyway, you're too late. Grimm's beaten you to the kind

331

of stories you'd tell – with witches and trolls and wicked queens.'

She grinned, unabashed at being caught in a lie. 'All right, I want to write a novel. An adult novel about choices and the prices we pay for making the wrong choices. I should know enough about that.'

But Steven wasn't listening. 'Great view. Wonder what it's like in the winter?'

'Let's play house, Steven?'

'What?'

'Don't look alarmed. I only meant I brought a picnic lunch along.' There was a sliding glass door in the bank of floor-to-ceiling glass and she opened it a crack to let in the pine-scented mountain air. 'I'll bring in the hamper.'

Steven strolled around the house, thinking how great it would be to have a place like this. It reminded him of Ellen's house in California. Not in style or size, but in its privacy and isolation.

'Where have you gone?' Faye said from the main room. He went back in to find that she'd laid out a generous repast on a plaid rug on the floor. Sandwiches, chips, and a thermos of coffee. 'Do you still like deviled eggs?'

'Love them,' he said.

'I brought lots,' Faye said, opening a plastic container.

Steven ate contentedly, watching a vivid blue bird flitting around in a bush just outside the window. Gilly would have known what kind of bird it was. Gilly ...

'I've got some wine, too. Your favorite,' Faye said, pouring a plastic cup full of a wine that was, indeed, his favorite.

Steven suddenly woke up to what was happening. All this food, his deviled eggs and his favorite wine. He wasn't sure whether he should be amused or frightened at how easily she'd taken him in. 'Funny how you just happened to have that along with you before you "accidentally" ran into me, isn't it?'

She handed him the glass and her hand lingered on his. 'Enjoy, Steven.'

'How did you know where I was?'

'You've always been able to see right through me, haven't you?' she said with a girlish laugh that made his skin crawl. 'I had my maid call Nina and say it was about an insurance policy that had been upgraded and the company had to have your agreement before it could go into effect. Once I had a phone number, the rest was easy.'

'Easy, but pointless.'

She moved closer, took his hand. 'I needed to see you, Steven. To assure myself that my past was real. That I hadn't always been the crazy bitch I'd acted like last year.'

'But you have been,' Steven said brutally. 'You just kept it under wraps better.'

Suddenly she was crying, burrowing into his unwilling embrace. 'Steven, please say you don't mean that. I know I behaved badly, but I'm not a bad person. Not down deep.'

Before he could respond, her lips were on his, her hands were up under his sweater, caressing his back. 'Oh, Steven, Steven, we've been friends for ever. Be my friend now.'

He tried to pull away, for once not the least stimulated by a woman's attention. 'Faye, stop it. This is ridiculous.'

'No, my dear, this is fate. You and I go so far back. We know each other so well, in all but this one way.'

Her hand was on the zipper of his jeans. He grabbed her wrist and stopped her. 'I'm not interested.'

'Of course you are. Just enjoy yourself. I'm good, Steven. You won't be sorry.'

'For God's sake, Faye. What is the point? Can't you find anybody else to get it off with?'

'I don't want anybody else, Steven. I want you. I love you, Steven.'

'Bullshit! You don't love anybody but yourself.'

'I do love you,' she said, her hands working frantically at his clothing. 'I always have. I just never realized it until last year. Make love to me, Steven. You'll see. We'll be perfect together. It'll be you and me, my darling. Us against the world.'

'Against Anthony, you mean.'

'I don't want to talk about Anthony. I want you.'

He shoved himself back, away from her greedy hands. 'I don't know what the plan is, and I don't want to know. But you can't use me as a weapon against Anthony.'

'Will you stop yammering on about him? This hasn't got anything to do with anybody but us.'

'Faye, the very worst of this is your insulting assumption that I'm too stupid to see through it.'

'Steven, you want me.'

'And that's wrong, too.' He stood up.

She stood, too. 'Yes, you do. I know what men want.' With that, she crossed her arms, grabbed the bottom edge of her sweater and pulled it up and off. She stood before him smiling seductively, her naked breasts thrust out for his appreciation.

He was desperate to get away and the only way he knew was to hurt her badly enough to make her stop this indecent charade. There weren't many ways to hurt Faye, but he hit on one.

'Why, Faye,' he said coolly, 'you're starting to sag badly. You really ought to see a plastic surgeon. You look like one of those natives in the *National Geographic*.'

She couldn't have been more insulted if he'd thrown a bucket of slops in her face. She came at him. 'You slimy bastard! Self-righteous prick!'

'Ah, that's the Faye I know,' he said, dodging the slap she swung at him.

She stopped, gathering her forces, then smiled wickedly. 'You could just pretend, Steven. Pretend I'm your precious Gilly.'

Now it was his turn to be shocked.

'You thought I didn't know? You stupid bastard. The world knows you're in love with her. You're so damned obvious. Slobbering over your best friend's wife. You think *I'm* wicked? The choirboy with the hard-on for his precious Gilly. Do you do it when Anthony's at work? Or is it a threesome? Gilly's slut enough to service both of you, I'm sure. The innocent-looking ones usually are. After all, what are best friends for?'

'Shut up, Faye.' It actually crossed his mind to kill her. It was only the thought of getting caught that kept him from grabbing her by the neck. He spotted her purse where she'd flung it in the corner. He'd get the car keys. He'd get out of here, out where he could breathe something other than her poison before it choked him.

She saw his glance, ran for the purse herself. She opened it, took out the keys and jerked the sliding glass door open. She flung the keys as far as she could. 'You can't get away from me, Steven.'

He started toward the door, Faye still raving behind him. 'I'm going to destroy him, Steven. I'm going to do it. It's the only thing I have left to live for. And now I'm going to take you out with him. Listen to me, you pious jerk! I'm going to destroy all of you! Count your days!'

Steven walked quickly away, his legs operating without any conscious help from his mind. Her wickedness clung to him like a fetid odor. A few minutes later, he heard a car coming. He glanced back. Her rented Ford was tearing down the drive at a maniac speed. Of course she'd had another set of keys. Faye never made a dramatic gesture without a backup plan.

She sped past, veering toward him as he leaped out of the way. He heard her scream through the open window, 'Fool!'

The tires threw up a rock that struck his forehead.

It took Steven two hours to get back to the Stanley, pack and flee. And during that time, as he trudged along the road back to Estes Park, he realized what the worst of the distasteful scene with Faye had been. It wasn't that she'd meant to use him against Anthony; that was no surprise and had no chance of success. Faye was canny and smart, but had no understanding of human nature – not of his nature, at any rate. And attempting to seduce him would have been funny if it hadn't been so disgusting.

No, the worst was, she'd poisoned his mind, his spirit, with a simple, truthful fact. She'd said he was in love with Gilly. Until that second, Steven had never admitted it. He'd been worried and alarmed by his physical attraction to her, but had taken it as one more example of his lust getting the better of his soul. But love? No, he'd never let the concept come into his thoughts.

And in that accusation, he knew now, she was right. He did love Gilly. It had been a slow, insidious process. Joke by joke, dinner by dinner, crisis by crisis, day by day, he'd come to love her. There was hardly a part of him now that didn't have a thread of Gilly running through it. When he saw a flower or bird, he thought of Gilly. She always knew what kind it was and had some interesting little story about its behavior, habits or name. When he witnessed a tender scene between strangers, he wanted to tell Gilly about it. When he heard a funny story, he couldn't wait to repeat it to her and listen to her laughter bubble up. He ate, and almost liked, spinach now because Gilly believed in its nutritional benefits. He was wearing a blue sweater she'd given him for Christmas because she said it matched his eyes perfectly.

For once, and only briefly, he allowed himself to think about her without the fact of Anthony intruding. But that was wrong, and immediately he brought Anthony back on his mental stage. He loved Anthony, too. Not in the same way, but as much, probably more, than he loved Gilly. And he *couldn't* love them both. At least, he couldn't act on his love of Gilly, not even in the most guarded, subtle way, without betraying Anthony.

If even Faye, nasty-minded and insensitive, had seen it, it was only a matter of time before Anthony suspected. It would ruin the friendship that was the core of his life.

He had to choose between them and there was no question of what that choice had to be. He had to tear Gilly out of his life, pull her influence out by the roots.

PART FIVE

Steven

1978-86

'Now turn we unto Queen Guenever and to the fair Lady Elaine, that when Dame Elaine heard the Queen so rebuke Sir Launcelot, and also she saw how he swooned, then she said unto Queen Guenever: Madam, ye are greatly to blame for Sir Launcelot, for now have ye lost him, for I saw and heard by his countenance that he is mad for ever. Alas, madam, ye do great sin, and to yourself great dishonour, for ye have a lord of your own, and therefore it is your part to love him; for there is no queen in this world hath such another king as ye have.'

Le Morte d'Arthur by Sir Thomas Malory,
edited by Isreal Gollancz, 1897

Chapter Twenty-one

'Well, will you look at this!' Anthony said, passing the wedding invitation across the breakfast table to Gilly. 'You remember Don Shermerhorn, don't you? I think you met him once. He's the young man we sent down to run that clinic in Alabama. And the bride is the daughter of the town doctor down there.'

'Will we go? September.' She got up and went to the bookshelf in the kitchen where she kept her gardening references. Anthony knew she was finding out if there were any gardens she could visit on the same trip. He made his escape.

It was the talk of the office. Don Shermerhorn was well liked at Samaritan. His occasional trips to report to the board were marked by a certain amount of squabbling among the staff as to whose apartment he'd stay at while he was in town and who'd get to have dinner with him. This morning a couple of secretaries were looking distinctly disappointed at the news, but on the whole everyone was pleased.

'Steven, did you get the invitation to Shermerhorn's wedding?' Anthony said, coming into the boardroom. It was the day for their weekly meeting.

'What? Yeah. Nice for him,' Steven said, looking up. He was attempting to rearrange an armload of file folders and was frowning fiercely.

'Where have you been, Steven?'

'What do you mean? Right here in the office. You've seen me.'

'I mean outside the office. You haven't come to the house for months. Gilly says you don't like us anymore. Here, give me those. You've never been any good at alphabetizing,' Anthony said, taking the disorganized jumble of files from him.

'That's why the secretarial pool wouldn't accept me,' Steven said with a laugh, releasing the mess for Anthony to sort out.

'So, where have you been keeping yourself? The office grapevine says you took a stunning redhead to a business dinner last week.'

'Oh? That was Dianna Jarvis. She's a volunteer for the Danning Home. I wanted her to tell some of our contributors what the volunteers do.'

'Strictly business then?' Anthony said. He was getting irritated with the files as well. 'Your problem is you don't label them consistently. I'll have to have Nina straighten you out.' He set aside the pile of folders. 'About this Dianna Jarvis.'

'She's gorgeous, smart, sensitive.'

Anthony stared at him with surprise and pleasure. 'This sounds serious!'

'I think it is,' Steven admitted.

'Wow! Gilly will be thrilled. When do we get to meet her? How about dinner Friday? Gilly's got some floral triumph she's dying to show off and has been making noises about a dinner party.'

The rest of the working board members were drifting in. Nina was bustling around, trying to herd them to the table. Her glance fell on the file folders. 'Are these yours?' she asked Steven.

'Guilty,' he said, hanging his head in mock embarrassment.

She gathered them up. 'I'll have a talk with your secretary,' she said ominously.

'No, no! They're my own from home. They're not her fault,' Steven said, imagining a bloody secretarial confrontation.

Most of the working board were in place when a visitor arrived.

'Well, Anthony, what have you got to say for yourself?' Betsy Graves demanded from the doorway.

Betsy had remained on the official list of board members, mainly because Anthony was afraid if he removed her she'd make a scene. But she never attended meetings. She and Anthony had unofficially adopted a policy of ignoring one another's existence. He hadn't laid eyes on her for at least four years.

'Betsy! What a surprise. We're just about to have a board meeting.'

'I know that. Why do you think I'm here?'

Why was she here was a question that troubled Anthony.

There was some shuffling of chairs to make room for her and Anthony studied her while it was going on. Betsy, he discovered to his pleasure, was getting matronly. The drapey pink dress didn't quite disguise the added weight, the chunkiness of her waist, the very slightly wrinkled look of her neck. Her rouge was overdone, her hair too teased and lacquered. He wondered nastily if she'd yet started having to pay the beautiful young men who surrounded her. If not, it was just a matter of time.

'Betsy, since your visit is unusual, we'll start with your business,' he said, thinking it was better to have it over with, whatever it was.

She arranged herself in a chair. 'I want to know just what you think you're doing to my son.'

That took him completely by surprise. 'Harry's on a fund-raising trip to California.'

'I'm not talking about Harry. I know perfectly well where he is.'

'But Wayne doesn't work for us anymore.'

'Don't be stupid. I know that! I'm talking about Donald. It's disgraceful the way he's been treated ...'

Anthony couldn't imagine what she was raving about. Who was Donald? Wasn't he the one they shipped off to

341

an uncle or cousin or somebody when he was still a kid? He'd never met the boy. '... such a minor job,' she was going on loudly. 'I didn't mind so much, but now he's marrying this nobody girl and it's all your fault. We don't know a thing about her family. Southern upstarts, that's all they are. Claims her father is a doctor, but I'd like to see his credentials, that's all I say. Probably just a bunch of barefoot hicks. And I want him to have a decent salary now that you've done this to him.'

Anthony couldn't believe what he was thinking. 'You aren't talking about Don Shermerhorn, are you?'

'Can't you hear?' she demanded.

'Don Shermerhorn's your son?'

'Of course he is! Why would I care otherwise?' She made a dramatic gesture that upset a coffee cup all over Anthony's meeting notes.

While several of the men ran for napkins to blot up the spill (at least one tried unobtrusively to escape, but Nina stopped him), Anthony said, 'But his name's Shermerhorn, not Graves.'

'He took his uncle's name when he went to live with him,' Betsy explained with exaggerated patience.

'But he went to Africa, didn't he?'

'That's where they keep Egypt. Look at a map!' Betsy snapped. 'Are you trying to tell me you hadn't figured out who he really was?'

'I swear I didn't know. Why didn't he tell me himself?'

Betsy waved her hand and several more coffee cups were hastily moved out of her range. 'Some idealistic bullshit about making it on his own merits. I told him how stupid that was, that you'd taken on Wayne and Harry and you'd surely give him a job, but he said that was just the point. So, what are you going to do about all this? It's disgraceful to have your own nephew, a boy of his social background, working in such a menial capacity and for such a pittance of a salary.'

'What we going to do?' Anthony mused. 'Well, first we'll go to the wedding. Then, if he wants a change of assignment or salary, he can ask for it himself,' he said with a grin. He got up and came round to where she was sitting and almost lifted her out of her chair. 'Betsy, it was so good of you to come share your information and opinions with us. Do feel free to drop in again.'

Gilly didn't take the news about Dianna Jarvis like Anthony thought she would.

'What do you know about her?' she asked coolly.

'Only what Steven's said. She must really be something. Gilly, you don't seem happy to hear this.'

'I'm just wary. Nobody else seems to know her. What if she's just after his money.'

'Why would you assume that?'

'I'm not assuming it, just considering it as a possibility.'

'Gilly, Steven's not stupid. He'd see through a person like that.'

'I don't know. Men never seem to—'

'Gilly, he's happy. Don't you want that for him?'

'Yes, naturally I do. But he was happy with us, being our friend,' she replied. 'What does he need her for?'

'Besides the obvious?'

'Oh, Anthony. Don't be vulgar.'

'You're jealous!' he said with a laugh.

'I am not!'

'You are, too.'

'Well then, so are you. Or you should be. You know we haven't seen him for months and you've minded that just as much as I have. And it's her fault. He doesn't have time for us anymore. And if he's really serious and marries her, he won't need us at all.'

'Not necessarily,' Anthony said. 'We're married and that doesn't stop us from liking him and wanting him around.'

'I don't like it. Things were fine as they were. Why do they have to change?'

'Because they do and you know it. What if your gardens never changed?'

'That's different.'

'No, not much, Gilly. I've invited them to dinner Friday. Make a special effort to like her, will you? Steven will be hurt if you don't.'

She hesitated, then said, 'Of course I will. I'm being a selfish bitch. How do you stand me?'

'Very easily,' he said, taking her in his arms.

The dinner didn't go well.

Gilly was so aggressively hospitable that it amounted almost to rudeness. She insisted on regaling Dianna Jarvis with a wealth of stories which, ostensibly meant to be entertaining, actually proved what an intimate, close little circle she and Steven and Anthony made. Anthony was perplexed and irritated, and he wasn't sure just who he was most irritated with. Steven was sullen and snappish and Dianna, thoroughly intimidated, acted like she had the personality of a sick canary. Anthony really wanted to like her, but couldn't. Steven needed a practical woman with spirit. This one seemed merely to echo his weaknesses without bringing any strengths to the relationship. She was dreamy, shy, introspective. Or maybe she was just overwhelmed by Gilly. It was an endless evening.

Anthony recognized that Gilly had behaved badly, but he hadn't the heart to chide her. If Dianna had any backbone she'd have stood up to Gilly's smiling attack. And while Anthony himself wasn't jealous, he was beginning to understand Gilly's jealousy – or so he thought. They had been a great threesome, he and Gilly and Steven. And Dianna Jarvis put a damper on their enjoyment of each other. He wanted Steven to be happy and if this innocuous young woman made him happy, good. But she was so boring! So sticky-sweet *nice*!

'Is he going to marry her?' Gilly asked when she came up to bed.

'I hope not,' Anthony said honestly.

'I didn't like her.'

'I didn't like any of us tonight,' Anthony said, climbing into his side of the bed and picking up a book on non-profit tax law he'd been working his way through for a week. 'He'll be bringing her to Donald's wedding. We've got to make an effort to get to know her better. Maybe we'll learn to like her.'

'She's not good enough for him,' Gilly said, savagely plumping her pillows.

The gathering of the Herron/Graves/Wentworth family for the wedding had a number of other impacts on Samaritan. Wayne was there, of course, for his brother's wedding and in the course of socializing talked to Anthony about having his old job back. Anthony was happy to welcome him back to the fold and wouldn't even let him grovel.

Fortunately, Faye didn't turn up. Donald didn't care, because he had only the vaguest recollection of his aunt and, having heard of her actions, didn't want to make her acquaintance anyway.

At the family gathering Anthony saw Martin, the boy Betsy claimed was his son. Martin Graves was approaching his fourteenth birthday now. The child was turning into a man; a man who promised to be tall, broad-shouldered and fair-haired. More important, there was a distinct similarity between Martin and Anthony – at least in Anthony's eyes – in the boy's hairline, set of eyebrows, shape of hands. All the tiny characteristics which, taken together, create a whole person. Anthony had the feeling that a snapshot of himself at that age would have had a startling resemblance to Martin Graves. And if someone had turned up a picture of Max Herron in his teens, it would have looked like both of them. The similarities didn't originate maternally.

No one else made any comment about the likeness. Anthony hoped that what was so obvious to him wasn't to anyone else. Why should they notice? he told himself. No one had known him as a gangling boy. But sooner or later they would start to see it.

During a pig roast the day before the wedding, Anthony decided he was going to have to tell Gilly sooner or later about Martin and that it might as well be sooner. Quite uncharacteristically, he made himself sick with worry over how to present to his wife the fact that he not only had an illegitimate child, but that the child's mother was his own half-sister.

'You're not eating a thing, Anthony. Are you getting sick?' Gilly asked with concern.

'No. Yes. Gilly, I have to talk to you.'

'Oh, dear. That sounds serious,' she said, taking a last bite of her potato salad.

'Let's go for a ride in the country. Get away from everybody for a while.'

'Not too far. Have you seen the desserts? I don't want to miss them.'

He felt like a criminal; taking her away from the fun when she was so happy just to crush her with his terrible admission. But it had to be done. He was blowing up like a balloon with the awful assurance that Martin really was his child. He'd never thoroughly believed it before, not heart-deep, and now that he did, he couldn't stand knowing and keeping it from her.

He'd driven only a mile or so when Gilly said, 'Pull off here. There are some nice picnic tables.'

It was a small public park. They sat down at a table, across from each other. Anthony leaned forward and took Gilly's hands. 'My darling Gilly, I have something awful to tell you. Now, I want you to promise that no matter how shocked and sickened you are, that you don't say anything until I—'

'Is this about Martin Graves?' she asked.

Anthony was so dumbfounded he couldn't speak.

'He's your son, isn't he?' she said calmly.

Anthony nodded. 'How – how did you know?'

346

'I saw him. That was all it took.'

'Is it that obvious?'

She squeezed his hands reassuringly. 'Only to me, darling. The few times you've ever mentioned him, you've gone all stiff and white around the lips. I've always wondered why you hate Betsy so much. When I saw him yesterday, I was suddenly sure I knew why.'

'And you don't hate me? You must be disgusted. I am. She's my half-sister, for God's sake!'

'Anthony, I'm not stupid. I can count. You've told me several times about being summoned to Birches years before you knew your relationship to your biological father. Don't you remember me asking you just when that visit was the last time you brought it up? I made a point of finding out how old Martin is. It's a simple matter of subtraction. I've met Betsy and I could tell you precisely what happened. You were very young and thrown among strangers. She must have been very beautiful then and as free with her favors then as now. She seduced you. Neither of you knew your true relationship.'

'Oh God, Gilly. You can't imagine the relief!' he said, his joints feeling rubbery with the release of tension. 'I was so afraid you'd hate me, that I'd lose you when you found out.'

'I do hate you a little. For not telling me your worries sooner. That's been the worst part. Waiting for you to get round to telling me and wondering if you ever would. I hate it when people I love keep secrets from me. Why didn't you talk about this before, Anthony? I'd have understood.'

'Because I was afraid you wouldn't. I was terrified that you'd be disgusted with me.'

'But you told me today. Why is today different?'

'Because today I know for sure that he's mine. I never believed it a hundred per cent.'

'What difference will it make?' Gilly asked.

'What do you mean?'

'I'm not sure. Does it make anything different?'

347

Anthony thought about it for a long moment. 'I don't think so, except between us. It's my only secret and now you know it.'

'I'm glad.'

'Not half as glad as I am that I had the miraculous good fortune to find you. What would my life have been like—'

'Anthony?'

'Yes?'

'Would you mind terribly if we went back? I'm really interested in trying some of those desserts and getting some new recipes.'

He got up, came round the battered picnic table and hugged her. 'The best thing about you is that you've got your priorities straight. God, I love you, Gilly.'

He'd made a joke of it, but he was quite sincere. Her refusal to agonize over the unchangeable was one of her best assets. He wasn't much given to agonizing, so he'd never benefited from that quality, but he'd seen her do it to Steven over and over again. 'Can anything be changed by worrying about this?' she'd ask him and when he admitted it couldn't, she'd briskly dispose of it. 'Then let's not waste adrenaline,' she'd say and move onto happier subjects than whatever was troubling him.

Anthony knew her practical astringency was good for Steven. He'd never appreciated, until today, how comforting it could be to him.

It wasn't until many years later that Steven was able to look back on those times without his heart feeling it would break all over again. But when he was able to analyze it, he realized that it was during the wedding trip to Alabama that his life started to unravel. That was when the tragedy that would engulf them all someday started lapping at their ankles. And it was his fault.

It started after the wedding at the reception dance held at the local country club. He'd had too much champagne for his own good; they all had. It was a very festive evening. In the end he hadn't invited Dianna along; her one introduction to Anthony and Gilly had been so disastrous he couldn't, in good conscience, throw her into all of them in a situation she couldn't escape. He should have missed her more than he did, he knew, but he was having a wonderful time. But as he finished his turn to dance with the bride, he suddenly felt the room was too noisy and too hot to stand a minute more and he slipped out through a service door to get some fresh air.

He ended up at the deserted swimming pool. Gilly was standing at the side of the pool, looking down into the calm water. 'Too much for you too?' he asked.

She looked round, startled. 'I needed some air. And time to think. Are you having a good time?'

'Great. They're a beautiful young couple, aren't they?'

She stepped away from the edge of the water and went to a deckchair where she had discarded her wrap, a spangled cobweb of fabric. He took it from her and draped it over her shoulders. And then, though he knew better, he let his hands linger on her shoulders. She was so small, so vibrant and warm. She seemed – no, it had to be his imagination – to lean towards him.

And then, without meaning to and knowing he shouldn't, he drew her near, and kissed her. He told himself later that he meant it only as a light, friendly gesture. But he knew he was lying to his own conscience, which only madmen can get away with.

She slipped her arms round his waist, holding him as she returned his kiss with fevor. And that was what truly shocked him – not that he was weak, he knew his weaknesses all too well, but that she was. Somewhere deep inside, he'd always believed that if he succumbed to his passion for her, she'd slap him back in place before he could embarrass them. That had been his moral safety net. Now he was hurtling toward the ground and it was gone.

He jerked back. 'Gilly, I'm sorry.'

She was as calm as a goddess. 'Don't be, my dear Steven.'

'This is awful. I didn't mean—' He couldn't go on. He turned and walked away. Almost ran.

He went from the country club to the house where he was staying and from there directly toward Kansas City in the rental car. He didn't want to see or talk to anyone he knew. He drove until five in the morning, when he was too tired to stay awake, then stopped at a Holiday Inn next to the highway. When he awoke around noon, feeling drugged with confusion and regret and guilt, he called Ellen.

'Steven, what's wrong?' she asked immediately.

'Nothing. Why should anything be wrong? I was just thinking about you and Gary and thought I'd give you a call.'

Another lie. He wanted to pour it out to someone who would soothe him, as she almost always did, but he couldn't even get near the subject without crying out with the anguish of it. Even if he could have brought himself to say any of it, where would he start? That he was hopelessly, incurably in love with his beloved friend's wife? That he now suspected that she was in love with him, too? Or at least physically attracted? That he was on the point of proposing to a lovely young woman who adored him and now knew he couldn't do it?

'Do you need me, Steven?' she asked softly. 'You don't have to tell me anything. I could come to Kansas City if you need me.'

Dear God, why couldn't he love *her*? She understood him. She'd never pressure him.

'No, I'm not home. It's really nothing. I just had the urge to call and see how everything is,' he said. He drew a deep breath, trying to sound normal and casual. 'I haven't heard from Gary for a while and I wondered how he's getting along.'

'He's fine. He's living in a commune. But you know that.'

'Yes, of course. Well, I better be on my way.' He was suddenly frantic to get away from her.

'Do that. Steven?'
'What?'
'I'm here. Whenever.'
'I know that. Goodbye, Ellen.'

When Steven got home, he broke off his relationship with
Dianna Jarvis. He was very kind, if not entirely honest.
He explained gently that although she was a perfect
person any man would be a fool to let go, there was something missing in him, something that kept him from
making the total commitment she deserved.

She took it all stoically and with the same distant
courtesy he employed. Yes, she understood. He had
no obligation to her. She was delighted to have had the
pleasure of knowing him, hoped they'd remain friends,
etc.

The next day she killed herself.

Chapter Twenty-two

Sunday night and the airport was mobbed with returning Thanksgiving travelers. Normally Nina didn't meet people at the airport; she sent a limo for them. But this guest was arriving at her urging and it was important that she be there, so she struggled through the crowds to the proper gate. Homebound travelers, replete with turkey and family gossip, were disembarking. Ellen was among the last.

'Nina, you haven't changed a bit,' Ellen said, not meaning it entirely as a compliment, but hoping Nina would take it that way.

'You have,' Nina said, looking at her with amazement. She'd been a pretty girl when Nina knew her in high school, pale and ethereal; she was quite a beautiful middle-aged woman, in a sturdy, tanned, back-to-nature way.

When they were finally alone in the back seat of the Lincoln, Ellen said, 'I'm so glad you called me.'

Nina was nearly wringing her hands. This had seemed a good idea before; now she was sick with worry that she was making things worse. 'I'm butting in and Steven will never forgive me if he finds out,' Nina said. 'Please don't give me away.'

'I wouldn't. I knew anyway that something was wrong. He called me one day shortly before – before it happened. I knew he was troubled. Tell me just what happened.'

'I really don't know very much,' Nina said. 'We all went to a wedding in Alabama. He disappeared suddenly. Nobody knew where or why. He was missing a couple days. The morning he came back to the office he looked terrible. Exhausted, unhappy. He said he'd broken off with a young woman he'd been seeing a lot of – Dianna Jarvis. Everybody assumed that she'd dumped him and it had really been a shock. Anyway, later the same day the police arrived to ask him some questions. She'd killed herself. Slit her wrists. Apparently she left a note mentioning Steven. Saying, I'm told, that she did it because he was her last chance at happiness and if he didn't want her, she didn't want to live. Something about going to be with her sister. There was a sister who killed herself, too. Steven told Anthony all this and Anthony told me.'

'What happened then?'

'Nothing. Steven went dead silent. Nearly mute. He kept coming to the office, worked himself nearly to death. It's been two months and he's still there, physically. But he's like a man walking a tightrope. Very intense, preoccupied, as if he's maintaining an excruciatingly careful balance. Ellen, I'm worried about him and he won't let me help him. I don't know if he needs a shrink or an exorcist or what. I'd find it, if I knew what it was. Anyway, I thought of you.'

Ellen sat back in the soft leather upholstery and lit a cigarette. She never smoked at home, only when she was out in the world. She inhaled and studied Nina. 'You're in love with him, aren't you?' she said. It wasn't really a question and there wasn't the least criticism in it.

Nina didn't say anything for a long moment. Not out of any reluctance to tell Ellen the truth, only because she wasn't sure what the truth was anymore. She wasn't much given to examining her feelings. It took her a while to crank up the machinery. 'I'm in the habit of loving him,' she said, striving for strict accuracy.

'So am I. But he doesn't want either of us. What does he want?'

'I don't know,' Nina said. That wasn't entirely true. She had the vaguest sort of suspicion, but wouldn't put it into words. It was a potential problem she kept tightly locked into one of the high-security compartments of her tidy brain.

'And you think I can help him?'

'I have no idea, but somebody must. I'm frantic about him; Anthony's frantic. We thought – '

' – that he needs me? It sounds like he does. But he doesn't know it. He never knows it. Nina, I'm glad you called me. I don't know what I can do, but I'd move heaven and earth to help him. Tell me, do other people know what Steven's and my relationship is? Do his friends know about Gary?'

'I don't think so. Anthony does, of course. And me.'

'So I explain myself as an old friend? Just that? '

'I think you'll have to ask him,' Nina said.

'Yes, you're quite right. Nina, you've turned out to be a very wise woman.'

'Gilly, I want to talk to you about Steven,' Anthony said a couple days later as they were having breakfast.

Gilly had thought about almost nothing but Steven for several months. She had been shocked when he kissed her and shocked at her own response, but she had quickly adjusted, even accepted the situation. She loved Steven, had loved him as Anthony did, for years. To her, the really surprising revelation that night of the wedding reception was that neither of them had recognized much earlier exactly what *kind* of love it had grown to be. It had been so obvious a course, so inevitable.

And she didn't really mind that much.

It was difficult to find anything all that bad about being loved by two men, two wonderful, exceptional men. That part of it was quite nice, really. Not that she'd ever betray Anthony by sleeping with Steven. That was a given. But she knew Steven was agonizing over it. That was why he'd broken off his relationship with that drippy Jarvis girl. Well, good! she'd told herself. She wasn't right for him anyway. Her suicide only proved what a morbid, unbalanced person she had been. Not that Gilly would have wished her dead for anything. She only wished her out of Steven's life.

'What about Steven?' she asked.

'A friend of his has come to visit. An old friend who might help get him out of this funk he's in.'

'I'm glad to hear it.'

'She's going to join Samaritan for a while.'

'She? This friend is a woman?'

'Yes. She's also – she's the mother of his child.' Anthony spat the last words out, knowing Gilly wasn't going to take well having had this kind of secret kept from her.

'What!'

'Gilly, Steven has a son named Gary. He's twenty-two, twenty-three years old.'

'That's not possible! Why are you saying such outrageous things, Anthony?'

'It is possible. He was just a kid.'

'And you've known about this for how long?'

Anthony didn't understand quite how he got on the defensive. 'For a long time. Since we started Samaritan.'

'And you never told me!' She got up from the table and started slam-stacking dishes.

'It wasn't my secret.'

'So it *was* a secret from me!'

'No, I didn't mean that.'

'Are they divorced?' Gilly asked.

'No, they never married.'

'Why is that?'

'I'm not sure I know. You'll have to ask him, but not soon, Gilly. Let him get over this Dianna Jarvis business before you question him.'

She leaned on the table, her face white with anger. 'How dare you patronize me that way!'

Anthony came round and tried to hug her, but she shrugged out of his embrace. 'Gilly, what are you so pissed at me for?'

'It's not just you. It's both of you. I thought we were

356

all friends,' she said, tears brimming. 'And now I discover there's been an enormous, important part of Steven's life that you've conspired to hide from me. As if I weren't important enough to either of you to share it. Or possibly I wasn't to be trusted.'

'Conspired? We didn't conspire. It just never came up.'

'Never came up! Anthony, you can be *such* a fool!'

With that, she flounced out of the room, snatched up her jacket and car keys and was gone before Anthony could catch up with her. He knew where she was going, either the garden centre or the bird seed place. He considered going after her, but decided not to. Whatever the hell was bugging her was something she had to deal with herself. There was no point in making a public scene to no purpose.

A week later, when Anthony was going over plans for the annual board meeting at Birches with Gilly, he said, 'Make space for Ellen MacLaughton, will you?'

'Who is that? Steven's . . . person.'

'Yes,' he said cautiously. There hadn't been any more blow-ups about her. Gilly had come back that morning with what looked like a ton of shelled sunflower seeds and said nothing more about it since.

'Very well,' she said calmly, making a notation in the notebook in which she kept her hostess plans.

'I think it's good for him to have her around,' Anthony went on, knowing the dictum 'Never Explain' was a good one, but unable to stop himself.

'Indeed?' she said, very coolly. She scribbled something in the margin of her notes. He was glad he couldn't see what it said.

Steven seemed happy in Ellen's presence and it scalded Gilly like acid. He still moved and spoke as though he were made of eggshells that might shatter at any moment, but he sometimes smiled when Ellen spoke to him and his eyes often followed her as she walked across a room. Gilly hated Ellen from first sight. She was a big, strapping woman who looked like an aging hippy in all those damned homespun-looking things. Gilly would have bet she never used moisturizer on that skin; it was going to look like an alligator in a few years. And the fact that Ellen didn't even disguise the gray coming into her long dark hair enraged her. Gilly had only two or three white hairs which she plucked out the moment they appeared. She wasn't going to look like a hag before her time.

Ellen, who had been around Steven enough to begin to suspect what Gilly's role was in his shaky emotional state, went out of her way to be gracious, at first. 'What a very lovely home you have, Mrs Wentworth. I'm very grateful to you for inviting me,' she said when she arrived on Steven's arm.

I didn't invite you, you pushy bitch, Gilly thought, but said, 'I'm always glad to make room for any old friend of Steven's.' Only the slightest emphasis on 'old'.

'I'm a positively ancient friend of Steven's,' Ellen said, acknowledging the jibe with a condescending smile that made Gilly want to slap her. 'Steven's told me all about you, but he didn't say how very pretty you are, Mrs Wentworth.'

'It probably slipped his mind,' Gilly said with a dazzling smile. 'So many things do. I don't know a thing about you, I'm sorry to say. We'll have to sit down and have a nice long talk sometime while you're here and really get to know each other.'

Steven didn't grasp the subtleties or innate viciousness of the battle, but sensed that things weren't going well. 'If you'll excuse me, I need to have a word with Anthony.'

Gilly showed Ellen to her room, with a few more well-delivered snipes on each side. Ellen managed to imply, in a most complimentary manner, of course, that Gilly was nothing more than a glorified domestic drudge. Gilly suggested, ever so politely, that they probably didn't have fine houses to worry about in Oklahoma or Alaska or wherever Ellen was from.

When they parted, each hated herself as much as she

hated the other for succumbing to such jealousy and pettiness. Gilly was furious that this woman should come right into her home and try to steal Steven's affections from her and Anthony, never mind that Anthony didn't realize that's what she was attempting to do. Men could be *so* dim! If this Ellen person had her way, she'd steal Steven away and Anthony would lose his closest friend. It was for Anthony's sake as much as her own that she wanted Ellen out of Steven's life. Like Dianna Jarvis, she was a 'fifth wheel' who would spoil the precious friendship the three of them had shared for so long. Granted, Steven was upset right now, not his old self. But that would pass. He'd get over Dianna's death, realize that it was a fatal flaw in the girl herself, not something that he had caused.

As for the kiss beside the pool, he'd come to see, as Gilly herself had, that the physical attraction that had flared between them was natural, controllable, flattering to both, really. It wasn't as though either of them would succumb to it. Nobody could command what they thought and felt. So long as they limited their behavior to the proper bounds, there was no sin on anyone's soul. But Steven was given to brooding and blaming himself for imagined shortcomings and she couldn't explain any of that to him if he were in Ellen's clutches. Ellen would take him away where his over-sensitive conscience would run riot. The comradeship the three of them had shared would be irretrievably spoiled. She *had* to do something.

It was for his own good.

Ellen saw Gilly as a greedy, sensuous young woman with too much time on her hands and a trivial need to be adored to distraction by every man she liked. She summed her up as promiscuous. She had no way of knowing that Gilly had never loved or even looked twice at any man besides her husband – except Steven. She believed that Gilly had no idea of the moral torture she was putting Steven through. And during that week at Birches, Ellen came to another realization: that she loved Steven wholeheartedly. All those decades ago she'd foolishly turned down his proposal. Now she was reaping the thin, bitter crop from that juvenile mistake.

She'd raised a beloved child and now he was gone, no longer in need of her nurturing. And it was her nature to nurture a loved one. She needed to save Steven from Gilly because he needed saving, and because she loved him more than herself. The woman was destroying him and had to be stopped.

Ellen had to get Steven into her bed and Gilly had to know.

Ellen and Steven hadn't slept together since she'd come to Samaritan. She knew that whatever his feelings for Gilly Wentworth, he wanted her, Ellen. For all their emotional misfires, they were extraordinarily sexually compatible. Always had been. She knew she could have him any time she wanted him, but she hadn't exerted the slight pressure necessary to bring it about because he was so emotionally overburdened already. She thought that the most he could handle was supportive affection. But having met Gilly, she thought stronger measures were called for. And if she added a bit to Steven's stress in the short term, it would be to his benefit in the long term. Unfortunately, Gilly had put Steven in a room across the hall from the master suite and Ellen was stuck as far away as the enormous house allowed. Still, she'd get round that. Somehow.

It was for his own good.

The week was hell for Steven. He hadn't been sleeping well since the trip to Alabama and fatigue was catching up with him, clouding his judgment, muddling his thoughts. He felt as if parts of his mental equipment were spinning off away from him. He was constantly groping wildly for an elusive thought, a misplaced word, a vanished concept. If only he could sleep. But what chance was there here? In a room merely a dozen feet from the room where Gilly and Anthony slept – made love, whispered endearments. Her very proximity was an aphrodisiac. He was jittery with frustration, both sexual and spiritual. His mind was at war with his body. That was it, he told himself. No wonder he couldn't rest. He was a battlefield. On constant red alert.

It was showing in his work, too. There had been a fire at one of the Herron paper mills, and he'd screwed up the insurance paperwork and caused everybody extra trouble before it was sorted out. He'd made several proposals at this very meeting, proposals that were dear to his heart, and he'd been short of the necessary documentation and information. Other people, worthy, deserving people, were being harmed by his inefficiency. He felt he was fucking up everything he touched.

He couldn't get a firm grip on anything he was doing. Projects, responsibilities, relationships had all become octopi with long tentacles tangling, weaving themselves in slimy knots. At night, when he desperately wanted to sleep, his mind was grappling with the loops and clumps, all of which were struggling to strangle him in their deadly grip. He was having spectacular nightmares from which he woke, startled and sweating, choked with a sense of doom so oppressive that several times he staggered up from bed and threw open the window to get cold, fresh air, which he gulped as if suffocating.

If it hadn't involved Gilly, he'd have gone to her for advice and comfort. She was so sensible, so gloriously down-to-earth in her thinking. He'd always been able to tell her about his problems, his upheavals of conscience, as she called them. She would listen patiently to all the laboriously thought out pro and cons, and then cut through the nonsense to the heart of the matter. But not with this. How could he say, 'I've fallen in love with you, my best friend's wife. It's a love that obsesses me. But put that consideration aside and tell me what to do.' He certainly couldn't talk to Anthony about it. Nor did he feel right about laying this burden on Ellen. He was aware and sensitive to the change in her feelings towards him.

They hadn't talked about it, but he knew from the way she looked at him, or gently touched his shoulder when he was tired or beleaguered that her feelings for him had changed.

No, there was no help from any of the people he'd normally call on. This was his own mess to sort out. He needed to simplify. Cut through the crap. Get a distance. Get away. Run away. No, just step back a safe distance. When this meeting was over, he'd go away somewhere all alone. Leave no address or phone number. Get a grip on it all.

The thought comforted him for a full half-hour before his mind started chewing it over and spitting out sour chunks. Go where? Overseas? What about transportation? What about clothes? What about his responsibilities at Samaritan and to his family? What if there were an emergency and he couldn't be reached? Who could handle that proposal for the music program for handicapped children? Where were those figures for the musicians' union rates? Had he left that file at home? At the office? What else was he missing? What had he done with the silver tie clasp Anthony had given him six Christmasses ago? Or was it seven?

Was this a nervous breakdown? he was wondering as he fell into a fitful sleep.

The crisis came the night before the last day of meetings. 'Come to my room tonight, Steven,' Ellen said as they were leaving the dinner table. It had been an old-fashioned chili supper with a square dance to follow. The furniture had been pulled back, the oriental carpets rolled up and the fiddle player was already starting to play. Ellen was sure they couldn't be overheard. 'Just to talk, Steven.'

'Oh, Ellen, I—'

'You look headachy and I have something that kills headaches on the spot. Promise. Midnight. Last door along the east hall on the third floor.'

Ellen had judged wrong about the sound. Though she was speaking quietly, Gilly and Nina had just come up behind them to ask them to help in asking around about a car in front with the lights left on. Nina saw Gilly stiffen and stop in her tracks. 'Is there something wrong?' Nina asked harshly.

Gilly snapped back into her hostess role. 'No, nothing. It just occurred to me that the car must belong to the band. I'll ask them.'

Steven obligingly participated in the dancing for as long as he had to, then slipped away. Putting on a heavy coat and muffler from the back hall, he let himself out of the house and went for a long walk, trying desperately hard *not* to think about anything. He wouldn't go to Ellen's room. Not in Gilly's house. Not anywhere if he could resist his own physical needs.

It was quarter to twelve when he finally became aware of how cold he was. He went back to the house and was surprised to find it nearly in darkness. Everyone must have decided to make it an early evening so they could shine in the last day's meetings. Thank God, Gilly always left the back door unlocked when there were guests and he didn't have to wake the place up. He put away the coat and muffler and crept silently through the house. His own room was dark except for the faint glow of a night light in the adjourning bathroom. Without turning on any other lights, he undressed and crawled into bed.

He smelled her, that faintly floral scent that always surrounded her, before he sensed the warmth of her body next to him.

'I was afraid you wouldn't be able to find my room,' Ellen said, reaching out and touching his cheek.

Gilly had risen stealthily so she wouldn't wake Anthony though he was a heavy sleeper and probably wouldn't stir for anything less than gunfire. Standing at the window, she'd seen Steven come back. She watched, twisting her hands in indecision. A few minutes later she heard the

363

faint creak of his door opening and closing across the hall. Opening her own door slightly, she hesitated.

She *had* to talk to him. His affection and dependence on Ellen had seemed to grow rather than diminish during the week and she'd heard him ask Anthony if he could take a month off after the meeting. He was going away somewhere with her. With that dreadful woman. She'd turn him against them. She and Anthony might never see him again. She didn't know what she'd say to him. She had faith it would come to her, but she had to say something. And what if it took more than talking? she asked herself, fingering the silky folds of her sleek black dressing gown. If she gave herself to him, he'd know how important he was to her – to them. It would be a sin; a betrayal of Anthony. But not really. Not really. Not if it were just the once, just to make Steven understand something beyond words. And it would only be once. She'd make sure he knew that.

Nina had been on edge all evening, ever since she and Gilly had overheard that snip of conversation between Ellen and Steven. She'd tried to keep an eye on all of them during the evening, but had lost track of Steven early on. Gilly's behavior had been alarming. She'd been hectic, over-bright, flushed. Anthony hadn't been aware of it, men never were tuned to women's moods. But to a woman's eye, Gilly had turned a corner of some kind. What corner and what direction she was heading Nina didn't know, but it worried her. She'd seen the attraction between Steven and Gilly grow for some time; it now seemed steamy in spite of the fact that nothing improper had ever happened – to her knowledge.

She didn't give a damn what kind of messes Gilly and Ellen got themselves into. They were both expendable. And even her long-standing and deep affection for Steven was overridden by her devotion to Anthony. Gilly couldn't be allowed to do anything that would hurt Anthony or damage his reputation.

She had, accordingly, set a chair by her doorway that night and watched the hallway through the crack. It was a long wait, but she was sure something was going to happen and she had to keep whatever situation arose under control. She saw Ellen go to Steven's room and had only a twinge of regret that it was Ellen and not herself sharing his bed. A few minutes later she saw Steven go by, her heart aching at the pain and exhaustion in his face. Another ten minutes passed before she was startled to see Gilly glide by in a slinky black peignoir.

Steven was kissing Ellen when he sensed a bar of light from the doorway. He caught a glimpse of a woman's form before the door closed. He nearly leaped out his skin a second later when Gilly said softly, 'Steven, I must talk to you.'

A reply froze in his throat.

Ellen became rigid under him momentarily, then slithered away to reach for the lamp. The next moment the room was full of light.

'I'm afraid Steven is busy at the moment, *Mrs* Wentworth,' Ellen said languidly.

'What are you doing here, you ... you whore!'

'Much more to the point, what are *you* doing here?'

'I needed to speak to Steven about something important.'

Steven was paralyzed with humiliation, for himself and for both of them.

Ellen leaned forward, wrapping her arms round her knees. She studied Gilly with contempt. 'You always conduct your meetings dressed like that, do you, dear?'

'You have no right to be here,' Gilly said, her voice thick with pain and anger.

'Stop,' Steven said weakly. It took all the energy he could summon to repress his disgust at himself.

'Think again, Mrs Wentworth. You are the unwelcome one.'

'Steven is *our* friend!' Gilly sobbed.

Suddenly Steven's mind's eye was filled by huge birds of prey. They had circled in and were tearing him in half, their talons digging holes in his flesh and suddenly the talons were tentacles.

Smothering.

Engulfing.

'You can't own people,' Ellen was saying.

Smothering.

Sticky.

Crushing him.

Splinters crackling loose.

Flying off.

'You have no right to come into my home and ...'

Gouging at his eyes, his genitals. The pain. The ripe, fishy stench of sin.

'I remind you that this is your husband's home as well and I doubt that he would approve ...'

He was spinning, falling.

Rocks hitting him.

Nothing to hold onto.

No way to break the fall.

Nina, outside the door, heard an eerie keening. Opening the door, she saw Steven rising from the bed, his eyes closed, face and arms raised to the ceiling, fists clenched. Ellen and Gilly were staring in fright at the naked agony. Gilly put her hands to her ears to keep from hearing the low, inhuman sound he was making. Ellen scrambled out of bed, clutching at the sheets and drawing back from him. He suddenly jackknifed forward, as if sick. He bent forward on hands and knees, shaking violently.

Nina ran forward. The other two were too shocked to move. Nina put her arms round him and looked up with loathing. 'Look what you've done, you bitches. Fools! You've fought over him like a scrap of meat.'

'Nina,' Gilly began, stepping forward.

'Keep your voice down,' Nina said in a vibrant hiss that stopped Gilly in her tracks. 'Go back to your own bed. Both of you. *Now!*'

She looked and sounded so fierce, so primitive with her arms round the naked man, that they both did as they were told.

'Steven, Steven, listen to me. It's all right. It's over. You'll be fine now. I promise,' they heard her saying to him as they left.

An hour later Nina came to Ellen's room. 'He's gone,' she said, her voice as bleak and white as her face.

Ellen, who had dressed and packed in the interval, knowing she must leave this house no matter what else happened, said, 'Where?'

'I don't know.' Nina sat down heavily on the dressing table bench. 'I got him back to bed. I went downstairs to get him a drink, thinking it might help calm him. When I got back, he'd gone. His bags are there, but the clothes he was wearing earlier tonight are missing.'

'But where could he go? Didn't he say anything to give you an idea?'

'He didn't say anything at all. Not a word. He was as silent and tense as a statue. I had to nearly break his joints to get him to bed. Then he just curled back up and turned away from me and shook.'

Ellen was throwing on her coat. 'Did you tell Gilly?'

'No. And I wouldn't have told you except that I don't have a car to go after him. You rented one at the station, didn't you?'

Ellen was rummaging in her purse for her keys. 'Yes, help me with my suitcases, will you?'

At the front door, Ellen paused for a second. 'Nina, I'll find him. I'll take good care of him.'

Nina nodded, too tired and doubtful to formulate an answer.

Chapter Twenty-three

Ellen stood at the kitchen sink, washing dishes and listening to a news program on the radio. She never turned it on when Steven was in the house and didn't often mind not being in communication with the rest of the world. But every now and then she liked to catch up. Just to make sure there hadn't been a nuclear war or something, she thought, smiling to herself. It was a year-in-review type of program: last January and February's record-breaking cold weather; the break-up of Ma Bell (which didn't matter much to people like her who had no phone); the airplane that fell into the Potomac River; President Reagan opening the World's Fair in Knoxville; the ERA amendment defeated.

She switched to a classical music station and let Mozart help her finish drying the plates. She'd already picked up most of the news on her weekly trips into town and very little of it mattered to her. She couldn't help but think of Samaritan when she heard of outside events. So many of the events that were newsworthy were catastrophes and that was when Samaritan went into full swing. Like the skywalk collapsing in that Kansas City hotel the year before and killing so many people. Or Mount St Helen's blowing up a few months before that. Those were the situations where the Samaritan people really showed what they could do. They always seemed to be on-site and helping people before the Red Cross or the Salvation Army could even find the place.

Steven must think about the organization, too. He'd gone to town with her often this last year. He must notice the headlines at the newsstands outside the barber shop and overhear the talk at the general store. But he never commented on what he heard and neither did she. It was one of the unspoken rules.

He passed by the window carrying buckets of feed for the goats and she leaned against the sink watching him go about his chores. How much he'd changed while he'd been here with her. Almost two full years now. The first weeks of that time had been terrible, of course. She'd caught up with him about a mile from Birches. He was walking in the snow. She ordered him to get in the car and he'd done so like a sleepwalker and almost immediately fallen asleep. She remembered now with a shudder how frightened she'd been for him. She started to drive toward the city to fly them both back to California, but worried that he'd go to pieces en route. That would involve other people, perhaps airline security people, she realized. He'd not only be taken away from her, but be humiliated when he came to his senses.

She drove them cross-country, taking a week. He'd slept almost the whole way. And hadn't spoken once.

It had been terrifying.

And even when she got him home he'd been like a zombie for months, sleeping twelve or fourteen hours a day and just sitting in a chair the rest of the time. She'd written to Nina immediately, assuring her that she'd taken Steven somewhere that he'd get excellent care, but she wasn't so sure after a few months that she could do him any good. She'd park him like an infant wherever she was working – at the kitchen table while she cooked, on a log in the meadow where the beehives were, on the fence round the corral where the goats were taken for milking. The thing he seemed to like best was sitting by the loom, watching her weave. She guessed that he liked the color and rhythm of the work.

That's when she'd seen the first sign that he'd taken a tottering step toward recovering. One day, after sitting and staring sightlessly for more than an hour, he'd reached out his hand toward the beater bar. In spite of her heart pounding in her throat, she'd said matter-of-factly, 'Yes, I need help with that. Will you operate it?' And he did. She made a place mat that day a yard and a half long because she couldn't bear to stop while he was interested.

From that day there had been a series of small steps. He still wasn't speaking except to answer direct questions, but his sleeping was down to about ten hours and occasionally he did something on his own, like going for short walks, running his own bath or rescuing one of the barn cats when it got its claws stuck in the screen door. She found him cuddling the grateful animal with his face buried in the young cat's soft fur. He was crying. She left them alone.

One day, it must have been a full six months after she brought him back, she went to his room and woke him from one of his many naps. 'Steven, I'm glad to have you here and I don't expect you to do any work, but you must not make extra work for me. You left your dirty boots and jeans jacket on the floor in the living room. Please clean the boots and put the jacket away.' She was both kind and authoritative.

He started regularly picking up after himself. One morning a week later she took him along on the milking and asked him to help her carry the pails. He not only did so, but went along the next day and helped without being asked. He spontaneously started clearing his own place at meals and helping her with the washing up. She wrote to Nina again, saying she had it on good authority that Steven was finally getting better. She led the younger woman to believe that he was in an institution someplace.

At Christmas that first year, he came to her room in the middle of the night. 'Ellen?' he said from the doorway.

'It's cold tonight, isn't it?' she said calmly. 'Come in with me and keep warm.'

And he did. She cuddled up to him and he slept. He came to her room every night after that, but they didn't make love for several weeks. And when they finally did, it was with terrible ferocity on his part and acceptance and forgiveness on hers. It was brutal, practically a rape except that she knew he would have stopped if she'd told him to. When he'd done pounding at her as though she were a demon to be tamed, he flung himself onto his back and said, 'Oh, God!'

She cuddled into the crook of his arm and said, 'Steven, I will only say this once. You need never talk to me about anything, but if you ever want to, I will listen. Just so you know.'

'Thank you, Ellen.' That was all he said.

In the middle of the night, he woke her, stroking her breast gently and nuzzling her neck. She arched against him, smiling in the dark at the knowledge that one of the devils had been exorcized.

After that, the improvement was rapid and gratifying. Within a month, his behavior would have seemed absolutely normal to anyone who didn't know him well. He worked, talked, functioned usefully. He talked, however, only of the surface aspects of their day-to-day life – the bees, the goats, the weather, why the pickup truck was backfiring, where to put the new pegs for the yarn in the loom room. He made love to her infrequently, but with great tenderness.

And now, a year later, he was a whole person again. A more self-confident, contented person than he'd ever been before. He'd apparently cured himself of the obsessive introspection that had blighted him since youth. He seemed to have found a level plane to live on and didn't allow himself to soar or sink. He didn't talk about the future or the past; it was as if he had no concept of such things. They lived for the present and enjoyed it. But how long could the present last?

Ellen was startled out of her reflections by the sound of the kitchen door opening. She quickly turned off the radio, thinking it was Steven, but it wasn't. 'Gary! Why didn't you tell me you were coming?'

'Sunshine had someone to visit near here. I hitched a ride. He'll be back for me in an hour.'

Ellen kept the disapproval out of her face. 'How nice.' She didn't like Sunshine, born Leonard, who headed the commune Gary lived in. The group, a sixties holdover that would have been out of place anywhere but California, claimed to be Christian Buddhists. But Sunshine struck her as a hoodlum who wouldn't know a religious tenet from a blackjack and was probably more familiar with the latter. She'd been far too lenient and understanding a mother so far suddenly to come over as the heavy parent at this stage.

They embraced. 'You crackle,' Ellen said.

'I stopped in town and got your mail to save you a trip,' he said, fishing envelopes out of his parka pocket as he was extricating himself from the garment. 'There's something with a Samaritan letterhead.' He sounded worried. Ellen hadn't shared with Gary what had caused Steven's breakdown and he thought it had something to do with Samaritan itself.

'Don't be concerned. Your father and his friend Anthony have been corresponding from time to time for almost a year now.'

'Do you think it's good for him?' Gary asked.

'It's not up to me. It's his decision.'

'You don't think his friend upsets him?'

'He carefully doesn't say anything upsetting.'

'How do you know?'

'Steven makes a point of leaving both Anthony's letters and his own replies out in plain sight so I can read them if I want. I sometimes do, and when I don't he reads from them to me. They write about their daily life. Neither prods very deeply.'

'Who started it, do you know?'

Ellen grinned. 'Didn't I tell you? I thought I had. Remember that day I told you about the old geezer coming to the door to ask for a glass of water and having an attack of some kind?'

'Yeah, you said you went for a doctor and when you got back, he'd disappeared.'

'He was a detective. Anthony hired him to see if Steven was here. Then Anthony wrote to him and explained how he knew where he was. I read that letter before giving it to Steven. It was nice. Just an expression of support and concern and a promise that no one else would know. He said he didn't want to tread on Steven's privacy, only to know he was alive. He's really very thoughtful. He rented a post office box just to correspond with Steven, so that not even his secretary would see Steven's letters if he chose to write back. Although I suspect Nina knows perfectly well that he's here.'

'I'm glad he's got a friend like that – and like you.'

'Gary!' Steven said, coming in the door. 'I didn't see you get here. Can you stay?'

The two men hugged each other briskly. Ellen watched, feeling downright sappy, her heart filling with love for both. Such a wholesome, healthy, good-looking pair they were, her men. Steven had put on weight, all of it muscle, and except for some gray at his temples, could have been an elder brother to his son. Now that Steven was fit and robust they looked very much alike. They had the same physique, the same observant cornflower-blue eyes with the dark brows, the same wide, intellectual foreheads.

'I can't stay long. Sunshine's coming back for me.'

'Come out and see what I've done to the barn. I'm building an extension on the west side.'

They went off and Ellen sat down at the kitchen table. She was surprised to find tears rolling down her cheeks. She wasn't sure whether she was crying because she was so content or because she feared such happiness couldn't last.

In April 1983, Ellen realized a new phase was beginning

in Steven's life. It wasn't anything she could pinpoint; merely a general increase in energy, a restlessness. He seemed to be setting his sights at a slightly longer distance. She was glad, and yet uneasy.

'I've got to get this mower blade sharpened,' he said one day. 'Our whetstone isn't good enough. It has to go to the hardware store.'

'I'm going to town the day after tomorrow,' Ellen said from the sink where she was washing her hair.

'It looks like more rain. If I don't get that meadow cut now, it'll take a scythe. I'll run the blade into town myself.'

'You don't want me to come along?' she asked, glad that he couldn't see her face. He'd never shown any willingness to go to town by himself.

'Sure, if you want.'

'Come to think of it, I better not. I've got a lot to do. Bring me some salt for my dyeing, will you?'

Steven was in town and looking for a parking place for the van when he finally realized he was on his own, and that gave him a heady sense of freedom. Not that he failed to appreciate everything Ellen had done for him, but lately he'd started to feel that she was constantly evaluating and assessing him. Well, of course she was. He'd been a lunatic and she'd brought him back. She had every right. Still, it was nice to get a break.

He had to circle the block three times to get a parking place. There were more tourists around every week. A new, very expensive resort had opened nearby last year and brought a crowd to town looking for beach towels, souvenirs and restaurants. In the latter, they must be severely disappointed, Steven thought as he dropped off the mower blade and went next door to Mabel's Cafe, the only restaurant in town, to wait for it to be sharpened. He ordered one of Mabel's leathery, overdone steaks as an antidote to months of vegetarianism and was doggedly chewing his way through it when he felt a hand on his shoulder.

375

'Steven? It is you, isn't it?'

'Rhys Jones!' Steven exclaimed, looking up into the kind, familiar face. 'Sit down. God, it's good to see you. What in the world are you doing here?'

'Just vacationing. You old son-of-a-gun, you look great! I thought you'd dropped off the face of the earth. Where have you been?'

'Living here. Up in the hills. A goat farm.'

Rhys laughed. 'A *goat* farm? I can't believe it.'

'Sit down, Rhys. Catch me up on everything.' Rhys picked up a greasy menu card. 'Don't bother with that. Get the chilli and the lemon pie. They're the only things here that are edible. So, tell me, how have you been?'

Ellen was frantic by the time she saw headlights approaching. It was past eleven at night and she'd been worrying about Steven since noon. Having no phone, she couldn't call around and ask for him. And he'd taken the van, so she wasn't able to drive to town and look for him. She'd considered hitchhiking to town, but decided that would look too frantic if there was nothing wrong. Certainly he was all right. If he'd had an accident or become ill, somebody would have come to fetch her.

She ran to meet the car. Steven bounced out and greeted her cheerfully. 'You're up late, aren't you?'

'I was waiting for you,' she said, sorry that she sounded so accusatory.

'Sorry. I ran into Rhys Jones in town. Do you remember meeting him at Birches? We got talking and I completely lost track of time. I asked Wanda Bell to stop by on her way home and tell you I'd be late.'

'She didn't stop here. You know she never remembers anything.'

'Yeah, I guess so. Come inside. Let me tell you about my talk with Rhys.'

He strode ahead, but she couldn't move at first. She wanted him to come back and tell her how very, very sorry he was for worrying her half out of her mind, that he regretted trusting an important message to a bimbo like Wanda Bell. She was angry and frightened – frightened by how casually and naturally he'd mentioned Birches. As if there were no dangerous associations with the word.

He was standing at the kitchen door, holding it open for her. She went in and started making them some peppermint tea. He sat down at the kitchen table. 'Rhys was telling me about some of the things they're doing at Samaritan in a lot more detail than Anthony's gone into. I hadn't known, for instance, that they've contracted to administer a huge number of local charities. They leave the familar name, so the donors aren't aware of the change, but Samaritan handles all the paperwork and banking. So far, Rhys says, the average administrative cost has gone down more than twenty per cent. As much as seventy per cent in some of the smaller ones. There's less duplication of effort, you see, more skilled people and much more money and expertise can go to the actual intended recipients of the funds.'

He talked for hours, lavishly spending all the verbal credits he'd saved up from two years of near silence. In the morning, he was still enthusiastic. 'Rhys was telling me about the music program he's trying to institute for inner city children ...'

She let him go on until he finally stopped to draw breath. 'You're going back, aren't you?'

He stared at her. 'No, of course not. Why would I?'

'You seem so excited about Samaritan.'

'Of course I am,' he said, patronizingly patient, she thought. 'It was an important part of my life for many years. It does excellent work. I'm happy to hear of its successes. Who wouldn't be?'

'So you're not leaving?'

He got up and took her in his arms. 'I'm not going anywhere. Everything I need is here.'

Not everything he loved; everything he needed, she thought.

After that night Steven stopped talking about Samaritan so much, but he made more trips to town and occasionally brought back a newspaper or a copy of *Time* to peruse. She threw them away the second he put them down. He started writing longer, more frequent letters to Anthony and didn't always remember to leave them and their replies out for Ellen to read. He became uncharacteristically ambitious about the farm and their life there. He talked about purchasing the adjoining parcel of land and increasing their goat herd, perhaps hiring some extra help.

'But I don't need to make more money and I don't want more goats and more responsibility,' she said.

One day she found him tinkering with her loom. 'I was thinking if you could widen this, you could do larger pieces and you wouldn't have to sew the strips together when you're making rugs,' he said.

'I *like* sewing the pieces together.'

He had organizing talents, long dormant, that were wasted on the small farm. Wasted on her. She began to accept the fact that he was only on loan to her. She'd suspected it all along, but hoped against hope that she could fulfil all his needs. Each day became borrowed time.

It ended in September.

They were sitting in the living room, going over some leaflets from the county extension office about bees. 'Ellen, we need to talk.'

'You're leaving. Going back to Samaritan.'

He nodded. 'I'll never be able to repay the moral debt I have to you—'

She waved her hands in front of her face. 'No, no. Don't say that.'

'I have to. You saved my life. My soul. But now that I have myself back, thanks to you, I've got to do what's right. Ellen, I can be useful to Samaritan, be an important part of helping many people. If I stay here, I'll only be hiding from life. Indulging my own needs.'

'And mine,' Ellen said so softly that he didn't hear her.

'Anthony needs me. He thinks Samaritan is stagnat-

378

ing in its own success. Getting fat and complacent.'

'Steven, I'm going to collect on part of that debt right now. You have to answer some questions to my satisfaction.'

He sat back, stunned but smiling. 'Shoot.'

'You're obviously back to normal, but you're proposing to go back to the same environment that drove you mad before. What makes you think it will be any different? Do you honestly think you're over Gilly?'

She expected him at least to flinch at the name that hadn't been mentioned for years. But he smiled confidently. 'Maybe so. Probably not. But that's not the point. The point is that she's my friend's wife and I will never have any claim on her. It's that simple. I don't know why it took me so damned long to figure it out. And Ellen, you're wrong about one thing: I'm not back to normal. Normal was dismal. I'm a new person, a much stronger person than I ever was. And that's because of you.'

She started stacking up the paperwork they'd been going over. 'You'll need new clothes. You should probably allow yourself a day in San Francisco. And a haircut. You can get that in town and then I can drive you—'

'Ellen, stop. Let me explain—'

She stood up and leaned across the table between them. 'Steven, shut up!'

Chapter Twenty-four

Steven's welcome back to Samaritan was gratifying. Both Rhys and Anthony had honored their promises to keep his whereabouts secret. No one had the slightest idea where he'd been. When asked, he smiled and said, 'A long vacation on a goat farm,' which people took to be a joke.

Samaritan was in new offices south of the city. Everything was fresh and modern, except an office Anthony took him to. It was Steven's office, all his belongings transported and set up just as they'd been when he left. 'I appreciate the thought, but it looks like a museum exhibit. All it needs is a rope across the doorway and a few placards. Do you mind if I redecorate this?' Steven asked with a laugh.

'Not at all. God! It's like breathing fresh air to have you back. Things are going to change now.'

'What needs changing, Anthony?'

Anthony sat down. 'Everything, I think.'

'On the plane I looked over those reports you sent me. It looks like Samaritan is in great shape. The amount of money flowing through is at least twice what we hoped for when we started.'

'But that's what I keep thinking about: when we started. Don't you remember the excitement, the idealism, the sense of active virtue? Everybody had it, right down to the boys in the mail room.'

'I certainly do remember. The nights we sat up talking, dreaming, drinking coffee until we were nearly berserk with caffeine and dreams. But we've all grown up, Anthony. And the eighties are a boring rerun of the fifties. The Age of Aquarius is over.'

'But I don't want it to be over. I want Samaritan to recapture the sense of excitement at what's going on. We're bringing in lots of money and using it extremely well, but we've become a big business. You walked through that central office – rows of desks, computer terminals, piles of paperwork, phones ringing and being answered by bored secretaries. It could be an insurance company or a Federal Reserve bank.'

'You've recruited good businessmen and women. That's why it runs so effectively. You can't blame business people for acting like what they are.'

'Steven, don't tell me—'

'I'm playing devil's advocate. I'd like to recapture those days, too.'

'So, how do we do it?'

'I don't know. I'm not sure we can. Give me time to get back in the swing and think.'

'Will you come by and think at our house for dinner?'

Steven hesitated only a second. No more hiding from problems. 'I'd love to. Are you sure it's convenient for Gilly?'

'Gilly'd give up anything but her gardens to get a chance to feed you. We've missed you, Steven.'

Steven prepared for seeing Gilly again with care, but without nervousness. He'd told Ellen the truth: he was a much stronger person now than he'd ever been. And it was mainly because he knew he couldn't face ever falling back into the screaming, suffocating black despair he'd experienced. Nothing, *nothing* could drive him back to that. No problem was important enough to agonize him back to madness. The essence of the uncomplicated life Ellen lived had permanently permeated his healing soul.

He thought he was prepared for the sight and sound of Gilly. But it was still a shock. She'd changed, matured to a new beauty. She'd cut her hair short, put on a little weight. But it flattered her. 'You look lovely, Gilly,' he said exchanging polite kisses of greeting. No, his feelings for her hadn't changed, he thought coolly as a jolt of physical longing struck him. But his ability to withstand them had.

'Oh, Steven, we're so glad you're back. So very glad. Oh, no, I'm getting all teary and stupid.' She pulled a handkerchief from the sleeve of her dress and dabbed at her eyes.

Steven laughed. 'There can't be another woman of your generation in the whole country who not only *has* cloth handkerchiefs, but actually keeps one handy in her sleeve. Gilly, you're wonderful. Don't ever change.'

She sniffed in mock offense. 'I should have known the first thing you'd do was make fun of me.'

'Show me your gardens,' he said, grinning.

'It's dark outside.'

'I don't care. I just want to hear you talk about compost and daffodils and what you're doing about mildew on the zinnias. I've decided your gardens are truly the one fixed point in the universe.'

Anthony laughed. 'Gilly'd ask them to hold off Armageddon until she finished spraying for aphids. I'll turn on the floodlights and we'll take the tour.'

Much later in the evening, when Anthony left the room to take a phone call, Gilly said, 'Steven, I'm sorry about ...' She stopped, clearly at a loss for words.

'You don't have to be scared of what you say to me, Gilly. I'm not going to go nuts again. And you have nothing to be sorry about. It was my problem and it's taken care of.'

'Thank you, Steven. It's been hell these years. I've blamed myself and felt terrible.'

'I wish I could have spared you.'

'Where were you all that time?'

'With Ellen at her farm in California.'

'I thought you probably were. But Anthony said he'd hired detectives and you weren't there. I think he ought to get his money back,' she added with a laugh. She looked

383

down, fiddling with her necklace. 'Will she be coming here to you?'

'No.'

'Are you in love with her?'

He waited until she looked up. 'Not enough. Not in the right way.'

Her reply, when she spoke, chilled him. 'Good.'

Steven didn't provide Anthony with a solution to Samaritan's complacency, at least not for some time. But having his friend back did wonders for him. In fact, Steven, enthusiastic and fresh from his absence, invigorated the board of directors, if not the whole organization. He and Anthony were back on the same wavelength. Except on one notable matter.

'You're hiring Van Graves? Are you crazy?' Steven asked when Anthony dropped this bombshell.

'I know he's not very likeable, but—'

'Likeable! He's as charming as Dracula!' Steven exclaimed, remembering vividly the sour, nasty blond boy.

'Funny. Nina compared him to Attila the Hun.'

'You should have listened to her. Why are you doing this?'

'I could only say this to you. Steven: you know I've always believed that association with virtue can engender virtue. And God knows, Van can use an improved attitude. Look on it as one of the charities we perform.'

Steven clapped him on the shoulder. 'People who know us both think that I'm the dreamy, unrealistic one and you're bedrock. Personally, I think all the rocks are in your head. You can't change him, Anthony.'

'We don't know that.'

'I think we do. Faye probably put him up to this.'

'Faye? Come on, Steven. Talk about obsessive. Nobody's heard from Faye for years. She spends her time wafting from Geneva to Palm Springs to Monte Carlo. Nina keeps track of her. Believe me, Faye's lost all interest in Samaritan.' His voice had risen a bit.

Steven smiled knowingly. 'Nina said the same thing, didn't she?'

'As a matter of fact, she did. I think you're both—' He stopped, stricken.

'Crazy? Say it, Anthony. There aren't any words you and I can't use with each other. But I'm not crazy anymore and Nina's the sanest person on earth.'

'It can't hurt to give him a chance,' Anthony said.

'Maybe not. But I'm going to go home tonight and build a big I Told You So. To be delivered at a future date.'

Steven had put Ellen in mental cold storage. Though he was determined not to let guilt get its claws into his throat again, he did feel a sense of accountability to her. Consequently, he dropped everything one day in the summer of 1984 when Nina came into a meeting and said that Ellen was phoning and insisting on speaking to him.

'Ellen, what's wrong?' he said, striding into his office and snatching up the phone.

'Steven, I need your help. Gary was here yesterday and told me he's preparing to make a permanent commitment to Sunshine's commune.'

'A permanent commitment? What the hell does that mean?'

'It means he's writing a will, leaving everything to the commune. Sunshine requires it as a condition.'

'A will? Gary doesn't have a bean.'

'But I do, Steven. I've got a hell of a lot of beans. And Gary's my heir.'

'You don't think ...'

'I don't know. But you've met Sunshine. He's tough. And unprincipled.'

'Ellen, get out of there. Now. Go to somewhere you've never been before. Somewhere safe. Call Nina and let her know where you are. I'll come to you when I've seen Gary.'

'Steven!' She was alarmed at how readily he'd leaped

ahead in her own train of thought.

'I don't mean to scare you, but walk out the door now. Lock the car doors. I'm leaving now.'

Steven hung up and went to Anthony's office. He laid out the bare facts to explain why he had to depart suddenly. 'You don't think you're taking an extreme view?' Anthony asked.

'Once, when I was still sick, Gary and Sunshine came to the farm. Gary was with his mother. I was sitting quietly in the woods near where Ellen had set out a rabbit snare. A harmless one. She wanted to see if she could tame a rabbit to keep it with the goats. Some crazy theory of hers about goats giving more milk – well, never mind. There must have been a rabbit in the snare, but I didn't notice it until I saw Sunshine wandering through the woods. He took a leak against a tree, then he saw the rabbit and picked it up and strangled it. For no reason and with obscene relish. It was the sickest thing I've ever seen a person do. He killed that helpless animal for the sheer pleasure of killing it and it didn't benefit him. I can easily imagine him killing Ellen, then Gary to get a couple million dollars.'

'What are you going to do?'

'I have to get Gary away from Sunshine.'

'Want a suggestion?'

'I'd fall on one.'

'Why don't you try to get Gary back here with us?'

'I don't think he'd do it. We are, as you've pointed out, a big business. A long way from love beads and long hair.'

'But you say he's genuinely interested in helping people.'

'His way of helping is mainly prayer.'

'Then shouldn't he have a shot at good works on a big scale? Just as a spiritual exercise? To see how the other side lives, so to speak. If you can get him away from this Sunshine—'

'You're right. Sunshine probably has a record a mile long. Maybe we could turn him in for something and get him out of the running. I don't think Gary's cut out for Samaritan, but I think he'd give it a try to please me. And he won't be dead wood. If he agrees, he'll work hard. He's not lazy, just other-worldly. Anthony, thanks. I think this'll work.'

Steven put it to Gary as a combination favor/novitiate. 'There are people in need in ways you can't possibly know about. Some of them may be the people for whom your God-given talents are intended to be used,' he told the young man. 'You've got decades of life to give to God. Please give just two years to me.'

Gary agreed with such faint-hearted objections that Steven suspected he'd given his son a way out that he was unwilling to admit he was looking for. Steven took him away before Sunshine could get at him with arguments.

Within half a day of Gary's departure from the commune, it was visited by Federal officers with a warrant for the arrest of Leonard Svetlic, wanted for the murder of a bank teller during a robbery in Florida some years earlier. Sunshine used profanities the men had never heard before, but went along with them without a fight.

Steven, nearly bursting with pride in his fine son, brought Gary back to Samaritan. Steven himself was so well-liked that Gary got a warm reception. It started cooling within days.

'He's a prig, pure and simple,' Gilly said to Anthony as they were getting ready for bed after having given a dinner party in Gary's honor. 'Imagine telling me I'd more truly serve my guests with fruit drinks than with liquor. The nerve!' She picked up a hairbrush and attacked her hair.

'He meant well.'

'Yes, he probably meant well when he yammered on at Rhys about how bad cigar smoking is for him and for everyone breathing the same air. Someone should have put a cigar down his throat. Self-righteous, opinionated *prig* of a boy. Did you see the way he picked at his food? As if I'd sprinkled it with chemicals.'

Anthony got into bed, pulled up the covers and pressed the heels of his hands to his eyebrows as if he had a headache. 'He's probably a vegetarian.'

'Why didn't somebody tell me that before I served tenderloin to fourteen people? Tell me that!'

'Steven thinks he walks on water.'

'Well, of course he would.' She stopped short. She was on the brink of saying, 'You think Martin is terrific, too.' After admitting to her that he was Martin's father, Anthony had taken a great deal more interest in the boy, even inviting him for a week's visit every summer at Birches. Unlike Gary, Martin wasn't too good to be true. Martin, now eighteen years old, was brash, conceited and sly. When he wasn't scowling at her, he was leering at her. It made her skin crawl to have him around.

Anthony made every imaginable excuse for him. He was brash because he had four older brothers; that's what familial competition did to a boy, Anthony claimed. If he seemed sly, it was only because he was uneasy around them. As for leering, Gilly didn't mention it, fearing Anthony would make some excuse to her own discredit – not meaning it that way, of course, but it was safer to stay away from the subject.

Martin had entered college at the University of Missouri to study journalism just this fall, however, and if he followed in his brilliant brothers' footsteps, he'd be there full time until he got his degree. It would probably be only three years instead of the usual four, because that's how Betsy's bright, obnoxious boys did things, but Gilly was glad to have him settled somewhere she wouldn't run into him.

'Don't you think Steven sees through him at all?' she asked. She removed her robe and folded it over the back of her dressing table chair.

'Not for a second,' Anthony said with assurance. He punched his pillow into shape and leaned back with a sigh.

'You don't think part of the appeal is that he's Ellen's son and Steven's linked to her?'

'He could have stayed with Ellen and he didn't.'

'Because he couldn't have Ellen and you both.'

'If Steven ever has to choose between me and a woman, it won't be Ellen,' Anthony said in a flat voice. He had his eyes closed.

Gilly froze. 'What do you mean by that?'

'Nothing. Turn the light off, will you? I'm beat.'

Three of Betsy's boys had gone from Gilly's dinner party to drinks at the Kansas City Country Club where they all belonged. No one who didn't know them would have taken them for brothers. Wayne was slight, dark and handsome in contrast to Van's nearly albino fairness. Plump, boyish Harry looked more like a cuddly teddy bear with each year that passed. Van and Wayne were as wound up as tops. 'Harry, you must have seen it tonight,' Wayne said.

Harry had been watching Tom Watson at a nearby table, hoping to get a chance to have a word with him about his golf swing. 'Saw what?' he said, wondering if Watson would mind giving a little free advice.

'Haven't you heard anything we've said?' Van asked. 'Gilly and Steven. The way they kept ogling each other at dinner.'

'Gilly was doing the ogling,' Wayne said.

'Whoever. I thought she was going to lay him right there in front of everybody.'

'Come on, you're making it all up,' Harry, ever the peacemaker, said. 'Gilly was being nice to everybody. She always is.'

'What a stupid prick you are!' Van went on. 'They were all over each other with their eyes.'

'Gilly was all over Steven,' Wayne corrected.

'Hold it,' Harry said. 'How come whatever it is, it's always Gilly's fault?'

'Well, a man takes what he's offered,' Wayne said. 'He can't be blamed for that.'

'He can't?' Harry asked. He supposed in Wayne's view that was a truism.

'They're sleeping together. You can tell,' Van said, his watery blue gaze on Wayne narrow and speculative. 'I think Anthony ought to know.'

'I agree,' Wayne replied.

'Hold it!' Harry exclaimed. 'What a pair of drunken old gossips you two are. Even if this were true, and I don't believe for a second that it is, what the hell good would it do anybody to tell Anthony?'

'He ought to know she's a slut. She's fooled him all these years. If his eyes were opened to what she's really like, he'd get rid of her,' Wayne explained.

'And he'd also have to get rid of your beloved Steven. Where would you be then, big brother?'

'What if he did?' Van asked, sneering. But the moment he saw Wayne's expression, he realized his mistake. Wayne was as devoted to Steven as he was to Anthony. Maybe even more so.

'What do you mean by that?' Wayne demanded of Harry.

'Just that you can't say a man is sleeping with his best friend's wife and it's all the wife's fault.'

'He'd have to forgive Steven,' Wayne said. 'After all, it *isn't* his fault. A woman throws herself at you, you're entitled to fuck her.'

'If you're speaking from personal experience, it's a wonder you haven't been hauled up for rape,' Harry said.

'So, what are we going to do?' Van asked, not wanting the subject to wander. He didn't like to see Wayne lose his momentum on side issues. Van didn't give a damn how Steven ended up. He only wanted to make life miserable for Anthony.

'Nothing,' Harry said firmly. 'It's none of our damned business. Wayne, you've always had a cob up your ass about Gilly. But Anthony loves her and it'd kill him if your accusations happened to be true.'

'It might hurt for a while,' Wayne admitted. 'But in the end, he'd be better off without her. I'm only thinking of Anthony.'

'The hell you are.'

Nina *was* thinking about Anthony. And Steven and Gilly. The evening had been very upsetting to her. She'd seen the way Steven and Gilly looked at each other – everybody had. Worse, she'd seen Anthony watching them with sad understanding. She often wondered when and if he'd notice the electricity between them.

She liked and respected Gilly. She was a good wife to Anthony. Almost as devoted to his welfare as Nina herself was. And Nina was the last person in the world to blame her for being attracted to Steven. Nina, like Gilly, loved them both. But in Nina's case, it wasn't sexual love. And that made all the difference. Sex was dynamite with invisible fuses that could be lighted without anyone knowing the explosion was coming.

Gilly wasn't at fault, but still, if she happened to step in front of a truck ... How much better it would be if she were out of the picture. Nina was frustrated with her own impotence. There was nothing she could do. Confrontation was out of the question. The only thing that kept this particular keg of dynamite under control was the fact that nobody openly admitted that it existed. She knew and loved all three of them and knew that they loved each other. That was the worst of it. There wasn't a 'bad guy' in this who could be exposed and eliminated.

No, she could see nothing she could do except be there for Anthony when he needed her. And he would need her.

Steven had been back at Samaritan for a little over a year before he got an idea to pump the enthusiasm back into the organization. It happened at a board meeting. A young woman with a rare and debilitating nerve disease had been cured through research funded by Samaritan. She'd written to thank the directors and a copy of her letter was in the agenda packet given to each director. While Rory was droning on about ways of saving yet more money on office supplies, Steven was skimming through the letter when a postscript caught his eye.

'By the way, this is the second time Samaritan has come to my rescue. When I was a child, our house was destroyed by a tornado while I was at school. A Samaritan volunteer put me back in touch with my family and found a motel for us to stay in until we could find somewhere else to live. She even took me shopping to replace my favorite doll. So I am doubly grateful for your help,' the woman had written.

Steven put the folder down, thinking that there must be a number of people who'd benefited from Samaritan's bounty in several unrelated ways.

All day long the thought kept coming back to him. That evening, he made some notes, and the next day went to see Anthony. He reminded Anthony of the letter and outlined his own reflections. 'She's an example that's been dropped in our laps. Now, don't say anything until I'm done. What I'm proposing is this: a sort of Samaritan poster family. A family who, through no fault of their own, has suffered several problems that Samaritan has helped with.'

'I can see that it would be a great fund-raising tool, but how do we find such a family?'

'That's the other idea I've got. Put a bounty on them.'

'What?'

'That's a crass way of putting it. What I mean is, what if you said to every Samaritan employee that they'd get something terrific – a trip round the world, a year's salary extra, I don't know what – if they were responsible for bringing the family to the attention of the board? If the incentive were big and attractive enough, you'd get everybody looking closely at the actual good the organization's money does and has been doing for years. A clerk whose normal job is to total columns of figures is going to be looking at the names beside them, wondering if she's seen them before, digging in the files, inadvertently learning bits of Samaritan's history.'

'God, Steven, I think you've got something here.'

'The people in the field would have the advantage of actually knowing the individuals they work with, but the central office staff would have an equal advantage of easy access to the files,' Steven said.

'And human nature being what it is, the field people would want a shot at the office people's advantage and vice versa. You'd have employees taking a greater interest in what other employees do. Great. Great! Steven, you've got it!'

'What about the incentive? Doesn't it need to be something people can share? What if a field worker and a secretary team up to find the Samaritan family? We don't want an incentive that puts them against each other. It should be something that encourages them to work together instead of competitively.'

They brainstormed for an hour, finally deciding that they needed time to put together all the details before they presented it to the rest of the board. They'd both seen perfectly good ideas fail to take root because they were sloppily presented. 'We need Nina in on this, but nobody else,' Anthony said.

Fortunately, Nina was enthusiastic about the idea and arranged a weekend retreat for the three of them to hammer out particulars of the proposal. It was she who came up with the 'prize' they were to present in their pitch: a year's right to a condo in Vail, Colorado, which could be used by the winners or rented out to other employees or both. To counter any accusations of Samaritan spending its funds improperly on this, Anthony insisted that he'd pay the cost of the condo out of his private income from Herron Paper.

'... the deadline would be one year from the announcement of the contest,' Anthony said at the conclusion of putting the proposal to the board. 'The minimum requirement for a qualifying family would be that the family has benefited both as a group and as individuals. At least four members of the family must be included. This can be grandparents, but not aunts or uncles or cousins unless they live with the family. With this, as with any other part of the proposal, the board may make refinements if you choose to implement the idea.'

He sat down.

There was a long silence, then a sudden babble of excited conversation. Steven and Anthony grinned at each other.

Chapter Twenty-five

Gilly was working in the garden.

In the years she'd worked on the grounds of the Kansas City mansion, she gradually converted a severe, soulless formal landscape into a breathtaking series of vistas. It had been a process of experimentation, hard work and diligent study. There was a bit of Gertrude Jekyll in her carefully careless herbaceous border along the south side of the house, shading as it did from cool blues and whites at the ends, moving into pinks and purples, and exploding in shattering reds and oranges in the central section. She had some isolated nooks of one-color schemes; 'rooms', as Vita Sackville-West had called them. Gilly's favorite was the moonlight garden, all scented white flowers – gardenias, tuberoses, nicotiana, carnations, lilies, roses. She liked to go there at dusk and get drunk on the perfume.

Some of her laborious experiments had been failures, too. She'd studied Reginald Farrer's book on English rock gardens until she had the stuffy Edwardian prose almost memorized. And yet her rock gardens, if not complete failures, were a source of little satisfaction. A rock garden is an essentially Oriental concept; an exercise in subtlety and restraint. One had to appreciate understatement and patience to plant and love a rock garden. Just as Gilly adored Rachmaninoff and was bored and mystified by the cleverness of Sondheim, she much preferred a blowsy, sprawling bank of heavy-headed, intoxicatingly scented peonies to the fragile, mincing loveliness of hothouse orchids. Not for her a miniature stand of bonsai trees or a dish garden of moss and one perfectly placed pebble.

This spring afternoon, she was putting in bedding plants, a border round the gazebo that was to be blindingly deep purple lobelia set off by sparking lemon yellow marigolds. She liked the way the intensely contrasting color combination almost made her eyes water. She'd set in the last plant and leaned back to assess the effect when she felt a hand on the back of her neck. 'Anthony! I didn't hear you coming. You're home early.' She stood and put her arms round him.

'You smell like compost,' he said.

'I know. I was going to shower before you got home.'

'I guess it's a measure of how much I love you that I'm beginning to like the smell of compost.'

'Oh, there's nothing quite like the odor of well-rotted sheep manure. Giorgio can't compete,' she said with a laugh. 'Sit down in that lawn chair while I water these, then you can come in and help me with my shower.'

She expected him to respond in a mock leering manner to this invitation, but he simply said, 'Yes, sure,' and sat down.

Anthony had been behaving oddly lately. He'd taken a week off to go to that ranch of his, wherever it was. He'd come back very thoughtful and preoccupied, but she knew he'd share whatever was on his mind with her when he was ready and not a minute before. Gilly attached the fine spray attachment to the hose and gave the plants a gentle soaking, then she turned off the water and came to sit in the chair beside his. He was staring at the garden. 'It's pretty, isn't it?' Gilly said. 'I think I'm going to put tangerine impatiens round the other side where it's so heavily shaded. What do you think?'

'Huh? Oh, yeah. Good idea.'

'You haven't taken in a word I'm saying and you wouldn't know impatiens from pipe tobacco. Anthony dear, what's wrong? What are you doing here so early?'

'I just wanted some time to think.'

'To think or to brood?'

He smiled at her. 'Brood.'

'About Samaritan?'

He nodded.

'But you've been so happy about the way everything's been going since you started the search for the family.'

'Oh, that's done wonders for the organization. The deadline's next month and there have been a number of families submitted. Gary's will probably be chosen.'

'Gary? Steven's son? I can't imagine him getting involved. What would he want with a condo?'

'I don't think he even knows there *is* a prize. He just liked the idea of finding a whole family that had been benefited.'

'So it's worked.'

'Almost too well.'

'Anthony, don't make me pull teeth. What's wrong?'

He stretched out his long legs and locked his hands behind his head. 'Wayne brought a proposal to the board this morning. A good idea, well thought out, logically presented. He must have been working on it for months. It's a great proposal. And I hate it.'

'Oh dear. What's the idea?'

'He wants to open regional offices. Branch offices. He pointed out that we have huge numbers of our people doing all their work in Texas and New York and California, but they all report back here. Rory backed him, naturally. Rory presented a yearly total on phone and air fares that was staggering. Wayne had done his homework. He'd checked out office rentals and presented a plan of six regional offices with one director at each to make the week to week decisions and just that one person reporting in monthly instead of everybody. His way would save hundreds of thousands of dollars. They'd network by computers – Wayne had a system priced – and be as effective as we are now.'

'You've sold me,' she said, touching his hair where the sunlight through the trees was dappling it. 'What's the flaw in the plan?'

'There's no flaw.'

'Then why are you upset?'

He sat up. 'Don't you see? Everything I wanted to accomplish with this competition – the old-fashioned excitement of doing good, of being in this together, of feeling a oneness – all of that's negated by breaking Samaritan into regional units. It's like taking a country and hacking it into bits. The feeling of nationalism, chauvinism, whatever you call it, is gone. Each regional unit is an entity of its own with its loyalties to its own. An employee wouldn't be part of Samaritan, he'd be employed by Samaritan/Atlanta or Samaritan/Seattle. The people in other offices would be complete strangers.'

'But Anthony, you have hundreds, probably thousands of employees, and an army of volunteers all over the country. You don't imagine they all have tea with each other at intervals, do you?'

'Of course not, but the way it is now, they at least have the opportunity to know each other. With the regional plan, they won't.'

'If you hate the idea this much, veto it. You have the power.'

'The power, but not the right.'

'What do you mean?'

'It's a conflict between what's good for me and Samaritan and what's good for the recipients of Samaritan's gifts. Samaritan can be a more effective benefactor with the regional plan. And after all, that's the whole point of its existence. So, it has to be Wayne's way. That's the right way.'

Gilly got up and arranged herself on his lap. 'Poor Anthony. I'm so sorry you're unhappy. Have you talked to Steven about this? Do you want me to invite him over tonight? Or maybe for the weekend? We could even all go up to Birches and you and he could thrash this out.'

'No. Thanks.' He shifted uncomfortably and she got up. 'Gilly, there's something else troubling me,' he said, getting up and pacing. 'Van and Wayne came to talk to me two weeks ago, and I've been thinking about what they said.'

'What nasty thing are they up to now?' she said lightly.

'Gilly, it was about you – and Steven.'

She sat down in the chair he'd vacated. 'What do you mean, me and Steven.'

'They claim that you and Steven are ... are having an affair.'

Gilly was on her feet. *'That's a lie!'*

'Calm down, Gilly.'

'Calm down? You make an accusation like that and tell me to calm down? Anthony, it's not true, you know that, don't you?'

'Of course I do. But Gilly—'

'Did you fire them?'

'No.'

'Oh, Anthony. Don't betray me this way. How could you let them say that and get away with it?'

'I've told them I'll hear no more. That it was inappropriate and if it's ever mentioned again, they'll have to go.'

Gilly buried her face in her hands, unable to hold back the tears. After all these years of resisting the temptation, to have such an accusation hurled in her face ...

Anthony took her in his arms. 'Don't cry. I didn't want to make you feel bad. I just thought you had to be warned.'

'Warned?' she said, looking up. 'Warned to watch my step? Don't sleep with my best friend or I'll find out? Is that what you're saying?'

'No,' he spoke very quietly. 'No, I'm saying the opposite. I'm saying if you ever do, make very sure I *don't* find out.'

Gilly was stunned. 'You don't think I would—'

'Gilly, let's be honest. Or at least, let me be honest for a minute, then we'll never talk about it again. I couldn't bear to choose between you and Steven. I love you both. It's easy for me, though. I can love my friend and my wife without any conflict of loyalties. But you – you love us both, too. And it's different for you.'

She looked up at him, stricken.

'No, don't say anything. Just let me get this off my chest. It's different and much harder for Steven than for either of us. Everything's harder for Steven.'

At that she smiled a little.

'Gilly, there are things I wouldn't like, but I could live with almost any situation rather than lose either of you,' he went on. 'We're something grand, the three of us. But I need you both in my life. I *must* have you both. I can't let anything jeopardize that. Do you know what I'm talking about?'

She didn't answer.

'Nor can I let anything jeopardize Samaritan. I *am* Samaritan, Gilly. Any scandal that touched me would harm it. Even in this liberated day and age, a private scandal would inevitably become public and ultimately hurt the people Samaritan exists to help. Contributors would say, "He can't even keep his own house in order." I wanted you to know where things stood. That's it. That's all I have to say.'

'Do I get to say anything?'

'Of course.'

'I love you, Anthony. More than I have words for.'

He put his hands on her shoulders. 'I know you do. I've never doubted that in all the years we've been married. That's what we've been talking about.'

The Samaritan Family was introduced to the public with great hoopla. They were, as everybody suspected, the result of Gary's research. They were a wholesome, appealing family. The Dorseys lived on a small farm outside St Louis. They grew eighty acres of pumpkins to augment Peter's earnings from his business, which supplied wine bottle labels to wineries all over the country. Gary found them when researching Samaritan's farm assistance program. The Dorseys' underinsured house had burned three years earlier and Samaritan had made one of their two per cent interest loans to cover the gap between the insurance coverage and the actual cost of replacement. Digging further, Gary had discovered that Peter Dorsey had attended college on a scholarship funded by the old paperboy version of Samaritan that Max Herron had administered.

Dorsey's wife Evie, a talented artist who designed most of the wine labels, had been in a car accident that injured her hand and had eventually recovered full use of it due to a therapy program funded by Samaritan. She'd later been employed as a consultant in colonial color in a village restored by Samaritan in Massachusetts. 'A double whammy!' as some of Gary's competition put it admiringly.

The Dorseys' son, a boy of seventeen, had got in trouble at school with drinking a year earlier and had attended a teen alcoholism recovery program that had been a special project of Rhys Jones. He was now president of his senior class and was getting ready to attend Princeton.

Unfortunately, all was still not well with the Dorseys. While driving his daughter to school one morning several years earlier, Peter Dorsey's car had been sideswiped by a tractor entering the highway. Both he and his daughter had been injured. They both had to have blood transfusions and now both were suffering from AIDS, presumably from the transfusions. Peter Dorsey was holding up fairly well so far, both physically and mentally. But the daughter, now thirteen, had been hospitalized several times with raging infections and was under the care of a psychologist who operated a clinic that Samaritan partially funded.

The Dorseys were, at first, unaware of all their connections to Samaritan, until Gary went to them. He received their permission to put them forward as the Samaritan Family. They were grateful for all the organization had done for them and were willing to bare their family secrets and woes in order that others might benefit. This was a great relief. Many of the Samaritan employees who had sought out multiple beneficiaries had discovered that Henry Ford was right when he said, 'Give the average man something, and you make an enemy of him.' It was disheartening to find out that some recipients were resentful, rather than grateful. But not so the Dorseys.

A mammoth publicity campaign was planned, photographs of the Dorseys were taken at their farm, at the clinic, at Samaritan's offices, press releases were sent out, interviews were carefully planned to coincide with the beginning of an enormous fund-raising effort to commence just before Thanksgiving. For the first time since the beginning, Anthony felt all the employees and volunteers were feeling the enthusiasm he and Steven had felt that day in a downtown hotel room when they started planning Samaritan's future.

It was heady stuff and Anthony actually forgot for days at a time his concern over Gilly and Steven.

Faye Brent sat on the sun deck of her home in Palm Springs. She was watching her current young man do his exercises. What a body he had, she thought. Too bad he had the brains of a retarded duck. Of course, if she ever found one with a good mind, he'd probably be out earning his own living instead of being content to be her kept man. 'He's a new one, isn't he?' a voice said behind her.

'Oh, Van. I didn't expect you so early. Go away, Buddy,' she called to the young man. 'I have business to talk over with my nephew.'

'No, let's go inside,' Van said, his watery blue eyes squinting into the sun.

They went into the cool, dim dining room. Van put some folders on the table. 'You saw the *Today* show?'

'Yes. A whole ten-minute segment on the Dorseys. Anthony must be in heaven. What have you found?'

'Not much. These are copies of all the Samaritan files

on all their claims. I also stole Saint Gary's notes from his meetings with them. You'll have to take it from there.'

Faye riffled through the papers. 'I'll be glad to. Glad to.' She put the folder down and took his arm. 'You're a good boy, Van.'

He shrugged off her grasp with a wolfish grin. 'No, I'm not. That's why you like me, auntie dear.'

The next year's winter board meeting at Birches was more of a celebration party than a business meeting. The holiday season had been a huge boon to Samaritan's funds. The Dorseys were well on their way to being folk heroes. The media had embraced them like long lost relatives, and the public had taken them to their hearts. Samaritan had to supply a staff of secretaries to handle the 'fan mail' they were receiving in bags. Now that the Dorseys had come to attention, a number of other families had turned themselves in as multiple recipients. The Samaritan board was considering having an annual Samaritan Family.

The plans for the regional offices were almost ready to implement and even Anthony, who still opposed the scheme for personal reasons, was finding himself caught up in the enthusiasm. Another change was planned as well: Samaritan was going to branch beyond national boundaries. Several communities on the borders of Mexico and Canada had applied for help that would have involved foreign nationals. Previously, Samaritan had resisted extending into other countries, but the board had voted to suspend this restriction. Anthony agreed, so long as aid was confined to North America. There was resistance to this limitation.

'How can we ignore the suffering in the rest of the world?' Wayne asked. 'Think what we could have done in Biafra, for instance.'

'True, but if we'd put our money there, we couldn't have done what we did here with those funds. If Samaritan has a failing, it's that our aims are too diffuse. We can't try to turn ourselves into a worldwide cure-all,' Anthony said firmly. He didn't like reminding people, even by implication, that he held veto power, but he didn't hesitate to use it on those few issues he felt strongly about.

'So, you're going to Mexico next week?' Wayne said at the formal dinner the night they adjourned the meeting. Everybody else would be leaving tomorrow. Only Anthony, Gilly, and Steven would stay on at Birches for another few days as they always did.

'No, I go the day after tomorrow,' Anthony said.

'What?' Gilly asked. 'I didn't know that.'

'I told you,' Anthony said mildly. 'Of course, it was while you were getting ready for this meeting. I should know better than to think you listen to me when you're planning a party – or a garden.'

Everybody laughed politely, except Gilly. 'Steven, are you going too?' she asked.

'No, I'm not needed on this trip.'

'Then I'm afraid I'm going to have to ask you to move to a hotel if you're planning to stay up here.'

A silence fell round the table. This rudeness was very unlike Gilly's usual easy-going charm.

Only Rhys Jones failed to pick up the tension. 'You're throwing Steven out of Birches, Gilly? You can't do that. It's his second home,' he said, thinking it was all a joke.

'Uncle Rhys, I know that it's old-fashioned in this day and age, but I think it would be highly improper for Steven to stay here with me. Think what Anthony's enemies might make of it.'

Now Rhys knew there was something wrong. 'Gilly, Anthony doesn't have any enemies.'

'Maybe not, but perhaps I do,' she said. Her gaze swept the table, paused a second at Steven and came firmly to rest on Wayne, who set his jaw and looked away.

Late that night, after everyone was asleep, Gilly dressed and went down to the kitchen to get herself a cup of hot chocolate. She decided that since she couldn't sleep anyway, she'd do a little tidying up. She emptied an ashtray, and was plumping pillows in the living room when Steven came down the stairs. 'God! I thought you were burglars!' he said in a whisper.

'A burglar who comes in and cleans up?' she said with a laugh. 'Want some hot chocolate?'

'No, thanks, but I'll fix myself a whisky and soda if you don't mind.' Steven put a small log on the fire, which had burned down to embers. As the dainty flames began to lick at the bark, he said, 'Gilly, what was that about at dinner? About how I had to leave Birches.'

Gilly sat down at the other end of the sofa and curled her feet under her. 'Would you have stayed here alone with me?' she said instead of answering.

He didn't reply for some moment, then said, 'No, I couldn't have.'

'Why not?'

He took a sip of his drink. 'Because of the temptation.'

They'd never openly talked about their attraction to each other and yet, for some reason, it seemed natural, like picking up an old conversation where it had been left off before.

Gilly put her hands round her cup of chocolate and stared into the fire. 'Apparently the "temptation", as you put it, has been as obvious to others as to us. Someone,' she considered naming Wayne and Van and decided against it, 'someone told Anthony that you and I were having an affair.'

'No!' He set his drink down on the end table so hard that it slopped over.

'It hardly seems fair, does it?' Gilly said. 'That we've fought it so hard and still get blamed.' Ever the homemaker, she handed him a wad of cocktail napkins and gestured at him to clean up his spill.

He mopped up the Scotch. 'Why didn't Anthony talk to me about this? I can't stand for him to think we've betrayed him. He didn't believe it, did he? Was he angry?'

'No, he didn't believe it and he wasn't angry. He knows, too.'

'Knows what?'

'How we feel. We must be awfully transparent.'

'I can't stand this. I have to talk to him. Right now.'

'No, Steven. Sit down. He won't want to talk about it anymore. It was one of those things that he got off his chest, then closed the book on. He said he could live with any situation, but he couldn't stand ever to be made to choose between us. And he said nothing must ever cause a scandal that would jeopardize Samaritan.'

'Gilly, you can't have this right. That sounds like – like "permission", for God's sake!'

'With a requirement of discretion,' Gilly said softly.

'Hell!' Steven said, getting up suddenly. 'I wish I didn't know this.'

Gilly stared into her chocolate. 'So do I.'

PART SIX

Anthony

March-August 1987

'That night came Arthur home, and while he
  climb'd,
All in a death-dumb autumn-dripping gloom,
The stairway to the hall, and look'd and saw
The great Queen's bower was dark, — about his feet
A voice clung sobbing till he question'd it,
What art thou?' and the voice about his feet
Sent up an answer, sobbing, "I am thy fool,
And I shall never make thee smile again."'

Idylls of the King, Tennyson

Chapter Twenty-six

They were very circumspect, meeting only rarely and in places where neither of them were known. They were careful to the point that their encounters assumed an almost cloak-and-dagger air. Gilly, who was acutely aware that Wayne and Van would go to any lengths to discredit her, would go shopping and slip out through another entrance to a store to take a cab to a hotel. She would register with cash and a convincing false name – no Mr and Mrs Smith for her – and claim that her husband was coming later with the luggage. She'd then call Steven and tell him the hotel room number so that he could speed through the lobby without talking to anyone.

To Steven, this furtiveness only increased the awful guilt he felt. Every time they met, he swore to himself he would never do it again and every time she called, he answered the summons. The exquisite pleasure of holding her naked body in his arms was a temptation he was unable to resist, no matter what his conscience shrieked at him. And while he was actually with her, his conscience was stilled, its voice swallowed up in the delicious aria of flesh to flesh.

It was, as Anthony had said, much easier for Gilly. She regarded her intense longing for Steven as highly inconvenient and unfortunate, but no more immoral than her need for flowers in her life. She could love a gently tumbling cascade of sweetly scented wild roses and still feel her heart swell at the sight of a stand of flamboyant scarlet canna lilies. So could she wholeheartedly love two men. Anthony, who had seen her at Stonehenge and knew that there was something primitively pragmatic in her, understood this better than Steven ever would.

This meeting was their fifth in as many months. 'I have to go,' Steven said, dragging himself from the bed where they had been for nearly two hours. 'We have a meeting at three.'

'You were careful that you weren't seen, weren't you?' Gilly said, stroking his back as he sat on the side of the bed.

'Naturally,' he said, leaning back against her hand. But he knew he hadn't been as cautious as he should be. 'Gilly, this has to stop. We really can't—'

'Not this again. Please, just enjoy the time we have together. It's so little.'

'How can I? How can you? We're betraying Anthony.'

Gilly sat up, clutching the sheets to her breasts. 'It's not betrayal. As long as Anthony doesn't know, it doesn't change anything. I love him as much as ever and so do you.'

'A tree falling in a forest – you aren't fooling yourself that he wouldn't mind, are you?'

'No, Steven, I'm not. He'd mind terribly, but only if he knew. Look, Anthony loathes liver and onions and can't even stand to be in the house if I've cooked it. But it's one of my favorite dishes. So, when I go out alone, I always order it. Do you suppose he minds? Of course not.'

'Gilly, that's the stupidest comparison I've ever heard.' He started dressing.

'I know. But it's the best I could come up with on short notice. Oh, Steven, please don't always make me feel like I'm a terrible drug you're addicted to.'

'But you are. I am.'

'Love isn't a bad addiction, Steven. It's a good one, like breathing and eating. It's what we're supposed to want. It's the point of life. You and I and Anthony are really very lucky. So few people find even one person in this world to truly love and we've each got two. Anthony grasps this. Why can't you?'

'I don't know that he does. I don't see how he could. Gilly, we have to stop this. Confess to him—'

She hurled herself at him and grabbed his arm so hard that her nails left prints in his skin. 'No! No, Steven! We must never do that. That would be the worst betrayal. He would have to choose between us. You could do nothing worse to him.'

He turned to face her. 'But this is *wrong*, Gilly!'

'Steven, listen to me. You and Anthony have things in common that I don't share. Your work at Samaritan, the very existence of Samaritan. It's a huge part of both your lives. It absorbs you. You live for it. And I'm not part of it, except as a cheerleader at the fringes. But that's fine. It's how it should be. You and Anthony share your obsession with Samaritan and I'm left out. Then Anthony and I have a home and a marriage that you don't share. And you and I share these few stolen hours every few weeks. Anthony isn't part of that. It works out evenly. Each relationship is just as dear and important as the others, and together the three of us have a wonderful friendship.'

He took her in his arms. 'The scariest part of all this is I find myself thinking you make sense.'

She snuggled close for a moment. 'That's because I do. Now, get dressed. You mustn't be late for your meeting.'

As always, Steven was ready to leave before Gilly. She was still in her slip when he kissed the back of her neck. She walked to the door with him and still had her arm round him when he opened it and a flash of light hit her in the eyes. She had only a second to realize what had happened before Steven slammed the door and leaned against it. 'The bastard! The nasty, filthy bastard!'

'Steven, what is it? What's happened?'

'The light was a camera flash. Van Graves is standing in the hall.'

'Oh, God!' Gilly exclaimed. 'I have to get to Anthony before he does. Stop him, Steven. Get the camera!' She was flinging on her clothing as she spoke.

411

Steven disappeared, but was back in a few minutes. 'He's gone. Gilly, I don't know what to say. This is too awful—'

'I must see Anthony. Get me a cab.'

'I'll come along.'

'No, you won't. No. This is something I must take care of. It's my fault. All my fault. I've ruined everything. All of us.' She was sobbing as she tore round the room throwing things into her handbag. She was so pale she looked dead. If Steven had ever doubted the sincerity of her love for Anthony, her frantic distress dispelled those doubts.

'He said to show you straight in when you got here,' Nina said to Gilly a short time later.

'He knew I was coming?' Gilly asked.

'I guess so,' Nina replied, trying to act businesslike and neutral. But she'd been eavesdropping when Van phoned Anthony from a convenience store down the block from the hotel. It was all she could do to keep herself from grabbing Gilly by the shoulders, shaking her until her teeth rattled and screaming, 'You've wrecked everything, you selfish bitch!'

Anthony was standing by the windows when Gilly came in. He gestured her to a chair without turning round.

'You know?' she asked, barely able to control her voice.

He nodded and spoke in a cold voice. 'In a way, it was my fault. Van told me he wanted to follow Steven to get proof. I was so sure, so goddamned fucking sure he was wrong, that I told him to go ahead. Almost dared him.'

Gilly was shaking so badly she had to sit down. 'Anthony, I'll go away. Today. Right now. You and Steven will never see me again. It's all my fault. I'll do anything you say. Just please tell me you'll try to forgive me some day.'

Anthony turned. 'The hell of it is, Gilly, I don't want you to go. I don't want to lose you. Or Steven. But you've

412

made me choose. Gilly, why? I told you, I asked you not to make me choose.'

She found the strength to run to him. She buried her face in his chest and sobbed. 'Anthony, what can I do? Name it. Tell me to go kill myself. I'll do it. Put me in jail. Put me in a nunnery, for heaven's sake. Knock me senseless. Do something terrible to me.'

'I don't want to do anything terrible to you,' he said, stroking her hair. 'I just want to go back to yesterday. I want to not know any of this. And it's too late.'

Gilly cupped his face in her hands. 'Oh, Anthony, I do love you so much. I'm so sorry—'

'It's not your fault. It's not Steven's or mine either. It's fate. I believe that. For some reason, it had to happen. I think the Prof knew. He didn't want me to marry you, you know. He said if I did something awful would happen. This has got to be it,' he said wryly.

Gilly sniffed and started looking for a handkerchief. Anthony handed her a box of tissues from the desk drawer.

'Anthony, we can't go back to yesterday,' she said.

'I know.'

'You didn't want to have to choose and I stupidly thought I didn't have to choose. That I could have everything I wanted just because I wanted it. But I'm not afraid to choose, Anthony. If I have to, I choose you. But you can put me out with the trash and I won't object. Anthony, my darling Anthony, it's up to you.'

Anthony walked to his desk and sat down. They were being careful now not to touch. 'What do you want, Gilly?'

'If I could choose, which I have no right to, I'd want to stay with you for ever. Just us – off somewhere.'

'I can't chuck it all for you, Gilly,' he said sadly.

'I know that. Then send me someplace, anywhere you want, somewhere that I'll never see Steven again. And visit me sometimes. I won't make demands.'

'I need time to think. Go to your father.'

'I couldn't face his disappointment! I have to be alone.

Anthony, remember that house on the island off the coast of Georgia that my great-uncle left me? I could go there.'

'Gilly, I told you I went to look at it and it's a dump. No heat but a fireplace, no running water. Every time there's a storm, half the island blows away. You'd hate it.'

'Good. I need to be someplace I hate. If you won't punish me for what I've done, I'll have to punish myself,' she said with a weak smile. 'Anthony, I'll go there and you can decide what to do. I'll wait for you to come to me, and if you decide not to, you won't ever need to hear from me again. Ever. But I'll be there the rest of my life, ready for you.'

'I don't think—'

'That's right. Don't think. Not about me. Not until you feel like it. I'm going now, Anthony. Will you kiss me goodbye?'

In March 1987, Martin Graves turned twenty-one. His mother, Betsy, sent her best wishes with a magnum of champagne from Bermuda. His Aunt Faye sent a card with ten 100 dollar bills tucked inside and a note saying she was having a tummy tuck and was sorry she couldn't be there to celebrate with him, but as soon as he got settled into his new journalism job she'd have a story for him that would set him up for life. 'Maybe Christmas, my dear? I hope so,' she wrote.

So he celebrated with his brothers in the trendy renovated condo that his mother had given him for graduation a couple months earlier.

Martin had grown up to look so much like Anthony that it was eerie. People who had known Anthony in his youth couldn't look at him without gawking. Even those who'd never laid eyes on Anthony Wentworth found Martin Graves a stunning-looking person. Some speculated that he would have been even better looking if he smiled, but few of his acquaintances had ever seen that happen. Martin was bright, rich, talented, handsome and well-educated, but he wasn't happy. Perhaps it was because all the other attributes had come to him so easily. Perhaps it was because he was the last of five similarly bright brothers, or because his mother was what she was. He thought it was because he was both son and nephew to Anthony Wentworth, whom he loathed.

'So, you're a grown-up now,' his brother Van said, pouring another round of drinks.

'None for me, thanks,' Donald said, putting his hand over his untouched glass of champagne. He hadn't ever thrown off his missionary uncle's influence about drinking. Nor had he ever spent much time with his brothers as a group. He was finding it a less than enjoyable experience. The only one he got along with very well was Harry, but then everybody got along well with him. Good old Harry, so cheerful and easy-going. But Wayne was too high-strung and flashy for Donald's tastes, and pale, sneaky Van was a downright psycho, in his view. It remained to be seen how young Martin would turn out, but Donald wasn't holding out much hope. Martin was as surly and discontented as Van. But Martin had it under tighter rein.

Van had left Samaritan suddenly a couple weeks before, which was a good thing. No chance of running into him in the halls anymore. And Martin apparently had no interest in joining Samaritan, which Donald approved of. Better that he go pursue his career ambitions, whatever they were, someplace else.

'Sorry, but I've really got to be going,' Donald said, getting up and looking around for his jacket. 'Happy birthday again, Martin.'

'I'll come with you. I've met this girl I want to tell you all about,' Harry said.

As soon as the door closed behind them, Van said, 'Mr Nice has to get his beauty rest.'

'Come on, Van. Donald's okay,' Wayne said. 'So, did you invite Anthony over tonight?' he asked Martin.

He'd almost slipped and said 'your father', for they all

knew Anthony was Martin's father even though they didn't talk about it openly. Each had his own private version of how this could be: none of which reflected badly on their mother. Wayne and Harry had whispered about it years ago and decided that it was nobody's fault, that they must have met before anybody knew who Anthony really was. They slid by the fact that their mother had been married to their father Ned at the time. Wayne didn't have much trouble with that aspect of it; he didn't see what was so bad about adultery anyway – so long as Gilly Wentworth wasn't committing it. Van had also thought about it and in his view, Anthony, the devil personified, had cruelly ravaged his poor innocent mother, dishonoring both her and his sainted father.

Martin knew, too. He'd heard the whispers, but he hadn't believed it until they all went to that godawful country wedding. He'd seen Anthony then as though seeing himself in a mirror. And he'd hated the sight because it had deprived him of Ned. He didn't really remember Ned, but he believed he did. His older brothers had made a saint of their father and Martin fancied himself the one that was most like him. But if he was Anthony's son, he couldn't be Ned's. In a dark part of his soul, a place where injustices were hoarded and emotional scabs picked, Martin thought Anthony had killed Ned, had spiritually kidnapped him from his real father. He wouldn't have described his feeling that way consciously, he never let himself examine his emotions that carefully, yet he hated Anthony and blamed him for every failure and injury he'd ever received.

'Yeah, I invited him,' Martin said, plunging a chip into the bowl of dip in the centre of the coffee table. 'But he couldn't come. Surprise, surprise.'

'So what did he give you?' Wayne asked.

Martin almost smiled as he pulled a set of pristine new car keys from his pocket. 'Look upon them and weep. A Porsche.'

'Wow!' Wayne said. 'Not bad, little brother.'

'He can't buy me,' Martin sneered.

'Buy you? Listen, it's a nice gift. What's the matter with just thinking he was being nice to you?' Wayne said.

'Sure. Who do you know that's *that* nice for no reason?'

'Get off it, Martin,' Wayne said. 'So why isn't he here?'

'Had to go to Georgia, he said,' Martin replied.

'Georgia?' Wayne and Van exclaimed in unison. It didn't occur to either of them that Martin might be lying, though it should have crossed their minds; they knew him well enough.

'Is that where his wife is?' Martin asked. 'I've been busy getting to know the ropes at the paper and I haven't kept up with Samaritan gossip for the last couple of months.'

Van explained about how he'd got a picture of Gilly in her underwear with her arm round Steven in a hotel room doorway. 'So that's why you're not there anymore?' Martin asked Van.

'Yeah, he fired me.'

'You can't blame him,' Wayne said. 'I told you not to involve yourself so directly. Instead of waiting and planning carefully, you just barged in. But he'll change his mind. It was the shock of realizing she was making an ass of him. You know, killing the messenger who brings bad news. Sooner or later, he'll realize it was for his own good.'

Both brothers looked at him pityingly for a moment. 'Uh-huh. That's why he's gone panting off after her to Georgia, is it?' Van drawled.

'I don't get it. She's just a damned slut and we proved it to him,' Wayne said. 'She was making an ass of Anthony and of Steven. You'd think they'd both see it now.'

'So where's Steven in all this?' Martin asked.

'I don't know,' Wayne said. 'He came in just after Gilly left Anthony's office that day and they had a long talk, but I can't get that damned Nina to say what happened and I know she was snooping like mad. After that, Steven just left. Hasn't been back to the office since. Van, we've

417

made a mess of this. Our whole aim was to get Gilly out of the picture, not Steven. We can't let it go this way.'

Van didn't disagree openly, but his aim had been quite different and had almost been fulfilled when he heard the agony in Anthony's voice on the phone that day. Just for a little extra thrill, he'd had the film developed immediately and sent a delivery boy over with an 8- by 10-inch glossy of the shot. That's when Anthony had fired him; he sent the picture back in tiny shreds with a note saying his severance pay was being prepared. He was delighted that Anthony and Steven had ended their friendship. It must be hell for Anthony and that had been his aim. Still, if Wayne thought the object was to keep harping on Gilly, that was okay. It would make Anthony even more miserable. Wayne was an asshole thinking Anthony would be grateful to him.

'So what are you going to do?' Martin asked, his eyes lighting up.

'I don't know. But it'll come to me,' Wayne said. 'Pour me some more of that stuff, would you?'

August in Georgia was impossibly hot, Steven decided as he rolled down the windows of the rental car at the Atlanta airport. He consulted the map once more, then set out. After a few miles, when he felt the air conditioning had started functioning, he rolled the windows back up and settled in for the long drive.

This was a trip he shouldn't be making, he thought. But he hadn't had any contact with Gilly or Anthony after that terrible day in February. Gilly's typed note had seemed like the promise of cool water in the arid desert of his life. Her words, 'Please come. I must see you,' had seemed panicky and distressed. He would never succumb to her physical charms and his own weakness again, but she was still a longtime friend. And if she were in need, he had to go to her.

There had been no recriminations when he went to Anthony's office. Just profound sadness on both their parts. They hadn't talked about themselves, or Gilly. Anthony had been sitting at the desk when Steven entered the room. He looked up and said, 'What do you think of this Jim Bakker business on the news?'

'I think he's a crook, or an imbecile, or both. I've always thought so,' Steven said, surprised at the question. Bakker's people had put out feelers about applying to Samaritan to help fund his Heritage Village. Steven had been assigned to investigate them and had given a blistering recommendation that Samaritan stay as far away from them as humanly possible.

'Don't you feel a little bit sorry for him?' Anthony asked. 'I do. He trusted people.'

'You don't think he's guilty of misuse of funds?' Steven said, still not understanding why in hell they were talking about Jim Bakker.

'Oh, I'm sure he is. But in a way, it doesn't matter. The press has gone into a feeding frenzy. The media have a long and often honorable history of debunking. He's their current victim. He probably deserves it. Sometimes people don't, however. Now poor little country bumpkin Jimmy Bakker's whole life is going to be dissected. If some old bitch tells a reporter he stole a candy bar from her drug store when he was eight years old, it's going to be a front page headline, whether it's true or not. Gilly just left.'

'I know. I waited until she'd gone. She asked me to.'

'A messenger just brought this.' He opened the envelope and tossed the picture on the desk.

'Oh, God!'

'I don't blame you, Steven.'

'I do.'

Anthony waved his hand, too emotionally exhausted to argue. 'The press will be looking for an opportunity to go after even bigger fish than Jim Bakker.'

'I'll send a secretarial service over to pick up the personal things in my office.'

'That's a good idea.' Anthony looked like death. He

looked like Max Herron had toward the end.

'Anthony ... There aren't words.'

'No, I guess not.'

And with that, Anthony had got up and opened the door of his office. Steven saw that Nina was sitting by the intercom, her hands covering her face, crying. At the door, he turned back to Anthony. Suddenly, Anthony clasped him in a bear hug, then shoved him away and closed the door.

And that was the last Steven had seen or heard of either of them. Until he got this curt, alarming note from Gilly.

Steven arrived at the ferry boat dock about four in the afternoon, only to find that the ferry to the island was at its island end and wouldn't return for another two hours. He parked his car in a line of others that were waiting and went to find a soft drink and hamburger to fill the time. The waterfront cafe was crowded. Eavesdropping, Steven discovered that there was a society wedding today on the island, and most of the young men in the restaurant were reporters, hoping to crash the party. Apparently the groom's father was a Hollywood agent and there were rumours that some of his famous clients were invited.

Steven took his food outside to eat, queasy at the smoke and gossip inside. Gazing idly at the passing scene, he spotted a flash of blond hair. Watching more closely, and with some alarm, he decided it wasn't his imagination; it was Van Graves. Had he turned into a movie star fan? Unlikely. Steven had just finished eating and was looking for somewhere to throw away his paper cup when he spotted Harry Graves. 'Harry? Harry Graves!'

Harry turned from tying up a high-tech speedboat and hurried to meet Steven. 'Great to see you, Steven.'

'What are you and Van doing here?'

'Van? Van's in San Francisco – or was it San Diego?'

'I just saw him down the street.'

'Must have been somebody who looks like him.'

'Nobody looks like Van,' Steven said with a laugh. 'So what are you doing here?'

'Gilly wanted her seed catalogs. Anthony said he couldn't stand to just ship them to her in a box, so I volunteered to bring them. She'll be glad to see you. She must be awfully lonesome here.'

'Has Anthony been here to see her?'

'No, not yet. But he probably will when some time has passed. It was a pretty tough blow. Sorry, Steven, but I s'pose you must realize that everybody knows what happened. Van made sure of that. But most people understand. You know, shit happens. We aren't any of us saints. Come on, I just ran over to get some bread and milk.'

Steven trailed him to the grocery store and then back to the boat. 'Is this Gilly's?' he asked.

'Lord, no! She's got a dinky little rowboat with oarlocks that shriek like banshees. I rented this one. Hop in.'

The island could be seen from the mainland, but they were halfway across before Steven could discern the grandeur of the houses. 'Not bad, for shacks on the beach,' he said.

'Summer houses for all those grand rich folk from Atlanta and Savannah, ah reckon,' Harry replied in a fake southern drawl.

'Which one is Gilly's?'

Harry laughed heartily. 'None of these. Wait till you see hers. It's down here.'

He turned the boat and they headed away from the mansions. There was nothing but scrub and sand until they reached the mouth of a shallow cove. At the back end of it was a weathered one-story house that looked like a pioneer settler had abandoned it years ago. But the roof had been recently repaired and fresh yellow boards marked where the dock decking had been replaced. The weeds were cut back away from the shell walk and the wide, sagging porch. As Harry pulled the speedboat in and tied it up next to the primitive rowboat, Gilly came out of the house and stopped short.

She was wearing jeans and a sleeveless white tunic

blouse that made her look like a girl. Her hair – some gray in it now, Steven noticed – was tied up away from her face with a red bandana. She wore no make-up or shoes and she looked wonderful. She stared back at him for a long moment before starting to approach. 'Steven, what a surprise.'

'Surprise?' Steven asked. 'You wrote to me.'

Gilly shook her head. 'No. I never did.'

Steven pulled the letter from his shirt pocket and handed it to her. She looked at it. 'I don't have a type-writer here. And if I did, I wouldn't type my signature.'

Harry was watching them as if they were a tennis match. 'Sounds like dirty work to me.'

'I'll go right back,' Steven said. Van was behind this. He was sure of it. He *had* seen him in town no matter where Harry thought he was supposed to be.

'Nonsense. You'll come have a drink with Harry and me and we'll fix dinner, then he can take you back.'

'Right,' Harry said. 'I'd like to see anybody claim anything went on with me here. I'm the world's premier wet blanket.'

They went in the house, got drinks and adjourned to a screened porch at the back. They talked impersonally about the weather, the town, Harry's new girl friend and Harry's new car. Finally Gilly said, 'I better throw together some dinner. Harry, did you bring the groceries in?'

Harry looked stricken. 'Oh, shit! I got so busy talking to Steven that I left them sitting on the dock in town. Damn! What a dope! I'll go right back.'

'Oh, Harry, don't bother. I must have something here we can eat, if it's only peanut butter and crackers.'

'No. It'll only take me a few minutes.'

They went to the dock with him and sat down side by side to watch him cross the water. 'I didn't see any gardens,' Steven said.

'No. I tried when I first got here, but nothing would grow. I was actually thinking about importing tons of good topsoil when I realized there was a reason nothing would grow. It's part of my sentence.'

'What do you mean?'

'I deprived Anthony of his peace of mind. I must be deprived of my gardens.'

'Do you hear from Anthony?'

'Not directly. He sends messages and money through Nina. All very businesslike.'

'He sends you money? Isn't it enough? I'll buy you a decent boat. I hate to think of you out here without a way to get to shore quickly if a storm blew up.'

'Anthony sends me more money than is decent. That boat is my choice. It hurts like hell to row it and it reminds me how I hurt him.'

Steven turned and looked at her, expecting self-pity, but her face was serene, accepting. She wasn't being pitiful or melodramatic; merely honest. 'Are we over each other, Gilly?'

She smiled. 'What do you think?'

'I'm not sure.'

She put her hand on his knee in a sisterly fashion. 'I think we've both realized that Anthony is better and more important to the world than either of us are. And that we had no right to harm him – '

' – by succumbing to our passion,' he finished.

Facing him, she still smiled, but shook her head sadly. 'No, by letting him find out. By letting that nasty psychopath Van Graves get to tell him.'

'Speaking of Van Graves, I saw him in town.'

She nodded. 'It starts to make sense. He's not through with Anthony. He thought by getting you here on a weekend when every reporter in Georgia is around he could fake a new round of scandal. He'll be disappointed.' She squinted into the dusk and pointed. 'What's happening out there?'

Harry's boat had nearly reached the opposite shore, but another boat was heading straight toward it. Suddenly Harry's boat disappeared in a ball of flame and the other boat veered away so sharply it nearly capsized. The sound of the explosion reached them only a second after the flare of orange.

'Oh, my God!' Gilly exclaimed. She and Steven leaped to their feet and into her rowboat. 'No! Sit there! You don't know how to row!' she screamed, grabbing the oars.

'Oh, God! I've really fucked it up!' Van was sobbing into the phone.

'Jesus! What's the matter with you?' Martin said. 'Where are you? What's all the noise behind you?'

'It's the damned Coast Guard and police and God knows what! It was Harry! Not them! I tried to stop him but—'

'Get a grip on yourself!' Martin said. He motioned to Faye and punched a button to operate the speaker phone. 'Now listen. We're here. There's no rush. Just tell us, calmly, what happened.'

There was the sound of ragged breathing and Van said with a painful attempt at logic, 'I did what we planned. Came here this morning. Rented a boat. Checked out her place. She had this dinky little piece of shit rowboat and a big fancy one. So I naturally figured they'd use the big one.'

'So far so good,' Martin said encouragingly.

'Yeah, yeah. So I waited until I saw the big boat tied up in town and I figured she'd come to pick him up. So I waited around, but I missed seeing them leave. But all of a sudden the boat's gone. So I went back across to the island—'

'Okay, okay. Calm down.'

'Anyway, there's no sign of them and I figure they're too busy screwing to notice me, but it was scary anyway. I pulled in next to the big boat and put that gadget you gave me on the engine. Then I got the hell out. So I get back into town and was still cruising around looking for a place to put this damned great tub of a boat and I see her boat coming from the cove. So I'm watching, waiting in a front row seat and then, as it gets closer—' He broke off with what sounded like a cough – or a sob.

'What? What happened?' Martin asked.

'*It was Harry in the boat!*'

'Harry! Our Harry? What in hell—'

'I don't know. I don't know what he was doing here. I headed out to try to stop him, but the damned thing blew sky high!'

'With Harry in it! Oh, Jesus! Is he hurt?'

'You fool!' Faye exclaimed, jerking Martin out of the way and shouting at the phone. 'Is he dead, Van?'

'I don't know. I don't know. They haven't found him. The wreckage is still on fire. Steven and Gilly showed up in the damned rowboat and I tried to get a reporter to talk to them. To take a picture of them together, but he acted like I was nuts. Then they were gone. God knows how. Steven's car is gone— Oh God, I've killed Harry!'

Faye breathed deeply through her teeth and then said with hypnotic calm, 'No, Van. You didn't kill Harry. Gilly and Steven killed him. It's their fault. Not yours. All of this is because of them – and Anthony. They don't deserve to get away with it. Now, listen to me and listen carefully. We aren't going to tell Wayne about this yet. Do you understand? I don't think he should know the whole story until we've thought it all out very carefully. Don't tell anybody there who you are. Are you listening to me, Van? Good. Now, hang up the phone, keep your mouth shut and get back to Kansas City as soon as you can. Charter a plane if you have to – no, that would draw too much attention. Just go to Atlanta and call us back from there.'

She hung up the phone. 'Martin, make another pot of coffee. We've got to figure out how to get our rightful advantage out of this. And Martin, I've got something I've been saving to tell you on a special occasion. I believe this is it. You know that Samaritan family, the Dorseys?'

Anthony had gone out for dinner and when he came home

there was a message on his answering machine. 'Anthony, this is Steven. I'm with Gilly. Somebody has tried to kill her and got Harry Graves instead. I'm bringing her back home in the morning. I'm bringing her back to *you*, Anthony. She'll explain it all. Erase this message and don't talk to anyone until you've seen her.'

'We think it must have been a suicide pact,' Faye was saying, patting Wayne on the shoulder. 'And somehow Harry used the boat. Maybe they didn't know he was going to take it. Maybe they'd changed their minds and didn't care.'

Wayne was shivering with shock. 'But what was Van doing there? What was Harry doing there?'

'Van had sent a letter to Steven. Trying to trap them together again. It was foolish—'

'But Harry wasn't in on that, was he?'

'No, Van didn't know Harry was there.'

'And Steven fell for this note? After what he'd already done to Anthony, he went back to her? What a fool he is.'

Over his head, Faye and Martin exchanged a quick look of victory.

'I still don't see – suicide? By blowing themselves up in a boat? Where would Steven get an explosive device? I want to hear this from Van. Where is he?'

'We don't know. He was supposed to come back here this morning. As soon as he gets here, we'll bring him over to see you.'

Anthony, Steven and Gilly were at the Kansas City house. Gilly was standing at the window of the living room, looking out at her sadly neglected gardens. Everything needed staking and deadheading and some Miracid wouldn't hurt the potted hibiscus plants. The perennials looked naked without the annuals she always planted among them to create borders and fill in blank spots.

'You'll have to have security people for her. And your-self,' Steven was saying. 'You're not thinking of sending her back to that island, are you?'

'Send her back? I never wanted her there in the first place. As for security, I've already called them and made arrangements. But I'm not sure there's a need.'

'Not sure there's a need? Van has lost his mind. He tried to kill her already.'

'But he won't try again,' Anthony said. 'The police were here just before you arrived. Van's dead, too. He kept bugging the rescue people to let him help and they kept trying to keep him out of their way. He must have tried to swim out and drowned.'

They accepted this in silence.

'Gilly's staying here, isn't she?' Steven finally said, standing and patting his pockets with exaggerated casual-ness for his car keys.

'I hope so,' Anthony said, looking at her.

Gilly, still in the jeans and white tunic she'd had on the day before, turned slowly from the window and looked at Anthony. 'I guess I'll have to. The garden needs so much work.'

Chapter Twenty-seven

Anthony stood on the porch and stared out over the Flint Hills. There had been frost last night, and it was amazing the difference it made in the colors. The white-faced, rust-colored Hereford cattle dotting the range were against a background of grass turned a soft ocher by the season. Here and there were subtle shadings of mauve and copper and gold with the occasional scarlet of sumac. He loved the landscape in all its seasons, but fall was his favorite. The Flint Hills reminded him of eastern Scotland, with their gently rolling landscape and magnificent barrenness. Usually this vast, uncluttered view acted as a tranquilizer; that's why he'd canceled his appointments and come down here for a few days away from the world.

And yet this time it wasn't working. So much was wrong; so much that he couldn't do anything about. His marriage was still intact, but had been seriously injured by the events of the previous March. Perhaps in time he and Gilly would both be able to forget. If only he could use some of his fortune to buy that necessary time. She'd been changed by it as much as he. Even her gardens were different. Less joyous, more restrained and confined.

He missed Steven in his life. At least that time before when Steven had disappeared for several years, Anthony had known the problem was Steven's alone and he always believed he'd come back. But this time, the problem was between the three of them and Anthony couldn't fool himself that it would cure itself. Their friendship, so dear to both of them, to all three of them, had withered and possibly died. Perhaps that, too, in time ... But the time hadn't come yet. He'd know when it had.

The Graves, individually and as a family, were much on his mind as well. Martin was a disappointment. His byline appeared frequently in the newspaper, but it was always heading an article that was savaging someone. He seemed to have a victim a month; some judge or police official or city council member would come to Martin's attention, get a few columns of vitriolic coverage that skimmed the cusp of libel, then the glare of Martin's attention would shine on another. How could a boy with so many advantages be so mean-spirited? Anthony wondered. *My only child*, his heart sometimes cried.

Wayne had gone to pieces about Harry, deciding that Steven, whom he had always idolized, was somehow to blame. Anthony had considered telling Wayne that the private investigators he'd hired had found bystanders who'd heard a strange-looking blond man muttering frantically to himself, 'I killed my brother. Oh, God, I've killed my own brother,' at the scene. But he knew Wayne wouldn't believe him, would twist it to be part of a diabolical plot. In the end, he'd had to tell Wayne that he was free to believe whatever he wanted, but if he talked about it to Anthony one more time, he'd have to leave Samaritan. Anthony knew Wayne was still seething silently.

Donald had left Samaritan after Harry's and Van's deaths. He'd said it was because he wanted to apply what he had learned at Samaritan to helping the Egyptians among whom he'd grown up. That's what he said, but Anthony thought there was more to it. He suspected that Donald thought that Samaritan had been responsible for his brothers' deaths.

Sometimes, in the bleakest moments, Anthony wondered about that. Was there a subterranean seam of wickedness underlying Samaritan that was now being revealed at the surface? Had there been a flaw from the beginning? Was there something he should have done or shouldn't have done years ago that was catching up with them now?

The phone rang and he went to answer it. That would be Nina, the only person who knew where he was. In a confusing, changing world, Nina was the one thing that never changed. 'Hello, Nina.'

'Anthony, sorry to bother you, but I just got a call from Gilly. She sounded upset and wanted you to call her.'

Anthony hung up and punched in the Kansas City phone number. 'Gilly? What's wrong?'

'Anthony, Martin was just here and it was dreadful. He said he was looking for you and when I said you were out of town, he insisted on coming in anyway. He made chitchat for a few minutes, then all of a sudden he – well, he made a pass at me.'

'Martin? Martin did that?'

'I tried to shake him off gently, but he just kept coming on. Anthony, he very nearly raped me before I managed to get that gun you keep in the kitchen drawer. I waved it around and he backed off.'

'Gilly, are you all right?'

'Yes, now I am. I locked up the house and called the security people back. I don't know what came over him. Do you think he's on drugs or something? Anthony, I don't know what to do.'

'Just stay put. I'll be there as soon as I can.'

'Anthony, he was raving. He kept talking about how he was going to take everything that was yours, me included. He says he has information that can destroy you and Samaritan and then he'll destroy me at his leisure.'

Anthony's stomach heaved. 'Information?'

He dialed Nina again and told her everything Gilly had said. 'I want you to set up an emergency board meeting at Birches. Two days from now. Can you do it? I want Martin there, too. I'm tired of waiting for things to get better and all the while they're going to hell. We're going to thrash this out. We'll see just what this information of his is. Check with the security people and make sure they don't let Gilly out of their sight. Have a woman sleep in her room with her.'

'Gilly's not going to Birches?'

'Not this time. There are going to be ugly things said and I don't want her in the middle of it. I want security at Birches, too. I think Martin's gone mad.'

'You want Wayne there?'

'Everybody on the board, including Wayne. He needs some sorting out, too.'

'What about Steven?'

Anthony was silent for a minute. Dear God, how he longed to have Steven at his side! 'We aren't Steven's problem anymore, Nina.'

'Ellen? This is Wayne Graves. I don't know if you remember me—'

'Of course. Steven's young friend.'

'Not much of a friend lately,' Wayne mumbled into the phone. 'Do you know where Steven is? I have to talk to him. I've called everywhere I can think of and I thought if anyone could find him, you could.'

'I'll do what I can. Where can he call you?'

'He can't. I'm in New York, but I'm getting ready to drive up to Connecticut. Tell Steven to come to Birches. Something awful's happening and Anthony needs him. My brother Martin's planning something and I don't think anybody knows how really nasty he can be.'

'Wayne, I really don't know where Steven is.'

'Please, Ellen, please help find him. I've got to go.'

The meeting didn't resemble anything Gilly had ever planned at Birches. A staff of caterers had been told to bring in enough sandwiches, chips and drinks for a one-day meeting, then get out. Nina had got cleaning people in to take off the dust sheets and check that there were enough towels and sheets, but they, too, had gone. Anthony didn't want any outsiders in the house to over-hear anything that might be said.

The directors had been summoned from all over the country, told only that there was a crisis and where to pick up their plane tickets. They had been arriving all morning, frazzled and put out. Anthony had remained in his study, not greeting them. Nina had just come in to speak to him when the doorbell and the phone both sounded at once. 'You get the door,' Anthony said, reaching for the phone.

It was Rory at the door. 'What in hell is this all about!' he demanded.

Nina filled him in as best she could and she showed him to his room. 'Anthony thought it would be best to get it out in the open before Martin printed something in that paper of his.'

'Information? What could that twerp know? I think it's all bluff. Samaritan's clean as snow. At least the books are.'

'If it's a bluff, Anthony and the board will call it and be done with it,' Nina said.

'Yeah, that's the best way to deal with a little bully like that kid.'

She left Rory shuffling through his papers, trying to get organized for an impromptu financial report, should one be asked for.

Anthony was sitting at the desk, his hand still resting on the phone when she got back to his study. 'Everybody's here but Wayne, and Martin,' she said. 'Anthony? Did you hear me?'

He looked up slowly. 'Wayne won't be here. That was the police calling. He was driving too fast on the Merritt Parkway. He hit that section under construction near Stamford and jumped the median. He died five minutes ago.'

Nina stared at him in horror.

Anthony put his hands out in supplication. 'Nina, what's happening? It's all gone wrong. What have I done?'

Nina was the first to get a grip on herself. 'Nothing.

You've done nothing wrong. I don't think you should tell the others. Not yet. Everybody's here but Martin. You need to make sure everyone understands the situation and your position before he arrives. Straighten your tie. Comb your hair! You're a mess,' she said, brutally jerking him back to reality.

But there was little time to outline more than the bare facts to the board before Martin arrived. 'So, you've got all your big guns out, have you?' he said as he entered the room.

'All right, Martin,' Anthony said. 'We're all here. At considerable inconvenience, I might add. Now, what's on your mind?'

Martin strolled once round the table, looking at each of them in turn. 'I've never liked you much, Rory. I think you'll have to go.'

'Bullshit,' Rory rumbled contemptuously.

'And I don't much like this house. It should be sold. Now, the Kansas City house, that's a different matter. I like that. I'll like living there.' He'd reached the far end of the table. He put his briefcase down on the floor and leaned on the table, looking at Anthony.

'Are you on drugs, Martin? I'll get you any help you need,' Anthony said.

'Drugs? No. But I could buy all I want with your money, couldn't I? I could buy anything I wanted. A small Central American country, perhaps. Why don't we get on with the agenda? First item, election of a new Chief Executive Officer.'

'What the hell are you talking about, boy?' Rory said.

'Oh, didn't anybody tell you? I'm taking over Samaritan.'

'Over my dead body,' Rory said.

'If you want it that way, it's okay by me.'

Rory turned to Anthony, but Anthony was looking round the table, detached, distracted. He saw faces filled with outrage, with disgust, with embarrassment at this incomprehensible scene. But he saw no answers, no understanding. 'Martin, you're sick,' he said finally.

'I'm sick? Me? No, you're the sick one. Your life is a shambles. Is your slut of a wife still sleeping with your friend, Anthony? Do you ever visit my brothers' graves?' He leaned forward. 'You're not fit to run a garbage truck, much less a multi-billion-dollar corporation. And you're not going to anymore. I'm going to take over Samaritan.'

'You're not,' Anthony said.

'If you and your pet directors don't hand it to me nicely, I'll destroy it,' Martin said. 'I have the means. Don't push your luck and make me use what I know.'

'You don't know a damned thing, you little rattlesnake,' Rory said, starting to rise from his chair.

'You don't think so?'

'We ought to call the police,' the man sitting next to Rory muttered. 'The man's a lunatic.'

'Oh, yeah? Well, listen to this, you old fart. That family, that Dorsey bunch Samaritan touted far and wide. You know how the father and the teenage daughter come to both have AIDS? The father got it and gave it to her. He's been molesting her since she was four.'

There was a sudden babble of conversation, which Anthony cut through. He stood up and pointed to Martin. 'That's not true and you know it.'

'No? How do you know it isn't? And do you happen to know what sort of money those people have in their bank accounts? I think you'd be surprised at the amount. It looks like Samaritan paid them to be the perfect family.'

'They weren't paid anything but their travel expenses,' Rory said.

'No? Then how come they've got over two hundred thousand in banks all over town?'

'Faye,' Anthony said quietly.

'Yes, dear Aunt Faye takes a great interest in Samaritan's fine work,' Martin smirked. 'After all, it was founded by the money that should have come to her and my mother.'

'Martin, none of this is true,' Anthony said.

'Possibly. But can you take the chance? All I need to do is send anonymous tips to a few of my reporter friends and I'll be on the cover of *Time* by next week. You know how these things are – people only hear the scandal, not the denial. Where there's smoke, there's fire, they'll say, clutching their wallets. You'll be yesterday's garbage, Anthony.'

'Martin, listen to me. I don't know why you hate me so much, but you're talking about casually destroying the reputations of everyone at this table. These are good, giving people who have put their hearts and souls into Samaritan. You're threatening to brand them all as charlatans and fakes. Not even you can be bitter enough to do that.'

'Can't I? Just watch.'

'How could you do this to me,' Anthony said. 'I'm your own father.'

There were those at the table who'd suspected this, but most of them were stunned. Jaws dropped and their astonished gazes shifted between Anthony and Martin with horror. Rory muttered, 'Holy shit!'

Martin paled and his forehead glistened with sweat. 'Oh, sure, throw that around. Are you afraid someone didn't already know? Is that why you're finally admitting it? All these years you were buying me cars and sending me money, why didn't you give me some plastic surgery instead, so I didn't have to go through life with this face! *Your face!* Didn't it ever occur to you, you big dumb shit, that I didn't want to go through life with your face, being your bastard – and a product of incest, besides! Dear God, I despise you!'

Anthony spoke through clenched teeth. 'Then you go right on despising me. I don't care anymore. I've lost everything dear to me but one thing – Samaritan. But I'm not going to let you play out your filthy revenge on everybody in this room. I'm responsible for my sins. Not them. You're not going to hurt these people, and you're not going

436

to deprive all the people Samaritan can benefit.'

'I don't give a damn about Samaritan and all your underdogs and misfits and sickos. The only welfare I'm concerned about is mine! I'm going to be in charge, or it's going to cease to exist and I don't care what happens to the rest of these fat cats. They're probably all crooks anyway. I've looked into some of them.' He pointed to the man sitting next to Anthony. 'You cheat on your income taxes. I've got proof. And you,' he swung his arm round to point to another, 'you're sleeping with your secretary and your fat complacent wife doesn't know it – yet.'

Both men were on their feet in an instant.

'No! Stop! Sit down, all of you!' Anthony ordered. 'Nina, get the security people in here.' As Nina darted out the door, he went on, 'Martin, you won't do this. I'm not half as stupid as you think. I've got a tape recorder under the table. I'll call a press conference and announce this vile attempt at blackmail. You won't ruin anybody. I'd dissolve Samaritan before I'd let you get your hands on a penny. It'll hurt Samaritan, but not as much as letting you turn your foul mouth loose.'

'You can't do that. Nobody will believe you.' There was panic in his voice and sweat was running down the sides of his face in rivulets.

'More people will believe me than a two-bit muck-raking reporter like you, Martin. You've let your success go to your head because none of your other victims have fought back. Well, I'm fighting back and I'm a better fighter than you think.'

The security guard came to the door. 'You wanted me, Mr Wentworth?'

'Take this man out of here. Lock him up in the basement for now,' Anthony said.

'Okay, come with me, buddy-boy,' the guard said, advancing on Martin.

'It's a bluff!' Martin screamed.

'I *never* bluff,' Anthony said calmly.

Martin glared at him, glared at the guard, then grabbed

his briefcase off the floor. He plunged his hand into it and pulled out a gun. 'Stay away from me. Don't touch me. Anthony, we can work something out. I didn't really mean it. Not all of it.' He edged round the table, coming closer to Anthony. The other men in the room were inching away from his line of fire.

'Listen, boy, no cause for that,' the security guard said, his own voice shaking. 'Just hand over the pop gun and I'm sure everything'll work out.'

'Put down the gun, Martin,' Anthony said firmly.

'I can't. I can't now!' Martin sobbed.

Rory had been coming up behind him stealthily. He accidentally stepped on a pencil which broke with a snap. Martin swung round, terrified, then swung back toward Anthony and fired the gun. Anthony was knocked back against the wall and looked down as if only mildly curious at the blood blossoming on his shirt like a rose opening. Then he crumpled. As he went down, the security guard fired at Martin, who was flung against a credenza. Droplets of blood spattered everybody.

The room was instant chaos.

Above the shouts of alarm, Nina screamed, 'Call an ambulance. Call the police. Quickly. Quickly! He's alive. Get back!' A space cleared round her as she knelt by Anthony.

Nina continued throwing out orders until the ambulance arrived. Martin was dead, they told her. She didn't seem to hear or care. She staunched the blood and knelt close to Anthony, whispering. He seemed to drift in and out of consciousness, but said nothing except to groan with pain. The ambulance attendants arrived only moments before the police. 'I'll go with him,' Nina told the police. 'The others can explain what happened.' She held Anthony's hand as the attendants placed him on a stretcher.

Another ambulance came a few minutes after the first and took Martin's body away. Then the police began questioning the board members. Shaken, they tried to co-operate, but kept breaking off to commiserate with each other. Finally Rory said, 'Where have they taken him? My brother?'

'The county hospital,' one of the police officers said. 'I'll call and see how he is.' He dialed, spoke to someone for a while, waited, spoke again and hung up. 'He didn't get there.'

'What?' Rory bellowed. 'You've lost him?'

'I'll sort this out,' the other officer said. He went into the kitchen to phone where they wouldn't all hang on him like helpless children. He was gone nearly twenty minutes. When he came back, he looked angry and frustrated. 'He didn't get to the county hospital. That woman who went with him insisted that they take him to a private hospital over by Bridgeport. The medical attendants left him there.'

'Yeah, so how is he?' Rory asked.

'They don't know. The hospital in Bridgeport claims it never happened. They say they haven't admitted a patient since nine o'clock last night.'

EPILOGUE

May 1992

It was a beautiful day, the kind Gilly would have loved. The spring air was full of the aromas of warm soil and newly cut grass. Someone had put a fragile blanket of hothouse-grown lobelia over her coffin. The homeless shelter had hired a beat-up bus and several of the people she'd been so kind to over the years had attended the funeral, but they'd drifted away now. Only two people stood looking at each other over the dark walnut coffin and the rich purple flowers.

Steven reached out and picked a small sprig of the lobelia and put it between two bills in his wallet.

'It was her favorite flower,' Nina said.

'I never knew that. I should have. Was it you who sent me the telegram?'

'Yes. I thought you'd want to say goodbye to her.'

'I said goodbye a long time ago. But I'm glad you let me know. What did she die of?'

'TB, the people at the shelter told me. She's been working there ever since—' She didn't have to say since what. 'She took a little apartment down at Thirty-fourth and Main and worked at the shelter every day. They said she refused to see a doctor.'

Steven nodded. 'She would. Even in dying she'd be selfish and melodramatic.' They were harsh words, but the

441

softness in his voice made them seem more a fond assessment than a criticism. 'How have you been, Nina? What do you do now?'

'Not very much. And you?'

'I'm back in the paper business, but of course you know that. You knew where to find me. Do you ever hear anything about Samaritan?'

'There's nothing to hear. It's officially dissolved now. The directors met for the last time about three years ago to sign the papers to distribute the remaining assets to other charities.'

Steven walked over to a stone bench under a small copse of dogwood trees. 'Can you sit for a while?'

Nina glanced down the hill where a white limo with smoked glass windows was parked. 'Yes, just for a minute.'

'You know,' Steven said, sitting down and stretching his legs out in front of himself, 'Wayne called Ellen that day to track me down. I was on my way to Birches when it happened. I got caught up in the traffic from his wreck. I didn't know it was him. By the time I got there, everybody but Rory had gone. I've always wished I'd at least taken the time to call Anthony and tell him I was on my way.'

'He would have been pleased to know that you came.'

'How's Rory?' he asked.

'He went back to ranching. He's running the place that used to belong to Dr Lisle.'

'And Faye?' he asked.

'I don't know. She dropped out of sight when Samaritan went under.'

The cemetery attendants had come and were cranking the mechanism that let Gilly's coffin down into the ground. Nina and Steven watched silently. Finally he said, 'About Anthony, is there a grave I can visit? Where is he?'

Nina paused, glanced again at the limo, and answered carefully. 'Years and years ago, he bought a ranch down in the Flint Hills in Kansas. A place where he could find

442

privacy and peace. He's ... he's at his final rest there.'

He didn't notice how cautiously she had chosen her words. 'It was a nine-day wonder, the disappearing body. How did you do it? *Why* did you do it?'

'It's a long story. Maybe another time,' she said, standing up and brushing off the back of her skirt. 'Where do you go from here?'

'Just back to the airport.'

'Can I give you a lift?'

He stood up. 'Thanks, no. I'm going to stay here for a few more minutes. I'll walk somewhere and get a cab.'

They shook hands, felt foolish for a moment, then embraced awkwardly. Nina kissed his cheek. 'Goodbye, Steven.'

Then she turned and walked down the path to the limo. She didn't look back until the driver opened the door for her. She glanced at Steven sitting on the bench just up the hill, then she slid into the car.

'He was on his way to Birches and was held up in the traffic from Wayne's accident,' she said.

The man beside her in the back seat of the limo had a deeply tanned face and prematurely white hair. 'Was he, now?' He was looking past her at Steven, who had stood up and was starting down the path.

'I offered him a ride, but he wouldn't come with me.' She put her hand on his. 'Anthony ...'

He smiled a little, squeezed her hand, then reached for the door handle.